彩圖

# 初級英文文法

## Let's See! 四版

Grammar G

Expressions without "the"
不加the的情況

have the breakfast

Talking in general
名詞的泛指用法

sushi

the sushi

Uncountable nouns
不可數名詞

coffee

cheese

Countable nouns
可數名詞

some apples

Reflexive pronouns
反身代名詞

lick itself

Counting an uncountable noun
不可數名詞的計算

a box of chocolate

作者 Alex Rath Ph.D.　譯者 謝右／丁宥榆
審訂 Dennis Le Boeuf & Liming Jing

MP3

寂天雲 APP

如何下載 MP3 音檔

❶ 寂天雲 APP 聆聽：掃描書上 QR Code 下載
「寂天雲－英日語學習隨身聽」APP。加入會員
後，用 APP 內建掃描器再次掃描書上 QR
Code，即可使用 APP 聆聽音檔。

❷ 官網下載音檔：請上「寂天閱讀網」
（www.icosmos.com.tw），註冊會員／登入後，
搜尋本書，進入本書頁面，點選「MP3 下載」
下載音檔，存於電腦等其他播放器聆聽使用。

U0033648

# Contents

## Part 3　Present Tenses 現在時態

## Part 12  Prepositions 介系詞

## Part 13  Conjunctions 連接詞

## Part 14  Numbers, Time, and Dates 數字、時間和日期

# Part 1 Nouns and Articles 名詞和冠詞

## Unit 1

### Countable Nouns:
### Plural Forms of Regular Nouns (1)
### 可數名詞：規則名詞的複數形（1）

**1** 表示人、事、物、地方名稱的詞彙就是**名詞**。有些名詞可用數量計算；有些名詞不可以。可用數量計算的名詞稱為**可數名詞**，不能計算的稱為**不可數名詞**。

可數

**a dog** 狗　　　**an apple** 蘋果

不可數

**hair** 頭髮　　　**snow** 雪

**2** **可數名詞**通常有**單數**（singular）和**複數**（plural）兩種形式。

單數（一個）　　　複數（兩個以上）

**a cat** 一隻貓　　　**four cats** 四隻貓

**one hairbrush**　　**two hairbrushes**
一支梳子　　　兩支梳子
**one television**　　**two televisions**
一台電視　　　兩台電視
**a scanner**　　　**two scanners**
一台掃描器　　　兩台掃描器

**3** 大部分**名詞**的**複數形**是在字尾加 **s**。

**student** 學生　　　**students**

- **book** 書　　→ ¹_____
- **phone** 電話　→ ²_____
- **table** 桌子　→ ³_____

**4** 當名詞字尾是 **s、x、z、sh** 或 **ch** 時，複數形加 **es**。

**glass** 玻璃杯　　　**glasses**

fox → fox**es** 狐狸
quiz → quizz**es** 測驗
lunch → lunch**es** 午餐
bush → bush**es** 灌木

### 字尾 s 和 es 的發音

❶ 名詞字尾發**無聲子音**（/f/、/k/、/p/、/t/）時，s 的讀音為 /s/。
- **cups** /kʌps/ 杯子　**banks** /bæŋks/ 銀行

❷ 名詞字尾發**有聲子音**或**母音**時，s 的讀音為 /z/。
- **computers** /kəmˋpjutɚz/ 電腦
- **dogs** /dɔgz/ 狗

❸ 名詞字尾是 s、x、z、ch、sh 時，es 的讀音為 /ɪz/。
- **bosses** /ˋbɔsɪz/ 老闆
- **sandwiches** /ˋsændwɪtʃɪz/ 三明治

## Practice

**1**

請將右列單數名詞改成「複數」形態。

1. dog ................................
2. star ................................
3. dot ................................
4. glass ................................
5. clock ................................
6. witch ................................
7. fax ................................
8. banana ................................
9. fuzz ................................
10. crown ................................

11. mop ................................
12. dish ................................
13. mug ................................
14. sponge ................................
15. slash ................................
16. kite ................................
17. ruler ................................
18. branch ................................
19. box ................................
20. fan ................................

**2**

選出圖中各種物品或身體部位所對應的名詞，並寫出它們的複數形。

shoe
hand
tree
path
shirt
plant
leg

1. ................................
2. ................................
3. ................................
4. ................................
5. ................................
6. ................................
7. ................................

**3**

將右列名詞改為複數形，並依字尾 s 或 es 的發音填入正確的空格內。

watch
mother
cat
lunch
month
eraser
job
fox
park
store
bush
cup

**①** /s/
................................
................................
................................
................................

**②** /z/
................................
................................
................................
................................

**③** /ɪz/
*watches*
................................
................................
................................

## Unit 2

Countable Nouns:
Plural Forms of Regular Nouns (2)

可數名詞：規則名詞的複數形（2）

**1** 名詞字尾是「**子音 + y**」時，複數形須去 y 加 ies。

**baby** 嬰兒

**babies**

lady → ladies 女士
cherry → cherries 櫻桃
country → countries 國家
story → stories 故事

- candy 糖果 → ¹ _____
- city 城市 → ² _____

**2** 字尾是 f 或 fe 的名詞，複數形須去掉 f 或 fe，再加上 ves。也有例外。

leaf → leaves 葉子
knife → knives 刀子
thief → thieves 小偷

例外　直接加 s
▲ a giraffe
◀ two giraffes

**giraffe 有兩種複數形式：**
① 字尾加 s（giraffes）
② 單複數同形（two giraffe）

- half 一半 → ³ _____
- wife 妻子 → ⁴ _____

**3** 某些字尾是「**子音 + o**」的名詞，複數形要加上 es，但並非全部如此。

tomato → tomatoes 番茄
potato → potatoes 馬鈴薯
echo → echoes 回音
hero → heroes 英雄

例外
- photo → photos 照片
- piano → pianos 鋼琴

**4** 字尾如果是「**母音 + o**」的名詞，複數形只要加 s。

**kangaroo 有兩種複數形式：**
① 字尾加 s（two kangaroos）
② 單複數同形（two kangaroo）

kangaroos

**kangaroo** 袋鼠

zoo → zoos 動物園
radio → radios 收音機
video → videos 影片

**5** 某些名詞永遠都是以**複數**形出現。

**clothes** 衣服

**jeans** 牛仔褲

**scissors** 剪刀

**glasses** 眼鏡

**shorts** 短褲

- thanks 感謝
- billiards 撞球
- news 新聞
- earnings 收入
- underpants 女用內褲
- briefs 短內褲
- pants 褲子〔美〕
- trousers 長褲〔英〕
- physics 物理學
- mathematics 數學

**1**

請將右列單數名詞改成「複數」形態。

1. party ........................
2. leaf ........................
3. photo ........................
4. county ........................
5. army ........................

6. spy ........................
7. wolf ........................
8. tuxedo ........................
9. shelf ........................
10. piano ........................

**2**

找出必須以複數形表現的物品，並寫出正確的名稱。其他的請打✕。

1. ........................
2. ........................
3. ........................

4. ........................
5. ........................

**3**

將錯誤的句子打✕，並寫出正確的句子。若句子無誤，則在方框內打✓。

1. I took some photos of the lake yesterday.

☐ _____

2. The scissors are in the drawer.

☐ _____

3. Be careful. Those knifes are very sharp.

☐ _____

4. Leafs keep falling from the trees.

☐ _____

5. People say cats have nine lifes.

☐ _____

6. I can't find the cloth I wore yesterday.

☐ _____

7. My father needs to wear glass to read newspapers.

☐ _____

8. You can find three librarys in this city.

☐ _____

## Unit **3**

Countable Nouns:
Irregular Nouns and Other Plural Nouns

**可數名詞：不規則名詞與其他複數名詞**

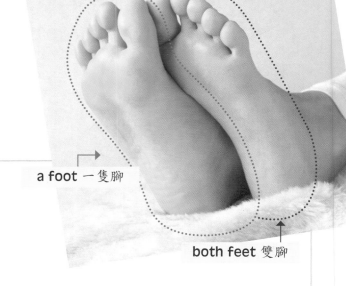

a foot 一隻腳

both feet 雙腳

**1** 某些名詞的複數形為**不規則變化**。

a child 小孩　　　seven children

a mouse 老鼠　　　three mice

| 單數 | | 複數 | |
|---|---|---|---|
| man | → | men | 男人 |
| woman | → | women | 女人 |
| goose | → | geese | 鵝 |
| louse | → | lice | 虱子 |
| tooth | → | teeth | 牙齒 |
| ox | → | oxen | 牛 |

**2** 某些名詞的**單複數同形**，它們也屬於不規則變化的名詞。

one sheep 一隻羊　　　many sheep 許多隻羊

| 單數 | 複數 |
|---|---|
| one deer 一頭鹿 | → two deer |
| one species 一個物種 | → two [1]_____ |
| one aircraft 一架飛機 | → two [2]_____ |
| one bison 一頭野牛 | → two [3]_____ |
| one moose 一頭麋鹿 | → two [4]_____ |

**3** 魚類的複數形有兩種：fish 和 fishes。指**同類魚**或**泛指魚**時，複數形只能用 **fish**；指**多種不同類的魚**時，通常也用 **fish**，但也可以用 **fishes**。

one fish 一條魚

three fish 三條魚

three fish / three fishes 三種魚

| 單數 | 複數 |
|---|---|
| one salmon 一條鮭魚 | → three salmon/salmons 三條鮭魚 |
| one trout 一條鱒魚 | → two [5]_____ 兩條鱒魚 |

# Practice

**1**

寫出右列各種名詞的
複數形。

1. _____    2. _____    3. _____

4. _____    5. _____    6. _____

**2**

選出正確答案。

_____ 1. Bob used to count _____ to get to sleep.
   Ⓐ a sheep        Ⓑ sheeps        Ⓒ sheep

_____ 2. Who are those _____ standing in front of the gate?
   Ⓐ woman        Ⓑ women        Ⓒ womans

_____ 3. Mom told me to brush my _____ twice a day.
   Ⓐ tooth        Ⓑ tooths        Ⓒ teeth

_____ 4. Rhinos and pandas are two of the endangered _____.
   Ⓐ species        Ⓑ specieses        Ⓒ specy

_____ 5. Sometimes _____ are not afraid of cats.
   Ⓐ mouse        Ⓑ mouses        Ⓒ mice

_____ 6. Some _____ in that remote village do not have enough
   food to eat.
   Ⓐ children        Ⓑ child        Ⓒ childs

_____ 7. Jim likes to jog in bare _____.
   Ⓐ foot        Ⓑ feet        Ⓒ foots

_____ 8. The airline bought six _____ from France.
   Ⓐ aircraft        Ⓑ aircrafts        Ⓒ aircreft

## Unit 4

A, An
不定冠詞

**1** 冠詞是一種用來修飾名詞的詞，分為「定冠詞」the 和「不定冠詞」a、an，它們的功能很像形容詞。在**非特定的單數可數名詞**前面通常要加**不定冠詞 a 或 an**。

a tree 一棵樹   an elephant 一頭大象

**Have you ever eaten a worm?**
你吃過蟲嗎？

**2** a 和 an 只用於「**單數可數名詞**」前面。複數名詞前面不可以加 a 或 an。

**We saw two turtles.**
我們看到兩隻海龜。

*Detective Conan* and *Demon Slayer* are Japanese cartoons.
《名偵探柯南》和《鬼滅之刃》都是日本卡通。

**3** a 和 an 可以用來分類人物、地方或事物。

**A blog is an online web log.**
部落格是一種網路日誌。

**A whale is a mammal.**
鯨魚是哺乳類動物。

**4** 字首發音為「**子音**」時（如 b、c、d、f 和 g 等），前面的不定冠詞用 **a**；
字首發音為「**母音**」時（如 a、e、i、o 和 u 等），前面的不定冠詞則用 **an**。

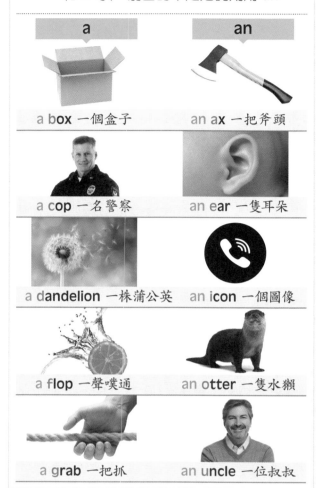

| a | an |
|---|---|
| a box 一個盒子 | an ax 一把斧頭 |
| a cop 一名警察 | an ear 一隻耳朵 |
| a dandelion 一株蒲公英 | an icon 一個圖像 |
| a flop 一聲噗通 | an otter 一隻水獺 |
| a grab 一把抓 | an uncle 一位叔叔 |

**5** 有些字的**字首拼寫雖然是子音**，卻**發母音**；有些字的字首**拼寫雖然是母音**，卻**發子音**。要用 a 或 an，請以發音為準。

an honest alien
一位誠懇的外星人

↳ 字首的 h 有時不發音，這個字就變成母音開頭，所以前面要用 an。

a UFO 一個飛碟

↳ u 的發音有時為 /ju/，是子音，所以前面要用 a。

字首 h
an hour 一小時
a herd 一群

字首 u
an umbrella 一把雨傘
a universe 一個宇宙

# Practice

**1** 用 a 或 an 寫出 Lydia 和 Trent 在超市裡購買的商品名稱。

lightbulb
orange
magazine
umbrella
lamp
fish
ice cube tray

Lydia bought . . .

▷ .................................

▷ .................................

▷ .................................

▷ .................................

Trent bought . . .

▷ .................................

▷ .................................

▷ .................................

**2** 自列表選出適當的詞彙，加上 a 或 an，完成右列句子。

art museum
glass of beer
owl
cup of coffee
café
cab
opera

1. I could walk home, but I would rather take ........................ .

2. We don't have any wine. Do you want ........................?

3. I'm having an espresso. Would you like ........................?

4. Have you ever been to ........................?

5. She spent more than 5 years composing ........................ based on a novel about Africa.

6. We had a lunch at ........................ in Montmartre.

7. In her dream she saw ........................ sitting on a branch of a tree.

Unit **5**

A, An, The
不定冠詞和定冠詞

**1** a、an 稱為**不定冠詞**,用於**非特指的名詞**前。當我們用 a、an 時,並沒有要對方清楚知道所指的是哪一個。

There's a movie theater near here.
這附近有間電影院。

Let's watch a horror movie.
我們去看恐怖片吧。

- Are you going to watch [^1]......... action movie?
  你要去看動作片嗎?
- Let's dine in [^2]......... Chinese restaurant tonight.
  我們今天晚上去吃中國菜吧。

**2** the 稱為**定冠詞**,用來**特別指某一個名詞**。用 the 表示你認為對方清楚知道所指的是哪一個。

That's Mark standing outside the theater.
馬克正站在那間戲院的外面。

The laptop I just bought was expensive.
我剛買的筆記型電腦很貴。

- We rented two movies. Let's watch [^3]......... Chris movie first.
  我們租了兩部片子,先來看克里斯演的那部吧。
- Let's go to [^4]......... newly-opened Italian restaurant.
  我們去那家新開的義大利餐廳吧。

**3** 再來比較一次用 a/an 和 the 的差別。

Are you going to watch a movie?
你打算看部電影嗎?

↳ 並不確定是哪一部電影。

Are you going to watch the movie? 你要看這部電影嗎?

↳ 確定知道是哪一部電影。

There's a talk show at eight tonight.
今天晚上八點有個脫口秀。

Sam is watching *The Ellen Show*.
山姆正在看艾倫秀。

**4** 此外,我們經常在文章中第一次提到某物時用 a/an,再次提及時用 the。

When Jane entered the forest, she saw a unicorn. She followed the unicorn to a green lake.
珍走進森林,看到一隻獨角獸,於是她尾隨獨角獸,來到一座綠色的湖泊邊。

Ted: Kevin's father bought a bicycle for him last week.

Susan: Really? Is the bicycle expensive?

泰德: 凱文的爸爸上星期買了一台腳踏車給他。

蘇珊: 真的嗎?那台腳踏車貴不貴啊?

## Practice

用 a、an 或 the
填空，完成對話。

1. David: Is there _____ public library in town?
   Janet: Yes, there is one.
   David: Would you like to go to _____ library tomorrow?
   Janet: OK.

2. Joe: Where is _____ remote control?
   Kay: _____ remote control is on _____ table.
   Joe: Where is _____ gamepad?
   Kay: _____ gamepad is on _____ sofa.

3. Nancy: Did you see that woman?
   Phil: What woman?
   Nancy: _____ woman who is looking at _____ cellphone.
   Phil: Oh, yes.

4. Amy: Where is Mom?
   Tony: She's in _____ kitchen.
   Amy: What is she doing in _____ kitchen?
   Tony: She's making _____ sandwich.

5. Jim: How do you like your new office building?
   Kelly: I like it. It has _____ big conference room.
   Jim: Do you use _____ conference room a lot?
   Kelly: Yes, I use it every day.

**2**

請選出正確的答案
填入空格。

1. a channel   the channel
   Ⓐ Please change _____.
   Ⓑ Please find _____ with something good on it.

2. a movie   the movie
   Ⓐ Do you want to watch _____ on cable?
   Ⓑ Do you want to watch _____ we talked about last night?

3. a sandwich   the sandwich
   Ⓐ Do you want to eat _____?
   Ⓑ Are you going to eat _____ I made for you?

4. a soda   the soda
   Ⓐ Do you want _____ with your sandwich?
   Ⓑ Do you want _____ you bought at the store?

Part 1 名詞和冠詞 5 不定冠詞和定冠詞

# Unit 6

## Uncountable Nouns
## 不可數名詞

**1** 　**不可用數量計算**的名詞，則稱為不可數名詞，前面不可以加數字。

~~one~~ powder
~~two~~ powder　粉末

~~one~~ makeup
~~two~~ makeup　化妝品

**2** 　不可數名詞意指無法分成個體的名詞，表示**概念、狀態、品質、感情或物質材料**。

cheese 起司　　　coffee 咖啡

- beer 啤酒
- butter 奶油
- beauty 美麗
- courage 勇氣
- love 愛
- horror 恐懼
- luggage 行李
- equipment 裝備
- cosmetics 化妝品
- truth 真理

**3** 　不可數名詞只有一種形式，通常作**單數形**，沒有複數形。

homework 功課　　　milk 牛奶
~~homeworks~~　　　　~~milks~~

**4** 　不可數名詞前面可不加任何限定詞，動詞必須使用**單數動詞**，如 be 動詞 is。可數名詞則視名詞的單複數決定動詞的單複數，複數使用 are。

Is education free in your country?
在你們國家受教育是免費的嗎？

Money is important for basic commodities.
↳ 不可數名詞 education 和 money 前面不加限定詞，並使用單數動詞 is。

要買到基本的生活用品，錢是很重要的。

**比較**

Where is your grammar book?
你的文法書在哪裡？
Where are your grammar books?
↳ 可數名詞視單複數決定用 is 或 are。
你的文法書在哪裡？

**錯誤**

✗ His furnitures are old. 他的家具都很舊。
✗ His meat are fresh. 他賣的肉都很新鮮。

**5** 　有些名詞會同時具有可數和不可數的形式，但意義不同。

How many cakes do you want to get?
　　　　　↳ 指一塊一塊的蛋糕
你想要幾個蛋糕？

Cake is fattening. 蛋糕使人發胖。
　↳ 指蛋糕整體

Who is that lady with long hair?
那個長頭髮的小姐是誰？　↳ 指頭髮整體

There is a hair in my soup.
　　　　↳ 指一根一根的頭髮
我的湯裡有一根頭髮。

There are some dog hairs on the sofa.
沙發上有一些狗毛。　　↳ 指一根一根的毛髮

## Practice

**1**

將右列單字歸類為可數或不可數名詞，並在可數名詞前正確的加上 a 或 an，不可數名詞則不用加。

可數 | 不可數

...........................

...........................

...........................

comb

newspaper

hairdryer

shampoo

sugar

bread

**2**

在第一格填上正確的動詞（is 或 are），並在第二格填上正確的冠詞（a 或 an），若不需要冠詞請打 ✗。

1. There _____ _____ some water in the bottle.
2. There _____ _____ some cream rinse in the bathroom.
3. There _____ _____ jar of cold cream on the sink.
4. Those women _____ _____ buyers for the company.
5. That man _____ _____ sales representative.
6. That _____ _____ beautiful bottle.
7. That _____ _____ inexpensive makeup case.
8. There _____ _____ sale on eyeliners.

**3**

改正右列句子的錯誤，若句子無誤，則在後面寫上 OK。

1. How often do you cut your ~~hairs~~? _____ *hair* _____
2. I am thinking of buying some jewelries. _____
3. Where do you buy your makeups? _____
4. How much skin cream do you use? _____
5. I am buying some cosmetic at a department store.

   _____
6. It takes a lot of courages for Tom to do this. _____
7. Beauty is only skin deep. _____

Counting an Uncountable Noun
不可數名詞的計算

**1** 不可數名詞的數量，可以用可計算的**量詞**來表示。

**量詞**

- **bottle** 瓶
- **tube** 管
- **box** 箱；盒
- **can** 罐
- **jar** 廣口瓶
- **packet** 包；袋
- **bowl** 碗
- **bar** 塊
- **carton** 紙盒
- **stick** 根
- **pot** 壺
- **piece** 個；件

two tubes of
**toothpaste**
兩條牙膏

a bottle of
**perfume**
一瓶香水

a box of
**chocolate**
一盒巧克力

a can of
**hairspray**
一罐髮霧

a bowl of
**rice**
一碗飯

a bar of
**soap**
一塊肥皂

a jar of
**jam**
一罐果醬

a carton of
**milk**
一瓶牛奶

three sticks of
**incense**
三支香

**2** 在不可數名詞前，常用 some 作限定詞，但**不能用 a 或 an**。

We have <u>some</u> information about him.
我們有一些關於他的消息。

There's <u>some</u> rice on the counter.
櫃臺上有一些米。

**錯誤**

- We have ~~an information~~.
- There's ~~a rice~~ on the counter.

- We need [1] _____ advice.
  我們需要一點建議。
- Please buy me [2] _____ bread.
  請幫我買一點麵包。

**3** 不可數名詞前面用 some 表示**數量不確定**，用量詞表示**具體的數量**。

| 數量不確定 | 具體的數量 |
| --- | --- |
| **She's got** some **wine.** 她有一些葡萄酒。 | **She's got** a bottle of **wine.** 她有一瓶葡萄酒。 |
| **There's** some **spaghetti on the stove.** 爐子上有一些義大利麵。 | **There are** two **boxes of spaghetti in the cupboard.** 櫃子裡有兩盒義大利麵。 |

**比較**

a stick of
**glue**

a bottle of
**glue**

a tube of
**glue**

## Practice

**1**

請將物品正確的數量搭配表中量詞填入空格；不需要使用 **of** 片語的，請填入 some。注意量詞的單複數。

bowl of
stick of
jar of
tube of
bar of
carton of
can of
bottle of
some
piece of

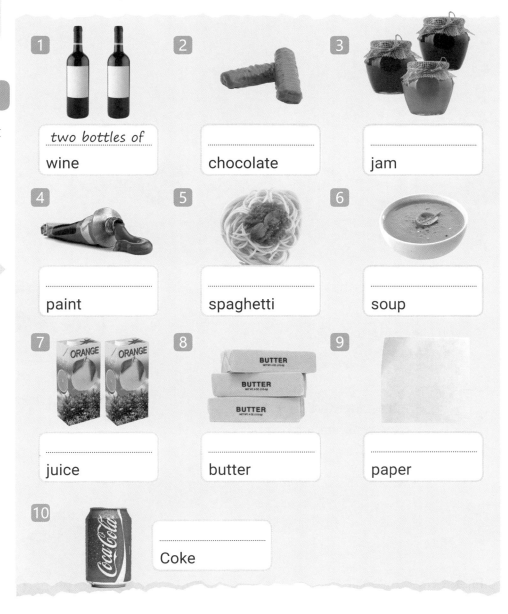

1 *two bottles of* wine

2 _____ chocolate

3 _____ jam

4 _____ paint

5 _____ spaghetti

6 _____ soup

7 _____ juice

8 _____ butter

9 _____ paper

10 _____ Coke

**2**

改正右列句子的錯誤。

1. Where can I buy a chocolate?

   ..................................................................................................

2. How many luggages do you have?

   ..................................................................................................

3. It's too quiet. I need a music.

   ..................................................................................................

4. How many bowls of perfume did you get?

   ..................................................................................................

5. Can you buy me two breads?

   ..................................................................................................

6. My brother wants to buy a new furniture.

   ..................................................................................................

# Unit 8

## Talking in General
名詞的泛指用法

**1** 一般來說，名詞前若沒有 the，是泛指事物的**總體**。

**Pubs are noisy.**
酒吧很嘈雜。

**Apples are good for health.**
蘋果對健康很好。

**Do you like going to cafés?**
你喜歡去咖啡廳嗎？

- ¹_____ are expensive. 車子很貴。
- ²_____ are grass-eating animals.
  山羊是草食性動物。

**2** 名詞前面加 the，是特別指某**具體事物**。

**Please try the cookies.**
請吃吃看這些餅乾。

**Take the apples.**
拿這些蘋果吧。

- ³_____ in this showroom are very expensive.
  這個展場裡的車子很貴。

**3** 再來比較一次有沒有 the 的差別。

**I love to eat sushi.**
我喜歡吃壽司。

**The sushi is not fresh.**
這些壽司不新鮮。

**Furniture is hard to move.**
家具很難搬移。

**The furniture is in the truck.**
這批家具在貨車上。

- ⁴_____ are here to see you.
  警察來探視你了。

22

## Practice

**1**

貓貓都喜歡些什麼？
根據圖示，並利用下
表提示，造句解釋貓
貓喜歡什麼和不喜歡
什麼。

balls of yarn
showers
dogs
fish
boxes
vets

Cats like . . .

Cats don't like . . .

1. ............................................................
2. ............................................................
3. ............................................................
4. ............................................................
5. ............................................................
6. ............................................................

**2**

選出正確的答案填入
空格中。

1. Coffee   The coffee
   Ⓐ ............................................ keeps you awake at night.
   Ⓑ ............................................ is in the pot next to the cups.

2. money   the money
   Ⓐ You need ............................................ to live.
   Ⓑ I gave ............................................ to the landlord.

3. Rice   The rice
   Ⓐ ............................................ is the most important grain crop.
   Ⓑ ............................................ is cooked with butter and parsley.

4. attendance   the class attendance
   Ⓐ The class has low ............................................ .
   Ⓑ I entered ............................................ into the computer.

Part 1 名詞和冠詞

8 名詞的泛指用法

23

## Unit 9

### Proper Nouns
### 專有名詞

名稱中有「... of ...」者，則一定要加 the。

I studied at the University of Michigan.
我在密西根大學念書。

I went on vacation to the Bay of Fundy.
我到芬地灣度假。

**1** 特定人、事物、地方、國家的名稱屬於專有名詞，首字母必須**大寫**。

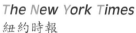

*The New York Times* ▼
紐約時報

Shawn Mendes ▼
尚恩‧曼德斯

Australia ▼
澳洲

Tower Bridge ▼
倫敦塔橋

**2** 大多數專有名詞的前面**不加 the**。

❶ **Names** 人名
~~The~~ Mike is my uncle. 麥克是我叔叔。

❷ **Days of the week** 星期
Tomorrow is ~~the~~ Saturday. 明天是星期六。

❸ **Months of the year** 月分
My favorite month is ~~the~~ September.
九月是我最喜歡的月分。

❹ **Languages and nationalities**
語言和國籍
~~The~~ Russian is a difficult language.
俄語是一種很困難的語言。

❺ **Countries, continents, and regions**
國家、洲和地區名稱
Did you like your trip to ~~the~~ France?
你喜歡那趟法國之行嗎？
~~The~~ Canada is in ~~the~~ North America.
加拿大在北美洲。

❻ **Villages, towns, and cities**
村、鎮和城市名稱
~~The~~ Toronto is the biggest city in Canada.
多倫多是加拿大最大的城市。

❼ **Street / road / avenue names**
街、道路、大道名
I have a friend who lives on ~~the~~ Washington Street. 我有個朋友住在華盛頓街。

❽ **Place names** 地方名
I know a student at ~~the~~ Seattle University.
我認識一名西雅圖大學的學生。

❾ **Lake** 湖泊
~~The~~ Lake Michigan is located entirely within the United States.
密西根湖完全位於美國境內。

**3** 有些專有名詞必須**加 the**。

❶ **Hotels, restaurants, and pubs** 飯店、
餐廳和酒吧
The Ritz Carlton is a famous hotel.
麗池卡爾登度假酒店是間知名的飯店。

❷ **Cinemas** 電影院
*Tenet* is showing at the New Art Cinema.
《天能》正在新藝術電影院上映。

❸ **Theaters** 劇院
How do I get to the Goodman Theater?
我要如何到古德曼劇院？

❹ **Seas and oceans** 海和洋
Is the Mediterranean a sea or an ocean?
地中海是海還是洋？

❺ **Rivers** 河流
The longest river in South America is the Amazon. 亞馬遜河是南美洲最長的河。

## Practice

**1**

請在必要的地方，填上 the；若不必要，則畫上「╳」。

1. ............... University of Cambridge
2. ............... Jason
3. ............... Wednesday
4. ............... February
5. ............... Sheraton Hotel
6. ............... France
7. ............... Asia
8. ............... Whitewater Pub
9. ............... Tokyo
10. ............... Budapest Café
11. ............... River Thames
12. ............... Oprah Winfrey
13. ............... West River
14. ............... Pacific Ocean
15. ............... Los Angeles County Museum of Art
16. ............... Lake Michigan
17. ............... Century Cinema
18. ............... Jackson Avenue
19. ............... Ireland
20. ............... Korean

**2**

將右列句子改寫為正確的句子。

1. "What are you reading?" "I'm reading *china post*."

   → ..................................................................................................
   ..................................................................................................

2. Is mary going to japan with you?

   → ..................................................................................................

3. jane has a project due in the october.

   → ..................................................................................................

4. Why don't we see the latest movie in miramar cinema?

   → ..................................................................................................
   ..................................................................................................

5. Is the yellow river the longest river in china?

   → ..................................................................................................

6. Excuse me, how do I get to the maple street?

   → ..................................................................................................

7. Are you going to evanston public library?

   → ..................................................................................................

## Unit 10

### Expressions With and Without "The" (1)
### 加 The 與不加 The 的情況（1）

**1** 娛樂消遣的場所和活動名稱要加 the。

**go to** the **movie theater** 去電影院
**be at** the **movie theater** 在電影院

**listen to** the **radio** 聽廣播
**be on** the **radio** 廣播中

**watch** the **broadcast** 看轉播
**will be in** the **broadcast** 即將轉播

We go to the **theater** whenever there is a good movie.
只要有好電影，我們就會去電影院看。

How often do you go to the **cinema for art films?** 你多久會去戲院看一次藝術電影？

**2** 電視前面不加 the。但是若 TV 指一台具體的「電視機」時，則需加 the。

They're watching TV. 他們在看電視。

The movie is on TV tonight.
這部電影今晚會在電視上播映。

Your glasses are next to the TV.
你的眼鏡在電視機旁邊。

**3** 天氣類型需加 the。

I hate getting caught in the **rain**.
我討厭淋雨。

I wear sunscreen if I am going to be in the **sun**.
如果會曬到太陽，我就會擦隔離霜。

The **weather** is nasty today.
今天天氣很差。

**4** 三餐前面不加 the。

have/eat **breakfast** 吃早餐

have/eat **lunch** 吃午餐

have/eat **dinner** 吃晚餐

It is important to eat ~~the~~ breakfast every morning.
每天早上吃早餐是很重要的。

**5** 帶有介系詞 on 或 by 的交通工具前面不加 the。

on **foot** 走路
by **car** 開車
by **bicycle** 騎腳踏車
by **train** 搭火車
by **scooter** 騎機車
by **subway** 搭地鐵
by **bus** 搭公車
by **plane** 搭飛機

Going on ~~the~~ foot is much better than taking a bus. 走路比搭公車好多了。

If you go by ~~the~~ car, be prepared for traffic jams.
假如你開車去，要有塞車的心理準備。

## Practice

**1**

依據圖示，自下表選出適當的詞彙，完成右列句子，並視需要加上 the。

breakfast
TV
radio
rain
theater
car

1. What's that music you're listening to on ........................?

2. Last weekend, Tom and Patti went to .........................

3. It'll be quicker if we go by .........................

4. Every morning we have cereal and milk for .........................

5. The laundry got all wet because of .........................

6. Is there anything good on ........................ tonight?

**2**

在必要的地方加 the；在不必要的地方畫上「╳」。

1. This morning I got caught by ........... rain.
2. When was the last time you went to ........... cinema?
3. I'm so busy that I don't have time to eat ........... lunch.
4. While I was driving, I heard a beautiful song on ........... radio.
5. We could go on ........... foot, but going by ........... cab will be faster.
6. There is a fashion show on ........... TV tonight.

Expressions With and Without "The" (2)

加 The 與不加 The 的情況（2）

**1** 樂器名稱需加 the。

play the cello 彈大提琴    play the piano 彈鋼琴

play the guitar 彈吉他

**He has been playing** the **violin for 12 years.**
他拉小提琴已經 12 年了。

**2** 以下**泛稱性的自然環境地點**，一般要加 the。

**I like living in** the **country.**
我喜歡住在鄉下。

**He commutes from** the **suburbs to** the **city every day.** 他每天從郊區通勤到城裡。

**They have a house in** the **city.**
他們在市區有間房子。

**I used to swim in** the **sea.**
我以前常在海裡游泳。

**3** 某些**社會機構名稱**不用加 the。

**go to** church
上教堂作禮拜
**at** church
上教堂作禮拜
**in** church
上教堂作禮拜

**go to** school 上學
**be at** school 在上學
（相對於在家或在校外）
**be in** school 在上學
（相對於有工作）

**go to** court 上法庭      **go to** jail 去坐牢
**be at** court 在庭上      **be in** jail 進牢裡
**be in** court 在庭上      **go to** prison 進監獄
                        **be in** prison 進監獄

- **Right now he is** [1] _____.
  此刻他在教堂作禮拜。
- **When do you have to be**
  [2] _____ ?
  你什麼時候要到學校上課？

**4** 有些**社會機構名稱**可加 the，也可不加。

**go to** (a) **hospital**       **go to** (a) **university**
**go to** the **hospital**       **go to** the **university**
去醫院                        上大學（和 school、
↳ 美式須用 the：               church 的用法一樣）
  go to the hospital          ↳ go to the university
                               指特定某所大學
                               go to university
                               泛指「上大學」

## Practice

**1**

依據圖示，自下表選出適當的詞彙，完成右列句子，並視需要加上 the。

church
university
violin
court
hospital
city

1. Do you prefer to live in the country or in ........................... .

2. She wants to learn to play ........................... .

3. I didn't see you in ........................... last Sunday.

4. Jimmy left his home and went to ........................... last month.

5. The lawyer spent a lot of time at ........................... for this case.

6. Grandma is sick and has been in ........................... for a week.

**2**

在必要的地方加 the；在不必要的地方畫上「✕」。

1. I love the beach, but I don't like lying in ............... sun.
2. They go to ............... church once a year on Christmas Eve.
3. He can play ............... guitar, ............... bass, and ............... piano.
4. He is studying electronics in ............... college.
5. First he was in ............... jail and now he is in ............... prison.
6. Are you going to show your guest around ............... town?
7. Terri and Craig love riding bicycles in ............... countryside.
8. They are going to ............... court for a murder case.

# Unit 12

## Other Expressions Without "The"
## 其他不需要加 The 的情況

**play American football**
打美式足球

### 1  從事某種球類運動不用加 the。

**play basketball** 打籃球

**play volleyball** 打排球

**play soccer** 踢足球

**play baseball** 打棒球

**My family used to play** badminton **every Sunday.**
我家人以前每週日都會去打羽球。

**I'm learning** tennis. 我在學網球。

**Is** golf **very popular in your country?**
你們國家盛行高爾夫球嗎?

### 2  某些慣用語前面不加 the。

go to work 上班       be at work 工作中
go home 回家          be at home 在家
go to bed 去睡覺      be in bed 在床上

**I have to go to work early this morning.**
我今天一早就得去上班。

### 3  學科的名稱前面不加 the。

**My favorite subject is the math.**
數學是我最喜歡的科目。

**Daniel is studying the geography.**
丹尼爾正在唸地理。

**I'm good at** physics **and** chemistry.
我擅長的科目是物理和化學。

### 4  季節名稱通常不加 the,但也有例外。

**It will soon be** spring **again.**
春天又將到臨。

**My family likes to relax on a tropical island in** summer.
我們家夏天時喜歡到熱帶島嶼上度假。

**I love** autumn **the best.**
秋天是我最愛的季節。

例外

**She will be leaving for New York in the fall.**
她將於這個秋天啟程前往紐約。
↳ fall 無論如何都要加 the。

**Joan and Matt first met in the winter of 2005.**
瓊和麥特初次相遇於 2005 年的冬天。
↳ 特別指某個冬天(春天、夏天、秋天)時就要加 the。

# Practice

**1**

依據圖示，自下表選出適當的詞彙，完成右列句子，並視需要加上 the。

math
tennis
home
work
winter

1. She's not home right now. She's at _____ .

2. Hey, why not play _____ with me this afternoon?

3. Birds will fly south before _____ comes.

4. Dora's always been good at _____ .

5. She decided to cancel her date and just stay at _____ and read.

**2**

在必要的地方加 the；在不必要的地方畫上「✗」。

1. If I'm tired, I go to _____ bed and sleep 12 hours straight.
2. She will be going to _____ college in _____ fall.
3. I love _____ autumn better than _____ summer.
4. Billy had surgery this morning, and he has to stay in _____ bed for the next two days.
5. Is _____ soccer popular among the students in your class?
6. Are you good at _____ English grammar?

**3**

依據事實，回答右列問題。

1. What's your favorite sport?
   → _____
2. What's your favorite subject?
   → _____
3. What's your favorite season?
   → _____
4. What subject do you dislike the most?
   → _____
5. What season do you dislike the most?
   → _____

# Unit 13

Possessive：'s
所有格：'s

**1** 用來表示所有權或彼此關係的詞彙或格式，稱為**所有格**。

Susan's **apples**
蘇珊的蘋果

John's **lunch**
約翰的午餐

**2** **單數名詞**和**人名**的後面加「 's 」，即成為所有格。

**Cathy's cat** 凱西的貓

**his sister's book** 他姐的書

**3** **複數名詞**或**複數人名**的所有格只要加「 ' 」。

the brothers' **restaurant**
哥哥們的餐廳

the Jones' **dinner party**
瓊斯家的晚宴

**4** **字尾不是 s 結尾**的不規則複數名詞，也是加「 's 」變成所有格。

the **women's** snack
這些女人們的點心

the **children's** meal
孩子們的餐點

比較

my friend's party  一個朋友
我朋友的派對

my friends' party  多個朋友
我朋友們的派對

**5** 在**人和人**或**人和物**之間加所有格，表示**人和人**或**人和物**之間的關係。

Lily's **father** 莉莉的父親

my brother's **shirt** 我哥的襯衫

- That's ¹＿＿＿＿＿＿＿ car.
  那是我朋友的車。
- That's ²＿＿＿＿＿＿＿ sister.
  那是喬的姊妹。

**6** 如果**前後文的主詞都很清楚**，則所有格「 's 」或「 ' 」後面的名詞可以省略。

**Whose coffee is this? It's Jim's.**
這是誰的咖啡？吉姆的。　　↳ = Jim's coffee

**Whose cake is this? It's Jan's.**
這是誰的蛋糕？是珍的。　　↳ = Jan's cake

---

## 所有格「's」字尾發音

❶ 名詞字尾發無聲子音（/f/、/k/、/p/、/t/）時，「's」或「s'」的讀音為 /s/。
- a giraffe's **long neck** 長頸鹿的長脖子
  /dʒəˋræfs/

❷ 名詞字尾發有聲子音或母音時，「's」讀音為 /z/。
- my brother's **backpack** 我哥哥的背包
  /ˋbrʌðɚz/

❸ 名詞字尾是 s、x、z、ch、sh 時，「's」或「s'」的讀音為 /ɪz/。
- my boss's **desk** 我老闆的桌子
  /ˋbɔsɪz/
- the fox's **tail** 狐狸的尾巴
  /ˋfɑksɪz/
- Josh's **reward points** 喬許的兌換點數
  /ˋdʒɑʃɪz/

## Practice

**1**

右列物品可能會是誰的？請依圖示，分別用完整句子和簡答來回答問題。

 Catherine
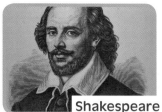 Shakespeare
 Kevin Durant
 Tim Cook
 the wizard
 Kiki

1 
Whose key is it?
It is _Catherine's key_.
It is _Catherine's_.

2 
Whose collar is it?
It is _____.
It is _____.

3 
Whose pen and ink is it?
It is _____
_____.
It is _____.

4 
Whose briefcase is it?
It is _____.
It is _____.

5 
Whose magic wand is it?
It is _____
_____.
It is _____.

6 
Whose basketball is it?
It is _____
_____.
It is _____.

**2**

將表中的名詞改為所有格，並依字尾「's」的發音填入正確的空格內。

Jennifer
student
Alice
dish
bottle
aunt
Jeff
ox
lion
tank
kid
tax

1 /s/
_____
_____
_____
_____

2 /z/
_Jennifer's_
_____
_____
_____

3 /ɪz/
_____
_____
_____

Unit **14**

Possessive : The . . . Of . . .
所有格：The . . . Of . . .

**1** 通常**無生物**的所有格要用「of . . .」來表示。

the window of the room 房間的窗戶

the end of the road 路的盡頭

the cover of the magazine 雜誌的封面

- I like the color [1] _____.
  我喜歡這面牆壁的顏色。
- Janet is a student [2] _____.
  珍奈特是這所學校的學生。

**2** 表示**時間**或**度量**的名詞，則必須用「's」或「'」來表示所有格。

today's schedule 今天的行程

four hours' work 四小時的工作

a year's membership 一年的會員資格

two dollars' worth 兩塊美金的價值

**3** **擬人化**的名詞也必須用「's」或「'」來表示所有格。

heaven's will 天意

Mars' surface 火星地表

life's miracle 生命奇蹟

the world's economy 全球經濟

**4** 即使名詞屬於**生物**，有時也可以用「of . . .」來表示關係或所有權；但「's」或「'」的所有格形式更常見，也更為自然。

the smile of the dog = the dog's smile
狗狗的笑容                              ↳ 用法更常見、自然

the leaves of the tree = the tree's leaves
這棵樹的葉子

the son of Tim = Tim's son
提姆的兒子

- the toys [3] _____
  = the boy's toys 男孩的玩具
- the tail [4] _____
  = the pig's tail 豬的尾巴

## Practice

**1**

將右列「of . . .」的用法改寫為「's」
或「'」的所有格。

1. the schoolbag of the student

   → .............................................

   .............................................

2. the iPad of Jenny

   → .............................................

   .............................................

3. the newspaper of Grandpa

   → .............................................

   .............................................

4. the laptop of David

   → .............................................

   .............................................

5. the headphones of my sister

   → .............................................

   .............................................

6. the umbrella of my brother

   → .............................................

   .............................................

7. the cell phone of the manager

   → .............................................

   .............................................

8. the scarf of my mother

   → .............................................

   .............................................

9. the book of Liz

   → .............................................

   .............................................

**2**

自左右兩個列表中各選出相關的詞彙，並用「the . . . of . . .」描述它們之間的附屬關係。

| | | |
|---|---|---|
| pile | 1. *the light of the sun* | the sun |
| light | 2. .......................... | trash |
| ninth symphony | 3. .......................... | the computer |
| keyboard | 4. .......................... | the president |
| speech | 5. .......................... | Beethoven |

35

**1** 下列物品名稱，哪些是可數名詞？哪些是不可數名詞？請在可數名詞的空格內寫上 C（countable），不可數名詞的空格內寫上 U（uncountable）。

→ Unit 1, 6 重點複習

| | | | | |
|---|---|---|---|---|
| 1 | 2 | 3 | 4 | 5 |
| _C_ belt | helicopter | marker | cloth | mayonnaise |
| 6 | 7 | 8 | 9 | 10 |
| cloud | water | castle | bread | dolphin |
| 11 | 12 | 13 | 14 | 15 |
| paper | swimming pool | olive oil | pearl | sugar |

**2** 依據題意，自圖片中選出正確的單字，改成複數名詞來填空。

→ Unit 1, 3 重點複習

1. I heard lots of _____ running around above the ceiling of my room.

2. I really don't like washing _____.

3. This store sells some clocks and _____.

4. My little brother loves to eat _____ for dessert.

5. There aren't many _____ this year.

6. Do little _____ drink milk from their mother?

7. _____ have an important role in many fairy tales.

8. Archaeologists found several dinosaur _____ on this spot.

9. Mom is cooking two _____ for dinner.

10. Iris wrote several _____ while she was traveling in Europe.

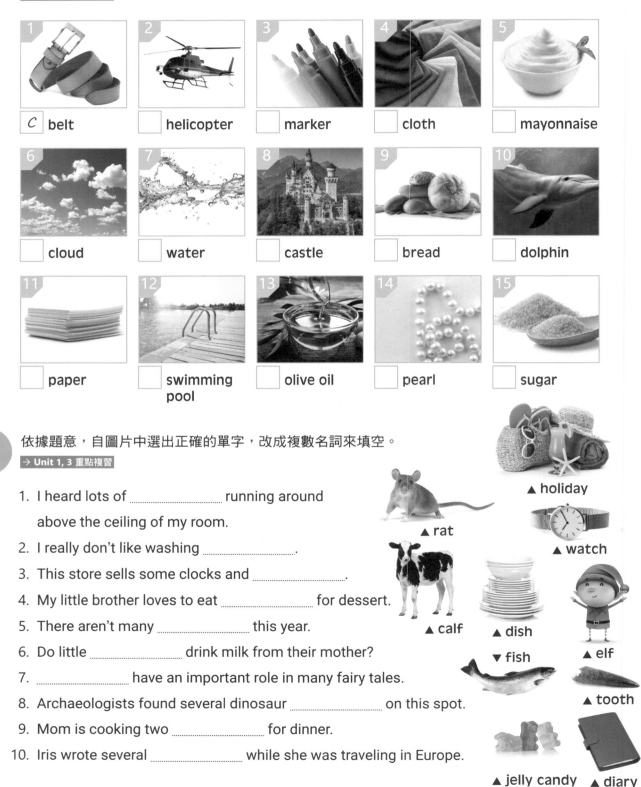

▲ holiday
▲ rat
▲ watch
▲ calf
▲ dish
▼ fish
▲ elf
▲ tooth
▲ jelly candy    ▲ diary

**3** 運用圖中的單字填空，並根據內文做正確的單複數形變化，或加上 a、an、the。
→ Unit 4–5 重點複習

**carrot**

1. Give the rabbit _____ .
2. I left _____ on the grass for the rabbit.
3. _____ are a healthy food.

**lion**

4. They have a statue of _____ .
5. The statue of _____ is very old.
6. _____ are a symbol of power.

**sugar**

7. I like _____ in my tea.
8. Where is _____ ?

**banana**

9. Would you like _____ ?
10. Who gets _____ ?

**keyboard**

11. He reached out his hands to _____ and typed some words.
12. Can you stop at the electronics store to buy _____ ?

**music**

13. _____ distracts me when I am studying.
14. What is _____ you are playing?

**4** 選出符合題意的詞彙，以正確的形式（加上 a、an、the，或改為複數名詞，或完全不需要冠詞等）來填空完成句子。可重複使用詞彙。
→ Unit 1, 4–5, 8 重點複習

Johnny lives in ❶_____.
He commutes from his place to work by
❷_____ every day. He loves
playing ❸_____.
Tonight there is going to be a football game
on ❹_____ . So he plans to go
❺_____ early. He will also buy two
cheeseburgers and some French fries for
❻_____ . He will not go to
❼_____ until the game is over.

bed                    dinner

TV                     football

car                    suburbs

home

Muhammad is ❽_____. He
told me that ❾_____, the
longest river in the world, plays an important
role in the life of all ❿_____.
However, some geographers from
⓫_____ and Peru are claiming that
⓬_____ is the longest river
in the world by now. They are claiming that
they've found ⓭_____ of the river,
and the length of the river makes it the longest
one. Debates between ⓮_____ go
on. No matter which river is the longest one
on earth, they are popular sites for
⓯_____ from all over the world.

Egyptian          new source          Brazil

Amazon River          scientist

tourist          Nile River

**5** 圈選正確的答案。
→ Unit 4–5, 8 重點複習

1. Do you have  camera   a camera   an camera   some camera ?

2. We are having  potatoes   a potatoes   an potatoes   some potato  for dinner.

3. She has long  hair   a hair   an hair   hairs .

4. Please help me carry  a boxes   a box   an box   some box .

5. We already have  a loaves   a loaf   an loaf   some loafs  of bread.

6. There is  lots of snow   a snow   an snow   snows  in the mountains.

7. Where  is   are  your watch?

8. How many people  is   are  coming?

9.  Is   Are  this rice expensive?


**6** 根據題目所提供的內容，以「's」和「the . . . of . . .」這兩種形式來表達所有格；
若該題目不適合以某一形式表達，則畫上「╳」。
→ Unit 13–14 重點複習

1 **Ned**

suitcase

Ⓐ *Ned's suitcase*

Ⓑ *the suitcase of Ned*

2 **my father**

jacket

Ⓐ

Ⓑ

3 **my sister**

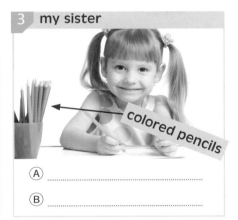

colored pencils

Ⓐ

Ⓑ

4 **bathroom**

corner

Ⓐ

Ⓑ

5 **Edward**

brother

Ⓐ

Ⓑ

6 **vacation**

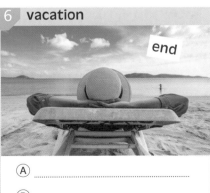

end

Ⓐ

Ⓑ

**7** 將下列圖中的各項物品名稱，依據其適合的量詞，填入正確的空格內。

→ Unit 7 重點複習

| tuna | soy sauce | grapes | wine | luggage | shaving cream |
| cheese | watercolor | potato chips | jewelry | pickles | cleansing foam |
| tea | lotion | peanut butter | soda | coffee | salad |
| soup | strawberry jam | ketchup | rice | cookies | ointment |

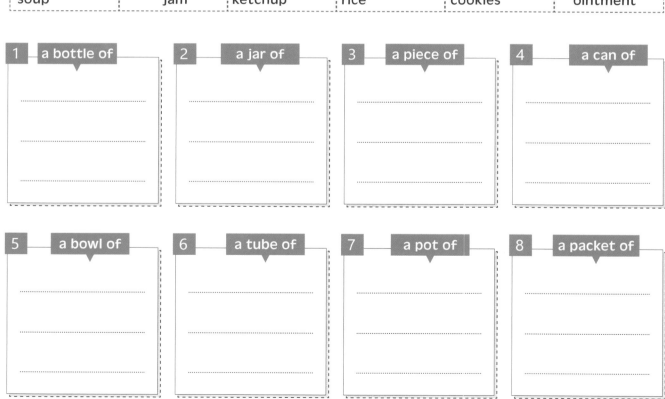

| 1 a bottle of | 2 a jar of | 3 a piece of | 4 a can of |
| 5 a bowl of | 6 a tube of | 7 a pot of | 8 a packet of |

**8** 下列名詞類別是否需要加「the」？在需要 the 的類別上將「the」打勾；在不需要 the 的類別上將「the」打叉，並各舉兩個例子。

→ Unit 9–11 重點複習

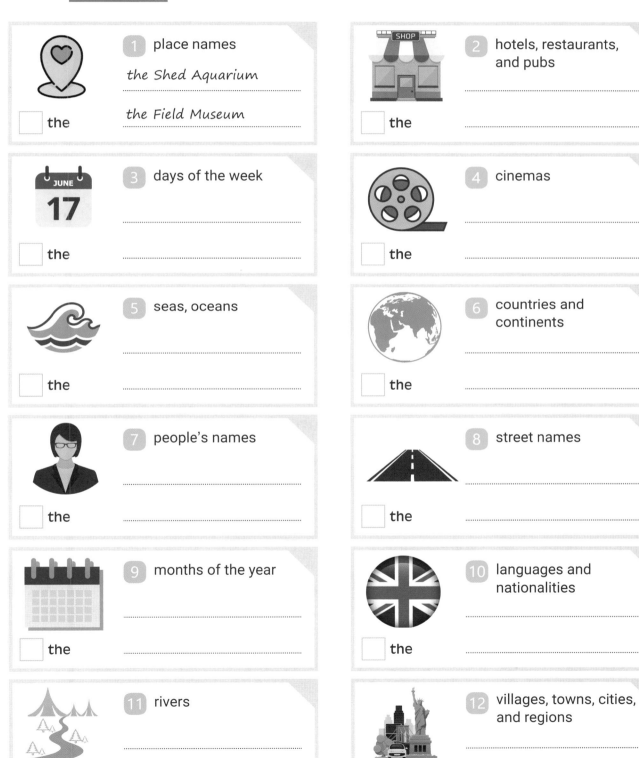

1 place names

the Shed Aquarium

the Field Museum

☐ the

2 hotels, restaurants, and pubs

☐ the

3 days of the week

☐ the

4 cinemas

☐ the

5 seas, oceans

☐ the

6 countries and continents

☐ the

7 people's names

☐ the

8 street names

☐ the

9 months of the year

☐ the

10 languages and nationalities

☐ the

11 rivers

☐ the

12 villages, towns, cities, and regions

☐ the

## Part 2 Pronouns 代名詞

## Unit 16

### Personal Pronouns: Subject Pronouns
### 人稱代名詞：主詞代名詞

**1** 用來代替名詞的詞稱為**代名詞**。其中一種具有人稱區別的代名詞稱為**人稱代名詞**，用來指人或事物。

Tim is English. He's from London.
                 ↳ 是人稱代名詞，代替 Tim。
提姆是英國人，他是從倫敦來的。

The cell phone on the desk is mine.
桌上的手機是我的。    ↳ 人稱代名詞，
                          等於 my cell
                          phone。

**2** 人稱代名詞有三種型態，分別為**主詞代名詞**、**受詞代名詞**和**所有格代名詞**。

| 主詞代名詞 | | 受詞代名詞 | | 所有格代名詞 | | 所有格形容詞 | |
|---|---|---|---|---|---|---|---|
| I | 我 | me | 我 | mine | 我的 | my | 我的 |
| we | 我們 | us | 我們 | ours | 我們的 | our | 我們的 |
| you | 你 | you | 你 | yours | 你的 | your | 你的 |
| you | 你們 | you | 你們 | yours | 你們的 | your | 你們的 |
| he | 他 | him | 他 | his | 他的 | his | 他的 |
| she | 她 | her | 她 | hers | 她的 | her | 她的 |
| it | 它 | it | 它 | | | its | 它的 |
| they | 他們 | them | 他們 | theirs | 他們的 | their | 他們的 |

↳ 所有格形容詞雖然不是代名詞，但是卻與所有格代名詞相關且容易混淆，請看 Unit 18 的詳細說明。

**3** 主詞代名詞有單數，也有複數。

**4** 主詞代名詞可用來表示自己、和自己對話的人、對話中已提過的人或事，以及已知事物。
在句中通常當主詞用，不能省略。

I've got a job in Los Angeles.
我在洛杉磯工作。

What are you looking for?
你在找什麼？

We are going to buy some fruit.
我們要去買一些水果。

Annie isn't in town. She's on vacation.
安妮不在城裡，她去度假了。

Cindy and Melissa aren't on-line. They're at a pub.
辛蒂和梅麗莎並沒有在線上，她們在酒吧。

**5** it 是個**單數**、**中性**的主詞代名詞。可以**泛指一般的事物**、**動物**，也可以用來代表**時間**、**日期**、**天氣**和**距離**。
（確定性別的寵物，也常用 he 或 she。）

| general | 一般事物 | It's a giant ship. 那是一艘巨輪。 |
|---|---|---|
| time | 時間 | It's 3 o'clock. 現在時間是三點。 |
| days | 星期 | It's Tuesday. 今天是星期二。 |
| weather | 天氣 | It's rainy. 今天是雨天。 |
| distance | 距離 | It's 5 blocks to the bus stop. 公車站在五條街外。 |

◆ 主詞代名詞可以和動詞 am、is、are、have got、has got 一起縮寫。

| I'm | he's | I've got | he's got |
|---|---|---|---|
| we're | she's | we've got | she's got |
| you're | it's | you've got | it's got |
| they're | | they've got | |

## Practice

**1**

請依圖示，在空格處填上 I、you、he、she、it、we 或 they，完成句子。

◀ 1. _____'m on the phone.

◀ 2. _____'re taller than me.

▲ 3. _____'s got cool hair.

▲ 4. _____'s raining hard.

▲ 5. _____'s a tall building.

▲ 6. _____'re going surfing.

▲ 7. _____'re going to jump.

▲ 8. _____'s running.

▲ 9. _____'s got a new car.

**2**

請依圖示，在空格處填上 I、you、he、she、it、we 或 they，完成句子。

1. These are my parents. _____'re both in excellent health.

2. My dad is retired. _____'s 75 years old.

3. My mom helps take care of our kids. _____'s a big help.

4. My son is Sam. _____'s a very good student.

5. My daughter is Mary. _____'s learning to play the violin.

6. My dog is Fred. _____'s cute.

7. We just bought a summer house. _____'s in Hawaii.

8. That's us. _____'re a happy family.

Unit **17**

## Personal Pronouns: Object Pronouns
## 人稱代名詞：受詞代名詞

**1** 受詞代名詞也是人稱代名詞的一種，通常作受詞用，不能省略。受詞代名詞**有單數**，也有**複數**。

| 單數 | | 複數 | |
|---|---|---|---|
| me | 我 | us | 我們 |
| you | 你 | you | 你們 |
| him | 他 | | |
| her | 她 | them | 他們 |
| it | 它 | | |

**Danny is at the party. Did you see** him?
丹尼在派對裡。你有看到他嗎？

**Betty and Judy are doing their homework. Can you help** them?
貝蒂和茱蒂正在做功課。你可以幫她們嗎？

**2** 介系詞片語中，受詞代名詞需放在**介系詞後面**。

**When is Doug leaving? I want to go with** him.
道格什麼時候會離開？我要跟他一起走。

**Have you seen Barb? I am** looking for her.
你有看到芭波嗎？我在找她。

**The whole family is here. Have you talked to them?** 這一家人都在這裡。你和他們談過了嗎？

**3** 受詞代名詞可以直接放在**動詞**（如：see、help、like）**後面**，不加介系詞。

**We're waiting for Sam. Did you see** him?
我們在等山姆，你看到他了嗎？　　↳ him 指的是 Sam

**I'm supposed to meet my daughter here. I'm** helping her **move to a new apartment.**　↳ her 指的是 the daughter
我約好在這裡和我女兒見面，我要幫她搬家到新公寓。

**Jack** told me **that he was sick.**
傑克告訴我他生病了。

**Jennifer doesn't** like us.
珍妮佛不喜歡我們。

**Did you see my headphones? I need them right now.**
你有沒有看到我的耳機？我現在需要它。

**I'll** give you **a call tomorrow morning.**
我明天早上打電話給你。

**I love to eat lobsters. Do you like** them?
我喜歡吃龍蝦。你呢？　↳ them 指的是 lobsters

- **Janet needs some help. Can you help** ___1___?
珍奈特需要幫助，你可以幫她嗎？
- **Steven and Naomi are very friendly. I like** ___2___ **very much.**
史蒂文和娜歐蜜都很和善，我很喜歡他們。

- A **Which letter is for Mary?**
  B **This one is for** ___3___?
  A 哪一封是瑪莉的信？
  B 這封是她的。
- **Here are some photos of Bill and Theresa. Do you want to see a photo of** ___4___?
這裡有一些比爾和泰瑞莎的照片，你想要看他們的照片嗎？

## Practice

### 1

請依據事實，用右邊列表的句型來回答問題。

I like him/her/them/it

I don't like him/her/them/it

1. How do you like Cristiano Ronaldo?
   *I like him.*

2. How do you like hiking?
   _____

3. How do you like ice cream?
   _____

4. How do you like washing clothes?
   _____

5. How do you like flowers?
   _____

6. How do you like Taylor Swift?
   _____

### 2

在空格處填上 me、you、him、her、it、us 或 them 來完成這篇日記。

Dear Diary,

  I went to a café with my best friend tonight. Becky brought her camera and got a cute guy to take our picture. That's ❶_____ in the picture. The guy seemed to like ❷_____. After he sat down at the table with his friends, I spent a lot of time watching ❸_____. He looked back at ❹_____. Becky waved at ❺_____ and he smiled back at ❻_____. I told Becky that we should go sit with ❼_____. She liked the idea, but said we should not do ❽_____. Becky said we should make ❾_____ come and sit with ❿_____. The guy left before we could decide how to get ⓫_____ to come over. I felt like it was over for ⓬_____ and wanted to go home. So we left. I liked the café and wanted to go back again.

## Unit 18

**Personal Pronouns : Possessive Pronouns and Possessive Adjectives**

**人稱代名詞：所有格代名詞與所有格形容詞**

**1** 所有格形容詞用來表示物品的所有權，有單數，也有複數。

| 單數 | | 複數 | |
|---|---|---|---|
| my | 我的 | our | 我們的 |
| your | 你的 | your | 你們的 |
| his | 他的 | their | 他們的 |
| her | 她的 | | |
| its | 它的 | | |

**Where is** his **car?**
他的車子在哪裡？

**Those are** our **roller blades.**
那是我們的直排輪溜冰鞋。

**Who is** your **friend?**
誰是你的朋友？

**2** 所有格形容詞用來代替某個名詞的所有格，必須放在其他名詞前面。

**I just saw Jason and** his **father in the park.**
↳ = Jason's，放在名詞 father 前面。
我剛才在公園裡看到傑森和他爸爸。

**Brenda and** her **twin sister are playing.**
↳ = Brenda's，放在名詞 twin sister 前面。
布蘭妲和她的雙胞胎姊妹正在玩耍。

**This is** my **lovely dog.** Its **name is Michael.**
這是我的寶貝狗狗，牠的名字叫麥可。

• **Mr. and Mrs. Smith are celebrating**
¹＿＿＿＿ **twentieth wedding anniversary in a fancy restaurant.**
史密斯夫婦正在一間高級餐廳慶祝他們的結婚二十週年紀念。

**3** 所有格代名詞用來表示物品的所有權，有單數，也有複數。

| 單數 | | 複數 | |
|---|---|---|---|
| mine | 我的 | ours | 我們的 |
| yours | 你的 | yours | 你們的 |
| his | 他的 | theirs | 他們的 |
| hers | 她的 | | |

**Rita: This is my coffee.** 麗塔：這是我的咖啡。
**Andy: Where is** mine**?** 安迪：那我的呢？

**George and Annie have been served their food, but we are still waiting for** ours**.**
喬治和安妮已經拿到他們的餐點，但我們的還沒拿到。

**4** **所有格代名詞**經常用來代替已經出現過的名詞，避免重複，後面不加名詞。

**Where's my mug? Is this** mine**?**
我的馬克杯呢？這是我的嗎？ ↳ 代替已經出現過的 my mug。

**I found my coat. Where is** yours**?**
我找到我的外套了，你的呢？ ↳ = your coat，避免重複 coat。

**These are our tickets. Did you bring** yours**?** 這是我們的票，你們的有帶來嗎？

**Isn't this a family party? We brought our whole family. Where is** theirs**?**
這不是家庭派對嗎？我們全家都來了，他們家的人呢？

• **This isn't Sam's mobile phone.** ²＿＿＿＿ **is black.** 這不是山姆的手機，他的是黑色的。

• **This is our bus stop. What's** ³＿＿＿＿**?**
我們要在這站下車，你的站呢？

**5** 所有格代名詞也可以視為一個**完整的名詞片語**，單獨存在。

Ⓐ **Are these** ours**?** 這些是我們的嗎？

Ⓑ **Yes, these are** yours**.**
是的，這些是你們的。

## Practice

**1**

一對兄妹的媽媽正在做簡短的家庭介紹。請在空格處填上 my、your、his、her、our 或 their，幫她完成這段簡介。

1. _____ name is Jane. My husband is Jerry.
2. These are _____ two kids, Jimmy and Sara.
3. Jimmy is eight years old. Those are _____ trains and cars.
4. Sara is six years old. Those are _____ dolls and stuffed animals.
5. They don't play with _____ blocks anymore.
6. Jimmy and Sara don't like cleaning up _____ room.
7. _____ house is usually a mess, but today it is clean.
8. I made Jimmy pick up _____ side and Sara cleaned up _____ side of _____ room.

**2**

請依圖示，在空格處填上「所有格代名詞」或「所有格形容詞」，完成句子。

1
Dad : Amy, it's not _____ doll. It's Nancy's doll.
Amy : I'm sorry. I didn't know it's _____ (= her doll). I'll give it back to her.

2
Joe : Have you seen _____ dog? I can't find it anywhere. It's a Shiba Inu.
May : No, I haven't seen _____ dog.

Jessica : Is this _____ watch?
Nick : Yes, that's _____ (= my watch).

4
The cat is playing _____ toy.

5
Mr. Anderson, that's not your office. _____ (= your office) is down there.

## Unit 19

Indefinite Pronouns and Adjectives:
Some, Any

不定代名詞與不定形容詞：Some、Any

**1** 不定代名詞用來指**不確定、未知的人或事物**。不定代名詞有很多種。

- some 一些
- any 任何
- few 一些
- one 一個
- many 許多
- much 許多
- something 某物
- somebody 某人
- anyone 任何人
- nothing 沒有事
- anything 任何事
- everywhere 到處

**2** some 和 any 可以當**形容詞**，用來形容不確定數量的名詞。

There are some **squirrels** in the tree.
樹上有一些松鼠。

There aren't any **squirrels** in the tree.
樹上沒有任何松鼠。

Are there any **squirrels** in the tree?
樹上有松鼠嗎？

**3** some 和 any 可以接**複數名詞**或**不可數名詞**。

複數名詞

some apples 一些蘋果
any apples 任何蘋果

some carrots
一些胡蘿蔔
any carrots
任何胡蘿蔔

不可數名詞

some beer 一些啤酒
any beer 任何啤酒

some wine 一些酒
any wine 任何酒

**4** some 通常用於**肯定句**，any 則用於**否定句和疑問句**。

We have some **rice**, but we **don't** have any **soft drinks**. 我們有一點白飯，但是沒有飲料。

Are there any **potato chips** in the cabinet?
櫃子裡有洋芋片嗎？

- I need ¹ _____ **help**. 我需要幫助。
- Jack doesn't want to make ² _____ **mistakes**. 傑克不想犯錯。
- Do you have ³ _____ **cameras**? 你有相機嗎？

**5** 如果疑問句是屬於**禮貌性的詢問**，希望得到**肯定**的答案，那就可以用 some。

Could I have some **rice**, please?
可以盛點飯給我嗎？

Would you like some **rice**?
你要不要吃點飯？

**6** 若已**清楚知道所指名詞**為何，some 和 any 後面接的名詞**可以省略**，也就是把 some 跟 any 當作**代名詞**使用。

Linda: He is selling lottery tickets. Would you like some (lottery tickets)?

Bob: No, I don't want any (lottery tickets).

琳達：他正在賣樂透彩，你要買一些嗎？
鮑伯：不，我不想買。

**7** 若需要特別加強語氣，可用 no 來替代 **not any**。另外，否定詞出現在句首時，通常會用 no 來替代 not any。

There isn't any **room** in the car.
= There is no **room** in the car.
車上沒位子了。

There isn't any **time**. = There is no **time**.
我們沒時間了。

No one likes his new hairstyle.
沒人喜歡他的新髮型。

## Practice

**1** 冰箱裡有什麼、沒有什麼？依據圖示，自表中選出適當的句型造句。

> There's some . . .
> There are some . . .
> There isn't any . . .
> There aren't any . . .

 eggs
1. There aren't any eggs.

 bottled water
4. _____

meat
2. _____

 vegetables
5. _____

ice
3. _____

 milk
6. _____

**2** 利用括號內的字，改寫右列的否定句。

\* 注意：**have / has got**是英式句型。美式不用這種句型。

1. There isn't any space. (no) → _____
2. We've got no newspapers. (any) → _____
3. She hasn't got any money. (no) → _____
4. There are no boxes. (any) → _____
5. I've got no blank disks. (any) → _____
6. He has no bonus points. (any) → _____

**3** 用 **some**、**any** 或 **no** 填空，完成句子。

1

Would you like _____ cookies?

2

Could I have _____ bread, please?

3

There isn't _____ tea.

4

Can I have _____ nuts, please?

5

Hurry up! I've got _____ time.

6

Have you got _____ chocolate chip ice cream?

## Part 2 Pronouns 代名詞

### Unit 20

Indefinite Pronouns and Adjectives:
Many, Much, A Lot Of, Enough

不定代名詞與不定形容詞：Many、
Much、A Lot Of、Enough

**1** much、many 和 a lot of 用來表示東西的數量很多，經常當**形容詞**使用。much 用於**不可數名詞**。

Ⓐ **How** much **dirt is on the rug?**
地毯上有多少灰塵？

Ⓑ **There isn't** much dirt. 不太多。

**How** much **money does it cost?**
這要多少錢？

▲much dirt

**2** many 用於**複數可數名詞**。

Ⓐ **How** many **stones are on the floor?** 地板上有多少石頭？

Ⓑ **There aren't** many stones.
沒有很多石頭。

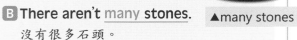
▲many stones

**How** many **card games do you know?**
你知道幾種紙牌遊戲？

**3** 一般對話中，**肯定句**通常用 a lot of 或 lots of 來表示「東西的數量很多」。可用於**不可數名詞**，也可用於**複數可數名詞**。

**There's** a lot of **juice.** 有很多果汁。
**There are** a lot of **bottles.** 有很多瓶子。
**Jimmy added** lots of **black pepper to the soup.** 吉米在湯裡加了很多黑胡椒。
**Sam bought** lots of **guavas.**
山姆買了好多芭樂。

**4** too much 和 too many 可用來表示「某件物品的數量已超過足夠的或希望的量」。

too much **homework** 太多作業
too many **projects** 太多案子

**5** enough（足夠的）可用於**複數可數名詞**，也可用於**不可數名詞**。

**I can't paint the house. I don't have** enough **time.**
我沒辦法油漆這間屋子，我的時間不夠。

**Do you have** enough **Parmesan cheese?**
你有足夠的帕瑪森乾酪嗎？

**We have** enough **paint brushes. We don't need any more.**
我們已經有足夠的油漆刷子，不需要更多了。

**6** 用 enough 表「**足夠的數量**」，是一個固定量的最低限度；a lot of 則代表「**較大的數量**」，是一個固定量的最大限度。

| enough **tea** | ↔ | a lot of **tea** |
|---|---|---|
| 足夠的茶 | | 很多茶 |
| enough **apples** | ↔ | a lot of **apples** |
| 足夠的蘋果 | | 很多蘋果 |

**7** much、many、a lot 和 enough 都可以**單獨存在**，指涉之前所指的名詞。也就是作**代名詞**用。

**There's some pressure, but not** much.
壓力是有一點，但是不太大。
↳ = much pressure

**We have some magazines, but not** a lot.
我們有一些雜誌，但是不多。
↳ = a lot of magazines

**We don't need any tissues. We've got** enough. 我們不用面紙，我們有的已經夠了。
↳ = enough tissues

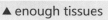

▲ enough tissues　　▲ too many tissues

50

## Practice

**1**

假設你在右列電器與相關用品部門工作,你會如何詢問顧客的需求?自下表選出適當詞彙,依照範例句型造句。

air conditioners
cell phone batteries
detergent
cameras
light bulbs
televisions
water filters

1. Video Equipment 影音設備部
   → *How many televisions do you want?*

2. Telecommunications 電信通訊部
   → _____

3. Cameras and Accessories 攝影器材部
   → _____

4. Washing Machines and Accessories 洗衣機及相關用品部
   → _____

5. Lighting 照明器材部
   → _____

6. Heating and Cooling 冷暖器材部
   → _____

7. Water Treatment 水處理設備部門
   → _____

**2**  用 too much、too many 和 enough 描述圖中人物平常的消費習慣。

 1 He eats _____ junk food.

 2 She buys _____ clothing.

 3 He has _____ video games.

 4 She has _____ teddy bears.

 5 She eats _____ dessert.

 6 She watches _____ TV.

 7 She doesn't have _____ money for the toy she wants.

## Unit 21

Indefinite Pronouns and Adjectives:
Little, A Little, Few, A Few

不定代名詞與不定形容詞：
Little、A Little、Few、A Few

**1** little、a little、few、a few 都是用來表示**數量**的代名詞兼形容詞。

little **food** 沒什麼食物

a little **sugar** 少許糖

few **things** 沒多少事

a few **cups** 幾個杯子

**2** a little 和 a few 的意思都是「一點點」，a little 用於**不可數名詞**，a few 用於**複數可數名詞**。

We have a little **food** and a few **soft drinks**. 我們有一些食物和一些飲料。

We have lots of spaghetti, but only a little **sauce** and just a few **meatballs**.

我們有很多義大利麵，但卻只有一點醬汁和一些肉丸。

• There is ¹_____ seaweed in the tank.
魚缸裡有一些水草。

• I have ²_____ English novels.
Do you want to read one?
我有幾本英文小說，你要看嗎？

**3** little 和 few 的意思是「**幾乎沒有**」，little 用於**不可數名詞**，few 用於**複數可數名詞**。

There are few people she likes.
She loves only herself.
她沒有什麼喜歡的人。
她只愛她自己。

Jack got little help from his brother.
傑克的哥哥沒有幫他什麼忙。

• She is arrogant, and ³_____ people like her. (few)

• There is ⁴_____ traffic in some rural areas. (little)

**4** little、a little、few、a few 都可**單獨存在**，指涉之前所指的名詞。也就是當作**代名詞**使用。

Few of us can speak German.
我們沒幾個人會說德文。

Only a few of the students agreed to participate in the charity event on Sunday.
只有少數學生願意參與週日的慈善活動。

Ted drank a little of the wine on the table, so there is little left.
泰德喝了一些桌上的酒，所以所剩無多了。

**5** much 是 little 的反義字；many 則是 few 的反義字。

| much **tea** | ⟷ | little **tea** |
|---|---|---|
| 很多茶 | | 沒有什麼茶 |
| many **apples** | ⟷ | few **apples** |
| 很多蘋果 | | 沒有幾個蘋果 |

## Practice

**1**

依照圖示，描述相關物品的數量。你可以從下表挑出最適當的用語，完成句子。

There are a few . . .
There are a lot of . . .
There are many . . .
There isn't much . . .
There's a little . . .
There's a lot of . . .

1 ▶ bananas

_There are a lot of bananas._

2 ▶ books

......................................
......................................

3 ▶ masks

......................................
......................................

4 ▶ beer
......................................
......................................

5 ▶ sandwiches
......................................
......................................

6 ▶ gift boxes

......................................
......................................

7 ▶ candles
......................................
......................................

8 ▶ passion fruit
......................................
......................................

**2**

依據圖示，用下表詞彙完成右列段落。

little
a little
few
a few
much
many
a lot of

There is not ❶...................... furniture in this room. There are only ❷...................... chairs and a cushion. ❸...................... dirt can be found on the floor. The curtains are open, and the large window allows ❹...................... light to come into the room.

There are ❺...................... tables and chairs in the square. It's getting dark. I think we're expecting ❻...................... rain later, but the weather broadcast says there won't be much rain.

## Unit 22

Indefinite Pronouns:
One, Ones, and Some Compound Pronouns
不定代名詞：
One、Ones 與一些複合代名詞

**1** one 和 ones 都可以當**代名詞**，
one 替代重複出現的**可數單數名詞**；
ones 替代重複出現的**複數名詞**。

可數單數名詞　　　　複數名詞

peanut 花生　　　　peanuts
↓　　　　　　　　　↓
one　　　　　　　　ones

I am getting a glass of orange juice.
Do you want one?
↳ = a glass of orange juice
我要去拿一杯柳橙汁，你要嗎？

My house is the small one.
↳ = house
我家是小的那間。

Do you like large cars or small ones?
↳ = cars
你喜歡大車還是小車？

Where did you take those photographs,
the ones on the wall?
↳ = photographs
牆上的那些照片，你是在哪裡拍的？

**2** one 和 ones 只能替代**可數名詞**。

I want to buy a cup of coffee. Would you
like one? 我想要買一杯咖啡，你要嗎？
↳ = a cup of coffee；單數可數名詞

We have lots of snacks.
Try the ones on the table.
↳ = snacks；複數可數名詞
我們有很多點心，吃吃看桌上這些吧。

**3** 疑問詞 which 後面可以接 one 或
ones，來表示「哪一個」或「哪
一些」。

We have lots of soft
drinks. Which one would
↳ = Which soft drinks
you like, Fanta, Pepsi,
or Coke?
我們有很多種軟性飲料，
你要哪一種，芬達、百事
可樂還是可口可樂？

We have many on-line games here at the
cyber café. Which ones do you like to
play? ↳ = Which on-line games
我們網咖有很多線上遊戲，你想要玩哪幾種？

**4** 不定代名詞還包含了一些由 every-、
some-、any- 和 no- 四種字首所組成
的複合代名詞，可以說是代名詞中最
大的群組。（請見 Unit 23–25 詳述）

|  | every- | some- | any- | no- |
|---|---|---|---|---|
| -one | everyone | someone | anyone | no one |
| -body | everybody | somebody | anybody | nobody |
| -thing | everything | something | anything | nothing |
| -where | everywhere | somewhere | anywhere | nowhere |

- My desk is the [1] _____ on the left.
  我的桌子是左邊的那一個。
- These pictures are the [2] _____ you
  wanted. 這些照片是你想要的那些。

## Practice

**1**

請依照圖示，在空格填上 one 或 ones 完成對話。

**1**

| | |
|---|---|
| Mother : | Sweetheart, which _____ would you like? |
| Girl : | I want the small _____. |
| Mother : | Wouldn't you like the big _____? |
| Girl : | No way! That's for big girls. |

---

**2**

| | |
|---|---|
| Jane : | Which _____ did you catch? |
| Joe : | I caught the little _____. |
| Jane : | You should buy the large _____ from that guy or you'll go hungry. |

---

**3**

| | |
|---|---|
| Mia : | How much are the _____ on the left? |
| Peter : | They are extremely expensive. |
| Mia : | Oh. How much are the _____ on the right? |
| Peter : | They are very expensive, too. |
| Mia : | Do you have a cheap _____? |
| Peter : | No, madam. I am sorry. We don't have any cheap _____ in the store. |
| Mia : | OK. Thanks. I guess I can't get _____ here. |

Part 2 代名詞

22 不定代名詞：One、Ones 與一些複合代名詞

## Unit 23

Indefinite Pronouns:
Someone/Somebody, Anyone/Anybody

不定代名詞：Someone / Somebody
與 Anyone / Anybody

**1** somebody 和 someone 都可以代表「**不確定的人**」，兩個字的意思完全相同。

Somebody **left an umbrella.**
有人留下了一把傘。

Someone **claimed the lost umbrella.**
有人說遺失的那把傘是他的。

**2** anybody 和 anyone 都可用來代表「**非特定的人**」，兩個字的意思完全相同。

Anybody **could have entered the contest.**
任何人都可以參加這場比賽。

Anyone **who enters the contest needs to pay $100.**
任何參加這場比賽的人都要繳 100 元。

I **thought I saw** somebody **at the door.**
我想我看見門口有個人。

I **didn't see** anyone **at the door.**
我沒有看見門口有任何人。

**3** somebody 和 anybody 都是**單數**，作主詞用時要接**單數動詞**。如果在同一句中再次提及，要用 **he or she**。（在非正式用法中，有些人也用複數代名詞 **they** 替代，並接複數動詞。）

Somebody **should call the police, shouldn't** they?
應該有人去叫警察的，不是嗎？（非正式用語）

Anybody **messes with the kid and** he or she **will have to answer to me.**
誰要是敢去招惹那個小孩，我將唯他／她是問。

**4** someone/somebody 和 anyone/anybody 的用法差別，和 some 與 any 的差別是一樣的。someone/somebody 通常用於**肯定句**。anyone/anybody 通常用於**否定句**和**疑問句**。

Somebody **called my private phone line.**
有人打我的專線電話。

Someone **called about delivering a package.**
有人打電話來問送包裹的事。

I **never gave** anybody **that phone number.**
我從未把那個電話號碼給任何人。

Hasn't anyone **delivered the package yet?**
已經有人送來包裹了嗎？

**5** 在**需要幫忙或支援**的狀況下，可以使用 somebody 和 someone，此時 someone 和 somebody 也可以用於**疑問句**。

Someone **will be right with you.**
馬上會有人來幫你。

Is there somebody **who can help me?**
有沒有人可以幫幫我？

**6** somebody、anybody 後面若接**動詞**，需使用**不定詞**（to V）形式，不用 -ing 形式。

If there is anybody **to talk to, I'll do the talking for us.**
如果有人能夠對談，我會去為我們發聲。

I **think Janet needs** somebody **to keep her company.** 我覺得珍奈特需要有個人來陪。

**7** somebody、anybody 是**單數**，複數則要用 some people。

Some people **are all talk and no action.**
有些人只會出一張嘴。

## Practice

**1**

用 someone 或 anyone 填空，完成句子。

1. Helen : I saw _____ in the alley last night.

   Peter : Oh?

   Helen : Did you see _____ in the alley last night?

   Peter : I didn't see _____ in the alley last night.

2. Ray : You don't look good. What's the matter?

   Elain : I lost my job. I'm so helpless, and there isn't

   _____ who can help me.

   Ray : There must be _____ who can help.

   Don't worry.

3. Jack : What is Sandy doing?

   Bella : She is talking to _____ on the phone.

   Jack : Is it _____ we know?

   Bella : No, it's _____ we've never heard of.

4. Vincent : Amanda, I asked you not to tell _____

   about my secret.

   Amanda : I didn't tell _____ about it.

   Vincent : Obviously, _____ besides you and

   me has known about it. I'm so painful. I really

   don't want _____ else to know.

5. Tom : _____ stole my notebook.

   Kenny : Who could possibly do that?

   Tom : It could be _____ in this classroom.

**2**

圈選正確答案。

1. Some people never **go / goes** out on the weekend.

2. Is there someone **talk / to talk** to about your problem?

3. **Someone / Anyone** mailed a box to me last week.

4. What would you do if **someone / anyone** tried to rob you in the street.

5. If **someone / anyone** sees Lisa, ask her to call me.

6. I can go by myself. I don't need anyone **to keep / keeping** me company.

7. I talked to **someone / anyone** in the personnel department about my job.

## Unit 24

Indefinite Pronouns: Something/
Somewhere, Anything/Anywhere

不定代名詞：Something / Somewhere
與 Anything / Anywhere

**1** something 和 anything 都是指「不特定的狀況或事物」。

Something is wrong with my car.
我的車子有點毛病。

At this point, I am willing to try anything.
到了這個時刻，我願意做任何嘗試。

**2** something 和 anything 這類的詞都是**單數**，要接**單數動詞**，在同一句中被再次提及時，也用單數代名詞 it 替代，並接**單數動詞**。

Something is walking towards us.
What is it?
有什麼東西往我們這邊走來，到底是什麼？

I will eat anything if it is good for my health.
只要對健康有益，我什麼都吃。

**3** something 和 anything 的用法差別，和 some 與 any 的差別一樣。
something 通常用於**肯定句**，
anything 通常用於**否定句**和**疑問句**。

There is something in my left shoe.
我左邊鞋子裡有東西。

Is there anything wrong with you?
You look sad.
發生了什麼事嗎？你看起來很難過。

We haven't had anything to drink for two days. 我們已經連續兩天沒東西喝了。

**4** somewhere、anywhere 用來指「非特定的地點場所」。

She lives somewhere in Florida.
她住在佛羅里達州的某處。

I don't want to go anywhere today.
我今天哪裡都不想去。

**5** 在**需要幫忙**或**支援**的狀況下，可以使用 something 和 somewhere。此時 something 和 somewhere 可以用於**疑問句**。

Is there something I can help you with while you wait?
你在等的時候需要我幫什麼忙嗎？

Is there somewhere safe in this town?
這個鎮上有哪裡是安全的嗎？

Is there somewhere we can meet?
有沒有什麼地方是我們可以碰面的？

**6** 如果表示「**無論什麼事**」、「**無論什麼地方**」時，anything 和 anywhere 也可以用於**肯定句**。

If you need anything, just let me know.
你如果需要任何東西，就告訴我。

My family would love to live anywhere in this city.
我們家想住在這個城市裡，哪裡都好。

We can meet anywhere.
我們到任何地方碰面都可以。

**7** something、anything 後面若接動詞，需使用**不定詞**（to V）形式，不用 -ing 形式。

A Would you like something to eat?
B Yes, bread and milk.
A 你想吃些什麼嗎？
B 想吃麵包和牛奶。

There isn't anything interesting to watch on TV tonight.
今天晚上沒有什麼有趣的電視節目。

**1**

利用下表中的不定代名詞和動詞來完成句子。

anything
something
anywhere
somewhere

to eat
to go
to do
to drink

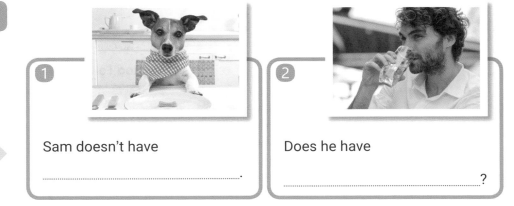

1
Sam doesn't have

_____.

2
Does he have

_____?

3
They don't have

_____.

4
He still has

_____.

**2**

圈選正確答案。

1. Don: Is there **something / anything** in your drawer?

   Lee: There isn't **something / anything** in my drawer.

2. I know somewhere for us **hide / to hide**.

3. There's **something / anything** in my eye that makes me uncomfortable.

4. I want to give you **something / anything** for your birthday.

5. I can't find my passport **somewhere / anywhere**.

6. Do you have anything **to read / reading**?

7. Joe: Where did you go yesterday?

   John: I didn't go **somewhere / anywhere**.

   John: Then what did you do?

   John: I didn't do **something / anything**, either.

   Joe: Didn't you have anything **doing / to do** at all?

   John: Oh, I did do one thing. I slept all day yesterday.

# Unit 25

Indefinite Pronouns：No One/Nobody/
Nothing/Nowhere, Everyone/Everybody/
Everything/Everywhere

不定代名詞：**No One** / **Nobody** / **Nothing** /
**Nowhere** 與 **Everyone** / **Everybody** /
**Everything** / **Everywhere**

**1** no one / nobody / nothing / nowhere
和 everyone / everybody / everything
/ everywhere 都可以作
**不定代名詞**使用，要與**單數動詞**搭配。

I **guess it was** nothing **important**.
我想這沒什麼重要的。

We **looked** everywhere, **but** nobody **was**
**there**. ↳ 注意，這個句子裡的 everywhere
是副詞的用法。

我們到處都找過了，但是那裡一個人也沒有。

Everything **is under control**.
一切都在掌握之中。

**2** no one 和 nobody 都是「**沒有人**」的
意思，兩者意義完全一樣。

There is nobody here.
這裡一個人影也沒有。

No one **came to give Ed a hand**.
沒人來幫艾德的忙。

**3** nobody 和 nothing 比 not anybody
和 not anything 的**語氣更強烈**。

| 語氣強烈 | 語氣和緩 |
|---|---|
| Nobody can help.<br>完全沒有人可以幫忙。 | There isn't anybody who can help.<br>沒有人可以幫忙。 |
| Nothing can be added.<br>完全沒什麼可以補充了。 | There isn't anything that can be added.<br>沒有什麼可以補充了。 |

**4** nowhere 和 everywhere 用來指
「**非特定的地點場所**」，這兩個字除
了當代名詞之外，也常作**副詞**使用。

There's nowhere **I can go to hide from him**.
↳ 代名詞

沒有地方可以讓我躲他。

My dog follows me everywhere **I go**.
我走到哪我的狗就跟我到哪。 ↳ 副詞

**5** no one / nobody / nothing / nowhere
後面常接**to加不定詞**格式，表示「沒有
人／沒有事／沒有地方可以……」。

There's no one **to talk to**.
沒有人可以跟我說話。

I **have** nobody **to turn to for help**.
我求助無門。

I **have** nowhere **to go and** nothing **to do**.
我沒有地方可以去，也沒有事情可做。

**6** no one / nobody / nothing / nowhere
本身已經具有**否定**意味，因此在句中**不
可搭配** not 或 never 這類的否定詞。同一
個句子中使用雙重否定是不被允許的。

~~I don't want to see nobody now.~~
I don't **want to see** anybody **now**.
我現在誰也不想見。

~~I never said nothing about this to Kenny.~~
I **said** nothing **about this to Kenny**.
我沒有對肯尼說過關於這個的事。

**7** everyone 和 every one 的差別在於，
everyone 等於 **everybody**，指「**人**」；
every one 可以指人或**物**，而且一定
要和 **of** 連用（every one of . . .）。
anyone 和 any one 的區別也是一樣。

Everyone **is excited about the coming**
**event on Sunday**.
人人都為即將到來的週日活動感到興奮。

Every one **of us will attend the meeting**.
我們都會去參加這個會議。

There isn't anyone **here who speaks**
**Chinese**. 這裡沒有人會說中文。

Does any one **of you play tennis?**
你們有人會打網球嗎？

## Practice

**1**

請利用括弧內的字，
改寫右列各句。

1. There isn't anybody at the office. (nobody)

   → There is nobody at the office.

2. There isn't anyone leaving today. (no one)

   →

3. There isn't anything to feed the fish. (nothing)

   →

4. There isn't anywhere to buy envelops around here. (nowhere)

   →

5. There is nobody here who can speak Japanese. (anybody)

   →

6. There is no one that can translate your letter. (anyone)

   →

7. There is nothing that will change the manager's mind. (anything)

   →

8. There is nowhere we can go to get out of the rain. (anywhere)

   →

**2**

將右列句子改寫為
正確的句子。

1. I don't have nowhere to go.

   →

2. Noone believed me.

   →

3. Everything are ready. Let's go.

   →

4. There is nothing eat.

   →

5. I never want to hurt nobody.

   →

6. Every one in this room will vote for me.

   →

7. Did you see my glasses? I can't find it nowhere.

   →

8. Any one who doesn't support this idea please raise your hand.

   →

## Unit 26

### This, That, These, Those
指示代名詞與指示形容詞

**1** 用來指明、指定名詞的代名詞，叫做**指示代名詞**。所指的人或物若是**單數**，用 this 或 that；所指的人或物若是**複數**，則用 these 或 those。

This is Mary's coat. 這是瑪莉的大衣。

That is Jason's watch. 那是傑森的手錶。

These are my dogs. They are Michael, Big Boy, and Fifi.
這些是我的狗，牠們叫做麥可、大寶和菲菲。

Those are my mother's friends.
那些人是我媽媽的朋友。

**2** 當所指人或物就**在說話者附近時**，用 this 或 these 表示。當所指人或物**離說話者較遠**時，則用 that 或 those 表示。

that tree　those trees

this tree　these trees

This is Mr. Jones. He is president of the Swan Company.
這位是瓊斯先生，他是天鵝公司的董事長。

Who are those men? 那些人是誰？

**3** 指示代名詞 this、that、these 和 those 可以**代替所指涉的名詞**，單獨存在。

This is the book I want.
↳ =this book
這本正是我想要的書。

That is not the book I want.
↳ =that book
那本不是我想要的書。

These are the books I was looking for.
↳ =these books
這些正是我在找的書。

Those are not the books I was looking for.
↳ =those books
那些不是我在找的書。

**4** this、that、these 和 those 除了作代名詞，也常作**形容詞**使用，此時後面會接**名詞**。

Look at this painting. 看看這幅畫。

Check out that sculpture. 檢查那座雕像。

I love these prints. 我喜歡這些圖片。

Let's go see those drawings.
我們去看那些畫。

**5** this、that、these 和 those 也可用來表示**時間**。「**正在發生的事**」或「**即將發生的事**」用 this 或 these，「**已經發生的事**」用 that 或 those。

We're going camping this weekend.
我們這個週末要去露營。

I'm quite busy these days. 我這幾天很忙。

I went downtown that night.
那天晚上我進城去了。

Don't you miss those summers?
你不懷念那幾年的夏天嗎？

## Practice

**1**

看圖用 this、that、these 或 those 填空，完成句子。

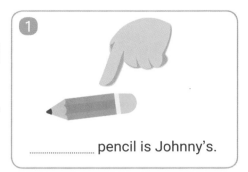

1　.......................... pencil is Johnny's.

2　.......................... tomatoes are sweet.

3　Whose bottle water is .......................... ?

4　.......................... pencil is Jenny's.

5　.......................... tomatoes are sour.

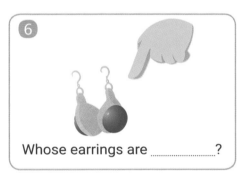

6　Whose earrings are .......................... ?

**2**

選出正確的答案。

1. Is **this / these** the book you want?

2. Do you recognize **that / those** man in the blue shirt?

3. Does our dog love **that / those** toys?

4. What are you up to **these / those** days?

5. We had a lot of snow **that / those** year.

6. We're going to have heavy rain **this / that** year.

7. **That / Those** children are hungry.

8. Will you move **this / these** boxes for me?

9. **This / That** was the end of the vacation.

10. Schoolchildren used chalk and slate boards in **these / those** days.

## Reflexive Pronouns and "Each Other"
## 反身代名詞與相互代名詞 Each Other

**1** 每個人稱代名詞都有一個相對應的**反身代名詞**。單數反身代名詞以 -self 結尾，複數反身代名詞則以 -selves 結尾。

|  | 人稱代名詞 | | 對應的反身代名詞 | |
|---|---|---|---|---|
| 單數 | I | 我 | myself | 我自己 |
|  | you | 你 | yourself | 你自己 |
|  | he | 他 | himself | 他自己 |
|  | she | 她 | herself | 她自己 |
|  | it | 它 | itself | 它自己 |
| 複數 | we | 我們 | ourselves | 我們自己 |
|  | you | 你們 | yourselves | 你們自己 |
|  | they | 他們 | themselves | 他們自己 |

**2** 當句中的**主詞和受詞一樣**時，就要使用反身代名詞當作受詞。

**You are feeling sorry for** yourself.
你在自怨自艾。

**The kids built the tree house by** themselves. 這群小孩們自己蓋了間樹屋。

**The children are now able to dress** themselves. 這些孩子現在會自己穿衣服了。

**Let me introduce** myself.
我來自我介紹一下吧。

**My aunt is looking at** herself **in the mirror.** 我姑姑正在看鏡中的自己。

**My cat likes to lick** itself.
我的貓喜歡舔自己。

**3** by myself 或 by yourself 這類的反身代名詞片語，意思是**獨自**（等於 alone），並無來自於別人的幫助或參與。

**I always go off by** myself **during lunch.**
**= I go places** alone **for lunch.**
午餐時我總是自個兒出去。

**Do you always eat lunch by** yourself **in your office?**
**= Do you always eat lunch** alone?
你都自己在辦公室吃午餐嗎？

**4** 反身代名詞有**強調主詞**的作用，加強敘述的重點。

**I finished the report.**
我把報告完成了。
↓
**I finished the report** myself.
我自己把報告完成了。

**My coworkers were supposed to help, but I finished the report all by** myself.
我同事本來應該要幫忙，但我卻靠自己完成了這份報告。

**5** **相互代名詞** each other 和反身代名詞很像，也是反指主詞，但是它表達了彼此之間互相的關係。

**They are taking a picture of** themselves.
她們在為她們自己拍照。

**They are taking pictures of** each other.
他們在幫彼此拍照。

**Dogs like to sniff** each other.
狗狗喜歡互相聞來聞去。

## Practice

**1**

請看圖並填入適當的反身代名詞。

I am brushing my teeth by
_____myself_____ .

Can you carry that box by
_____ ?

This book is not going to read
_____ .

The little boy cannot dress
_____ .

She always eats lunch by
_____ .

Are you going to drive
_____ to the
toy store?

I guess we have to
get the food by
_____ .

Micky and Lucky
can find food by
_____ .

**2**

請用 themselves 或 each other 造句說明圖中的情況。

1. They are talking to
_____ .

2. They are filming
_____ .

3. They are painting the wall
by _____ .

**1**  自右表選出正確的第一人稱單數代名詞填空，完成句子。
→ Unit 16, 18 重點複習

1. That's ＿＿＿＿＿＿ notebook computer.
2. This morning ＿＿＿＿＿＿ sent an email message to the boss.
3. The funny flash animation was ＿＿＿＿＿＿.
4. If you see someone in the chat room named Monster, that's ＿＿＿＿＿＿.
5. ＿＿＿＿＿＿ computer has a wireless connection to my cellphone.
6. ＿＿＿＿＿＿ use a bluetooth connection from my computer to my cell phone.
7. Wireless Internet access is better for ＿＿＿＿＿＿.
8. That laser mouse is ＿＿＿＿＿＿. It's also wireless.

| me |
| I |
| mine |
| my |

**2**  在空格內填入正確的人稱代名詞。
→ Unit 16, 18 重點複習

1. ＿＿＿＿＿＿ first name is Kevin. What's ＿＿＿＿＿＿ name?
2. My husband and ＿＿＿＿＿＿ have two children. ＿＿＿＿＿＿ children are John and Grace.
3. Jeanie is going out to get dinner. I am going with ＿＿＿＿＿＿.
4. Here's a photo of ＿＿＿＿＿＿ family. That's me on the left.
5. Winnie is in love with Arthur, but ＿＿＿＿＿＿ doesn't love ＿＿＿＿＿＿.
6. This is your hat. ＿＿＿＿＿＿ can't find ＿＿＿＿＿＿. Have ＿＿＿＿＿＿ seen ＿＿＿＿＿＿?
7. The Jones have ＿＿＿＿＿＿ air conditioner on. Let's turn on ＿＿＿＿＿＿.
8. I bought a new car. I like ＿＿＿＿＿＿ very much.
9. My cat caught two mice. ＿＿＿＿＿＿ is playing with ＿＿＿＿＿＿ now.
10. Kim and Tim have moved to a new apartment. ＿＿＿＿＿＿ new apartment is rather big. ＿＿＿＿＿＿ really love ＿＿＿＿＿＿.
11. Linda : Where is ＿＿＿＿＿＿ car?

    Anne : ＿＿＿＿＿＿ is broken.

    Linda : Then how will you go to school tomorrow?

    Anne : I don't know.

    Linda : Would you like to borrow ＿＿＿＿＿＿?

    Anne : That would be great.

**3** 下列各句的空格中，應填入可數名詞、不可數名詞還是兩者皆可？
請選出正確答案填入空格內。

→ Unit 19–21 重點複習

▼ green peppers
▲ wine

**1** Do you have any
<u>wine / green peppers</u> ?

▼ cookies
▲ bread

**2** Please have some
........................................ .

▼ ice cubes
▲ sugar

**3** There's no
........................................ .

▼ combs
▲ toothpaste

**4** There isn't any
........................................ .

▼ pies
▲ candy

**5** How much ........................................
did you get?

▼ grapes
▲ juice

**6** Did you get many
........................................ ?

▼ goats
▲ fish

**7** I saw a lot of
........................................ .

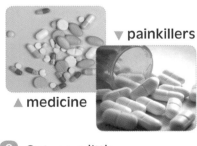

▼ painkillers
▲ medicine

**8** Get me a little
........................................ .

▼ fruit tarts
▲ chocolate cakes

**9** How about a few
........................................ ?

▼ soda
▲ soup

**10** Did you get enough
........................................ ?

▼ leek
▲ garlic

**11** How much ........................................
did you buy?

▼ notebooks
▲ homework

**12** We have many
........................................ .

**4** 檢查各句 any 和 some 的用法是否正確。在正確的句子後寫 **OK**；
不正確的請將錯誤用字畫掉，並於句後更正。
→ Unit 19 重點複習

1. We have any rice. ........................
2. Are there any spoons in the drawer? ........................
3. There isn't some orange juice in the refrigerator. ........................
4. Are there any cookies in the box? ........................
5. Could I have any coffee, please? ........................
6. Would you like some ham? ........................
7. We have lots of fruit. Would you like any? ........................
8. I already had some fruit at home. I don't need some now. ........................
9. There aren't some newspapers. ........................
10. There are any magazines. ........................

**5** 請用 one 或 ones 重寫以下句子。
→ Unit 22 重點複習

1️⃣ Who are these boxes for, the boxes you are carrying?
→ ........................
........................

2️⃣ Do you like the red socks or the yellow socks?
→ ........................
........................

3️⃣ My cubicle is the cubicle next to the manager's office.
→ ........................
........................
........................

4️⃣ I like the pink hat. Which hat do you like?
→ ........................
........................
........................

5️⃣ Our tennis balls are the tennis balls stored over there.
→ ........................
........................
........................

**6** 選出正確的答案。

→ Unit 20 重點複習

**1** ☐ We haven't got _____ time.

　Ⓐ many　　　　Ⓑ much

**2** ☐ We don't have _____ milk left.

　Ⓐ many　　　　Ⓑ much

**3** ☐ _____ information do you have?

　Ⓐ How many　　Ⓑ How much

**4** ☐ _____ people agree with you.

　Ⓐ Many　　　　Ⓑ Much

**5** ☐ He has _____ homework.

　Ⓐ too many　　Ⓑ too much

**6** ☐ He has _____ sandwiches.

　Ⓐ too many　　Ⓑ too much

**7** ☐ Do we have _____ headphones?

　Ⓐ lots of　　　Ⓑ little of

**8** ☐ There are _____ gifts for your family.

　Ⓐ many　　　　Ⓑ much

**9** ☐ You have _____ things to do.

　Ⓐ too many　　Ⓑ too much

**10** ☐ Do you have _____ experience with this?

　Ⓐ many　　　　Ⓑ much

**7** 從下表選出適當的字首搭配標籤裡的提示字根，填空完成以下句子。
→ Unit 23–25 重點複習

| some- | any- | no- | every- |
|-------|------|-----|--------|

**-where**

1. I've looked for my wallet ___everywhere___, but I can't find it.
2. My wallet is _____ to be seen.
3. It must be in the house because I haven't gone _____.
4. I have to go _____, and I need my wallet.

**-one**

5. I called Joe's house about the party, but _____ answered.
6. Do you know if _____ is going over there tonight?
7. _____ should answer the phone.
8. _____ else intends to go there tonight except me.

**-thing**

9. Sue tried to tell me _____ about a problem.
10. Have you heard _____ about Sue's problem?
11. There is probably _____ I can do, but I want to help.
12. Is _____ OK with her now?

**-body**

13. Hello. I'm home. Hey, where is _____?
14. Is _____ home? I am here.
15. There must be _____ here because the lights are on.
16. Well, if _____ is here, then I am going to leave. Bye-bye.

**8** 請看圖並利用表中的不定代名詞，完成下列對話。

→ Unit 23-25 重點複習

**1** **In the Musical Instrument Store**

| someone | anyone |
| no one | everyone |

Woman: I am looking for ❶_____ to give opera lessons to my son.

Man: We just sell musical instruments. ❷_____ here teaches opera.

Woman: Do you know ❸_____ who teaches opera?

Man: ❹_____ likes rock and pop. ❺_____ likes opera.

Woman: Maybe my son should try gospel singing.

**2** **In the Airport Parking Lot**

| somewhere | everywhere |
| anywhere | nowhere |

Woman: Your car is ❻_____ close by, right?

Man: I think so, but it could be ❼_____ in the parking lot.

Woman: It's ❽_____ to be seen. That's for sure.

Man: We haven't looked ❾_____. It could be ❿_____ else.

Woman: You keep looking. I am waiting here.

**3** **In the Principal's Office at School**

| something | everything |
| anything | nothing |

Woman: You must have done ⓫_____ wrong for your teacher to send you to the office.

Boy: I didn't do ⓬_____.

Woman: Are you sure there was ⓭_____ going on?

Boy: The teacher blames ⓮_____ on me.

**9** 選出正確的答案。
→ Unit 26 重點複習

........... 1. ..................... is not my cell phone. That is mine.
Ⓐ This 　　　Ⓑ That 　　　Ⓒ These

........... 2. We are going to the beach ................ weekend. Would you like to join us?
Ⓐ this 　　　Ⓑ that 　　　Ⓒ these

........... 3. Can you pass ................ glasses to me?
Ⓐ this 　　　Ⓑ that 　　　Ⓒ those

........... 4. Can you pass ................ bottle of black pepper to me?
Ⓐ this 　　　Ⓑ that 　　　Ⓒ those

........... 5. We had a lot of fun on ................ Christmas.
Ⓐ this 　　　Ⓑ that 　　　Ⓒ those

........... 6. ................ suitcase belongs to Heather.
Ⓐ This 　　　Ⓑ These 　　　Ⓒ Those

**10** 下列各句若正確，在句後寫上 OK。若句子有誤，畫掉錯誤的字並寫出
正確的反身代名詞或 each other。
→ Unit 27 重點複習

1. My brother made himself sick by eating too much ice cream. .....................

2. My sister made himself sick by eating two big pizzas. .....................

3. The dog is scratching itself. .....................

4. I jog every morning by me. .....................

5. You have only yourself to blame. .....................

6. We would have gone there us but we didn't have time. .....................

7. He can't possibly lift that sofa all by himself. .....................

8. Do you want to finish this project by yourself or do you need help? .....................

9. I helped him. He helped me. We helped ourselves. .....................

10. Don't fight about it. You two need to talk to each other if you are going to solve this problem. .....................

**11** 選出正確的答案。
→ Unit 19–21 重點複習

1. I have **a little / a few** business to do here.

2. You need to give **a few / a little** examples in your essay.

3. Let's not start now. I don't have **enough / a little** time.

4. He has **a lot of / many** courage.

5. Don't buy more food. We have **many / enough**.

6. Buy some new clothes, but not **a lot / much**.

7. There is **little / few** we could do.

8. **Little / Few** people would have done as much as you did.

9. There is **enough / few** salad for everybody.

10. He bought **much / many** games.

11. You had **a few / a little** telephone calls.

12. There are **a lot of / much** boxes in the garage.

13. There were **too many / too much** people in line.

14. I checked the batteries. We have **enough / much**.

## Unit 29

### Present Tenses of the Verb "Be"
### Be 動詞的現在時態

**1** am、is、are 是表示現在時態的 **be 動詞**，用於**現在簡單式**和**現在進行式**。

**My name is Yuki.** 我名叫 Yuki。

**This is my friend Akiko.**
他是我朋友 Akiko。

**Are you both Japanese?**
你們兩個都是日本人嗎？

**No, we aren't. I'm Japanese.
Akiko is Canadian.**
不是，我是日本人，Akiko 是加拿大人。

**2** am 只和代名詞 I 搭配使用。

**I am a student. I am learning English.**
我是學生，我正在學英語。

**I'm not home.** 我不在家。

**3** **單數名詞**以及**代名詞** he、she、it 則搭配 is 使用。

**The knife is very sharp.** 這把刀很利。

**She is a shy girl.** 她是個害羞的女孩。

**4** **複數名詞**以及**代名詞** we、you、they 要和 are 搭配使用。

**These cups are dirty.** 這些杯子很髒。

**We are both Chinese.**
我們兩個都是中國人。

**Are you interested in Chinese literature?**
你對中國文學有興趣嗎？

**They are just like their father.**
他們跟他們父親簡直一個樣。

| 肯定句的全形和縮寫 | | 否定句的全形和縮寫 | |
|---|---|---|---|
| I am | I'm | I am not | I'm not |
| you are | you're | you are not | you aren't |
| he is | he's | he is not | he isn't |
| she is | she's | she is not | she isn't |
| it is | it's | it is not | it isn't |
| we are | we're | we are not | we aren't |
| they are | they're | they are not | they aren't |

| 疑問句的句型 | 肯定和否定簡答的句型 | |
|---|---|---|
| Am I . . . ? | Yes, I am. | No, I'm not. |
| Are you . . . ? | Yes, you are. | No, you aren't. |
| Is he . . . ? | Yes, he is. | No, he isn't. |
| Is she . . . ? | Yes, she is. | No, she isn't. |
| Is it . . . ? | Yes, it is. | No, it isn't. |
| Are we . . . ? | Yes, we are. | No, we aren't. |
| Are they . . . ? | Yes, they are. | No, they aren't. |

**5** wh 疑問詞通常搭配 is 使用。

| 搭配疑問詞的全形和縮寫 | |
|---|---|
| who is | who's |
| what is | what's |
| when is | when's |
| where is | where's |
| why is | why's |
| how is | how's |

**Where is my backpack?**
我的背包在哪裡？

**How is everything?**
一切還順利嗎？

**Who is the man next to Will?**
威爾旁邊那個人是誰？

# Practice

## 1

利用 be 動詞的現在時態（am、is 或 are）填空，完成右列段落。

My name ❶＿＿＿＿＿＿ Eizo. I ❷＿＿＿＿＿＿ the singer in a band called the Rockets. My best friend ❸＿＿＿＿＿＿ Haruki, and he ❹＿＿＿＿＿＿ the guitar player. Ichiro ❺＿＿＿＿＿＿ the bass player. Kiyonobu ❻＿＿＿＿＿＿ the drummer. Ichiro and Kinonobu ❼＿＿＿＿＿＿ brothers. We ❽＿＿＿＿＿＿ a rock band. I ❾＿＿＿＿＿＿ trying to get the band a gig playing at a pub. The place ❿＿＿＿＿＿ called the Beer Bar. We ⓫＿＿＿＿＿＿ not making enough money from our music, so we ⓬＿＿＿＿＿＿ all working day jobs. That ⓭＿＿＿＿＿＿ the life of a musician. We ⓮＿＿＿＿＿＿ used to it.

## 2

請依你的真實情況，填上 am、am not、is、isn't、are 或 aren't。

1. I ＿＿＿＿＿＿ Taiwanese.
2. I ＿＿＿＿＿＿ a student.
3. I ＿＿＿＿＿＿ working.
4. My favorite subject ＿＿＿＿＿＿ English.
5. My only two languages ＿＿＿＿＿＿ Chinese and English.
6. My main interest ＿＿＿＿＿＿ business.
7. There ＿＿＿＿＿＿ lots of job openings in my area.
8. Language skills ＿＿＿＿＿＿ helpful.

## 3

依照提示和範例，描述圖中人物的國籍和職業。

Italian
American
Japanese
French
Canadian
Chinese

drummer
policeman
businessman
chef
violinist
singer

| 1 Karl | 2 Dominique | 3 Hiroko |
|---|---|---|

*Karl is Canadian.*
*He is a violinist.*

＿＿＿＿＿＿＿＿＿＿＿
＿＿＿＿＿＿＿＿＿＿＿

| 4 Lino | 5 Jane | 6 Mike |
|---|---|---|

Unit **30**

There Is, There Are

有……

**1** there is 和 there are 用來表示「可以看到或聽到某物的存在」。

There's **a clock** on the wall. 牆上有個時鐘。

There's **a spider** in the bathroom.
浴室裡有一隻蜘蛛。

There are **ants** in the kitchen.
廚房裡有螞蟻。

| there 搭配 be 動詞的全形和縮寫 ||
|---|---|
| there is | there's |
| there is not | there isn't |
| there are | there're |
| there are not | there aren't |

**2** 這種句型裡，真正的主詞位於 **be 動詞**後面。
be 動詞後面的主詞若為**不可數名詞**或**單數可數名詞**，則使用 there is 的句型。
主詞若是**物品**，再次提及這個主詞時可用 **it** 來代替。

There's **an umbrella** in the hall. It's in the closet.
走廊有一把傘，就在櫃子裡。　↳ 指走廊的那把傘。

There's **a phone call** for Jane. It's her friend Katie.
有一通電話找珍，是她朋友凱蒂打來的。　↳ 指打電話的人。

There isn't **any time** left.
沒有時間了。　↳ 不可數名詞 time 要搭配 there is 或 there isn't 使用。

**3** be 動詞後面的主詞若為**複數可數名詞**，則使用 there are 的句型。再次提及這個主詞時可用 **they** 來代替。

There are **some pens** in the living room. **They're** in the drawer under the phone.
　↳ 指客廳裡的那些筆。
客廳裡有一些筆，就在電話下的抽屜裡。

There are **several letters** for you. **They're** on your desk.
　↳ 指那些信件。
你有一些信，它們就放在你的書桌上。

• There are some glasses on the table, but _____ not clean.
  1
桌上有一些杯子，但是都不乾淨。

**4** 將 be 動詞移到句首，就構成了**疑問句**。

Steve: Is there **a broom** in the closet?
Susan: No, **there isn't**.
史帝夫：櫥櫃裡有掃把嗎？
蘇珊：　沒有。

Ted: Are there **any kangaroos** in the zoo?
Ann: No, **there aren't**.
泰德：　動物園有沒有袋鼠？
安：　　沒有。

• There is a dictionary on the shelf. _____ David's.
  2
架上有一本字典，那本字典是大衛的。

# Practice

### 1

依據圖示，並使用下表提供的文字，完成右列句子。

> there is
>
> there isn't
>
> there are
>
> there aren't

1. ........................... any broccoli on the top shelf.

2. ........................... some tomatoes on the bottom shelf.

3. ........................... any meat in the refrigerator.

4. ........................... a lot of grapes in the refrigerator.

5. ........................... still some room on the shelves of the refrigerator door.

6. ........................... a bottle of mineral water on the bottom shelf of the refrigerator door.

7. ........................... some cheese on the top shelf.

8. ........................... a carton of milk on the bottom shelf of the refrigerator door.

9. ........................... any chicken in the refrigerator.

10. ........................... some grapes on the bottom shelf.

11. ........................... any apple on the bottom shelf.

12. ........................... two oranges.

13. ........................... three guavas.

14. ........................... some watermelon.

15. ........................... any milk on the bottom shelf.

16. ........................... some vegetables on the bottom shelf.

### 2

用下列詞彙完成句子。

> is
>
> isn't
>
> are
>
> aren't
>
> it is
>
> they are
>
> it
>
> them

1. There ........................... some orange juice. ........................... in the refrigerator.

2. There ........................... any rice wine in the kitchen. Can you go buy some? You can buy ........................... at the grocery store on Tenth Street.

3. There ........................... a bottle of mouth wash in the bathroom. ........................... beside the sink.

4. There ........................... many stray dogs in the streets. ........................... very hungry.

5. There ........................... some fantastic programs on TV this weekend. ........................... on Channel 6.

6. There ........................... a lot of homework tonight. ........................... too much.

## Part 3 Present Tenses 現在時態

### Unit 31

Have Got

「擁有」的說法：Have Got

**1** have got 和 has got 只能用於**現在式**，是 have 和 has 比較不正式的說法，兩者意思相同。
但have / has got 主要用於英式，美式用 have / has 表示「**擁有**」。

I have got a new boyfriend. 英式
= I have a new boyfriend.
我有一個新男友。

He has got blue eyes.
= He has blue eyes.
他有一雙藍色的眼睛。

I've got an extra pencil. You can use it.
我有多一支鉛筆，你可以用。

**2** have got 和 has got 的**疑問句**，是把 have 和 has 移到**句首**。不能加助動詞 do 或 does。

Tim: Have you got a pencil, Sam?
Sam: No, I have only got an eraser.
提姆：山姆，你有沒有鉛筆？
山姆：沒有，我只有橡皮擦。

Has she got blonde hair?
= Does she have blonde hair?
她有一頭金髮嗎？

**3** 回答 have got 或 has got 的問句時，若採用**簡答**，不能用 have got、has got 或 haven't got、hasn't got，而要用 have、has 或 haven't、hasn't。

Josh: Has your wife got a job?
Tom: Yes, she has.
　　　↳ 不能用 Yes, she has got.
喬許：你老婆有工作嗎？
湯姆：有，她有。

Jason: Have you got a cellphone?
Helen: No, I haven't.
　　　↳ 不能用 No, she hasn't got.
傑森：你有手機嗎？
海倫：我沒有。

| 肯定句的全形和縮寫 | |
|---|---|
| I have got | I've got |
| you have got | you've got |
| he has got | he's got |
| she has got | she's got |
| it has got | it's got |
| we have got | we've got |
| they have got | they've got |

| 否定句的全形和縮寫 | |
|---|---|
| I have not got | I haven't got |
| you have not got | you haven't got |
| he has not got | he hasn't got |
| she has not got | she hasn't got |
| it has not got | it hasn't got |
| we have not got | we haven't got |
| they have not got | they haven't got |

| 疑問句的句型 | |
|---|---|
| Have I got . . . ? | Has it got . . . ? |
| Have you got . . . ? | Have we got . . . ? |
| Has he got . . . ? | Have they got . . . ? |
| Has she got . . . ? | |

| 肯定和否定的簡答方式 | |
|---|---|
| Yes, I have. | No, I haven't. |
| Yes, you have. | No, you haven't. |
| Yes, he has. | No, he hasn't. |
| Yes, she has. | No, she hasn't. |
| Yes, it has. | No, it hasn't. |
| Yes, we have. | No, we haven't. |
| Yes, they have. | No, they haven't. |

# Practice

**1**

根據圖示，找出相符的寵物名，並利用下表的句型造句。

hamster
pig
cat
snake
dog
parrot

She's got a hamster.

_____

_____

_____

_____

_____

**2**

利用 have / has got 和題目所提供的詞彙，寫出問句。

1. your family / cottage on Lake Michigan

   .................................................................................................

2. you / your own room

   .................................................................................................

3. you / your own closet

   .................................................................................................

4. How many cups / you

   .................................................................................................

5. How many TVs / your family

   .................................................................................................

6. How many cars / your brother

   .................................................................................................

## Unit **32**

### Present Simple Tense
### 現在簡單式

**1** 時態是用來表達某個**動作進行的時間和狀態**的動詞形式。以時間來看，可分為**現在式、過去式和未來式**。

past      present      future

**2** 現在簡單式用來表示**習慣**以及**重複發生的事**，經常和一些**頻率副詞**搭配使用。

I often eat squid. 我常吃烏賊。

I rarely eat meat. 我很少吃肉。

Peggy drinks coffee every day.
珮琪每天喝咖啡。

常用的頻率副詞：
① every day 每天
② usually 通常
③ often 經常
④ sometimes 有時
⑤ never 從不
⑥ yearly 一年一次
⑦ rarely 鮮少

**3** 現在簡單式的構成，如果主詞是**第一人稱代名詞 I、第二人稱代名詞 you** 或者**複數名詞**，就使用**動詞原形**。

I cook dinner every Thursday.
我每個星期四都會做晚餐。

My grandparents like oatmeal.
我的祖父母喜歡燕麥粥。

**4** 若主詞是**第三人稱單數名詞**或**代名詞**，則動詞則要使用加了s、es或ies的第三人稱單數動詞形式。

　　大多數動詞在字尾加s；字尾是s、ch、sh、x、z、o的動詞，加上es；字尾是**子音+ y**的動詞，刪除y，加ies。

Joe reads a book every day.
喬每天看書。

She sometimes goes jogging in the evening.
她有時傍晚會去慢跑。

The baby cries every night.
這嬰兒每晚哭鬧。

**5** 現在簡單式否定句的構成，如果主詞是**複數名詞**或者代名詞 I、you、we、they，就在句中加上 do not 或 don't；如果主詞是**第三人稱單數名詞**或**代名詞**，就在句中加上 does not 或 doesn't。

My wife doesn't cook dinner on Thursdays.
我太太星期四都不做晚餐。

They don't play tennis.
他們不打網球的。

I don't wash dishes.
我不洗碗的。

**6** 現在簡單式的疑問句，是在句首加上 do 或 does，並且動詞使用原形。回答也是用 do 或 does 來構成簡答。

Eve: Do you like cereal and milk for breakfast?
依芙： 你早餐喜歡吃牛奶麥片嗎？
Bob: I do. 鮑伯：喜歡。

Jude: Does Wendy drive to work every day?
裘德： 溫蒂每天開車上班嗎？
Sid: Yes, she does. 席德：是的。

| 否定句的全形和縮寫 | | 疑問句的句型 | 肯定和否定的簡答方式 | |
| --- | --- | --- | --- | --- |
| I do not | I don't | Do I . . . ? | Yes, I do. | No, I don't. |
| you do not | you don't | Do you . . . ? | Yes, you do. | No, you don't. |
| he does not | he doesn't | Does he . . . ? | Yes, he does. | No, he doesn't. |
| she does not | she doesn't | Does she . . . ? | Yes, she does. | No, she doesn't. |
| it does not | it doesn't | Does it . . . ? | Yes, it does. | No, it doesn't. |
| we do not | we don't | Do we . . . ? | Yes, we do. | No, we don't. |
| they do not | they don't | Do they . . . ? | Yes, they do. | No, they don't. |

# Practice

## 1

請寫出右列動詞的
第三人稱單數動詞。

1. eat _____
2. drink _____
3. walk _____
4. run _____
5. paint _____
6. bury _____
7. watch _____
8. carry _____
9. unbox _____
10. crunch _____
11. try _____
12. chase _____
13. cut _____
14. go _____
15. fix _____
16. teach _____

## 2

右列是 Bobby 和
Jenny 日常行程的描述，
請分辨其中哪些動詞是
「現在簡單式」，將它
們畫上底線。

**Bobby** ▶  I cook simple food every day. I usually heat food in the microwave oven. I often make sandwiches. I sometimes pour hot water on fast noodles. However, I don't wash dishes.

**Jenny** ▶ I usually get up at 6:00 in the morning. I eat breakfast at 6:30. I leave my house at 7:00. I walk to the bus stop. I take the 7:15 bus. I always get to work at 8:00. I have lunch at 12:30. I leave work at 5:30. I take the bus home. I arrive at my home about 6:30. I eat dinner at 7:00. I often fall asleep after the 11:00 news ends.

## 3

現在簡單式經常可以
用來說明工具的功
能。請依據圖示，自
下表選用適當的動
詞，用「現在簡單式」
造句說明每個工具的
功能。

cut
move
tighten
push
pound
make

1. A saw _____
   wood.

2. A wrench
   _____ bolts.

3. A drill _____
   holes.

4. A cart _____
   boxes.

5. A hammer
   _____ nails
   into wood.

6. A bulldozer
   _____ earth
   and stones.

# Unit 33

## Present Continuous Tense
## 現在進行式

**1** 現在進行式用來表示現在**持續不斷**或正在進行的動作，由「be 動詞 + V-ing」所構成。

I'm <u>making</u> a strawberry cake.
我正在做草莓蛋糕。

The sun is <u>rising</u>. 旭日正在升起。

Little Susie and Pinky are <u>playing</u> with their dolls. 小蘇西和蘋綺正在玩洋娃娃。

- It ¹ _____. 現在正在下雨。
- Watson ² _____ a novel.
  華生正在讀小說。

Rick is <u>putting</u> a jigsaw puzzle together.
瑞克正在玩拼圖。

**2** **動詞的進行式**是在字尾加上 ing，變化方式如下：

❶ 直接加上 ing。
clean → cleaning 清掃
study → studying 研讀
walk → walking 走路

❷ 字尾是 e 的動詞，去掉 e 再加 ing。
bake → baking 烘焙
rise → rising 升起
hope → hoping 希望

❸ 字尾是 ie 的動詞，把 ie 改成 y，再加 ing。
die → dying 死亡
lie → lying 說謊
tie → tying 捆

❹ 字尾是「單母音 + 單子音」的動詞，重複字尾子音，再加 ing。
stop → stopping 停止
hit → hitting 打

**3** 現在進行式的疑問句，只要將 **be** 動詞移到句首。

May: Hello? What <u>are</u> you <u>doing</u>?
Victor: I am <u>watching</u> TV.
May: <u>Are</u> you <u>doing</u> your homework?
Victor: Yes, I am. This is for the TV class.

梅： 哈囉！你在做什麼？
維多： 我在看電視。
梅： 你在做功課嗎？
維多： 對啊，這是電視廣播課的作業。

- ³ _____ you ⁴ _____ English now?
  你在唸英文嗎？
- ⁵ _____ he ⁶ _____ in the pool now? 他正在池子裡游泳嗎？

| 肯定句的全形和縮寫 | |
| --- | --- |
| I am thinking | I'm thinking |
| you are thinking | you're thinking |
| he is thinking | he's thinking |
| she is thinking | she's thinking |
| it is thinking | it's thinking |
| we are thinking | we're thinking |
| they are thinking | they're thinking |

| 否定句的全形和縮寫 | |
| --- | --- |
| I am not thinking | I'm not thinking |
| you are not thinking | you aren't thinking |
| he is not thinking | he isn't thinking |
| she is not thinking | she isn't thinking |
| it is not thinking | it isn't thinking |
| we are not thinking | we aren't thinking |
| they are not thinking | they aren't thinking |

| 疑問句的句型 | |
| --- | --- |
| Am I thinking . . . ? | Is it thinking . . . ? |
| Are you thinking . . . ? | Are we thinking . . . ? |
| Is he thinking . . . ? | Are they thinking . . . ? |
| Is she thinking . . . ? | |

| 肯定和否定的簡答方式 | |
| --- | --- |
| Yes, I am. | No, I'm not. |
| Yes, you are. | No, you aren't. |
| Yes, he is. | No, he isn't. |
| Yes, she is. | No, she isn't. |
| Yes, it is. | No, it isn't. |
| Yes, we are. | No, we aren't. |
| Yes, they are. | No, they aren't. |

## Practice

**1**

將右列動詞，加上 ing，並根據規則做必要的變化。

1. talk _____
2. care _____
3. stay _____
4. sleep _____
5. jog _____
6. eat _____
7. make _____
8. rob _____
9. advise _____
10. die _____

11. spit _____
12. stare _____
13. wait _____
14. clip _____
15. swim _____
16. cry _____
17. lie _____
18. plan _____
19. throw _____
20. speak _____

**2**

請依圖示，自下表選出適當的動詞，以「現在進行式」完成句子。

lie
walk
buy
run
picnic
sit
play
shine
eat

1. The girl _____ a dog.
2. The woman _____ fruits.
3. The sun _____.
4. The cat _____ with a ribbon.
5. The girls _____.
6. A surfboard _____ on the beach.
7. They _____.
8. The girl _____ ice cream.
9. Mike _____ on the lifeguard chair.

## Unit **34**

### Comparison Between the Present Continuous Tense and the Present Simple Tense

### 現在進行式和現在簡單式用法比較

**1** 現在進行式用來**描述說話當下正在發生的事**，或詢問某人當下正在做什麼。句子裡經常會出現 now 或 right now 這樣的詞。

Leslie is in the warehouse now. She's making an inventory.
雷思莉在倉庫裡，她正在開一張存貨清單。

Where is Leslie? Is she working in the warehouse?
雷思莉在哪裡？她在倉庫裡工作嗎？

**2** 現在簡單式用來描述一再重複的事情，與講話當下的狀況並無緊密關連。句子裡經常會出現 every day、usually、often、sometimes 這些頻率副詞。

Ian checks his email every day.
伊恩每天都會收電子郵件。

Does Ivana often update her blog?
伊凡娜有經常更新她的部落格嗎？

**3** 讓我們用同樣的動詞來比較看看。

現在進行式

I'm listening now. Please say it.
我正在聽，請說。

Stop, thief! He's stealing my bicycle.
站住，小偷！他正在偷我的腳踏車。

現在簡單式

I usually listen to heavy metal rock music.
我通常都聽重金屬搖滾樂。

He frequently steals things, and sooner or later he will get caught and put into jail.
他慣性地偷竊，遲早會被抓去關的。

**4** 問句中，「What are you doing?」用來詢問對方正在做什麼事；「What do you do?」則用來詢問一個人的**工作或職業**。

Jay : What are you doing?
Kay : I'm playing a computer game.
Jay : What do you do?
Kay : I am a computer game designer.
杰：你在做什麼？
凱：我正在玩電腦遊戲。
杰：你是做什麼的？
凱：我是電腦遊戲的設計師。

比較

Sarah is a freelance writer. She writes for several newspapers and magazines. She works hard for over 8 hours a day. Right now she is working on her computer. She is writing a story about a wind farm in Mongolia.

莎拉是一名自由作家。她為幾家報紙及雜誌寫文章。她一天認真工作超過八小時。她現在正在電腦前工作，寫一篇關於蒙古風力農場的報導。

比較

Jamie is a computer security specialist. He works for a computer security firm. He protects corporate data networks. He is watching a hacker trying to break into a computer right now. He is trying to stop the hacker at the moment.

傑米是一名電腦安全防禦專家，他在一家電腦防禦公司上班，負責保護公司的資料網。他現在正盯著一名試圖入侵的駭客，試著阻止他。

## Practice

**1**

自字彙表選出適當的動詞，並正確使用現在簡單式或現在進行式，填空完成句子。

| leave | drive | wish | drink | end | think | design | go |

Bob Jones is stuck in traffic. He's ❶＿＿＿＿＿＿ to work. Every day he ❷＿＿＿＿＿＿ at 8:00 in the morning. He is a microwave engineer. He ❸＿＿＿＿＿＿ communication systems for mobile phone operators. Whenever he ❹＿＿＿＿＿＿ up sitting in a traffic jam, he ❺＿＿＿＿＿＿ some coffee and listens to music. Right now he ❻＿＿＿＿＿＿ about how fast microwaves travel and how slow he ❼＿＿＿＿＿＿ in the traffic jam. He ❽＿＿＿＿＿＿ he were a speedy little microwave.

**2**

判斷以下句子應使用現在簡單式或現在進行式，利用題目提供的詞彙，組合造問句，根據事實做出簡答之後，再寫出完整的句子描述事實。

| 主詞 | 頻率副詞 | 動詞片語／形容詞 |
|---|---|---|

1. **you** **often** **listen to music**

   Q Do you often listen to music?

   A Yes, I do. I often listen to music.

2. **you** **at this moment** **watch TV**

   Q ＿＿＿＿＿＿＿＿＿＿＿＿

   A ＿＿＿＿＿＿＿＿＿＿＿＿

3. **it** **now** **hot**

   Q ＿＿＿＿＿＿＿＿＿＿＿＿

   A ＿＿＿＿＿＿＿＿＿＿＿＿

4. **it** **often / this time of year** **hot**

   Q ＿＿＿＿＿＿＿＿＿＿＿＿

   A ＿＿＿＿＿＿＿＿＿＿＿＿

5. **you** **every day** **drink coffee**

   Q ＿＿＿＿＿＿＿＿＿＿＿＿

   A ＿＿＿＿＿＿＿＿＿＿＿＿

6. **you** **right now** **drink tea**

   Q ＿＿＿＿＿＿＿＿＿＿＿＿

   A ＿＿＿＿＿＿＿＿＿＿＿＿

# Part 3 Present Tenses 現在時態

## Unit 35

### Verbs Not Normally Used in the Continuous Tense
### 通常不能用進行式的動詞

**1** 下列動詞，通常不會用於進行式，會用於**現在簡單式（或過去簡單式）**。

| | | |
|---|---|---|
| want | 想要 | I want a notebook. |
| believe | 相信 | I believe in you. |
| belong to | 屬於 | This bag belongs to you. |
| forget | 忘記 | I forget things easily. |
| hate | 恨 | I hate you. |
| know | 知道 | I know the answer. |
| like | 喜歡 | Dogs like meat. |
| mean | 意指 | I mean what I say. |
| need | 需要 | I need a dictionary. |
| own | 擁有 | Jack owns a sports car. |
| prefer | 寧願 | I prefer fish. |
| realize | 瞭解 | Do you realize how difficult it will be? |
| recognize | 認識 | I don't recognize you. |
| remember | 記得 | He remembers everything. |
| seem | 似乎 | You seem tired. |
| understand | 瞭解 | I understand you. |

**Can you understand our waiter? He has a funny accent.** 你懂我們服務生的意思嗎？他有一種奇怪的口音。

**2** 有些字不只一個意思。當它用於某種意思時，不能用進行式。
動詞 think 表示「用腦子想」的時候，可以用**進行式**；表示「相信／認為」時，就只能用**簡單式**。

**Give me a minute. I'm thinking.** 思考
給我一分鐘，我正在想。

**I think I will try a cinnamon raisin scone.**
我想我會試試肉桂葡萄乾司康餅。認為

**3** 動詞 have/has 不只一種意思：
當它表示「吃」的動作時，可以用**進行式**；當它表示「擁有」時，就只能用**簡單式**。

**Julie is having breakfast at the café.**
↳ 表「吃」，可用進行式。
茱麗正在咖啡廳吃早餐。

**Lily has a cottage by Deer Lake.**
↳ 表「有」，用簡單式。
莉莉在鹿湖旁有一間小屋。

**4** has got 和 have got 的意思是「**擁有**」，只能用於**現在簡單式**。

**Yvonne has got two sisters and three brothers.** 伊芳有兩個姊妹和三個兄弟。

**We have got a new house.** 我們有個新家。

**5** 一些**感官動詞**應使用**簡單式**，或者**加上 can**，而不用進行式。

smell 聞 　　　　hear 聽

see 看 　　　　taste 嚐

**I can smell something burning in the kitchen.** 我聞到廚房裡有燒焦的味道。

**I can see him coming this way.**
我看到他往這裡走來。

**This soup tastes delicious.**
這湯很好喝。

**Can you hear the man talking?**
你聽得到那個人說話嗎？

## Practice

**1**

請用「現在簡單式」
或「現在進行式」，
填空完成右列句子。

1. I _____ (eat) stewed prunes, but I really _____ (hate) stewed prunes.

2. Harry _____ (eat) a banana.
   He _____ (like) bananas.

3. Ron _____ (love) his weekend hiking trips.

4. The Jameson family _____ (like) to barbeque.

5. Jack and Jane _____ (make) sushi right now.
   They _____ (know) how to make sushi.

6. _____ you _____ (mean) we can leave now?

7. You _____ (seem) very tired. What _____ you _____ (do) right now?

8. _____ you _____ (go) to Sam's house?
   _____ you _____ (need) a ride?

9. Lucy _____ (carry) a backpack. This backpack _____ (belong) to her.

10. _____ you _____ (understand) what the teacher is saying?

11. John _____ (remember) to deliver a pot of chicken soup to his grandma every Saturday morning.

**2**

右列句子，若動詞的
用法正確，請在句後
寫上OK；
若錯誤，請刪掉錯誤
的用法並更正。

1. I am owning my own house. _____

2. This book belongs to Mary. _____

3. Mother is believing your story. _____

4. I often forget names. _____

5. I am having a snack. _____

6. The man is recognizing you. _____

7. The story is needing an ending. _____

8. You are seeming a little uncomfortable. _____

9. Are you feeling sick? _____

10. Do you have got a swimsuit? _____

# Unit 36

## Review Test of Units 29–35
### 單元 29–35 總複習

**1** 寫出下列動詞的「第三人稱現在式」和「現在進行式」。
→ Unit 32, 33 重點複習

| | | |
|---|---|---|
| 1. change *changes changing* | 11. tie |
| 2. visit | 12. apply |
| 3. turn | 13. jump |
| 4. jog | 14. enjoy |
| 5. mix | 15. steal |
| 6. cry | 16. swim |
| 7. have | 17. send |
| 8. cut | 18. taste |
| 9. fight | 19. finish |
| 10. feel | 20. study |

**2** 請用 is 或 are 以及題目所提供的字造問句;並根據事實回答。
→ Unit 29 重點複習

1. What / your favorite TV show
   Q  *What is your favorite TV show?*
   A  *The Simpsons.*

2. What / your favorite movie
   Q
   A

3. Who / your favorite actor
   Q
   A

4. Who / your favorite actress
   Q
   A

5. What / your favorite food
   Q
   A

6. What / your favorite juice

Q _____

A _____

7. Who / your parents

Q _____

A _____

8. Who / your brothers and sisters

Q _____

A _____

3 參考圖片回答問題。先用 is 或 are 完成問句,再依事實回答問題。
→ Unit 29 重點複習

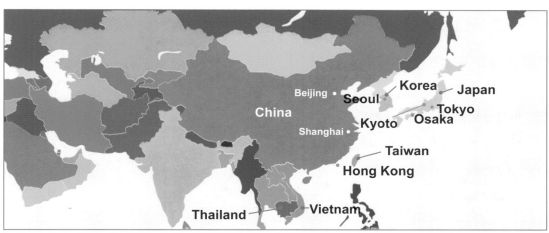

1. Q _Is_____ Seoul in Vietnam?

A _No, Seoul is in Korea._

2. Q _____ Thailand and Vietnam in East Asia?

A _____

3. Q _____ Hong Kong in Japan?

A _____

4. Q _____ Beijing and Shanghai in China?

A _____

5. Q _____ Osaka in Taiwan?

A _____

6. Q _____ Tokyo, Osaka, and Kyoto in Japan?

A _____

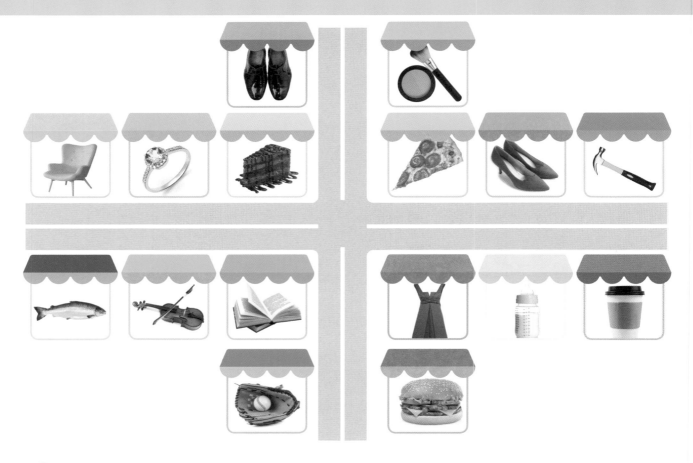

4 依據上面圖示，利用下表提供的句型來完成下列問答。
→ Unit 29 重點複習

| Is there |
| Are there |
| Yes, there is. |
| No, there isn't. |
| Yes, there are. |
| No, there aren't. |

1. Q  *Are there*  any men's shoe stores?
   A  *Yes, there are.*

2. Q _____ a wig store?
   A _____

3. Q _____ a computer store?
   A _____

4. Q _____ two bookstores?
   A _____

5. Q _____ any women's clothing stores?
   A _____

6. Q _____ any women's shoe stores?
   A _____

7. Q _____ three music stores?
   A _____

8. Q _____ a jewelry store?
   A _____

**5** 請正確填上 am、are、is、have 或 has。
→ Unit 29-31 重點複習

1. My name _____ Leo.
2. I _____ a security guard at a bank.
3. I _____ got a gun.
4. There _____n't any bullets in my gun.
5. If the bank _____ a problem, I call the police.
6. Uh oh! There _____ two bank robbers.

7. I _____ moving closer to the robbers.
8. They _____ reaching out to grab something.
9. Hands up! Oops! I made a mistake. They _____ vice presidents.
10. I _____ sorry. I made a mistake.

**6** 請用 is 或 are 以及題目所提供的字造問句；並根據事實，以肯定或否定句型簡答。
→ Unit 29 重點複習

1. you / university student

   Ⓠ *Are you a university student?*

   Ⓐ *Yes, I am. / No, I'm not.*

2. you / big reader

   Ⓠ _____

   Ⓐ _____

3. your birthday / coming soon

   Ⓠ _____

   Ⓐ _____

4. your favorite holiday / Chinese New Year

   Ⓠ _____

   Ⓐ _____

**7** 看圖用 there is 或 there are 來描述圖中有什麼物品。
→ Unit 30 重點複習

1. *There is an alarm clock on the dresser.*
2. _____
3. _____
4. _____
5. _____

**8** 用 do、does、don't、doesn't 和 work、works，填空完成句子。
→ Unit 32 重點複習

Jasmine: ❶_____ you ❷_____ or go to school?

Anthone: I ❸_____ go to school. I ❹_____ at a bank.

Jasmine: ❺_____ your friend George ❻_____ too?

Jasmine: Yes, he ❼_____ at the same bank as I do.

Jasmine: ❽_____ he ❾_____ in the same department as you do?

Anthone: No, he ❿_____. I ⓫_____ in the trust department.

He ⓬_____ in the foreign exchange department.

**9** 用 do 或 does 以及題目所提供的詞彙造問句，再依真實的情況簡答，
並寫出完整句子描述事實。
→ Unit 32 重點複習

1. you / watch many movies

   Ⓠ ........................................................................................................................

   Ⓐ ........................................................................................................................

2. your mother / work

   Ⓠ ........................................................................................................................

   Ⓐ ........................................................................................................................

3. your father / drive a car to work

   Ⓠ ........................................................................................................................

   Ⓐ ........................................................................................................................

4. your family / have a big house

   Ⓠ ........................................................................................................................

   Ⓐ ........................................................................................................................

5. your neighbors / have children

   Ⓠ ........................................................................................................................

   Ⓐ ........................................................................................................................

6. you / have a university degree

   Ⓠ ........................................................................................................................

   Ⓐ ........................................................................................................................

**10** 閱讀 Annabelle 的自我介紹，並從字彙表選出適當的詞彙，
造問句詢問她問題。
→ Unit 32 重點複習

Hi, my name is Annabelle, but I like my friends to call me Annie. I am from Singapore. I am working at a junior high school in Hong Kong. After school at 4:00 I usually go to my favorite café. I have a cup of black coffee, read a newspaper, and grade some papers. About 6:00, I take the bus home, have dinner, and watch TV. I go to bed early because I have to get up early. I have to be at school by 6:45 a.m. During the school year I am busy every day.

| go home |
| go home |
| come from |
| like to be called |
| drink at the café |
| have to be at school |
| go to the café |

1. What  *do you like to be called* _____?
2. Where _____?
3. What time _____?
4. What _____?
5. What time _____?
6. How _____?
7. What time _____?

**11** 用 have got 或 has got 改寫下列句子，若不能改寫，則畫上╳。
→ Unit 31 重點複習

1. Peter has a good car.

   → _____

2. Paul is having a haircut right now.

   → _____

   _____

3. Wendy has a brother and a sister.

   → _____

   _____

4. The Hamiltons have two cars.

   → _____

5. Ken has a lot of good ideas.

   → _____

   _____

6. My sister is having dinner with her friend right now.

   → _____

   _____

7. I have the answer sheet.

   → _____

**12** 請依圖示，自字彙表選出適當的動詞，以現在進行式完成句子。
→ **Unit 32 重點複習**

deliver
use
fix
change
talk
work

1. Sam _____ the suspension.
2. Peter _____ packages.
3. Joe _____ the tire.
4. Bill _____ on the phone.
5. Chuck and Debbie _____ the computer.
6. They _____ in the computer industry.

**13** 選出正確的答案。
→ **Unit 33–35 重點複習**

1. **I am going / I go** to the store now.

2. I usually **stop / stopping** at the store on my way home from work.

3. Frank is working at the store. **He often has / He's often having** the afternoon shift.

4. The store **is having / is having got** a big sale on diapers.

5. Frank **wants / is wanting** a break from selling baby supplies.

6. Frank is taking a break now. He **is having / has** some cookies and a glass of milk.

7. "Be quiet," Frank says to Joe. "**I'm thinking / I think** about something."

8. "**I have got / I am having** an idea," says Frank.

9. "**I don't believe / I'm not believing** you," says Joe.

10. "You're not thinking. **I can hear / I'm hearing** you snoring."

**14** 請將下列句子改成否定句和疑問句。
→ Unit 29-33 重點複習

1. We're tired.
   → ................................................................................................................................
   → ................................................................................................................................

2. You're rich.
   → ................................................................................................................................
   → ................................................................................................................................

3. There's a message for Jim.
   → ................................................................................................................................
   → ................................................................................................................................

4. It is a surprise.
   → ................................................................................................................................
   → ................................................................................................................................

5. They have got tickets.
   → ................................................................................................................................
   → ................................................................................................................................

6. You have got electric power.
   → ................................................................................................................................
   → ................................................................................................................................

7. She works out at the gym.
   → ................................................................................................................................
   → ................................................................................................................................

8. He usually drinks a fitness shake for breakfast.
   → ................................................................................................................................
   → ................................................................................................................................

9. We are playing baseball this weekend.
   → ................................................................................................................................
   → ................................................................................................................................

10. He realizes this is the end of the vacation.
    → ................................................................................................................................
    → ................................................................................................................................

## Unit 37

### Past Tenses of the Verb "Be"
### Be 動詞的過去時態

**1** was 和 were 是表示**過去時態**的 be 動詞，用來表示「**過去的某一狀況**」。也可以當作助動詞，與述語動詞的 -ing 形式一起構成**過去進行式**，表示「**過去某時刻正在發生的事**」。

I was on vacation last month.
I wasn't on sick leave.
我上個月是去度假，不是請病假。

Sam and Susie were in Berlin for a week.
山姆和蘇西在柏林待了一個禮拜。

It was raining all day yesterday.
昨天下了一整天的雨。

**2** **主詞**如果是**單數名詞**，或者是**代名詞** I、he、she、it，be 動詞則要用 was。

| I was | he was | she was | it was |

I was at home last night.
我昨天整晚都在家。

It was so much fun at the electronic music festival. 參加電子音樂節非常好玩。

Vicky was a law student for six years.
薇琪念了六年的法律。

- I ¹_____ in town yesterday.
  我昨天在鎮上。
- Janet and Mother ²_____ employed at the JJ Company for two years.
  珍奈特和媽媽曾經在 JJ 公司工作了兩年。
- It ³_____ snowing last night.
  昨晚一直下雪。
- They ⁴_____ not happy on the trip to Bali last month.
  他們上個月去峇里島玩得不太愉快。

| 否定句的全形和縮寫 | |
|---|---|
| I was not | I wasn't |
| you were not | you weren't |
| he was not | he wasn't |
| she was not | she wasn't |
| it was not | it wasn't |
| we were not | we weren't |
| they were not | they weren't |

| 疑問句的句型 | |
|---|---|
| Was I . . . ? | Was it . . . ? |
| Were you . . . ? | Were we . . . ? |
| Was he . . . ? | Were they . . . ? |
| Was she . . . ? | |

| 肯定和否定簡答的句型 | |
|---|---|
| Yes, I was. | No, I wasn't. |
| Yes, you were. | No, you weren't. |
| Yes, he was. | No, he wasn't. |
| Yes, she was. | No, she wasn't. |
| Yes, it was. | No, it wasn't. |
| Yes, we were. | No, we weren't. |
| Yes, they were. | No, they weren't. |

**3** **主詞**如果是**複數名詞**，或者是**代名詞** you、we、they，be 動詞則要用 were。

| you were | we were | they were |

Page: Were you and your friend in Berlin for the electronic music festival?

Craig: Yes, we were.

佩吉： 那時你和你朋友在柏林參加電子音樂節嗎？

克雷格：對啊。

They were not in school yesterday.
他們昨天不在學校裡。

## Practice

**1**

請判斷句中的時態，自下表選用正確的 be 動詞完成句子。

| is |
| --- |
| are |
| was |
| were |

1. Laura _____ a medical student for a long time. Now, she _____ a doctor.
2. Tammy _____ a cute little girl, and now she _____ a beautiful woman.
3. Today _____ a rainy day. Yesterday _____ a rainy day, too.
4. Today _____ January 1st, so yesterday _____ December 31st.
5. That _____ a big dog, but once it _____ a puppy.
6. Fluffy _____ such a busy little kitty, but now she _____ a lazy old cat.
7. The grapes _____ OK yesterday, but today they _____ overly ripe.
8. The new recruits _____ in Boot Camp last month. Now they _____ in technical school.
9. The thieves _____ in jail now. Last year they _____ not in jail.
10. We _____ so upset when we heard the news, but now we _____ feeling better.
11. Musicals _____ very popular in the past, and they _____ still popular today.
12. At one time, cell phones _____ uncommon, but now they _____ everywhere.

**2**

用 was 或 were 完成右列問句，依照實際情形做出簡答，並寫出完整句子描述事實。

1. __Were__ you busy yesterday?
   → _Yes, I was. I was very busy yesterday._
2. _____ you at school yesterday morning?
   → _____
3. _____ yesterday the busiest day of the week?
   → _____
4. _____ your father in the office last night?
   → _____
5. _____ you at your friend's house last Saturday?
   → _____
6. _____ your mother at home at 8 o'clock yesterday morning?
   → _____
7. _____ you in bed at 11 o'clock last night?
   → _____
8. _____ you at the bookstore at 6 o'clock yesterday evening?
   → _____

# Unit 38

## Past Simple Tense (1)
## 過去簡單式（1）

**1** 過去簡單式可用來表示「**過去曾經存在或發生過的事**」。這件事可以是短暫的單一事件，也可以是持續性或反覆發生的事件。

---

**Stella** called **a cab. The cab** drove **her home.**
史黛拉叫了一輛計程車。計程車載她回家。

Kelly: I went **to Paris on vacation.**
Sean: Did **your boyfriend Andrew** go?
Kelly: **Andrew** didn't go **with me.**
Sean: Did **you** go **alone?**
Kelly: No, I didn't. I went **with my new boyfriend, Henry.**

凱莉：我去了一趟巴黎度假。
席恩：你的男友安德魯有一起去嗎？
凱莉：安德魯沒有和我一起去。
席恩：那你是一個人去的囉？
凱莉：不是，我和我的新男友亨瑞一起去。

**2** 過去簡單式經常和一些表示**過去時間**的**副詞**搭配使用。

---

**I** walked **to the mall** yesterday.
昨天我走路去購物中心。

**Thomas Edison** invented **a lot of devices** in the 19th century.
愛迪生於十九世紀發明了許多裝置。

表示過去時間的副詞：
① yesterday 昨天
② last week 上週
③ last month 上個月
④ in 2005 在 2005 年
⑤ in the 20th century 在二十世紀

**3** **過去簡單式**的動詞要使用過去式動詞，其中規則動詞的過去式是在**字尾加上** ed。規則如下：

❶ 直接加上 **ed**。
visit → visited 參觀
wash → washed 洗
play → played 玩耍

❷ **字尾是 e 的動詞**只加 d。
love → loved 愛
dance → danced 跳舞
hate → hated 恨

❸ 字尾是「**子音 +y**」的動詞，去掉 y，再加 ied。
study → studied 研讀
fry → fried 油炸
copy → copied 影印

❹ 字尾是「**單母音 + 單子音**」的單音節動詞，重複字尾子音，再加 ed。
jog → jogged 慢跑
nod → nodded 點頭

### 規則動詞發音規則

規則動詞的過去式，字尾 ed 有 /ɪd/、/d/ 和 /t/ 三種發音，規則如下：
❶ 動詞字尾發**無聲子音** /f/、/k/、/p/ 時，ed 的讀音為 /t/。
· jumped /dʒʌmpt/ 跳 · laughed /læft/ 笑
❷ 動詞字尾發**有聲子音**或**母音**時，ed 讀音為 /d/。
· skimmed /skɪmd/ 撇過
· towed /toʊd/ 拖拉
❸ 動詞字尾發 /t/ 或 /d/ 的音時，ed 的讀音為 /ɪd/。
· visited /ˈvɪzɪtɪd/ 參觀
· needed /ˈnidɪd/ 需要

**4** **不規則動詞**的過去式，請一一記下它們的拼寫。

---

go → went 走
buy → bought 買
tell → told 告訴
make → made 做
run → ran 跑
get → got 拿取
choose → chose 選擇
hear → heard 聽到

cut → cut 切
hit → hit 打
read → read 讀
set → set 設立
cost → cost 花費
let → let 讓
put → put 放
shut → shut 關閉

## Practice

**1**

寫出右列動詞的過去式。

1. walk _____
2. run _____
3. cough _____
4. write _____
5. eat _____
6. drop _____
7. ask _____
8. pick _____
9. show _____
10. drink _____
11. wait _____

12. type _____
13. marry _____
14. fly _____
15. go _____
16. use _____
17. join _____
18. play _____
19. look _____
20. like _____
21. send _____
22. jog _____

**2**

依據圖示，自下表選出適當的動詞，用過去式來描述圖中人物做過什麼。

use
attend
receive
check
count
put

1. He _____ the money.

2. They _____ a meeting.

3. She _____ some email.

4. She _____ a photocopier.

5. He _____ the inventory.

6. He _____ a box on the shelf.

Past Simple Tense (2)
過去簡單式（2）

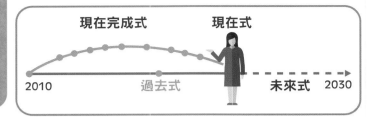

現在完成式　　現在式

2010　　過去式　　未來式　2030

**1** **過去簡單式**的否定句，是在主詞後面使用「did not + 動詞原形」或縮寫「didn't + 動詞原形」。

I didn't mean to hurt you.
我不是故意要傷害你。

She did not arrive on time.
她並未及時趕到。

Mark and Tanya didn't go to the market yesterday morning.
馬克和譚雅昨天早上並沒有去市場。

**2** **過去簡單式**的疑問句，是在句首加上 Did，**動詞**也要使用原形。

Did you call me this morning?
你今天早上有打電話找我嗎？

Did you lock Mr. Jones in his room?
你把瓊斯先生鎖在房間裡嗎？

Did your brother stay up late last night?
你哥哥昨晚是不是熬夜？

肯定簡答的句型，都是用「主詞 + did.」。
否定簡答的句型，都是用「主詞 + didn't」。

• Yes, I did.
• No, I didn't.

**過去簡單式經常用來說故事：**

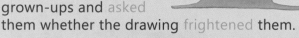

I showed my masterpiece to the grown-ups and asked them whether the drawing frightened them.

But they answered: "Frighten? Why should anyone be frightened by a hat?"

My drawing was not a picture of a hat. It was a picture of a boa constrictor digesting an elephant. But since the grown-ups were not able to understand it, I made another drawing: I drew the inside of the boa constrictor so that the grown-ups could see it clearly.

我把我的大作拿給大人們看，問他們這畫嚇不嚇人。他們卻回答：「嚇人？一頂帽子有什麼好嚇人的？」我畫的可不是什麼帽子，是一條大蟒蛇正在消化牠肚裡的一頭大象。好吧，既然大人們看不懂這張圖，我又畫了一張：我把大蟒蛇肚子裡的東西也畫出來，這下大人們就看得懂了。

**「過去簡單式」和「現在簡單式」的比較**

I am on vacation. I am in London now. Last night I went to the Tower of London. Last year I visited Paris. Two years ago I stayed in Rome for a week. I like Rome, but I like London better. I like vacations.

我正在度假，我現在人在倫敦。昨晚我去了倫敦塔。去年我去巴黎參觀，兩年前則在羅馬待了一週。我喜歡羅馬，但更愛倫敦。我很喜歡度假。

# Practice

**1**

用 did、didn't、have 或 had，完成右列句子。

1. Ken: _____ Harry sleep late?

   Joe: Harry _____ a late night, and he _____ to get up early, so he slept late.

2. Mia: _____ you _____ a lot of phone calls last night?

   Zoe: Yes, I _____. Every time I put my head on the pillow the phone rang.

3. Bob: When _____ you _____ the time to read the book?

   Bell: I read it on the airplane. I _____ it with me on my trip.

**2**

用 did 和題目提供的詞彙造問句，依照實際情況做出簡答，並寫出完整句子來描述事實。

1. you   see your friends last night

   Ⓠ *Did you see your friends last night?*

   Ⓐ *No, I didn't. I didn't see my friends last night.*

2. you   go to a movie last weekend

   Ⓠ _____

   Ⓐ _____

3. you   play basketball yesterday

   Ⓠ _____

   Ⓐ _____

4. you   graduate from university last year

   Ⓠ _____

   Ⓐ _____

5. you   move out of your parents' house last month

   Ⓠ _____

   Ⓐ _____

**3**

用過去式改寫括弧內的動詞，完成《小王子》的部分內容。

Once when I ❶ _____ (be) six years old I ❷ _____ (see) a magnificent picture in a book, called True Stories from Nature, about the primeval forest. It ❸ _____ (be) a picture of a boa constrictor in the act of swallowing an animal. Here is a copy of the drawing.

. . .

I ❹ _____ (ponder) deeply, then, over the adventures of the jungle. And after some work with a colored pencil I ❺ _____ (succeed) in making my first drawing. My drawing Number One. It looked like this:

# Unit 40

## Past Continuous Tense
## 過去進行式

**1** 過去進行式用來表「**過去某一時刻正在進行的事**」。

I was watching a vampire movie from 8:00 to 12:00 last night.

past        present

昨晚 8 點到 12 點之間，我在看一部吸血鬼的電影。

| 否定句的全形和縮寫 | |
| --- | --- |
| I was not watching | I wasn't watching |
| you were not watching | you weren't watching |
| he was not watching | he wasn't watching |
| she was not watching | she wasn't watching |
| it was not watching | it wasn't watching |
| we were not watching | we weren't watching |
| they were not watching | they weren't watching |

| 疑問句的句型 | |
| --- | --- |
| Was I watching . . . ? | Was it watching . . . ? |
| Were you watching . . . ? | Were we watching . . . ? |
| Was he watching . . . ? | Were they watching . . . ? |
| Was she watching . . . ? | |

| 肯定和否定簡答的句型 | |
| --- | --- |
| Yes, I was. | No, I wasn't. |
| Yes, you were. | No, you weren't. |
| Yes, he was. | No, he wasn't. |
| Yes, she was. | No, she wasn't. |
| Yes, it was. | No, it wasn't. |
| Yes, we were. | No, we weren't. |
| Yes, they were. | No, they weren't. |

**2** **過去進行式**由「be 動詞過去式 + V-ing」所構成。

**What** were **you** doing at 8:00 last night?
昨晚 8 點你在做什麼？

At 8:00 last night I was watching the news. It was a slow news day. The newscasters were talking about turtles. They were saying the sea turtles swim thousands of kilometers. It was boring so I turned off the TV.

昨晚 8 點，我正在看新聞。那天的新聞很無聊，當時播報員正在談論烏龜。他們介紹海龜可以游數千公里，這則新聞真是無趣，所以我就把電視關了。

「過去簡單式」和「過去進行式」的比較

❶ 過去進行式和過去簡單式經常連用，以**過去簡單式**描述某個動作，並以**過去進行式**描述該動作發生時的背景。

I was watching **the movie when you** called.
你打電話來的時候，我正在看電影。

❷ **when** 的後面可以用過去進行式也可以用過去簡單式，如果是較短暫的**動作**，就用**簡單式**，較長時間的動作就用**進行式**。

I called **when the movie** started.
電影開始播放後，我就打了電話。

**The phone** rang **when he** was taking **a bath.**
他在泡澡的時候，電話響了。

## Practice

**1**

將括弧內的動詞以「過去進行式」填空。

We ❶_____ (decorate) Debbie's apartment for her surprise birthday party when the door opened. Everybody froze. Trisha ❷_____ (hang) balloons. Francine ❸_____ (drape) streamers. Annabelle ❹_____ (arrange) the forks and plates for the cake. Julie ❺_____ (put) candles on the birthday cake. Gina ❻_____ (unpack) presents from the shopping bags. Cathy ❼_____ (put) a bow and ribbon on Debbie's cat. Everybody looked at Debbie coming through the doorway. Debbie had arrived from work early. She walked in, looked around, and said, "Surprise! What are you doing?" I said, "We are preparing your surprise birthday party. Now go back outside and then come in so we can yell "Surprise! Happy birthday!"

**2**

用動詞「do 的過去進行式」完成問句，詢問圖中人物在做什麼。

再依據圖示，自下表選出適當的動詞片語，用「過去進行式」造句回答問題。

talk on the phone
drink coffee
sleep soundly

1

**Q** *What was she doing* when the phone rang?
**A** *She was sleeping soundly.*

2

**Q** _____ while walking?
**A** _____

3

**Q** _____ while watching TV during breakfast?
**A** _____

## Unit 41

### Present Perfect Simple (1)
### 簡單現在完成式（1）

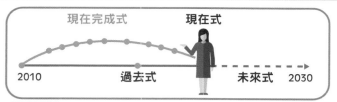

現在完成式　　　現在式
2010　　　　過去式　　　　未來式　　2030

**1** 簡單現在完成式經常被視為過去時態的一種，用來表示「**發生於過去，一直持續到現在的動作或事情**」。

**We have lived here since 2005.**
從 2005 年起，我們就一直住在這裡。

past
2005

moved to the house

2006

2007

2008

2009

2010

present
still living in the house

**2** **現在完成式**的動詞是由「have/has + 動詞的過去分詞」所構成。

**We have watched all her movies.**
↳ 我們對她的每一部電影都熟悉了。
我們已經看過她所有的電影。

**We haven't missed her TV show even once.** ↳ 她的電視節目我們還是每一次都看。
她的電視節目我們一次也沒錯過。

**He has been to the library three times today.** 他今天已經去圖書館三次了。

**3** 規則動詞的過去分詞和過去式同形；
不規則動詞的過去分詞必須逐一牢記。

#### 不規則動詞

| 原形 | 過去式 | 過去分詞 | |
|---|---|---|---|
| go | went | gone | 走 |
| buy | bought | bought | 買 |
| fall | fell | fallen | 落下 |
| rise | rose | risen | 升起 |
| build | built | built | 建立 |
| see | saw | seen | 看見 |
| write | wrote | written | 寫 |

| 肯定句的全形和縮寫 | |
|---|---|
| I have visited | I've visited |
| you have visited | you've visited |
| he has visited | he's visited |
| she has visited | she's visited |
| it has visited | it's visited |
| we have visited | we've visited |
| they have visited | they've visited |

| 否定句的全形和縮寫 | |
|---|---|
| I have not visited | I haven't visited |
| you have not visited | you haven't visited |
| he has not visited | he hasn't visited |
| she has not visited | she hasn't visited |
| it has not visited | it hasn't visited |
| we have not visited | we haven't visited |
| they have not visited | they haven't visited |

| 疑問句的句型 | |
|---|---|
| Have I visited . . . ? | Has it visited . . . ? |
| Have you visited . . . ? | Have we visited . . . ? |
| Has he visited . . . ? | Have they visited . . . ? |
| Has she visited . . . ? | |

| 肯定和否定的簡答 | |
|---|---|
| Yes, I have. | No, I haven't. |
| Yes, you have. | No, you haven't. |
| Yes, he has. | No, he hasn't. |
| Yes, she has. | No, she hasn't. |
| Yes, it has. | No, it hasn't. |
| Yes, we have. | No, we haven't. |
| Yes, they have. | No, they haven't. |

# Practice

**1**

寫出右列動詞的
「過去分詞」。

1. eat _____
2. see _____
3. write _____
4. go _____
5. love _____
6. come _____
7. fight _____
8. read _____
9. get _____
10. leave _____

11. bring _____
12. lend _____
13. cost _____
14. lose _____
15. hit _____
16. pay _____
17. find _____
18. take _____
19. ring _____
20. speak _____

**2**

從下表選出適當的動
詞，以「過去完成式」
填空，完成句子。

win
steal
arrive
teach
write
eat

1. Colonel Sanders _____ fried chicken all his life.
2. Mrs. Fredericks _____ at this school for 25 years.
3. Johnny Baxter _____ at the airport.
4. Kathy Stein _____ another first place ribbon.
5. John Newman _____ money from his friends.
6. Sidney Green _____ three books.

**3**

哪些動詞形式屬於
「現在完成式」？
將它們畫上底線。

Clive grew up in the country. He moved to the city in 2010. He <u>has lived</u> there since then.

He has worked in an Italian restaurant for a year and half.

He met his wife in the restaurant. They got married last month, and she moved in to his apartment. They have become a happy couple, but they haven't had a baby yet.

**Part 4 Past Tenses 過去時態**

## Unit 42

### Present Perfect Simple (2)
### 簡單現在完成式（2）

**1** 現在完成式常與 for（……多久）或 since（自……以來）連用，表示「事情延續的時間」。for 後面會接「一段時間」，since 後面則接「一個固定的時間點」。

We have been in line for 30 minutes.
我們已經排隊排了 30 分鐘了。

I have worked in Brazil for three years.
我已經在巴西工作了三年。

We have been here since 7:00.
我們從 7 點起就在這裡了。

**2** 現在完成式常與時間副詞 ever（曾經）或 never（從未）連用，表示「到現在為止已經發生或不曾發生某件事」。

Have you ever seen a movie star?
↳ 在你這一生中任何一刻
你曾經見過電影明星嗎？

I have never seen a movie star.
↳ 在我人生中從未有過
我從未見過任何一位電影明星。

**3** 現在完成式常與時間副詞 just（剛剛）、already（已經）或 yet（還沒）連用，來「指出或確認動作發生的時刻或狀況」。

Otto has just eaten the last cookie.
↳ 剛過不久（美式用過去簡單式：just ate）
奧圖剛把最後一塊餅乾吃掉。

We have already eaten at that restaurant.
↳ 之前（美式用過去簡單式：already ate）
我們已經在那家餐廳吃過飯了。

Ron hasn't finished eating yet.
朗恩還沒吃完。 ↳ 到目前為止

Have you finished reading the book yet?
↳ 到目前為止，注意：yet 只能用於否定句和疑問句。
你把這本書看完了嗎？

**4** 現在完成式可用來「談論直到目前為止的人生經驗」。

Have you ever been to Hollywood?
你去過好萊塢嗎？

Kevin has been to Hollywood and Beverly Hills.
凱文去過好萊塢和比佛利山莊。

**比較**

**have been 去過**

He has been to the library twice today.
↳ 他已經去過並回來了。
他今天去過圖書館兩次了。

**have gone 去了**

He is not at home. He has gone to the library.
↳ 他還沒回來。
他不在家，他去圖書館了。

**have been 去過**

Have you ever been to Brazil?
↳ 詢問對方過去的經驗。
你有去過巴西嗎？

**have gone 去了**

I hear Teddy has gone to Rio for Carnival.
↳ 泰迪現在人還在那裡。
我聽說泰迪到里約去參加嘉年華會了。

**5** 現在完成式可用來「談論一個目前可以看到結果的動作」。

Sally has gone to the movies.
↳ 結果是「She is at the movie theater. 她現在人在電影院。」
莎莉已經去看電影了。

Harriet has had dinner.
↳ 結果是「He is not hungry now. 他現在不餓。」
哈里特已經吃過晚餐。
↳ 美式用過去簡單式：Harriet had dinner.

**1**

請將括弧內的動詞以「現在完成式」來填空。

沒有動詞提示的空格，請填上 for 或 since。

1. I am an airplane pilot. I _____ (be) a pilot _____ I graduated from junior high school.

2. In high school I started making model airplanes. I _____ (build) model airplanes _____ 25 years.

3. I flew ultra-light airplanes _____ 8 years while I was in college.

4. I _____ (pilot) a dozen military aircraft during the time I was in the Air Force.

5. After leaving the Air Force, I _____ (work) for commercial airlines _____ over 20 years.

6. Ever since I was a kid, I _____ (dream) about going to the moon.

7. I _____ (wonder) if I will ever get to the moon, but I still have hopes.

8. _____ 2001, several companies _____ (start) to offer space tourism.

**2**

利用題目提供的字彙造問句，依據實際情況做出簡答，並寫出完整的句子來描述事實。

1. eat a worm

   Q *Have you ever eaten a worm?*

   A *No, I haven't. I haven't eaten a worm.*

2. be to Japan

   Q _____

   A _____

3. swim in the ocean

   Q _____

   A _____

4. cheat on an exam

   Q _____

   A _____

## Part 4  Past Tenses 過去時態

## Unit 43

### Comparison Between the Present Perfect Simple and the Past Simple
簡單現在完成式和過去簡單式的比較

---

**1**　簡單現在完成式和過去簡單式都用來表示**之前做過的行為或狀況**。

**簡單現在完成式**是「已於過去完成，對現在仍有持續影響的事情」

past　2017　2018　2019　2020　present

I have owned **the car for over four years.**
↳ 用現在完成式表示「現在還擁有這輛車」。
這輛車我已經開了四年以上。

**過去簡單式**則是「已經結束、完成的行為或動作，與現在並無關聯」。

past 2016　2017　2018　2019　2020　2021 present

I owned **the car for over four years.**
↳ 用過去式表示「過去曾經擁有，但現在已經不再擁有這輛車」。
那輛車我開了四年以上。

---

**2**　**現在完成式**往往和 ever 或 never 連用，表達「無確切時間的過去事件或經驗」。

I have never gone **swimming in a river.**
我從未在河裡游泳過。
Have **you** ever jumped **off a three-meter diving board?**
你曾經從三公尺高的跳台跳下來嗎？

---

**3**　**過去簡單式**則和表達過去時間的詞彙連用，表達「有確切時間的過去事件」。

Did **you** go **to your swimming class** last Saturday? 你上星期六有去上游泳課嗎？
I went **surfing twice** last month.
我上個月衝浪兩次。

**比較**

- Have you ever been to a baseball game? 你去看過棒球比賽嗎？
- Did you go to the baseball game yesterday? 你昨天有去看棒球賽嗎？

---

**4**　當句子使用 when 開頭的問句，應該使用**過去簡單式**。

When did **you** pass **your scuba diving test?** 你什麼時候通過水肺潛水的測驗？

---

**5**　現在完成式代表「仍在進行中的某件事」。
過去簡單式則表「過去發生的某件事，現在已不再持續」。

Willy has gone to **Amsterdam on vacation.**　↳ 他現在人在阿姆斯特丹。
威利已經到阿姆斯特丹去度假了。
Willy went to **Amsterdam on vacation.**
　　　↳ 他現在已經從阿姆斯特丹回來了。
威利到阿姆斯特丹度過假。

## Practice

**1**

根據圖示及內文，判斷動詞時態應該是「現在完成式」還是「過去簡單式」？

將括弧內的動詞以正確時態填入空格中。

Jimmy Jones ❶_____ (love) surfing since he was a teenager. He ❷_____ (be) to Phuket Island in Thailand six times. On his first visit in 1999, he ❸_____ (stay) at a popular beachfront hotel. He ❹_____ (go surfing) at all the beaches on the west coast. He really ❺_____ (like) the long white sand beaches on that side of the island. Later he ❻_____ (discover) cheaper hotels in Phuket City. He ❼_____ (rent) a small house in the city for a month on his last trip. He ❽_____ (learn) how to drive a motorcycle. He ❾_____ (visit) all the beaches along the southern coast. He also ❿_____ (enjoy) fishing since he was a kid. He ⓫_____ (fish) all over Phuket and the outlying islands. He last ⓬_____ (visit) Phuket in 2010. Since then, he ⓭_____ (go) to Hawaii for all of his vacations. Recently, however, Jimmy Jones ⓮_____ (talk) about going back to Phuket one more time.

**2**

請根據上一題內容，以正確時態完成關於 **Jimmy Jones** 的問句。

1. Ⓠ How long _____ a surfer?
   Ⓐ Since he was a teenager.

2. Ⓠ When _____ his first trip to Phuket?
   Ⓐ His first trip was in 1999.

3. Ⓠ How many times _____ to Phuket?
   Ⓐ He has been to Phuket six times.

4. Ⓠ _____ to Phuket between 1999 and 2010?
   Ⓐ Yes, he did. He went to Phuket between 1999 and 2010.

5. Ⓠ _____ at a beachfront hotel in 1999?
   Ⓐ Yes, he did. He stayed at a beachfront hotel in 1999.

6. Ⓠ _____ all the beaches on the island since 1999?
   Ⓐ No, he hasn't visited all the beaches.

7. Ⓠ _____ Jimmy Jones' last trip to Phuket?
   Ⓐ His last trip was in 2010.

## Unit 44 Review Test of Units 37–43
### 單元 37–43 總複習

**1** 寫出下列動詞的過去式和過去分詞。
→ Unit 38, 41 重點複習

1. drive _____ _____
2. go _____ _____
3. eat _____ _____
4. write _____ _____
5. think _____ _____
6. keep _____ _____
7. drink _____ _____
8. sleep _____ _____
9. make _____ _____
10. stand _____ _____

11. buy _____ _____
12. sing _____ _____
13. do _____ _____
14. hide _____ _____
15. fall _____ _____
16. say _____ _____
17. give _____ _____
18. sit _____ _____
19. shoot _____ _____
20. teach _____ _____

**2** 將括弧內的動詞以「過去簡單式」完成句子，並分別將句子改寫為「否定句」及「疑問句」。
→ Unit 38, 39 重點複習

1. I _____ (sail) on a friend's boat last weekend.
   → _____
   → _____

2. I _____ (see) a seal on the rocks.
   → _____
   → _____

3. We _____ (feed) the seagulls.
   → _____
   → _____

4. The seagull ........................... (like) the bread we threw to it.

→ .....................................................................................................

→ .....................................................................................................

5. We ........................... (fish) for our dinner.

→ .....................................................................................................

→ .....................................................................................................

6. My friend ........................... (cook) our dinner in the galley of the boat.

→ .....................................................................................................

→ .....................................................................................................

7. We ........................... (eat) on deck.

→ .....................................................................................................

→ .....................................................................................................

8. We ........................... (pass) the time chatting and watching the water.

→ .....................................................................................................

→ .....................................................................................................

**3** 規則動詞的過去式，有 /ɪd/、/d/ 和 /t/ 三種字尾發音，請將框內單字改寫為過去式，並依照字尾發音，填至正確的欄位內。
→ Unit 38 重點複習

| start | land | fix | hike | walk | march | call | order | cart | play | hand | brush |

**1** _____ /d/ _____

**2** _____ /t/ _____

**3** _____ /ɪd/ _____

**4** Catherine 總是日復一日的做著同樣的事情。請閱讀以下文章，並以過去式改寫該文章的內容。
→ Unit 38-39 重點複習

Catherine gets up every morning at 5:00. She takes a shower. Then she makes a cup of strong black coffee. She sits at her computer and checks her email. She answers her email and works on her computer until 7:30. At 7:30, she eats a light breakfast. After breakfast, she goes to work. She walks to work. She buys a cup of coffee and a newspaper on her way to work. She arrives promptly at 8:30 and is ready to start her day at the office.

Catherine got up at 5:00.

**5** 選出正確的答案。
→ Unit 38–40 重點複習

1. It **snowed / was snowing** when I **went / was going** to bed last night.

2. After I **fell / was falling** asleep, I **had / was having** a dream.

3. We **walked / were walking** to the pet store when we **saw / were seeing** an elephant.

4. When we **saw / were seeing** the elephant, my brother John **said / was saying** he wanted to ride on it.

5. While John was riding the elephant, he **fell / was falling** off.

6. John **broke / was breaking** his glasses when he **fell / was falling** off the elephant.

7. I **fed / was feeding** the elephant when I **heard / was hearing**, "There's Jumbo."

8. When I **woke / was waking** up, I **realized / was realizing** it was only a dream.

9. As I was lying in bed, I **started / was starting** to think about going to the zoo.

**6** 曼果公司的銷售團隊，正在一項一項核對「應做事項表」，看看他們是否已為這次的貿易展做好了準備。經理凱莉正在和約翰和喬安這兩名業務員說話。

根據右方列表，以「現在完成式」和「have . . . yet」的句型，造問句並做出簡答，並以「they have already . . .」或「they haven't . . . yet」的句型完整描述事實。
→ Unit 41–42 重點複習

1. Q *Have they picked up the flyers yet?*

   A *Yes, they have. They have already picked up the flyers.*

2. Q ......................................................................................
   A ......................................................................................

3. Q ......................................................................................
   A ......................................................................................

4. Q ......................................................................................
   A ......................................................................................

5. Q ......................................................................................
   A ......................................................................................

6. Q ......................................................................................
   A ......................................................................................

☑ pick up the flyers
☑ put out order pads
☐ get pens with our company logo
☑ set up the computer
☐ arrange flowers
☐ unpack boxes

**7** 回想你曾去過哪些地方度假？在哪一年？請依照範例，用「現在完成式 have been」的句型說出你去過的地方，再用過去式說明年分。
→ Unit 43 重點複習

1. _I have been to Tokyo. I went to Tokyo in 2008._
2. _____
3. _____
4. _____
5. _____
6. _____

**8** 將括弧中提示的動詞，以正確的時態完成句子。
→ Unit 37–43 重點複習

1. He _____ (be) sick yesterday, but he is feeling better today.
2. Today is Monday, and Jerry is at the office. Yesterday _____ (be) Sunday, and he _____ (be) at home.
3. Lydia _____ (have) a haircut yesterday, so she has short hair now.
4. Father _____ (buy) a new shirt yesterday, and he is wearing the new shirt today.
5. Sam _____ (sleep) well last night, so he is feeling energetic today.
6. Jill and Winnie _____ (go) to Canada. They are not at home now.
7. Uncle John _____ (keep) his dog for over ten years, but it _____ (die) of old age last month.
8. He _____ (register) for this school last week.
9. Mom: _____ you _____ (finish) your homework already?
   Tim: No, I _____ (finish) it yet.
10. She _____ (cook) dinner last night when the phone rang.
11. Lily: When _____ (do) you graduate from college?
    Sunny: In 2008.

114

**9** 選出正確的答案。

→ Unit 38–43 重點複習

........... 1. ..................... my new computer for one year.

Ⓐ I had      Ⓑ I've had

........... 2. ..................... my old cell phone two days ago.

Ⓐ I've sold      Ⓑ I sold

........... 3. ..................... at school last night.

Ⓐ We've been      Ⓑ We were

........... 4. The TV show ..................... about 30 minutes ago.

Ⓐ ended      Ⓑ has ended

........... 5. When did you ..................... that new hat?

Ⓐ get      Ⓑ got

........... 6. ..................... to Greece on vacation?

Ⓐ Did you go      Ⓑ Did you went

........... 7. Joey has worked in advertising ..................... ten years.

Ⓐ for      Ⓑ since

........... 8. Tommy has lived in Mumbai ..................... 1995.

Ⓐ since      Ⓑ for

........... 9. ..................... a painter since 1992.

Ⓐ I'm      Ⓑ I've been

## Unit 45

### Present Continuous for the Future
### 表示未來意義的現在進行式

**1** 現在進行式常用來表示「**未來計畫要做的行為**」，尤其是時間和地點已經確定的安排。這種用法裡，現在進行式並不具有正在進行的意味。

**What is Director Nelson** doing **next week?**
尼爾森董事下星期要做什麼？

**Mon.**

He is going **to a board meeting on Monday.**
他星期一要參加董事會議。

**Tue.**

He is meeting **with some international customers on Tuesday.**
他星期二要和國外客戶見面。

**Wed.**

He is flying **to Moscow on Wednesday.**
他星期三要飛去莫斯科。

**Thu.**

He is visiting **an old friend in Moscow on Thursday.**
他星期四要去拜訪一位住在莫斯科的老友。

**Fri.**

He's returning **on Friday.**
他星期五會回來。

**2** 現在進行式常用於表示「**未來之計畫、意圖、正要發生的行為**」，或是「**詢問未來的狀況**」。

I am having **lunch with Ricky on Friday.**
↳ 計畫
我星期五要和瑞奇一起吃午飯。

I am going **for a walk. Are you coming?**
↳ 正要進行的行為
我要去散步，你要來嗎？

I'm not waiting **any longer.**
↳ 堅決的意圖
我再也不等了。

**What** are you eating **for lunch tomorrow?** ↳ 對未來計畫的詢問
你明天午餐要吃什麼？

- I ¹ _____ a pizza for us later tonight.
  今晚晚一點我要幫我們叫一個披薩。
- Joan ² _____ baseball on Saturday. 瓊恩星期六要去打棒球。
- What ³ _____ you ⁴ _____ next summer? 你明年夏天打算做什麼？

## Practice

**1**

一對夫妻將要去度假。請利用圖片提供的資訊，以「現在進行式」完成問句，並回答問題。

Mark and Sharon

May 18, 2021

depart from Linz at 15:30

go on vacation

taking Aeroflot Airlines, Flight 345

arriving in Budapest at 17:30

1. Who _____*is going*_____ on vacation?
   → Mark and Sharon are going on vacation.

2. When _____ Mark and Sharon _____ on vacation?
   → 

3. Where _____ they _____ from?
   → 

4. Where _____ they _____ to?
   → 

5. What time _____ they _____?
   → 

6. What time _____ they _____ at their destination?
   → 

7. What airline _____ they _____?
   → 

8. What flight _____ they _____?
   → 

117

## Unit 46

### "Be Going To" for the Future
### Be Going To 表示未來意義的用法

| 肯定句的全形和縮寫 | |
| --- | --- |
| I am going to drive | I'm going to drive |
| you are going to drive | you're going to drive |
| he is going to drive | he's going to drive |
| she is going to drive | she's going to drive |
| it is going to drive | it's going to drive |
| we are going to drive | we're going to drive |
| they are going to drive | they're going to drive |

| 否定句的全形和縮寫 | |
| --- | --- |
| I am not going to drive | I'm not going to drive |
| you are not going to drive | you aren't going to drive |
| he is not going to drive | he isn't going to drive |
| she is not going to drive | she isn't going to drive |
| it is not going to drive | it isn't going to drive |
| we are not going to drive | we aren't going to drive |
| they are not going to drive | they aren't going to drive |

| 疑問句的句型 | |
| --- | --- |
| Am I going to drive? | Is it going to drive? |
| Are you going to drive? | Are we going to drive? |
| Is he going to drive? | Are they going to drive? |
| Is she going to drive? | |

| 肯定和否定的簡答 | |
| --- | --- |
| Yes, I am. | No, I'm not. |
| Yes, you are. | No, you aren't. |
| Yes, he is. | No, he isn't. |
| Yes, she is. | No, she isn't. |
| Yes, it is. | No, it isn't. |
| Yes, we are. | No, we aren't. |
| Yes, they are. | No, they aren't. |

**1** be going to 常用來表示**未來**意義。

Red Riding Hood, are you going to Grandma's house tomorrow?
小紅帽,妳明天要去奶奶家嗎?

Yes, Mr. Wolf, I am going to Grandma's house. 沒錯,大野狼先生,我要去奶奶家。

OK, I guess I am going to her house, too. 很好,我想我也要去她家一趟。

**2** be going to 可以用來表達「意圖」或「未來的決定」。

Are **you** going to get a job?
↳ 找工作的意圖
你要去找份工作嗎?

We **are** going to eat lunch in a few minutes.
↳ 幾分鐘內的決定
我們馬上就要吃午餐了。

- Lydia [1] _____ the bathroom after lunch.
莉迪雅吃完午飯後要打掃浴室。

- Lily [2] _____ Bali this summer.
莉莉今年夏天要去峇里島旅遊。

**3** be going to 可表示「預測未來即將發生的事」或「無法掌握而可能發生的事」。

Be careful or you're going to get hurt.
小心點,不然你會受傷。

It looks like we are going to get a visitor this evening. 看來今晚我們可能會有訪客。

It's going to rain at any minute.
隨時會下雨。

**4** be not going to 可用來表示「拒絕未來可能發生的事」。

I'm not going to drive you to the shopping mall.
我才不要載你去購物中心。

## Practice

**1**

請依圖示，對各個疑問句做出簡答，並用完整句子描述正確情況。

1. Is Santa Claus going to use a cell phone?
   *No, he isn't. He is going to use a laptop.*

2. Is the woman going to buy some vegetables?

3. Is the girl going to take a nap with her teddy bear?

4. Are the grandparents going to drink some milk?

5. Are the mother and daughter going to buy some toys?

6. Is the salesperson going to give the customers a pen?

**2**

依據事實，
用 be going to 或
be not going to
描述你今晚會不會做
這些事。

1. eat at a restaurant

2. watch a baseball game

3. read a book

4. play video games

5. write an email

## Part 5 Future Tenses 未來時態

## Unit 47

### Simple Future Tense "Will"
### 未來簡單式 Will

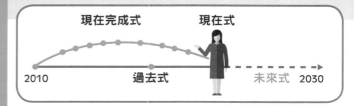

現在完成式　　現在式

2010　　過去式　　未來式　2030

---

**1** 未來簡單式用來表示「**預測未來要發生的事情**」或是「**提供未來資訊**」或「**意圖**」。句型是「will + 動詞原形」。

意願 I will weed the garden every Saturday.
我每個星期六會除花園的草。

意圖 I will plant peas this summer.
我今年夏天要種豌豆。

**2** will 通常會以縮寫「'll」的形式呈現。

She'll get married this summer.
她今年夏天要結婚了。

I'll go wherever the wedding is held.
不管婚禮在哪裡舉行，我都會去。

I'll take a pot roast out of the freezer to defrost.
我要從冰箱拿出燉牛肉來解凍。

**3** will 可用來表示「**在說話時剛做的決定**」。

I think I'll have a carrot. No, wait a minute, there are no carrots left. I think I'll eat a cucumber. Oh, I already finished the cucumbers. Maybe I'll quit eating salad.

我想我要吃一根胡蘿蔔，不，等等，已經沒有胡蘿蔔了。那我吃一根小黃瓜好了。我已經吃光所有的小黃瓜了。也許我該戒沙拉了。

肯定簡答的句型，都是用「主詞 + will」。
• Yes, I will.

否定簡答的句型，都是用「主詞 +won't」。
• No, I won't.

**4** will 常用來表示「**未來的生活**」。

Soon human beings will travel through space to the planets and beyond. We will live on the Moon, Mars, or maybe in another galaxy. I think I'll go to a nice little planet, not too far from my office on Earth.

很快人類就可以到外太空，甚至到更遠的星球去旅行。我們將會住在月球、火星或是其他的銀河上。我想我會選擇去一個離我地球辦公室不會太遠的美麗小行星上。

**5** will 的否定是 will not，縮寫為 won't，經常用來表示「**拒絕**」、「**不願意**」。

I won't give you any money.
我不會給你錢的。

No matter what I say, Mary just won't open the door.
不論我怎麼說，瑪麗就是不開門。

I won't forget you. 我不會忘記你的。

**6** will 常和 think （想）、hope（希望）、perhaps（或許）這些字搭配使用。

I think I'll eat that fish.
我想我會吃了那條魚。

I hope I will pass the exam.
我希望我會通過考試。

Perhaps he will visit his grandma this summer. 或許今夏他會去探望奶奶。

I doubt Johnny will tell the truth.
我不覺得強尼會說真話。

think 如果要表達**否定**的意思，通常會用「I don't think he/she/they will . . .」，而不會用「I think he/she/they won't . . .」這樣的句型。
• I don't think Vivian will like Sam.
我覺得薇薇安不會喜歡山姆。

## Practice

**1**

利用題目提供的主詞，和動詞片語，以 will 分別造出疑問句、肯定句和否定句。

1. scientist   clone humans in 50 years
   - → Will scientists clone humans in 50 years?
   - → Scientists will clone humans in 50 years.
   - → Scientists won't clone humans in 50 years.

2. robots   become family members in 80 years
   - → ...........................................................................
   - → ...........................................................................
   - → ...........................................................................

3. doctors   insert memory chips behind our ears
   - → ...........................................................................
   - → ...........................................................................
   - → ...........................................................................

4. police officers   scan our brains for criminal thoughts
   - → ...........................................................................
   - → ...........................................................................
   - → ...........................................................................

**2**

將題目提供的文字，分別以 I think、perhaps 和 I doubt 造句，並視情況使用「'll 的縮寫」形式。

1. I   live in another country
   - → I think I'll live in another country.
   - → Perhaps I'll live in another country.
   - → I doubt I'll live in another country.

2. my sister   learn how to drive
   - → ...........................................................................
   - → ...........................................................................
   - → ...........................................................................

3. Jerry   marry somebody from another country
   - → ...........................................................................
   - → ...........................................................................
   - → ...........................................................................

4. Tammy   not go abroad again
   - → ...........................................................................
   - → ...........................................................................
   - → ...........................................................................

Unit **48**

## Comparison Between "Will," "Be Going To," and the Present Continuous
### Will、Be Going To 和現在進行式的比較

**1** will 是「**突然決定的事件**」。

I've got a good idea. I'll buy her a
baseball cap.     ↳ 說話時刻做的決定
我想到一個好點子了，我要買個棒球帽給她。

Linda: The phone is ringing!
Nora: I'll get it.
琳達：電話響了！
諾拉：我來接。

**2** be going to 則是「**事先決定好的事件**」。

What am I going to buy Mom for her
birthday?     ↳ 正在想這件事
我媽生日的時候，要買什麼禮物給她呢？

I'm going to drive to the sporting
          ↳ 事前已做的決定
goods store. 我打算開車去運動用品店。

I am going to buy a present for Mom's
birthday.     ↳ 事前已做的決定
我要去買我媽的生日禮物。

I'm going to make a
          ↳ 事先做好的決定
cup of coffee.
我要泡杯咖啡。

I'll make a cup of coffee.
          ↳ 臨時做的決定
我來泡杯咖啡吧。

She'll fall off the swivel chair.
          ↳ 認為可能會發生的事
她可能會從旋轉椅上跌下來。

She's going to fall off the
swivel chair.   ↳ 有徵兆已經可以預見
她快要從旋轉椅上跌下來了。

**3** will 表示「**預測可能會發生的事情**」。

That guy looks like a thief. He'll steal
your wallet if you're not careful.
那傢伙看起來像小偷。如果你不小心一
點，他會偷走你的錢包。

Don't let Maggie know about this. She'll
tell Mom.
不要跟瑪姬說，她可能會告訴媽媽。

**4** be going to 表示「**從目前的狀況馬上可以預見的事情**」。

Watch out. He is going to steal your wallet.
小心，他打算要偷你的錢包。

Amy! You're going to crash into the tree!
艾美！你快撞到樹了。

**5** 現在進行式表示未來事件時，比較強調是一項「**安排**」；be going to 則強調「**意圖**」；will 則單純描述**未來事件**。

I'm flying to New York tomorrow morning.
          ↳ 機票已經買好
我明天早上就要飛去紐約。

I'm going to meet Mr. Simpson tomorrow
night.
我明天晚上打算與辛普森先生會面。

I will be in Mexico next week.
我下星期人在墨西哥。

## Practice

**1**

用括弧內提供的詞彙
改寫句子。

1. Will you go to the bookstore tomorrow? (be going to)

   → _____

2. Janet will help Cindy move in to her new house. (be going to)

   → _____

3. Are you going to play baseball this Saturday? (be + V-ing)

   → _____

4. He is going to cook dinner at 5:30. (will)

   → _____

5. She's going to fall into the water. (will)

   → _____

6. I will give him a call tonight. (be going to)

   → _____

7. When will you get up tomorrow morning? (be going to)

   → _____

8. I'll drive to Costco this afternoon. (be + V-ing)

   → _____

**2**

依提示用適當的動詞
形式完成句子。

1. She _____ (leave) for Rome tomorrow. ▶ 安排

2. The ice cream _____ (melt) if you don't finish it soon.
   ▶ 可能

3. I _____ (quit) tomorrow! ▶ 臨時起意

4. I _____ (quit) next month. I've been admitted to
   the university. ▶ 事先決定

5. I think I _____ (eat) a sandwich. ▶ 臨時起意

6. Mr. Lee _____ (have) dinner with Mr. Sun on Friday
   night. ▶ 安排

7. I _____ (find) a good job, and I
   _____ (make) a lot of money. ▶ 意圖

8. It _____ (rain) tomorrow. ▶ 單純描述未來事件

Review Test of Units 45–48
單元 45–48 總複習

根據題目提供的詞彙，以「現在進行式」完成肯定句，並將句子分別改寫為
「否定句」和「疑問句」。

→ Unit 1, 6 重點複習

1. I _____ (go) out for lunch tomorrow.

   → _____

   → _____

2. I _____ (plan) a birthday party for my grandmother.

   → _____

   → _____

3. She _____ (go) to take the dog for a walk after dinner.

   → _____

   → _____

4. Mike _____ (plan) to watch a baseball game later tonight.

   → _____

   → _____

5. Dr. Johnson _____ (meet) a patient at the clinic on Saturday.

   → _____

   → _____

6. Jack and Kim _____ (apply) for admission to a technical college.

   → _____

   → _____

7. I _____ (think) about having two kids after I get married.

   → _____

   → _____

8. Josh _____ (play) basketball this weekend.

   → _____

   → _____

9. My little brother _____ (plan) to sleep late on Sunday morning.

   → _____

   → _____

10. Father and I _____ (work) out at the gym on Sunday.

   → _____

   → _____

**2** 下列現在進行式的用法中，哪些是表示「正在進行的動作」？
哪些是表示「未來已經計畫好的事」？將表示正在進行的動作之句子寫上 C（continuous），
表示未來計畫之句子寫上 F（future）。

→ Unit 45 重點複習

........... 1. I'm eating out on Saturday night.

........... 2. Are you watching TV?

........... 3. Jennifer is making a doll now.

........... 4. Grandpa is watching a baseball game on TV at the moment.

........... 5. What are you doing now?

........... 6. I'm going downtown this Thursday.

........... 7. He's going on a date with Paula tonight.

........... 8. We're having dinner with the Smiths now.


**3** 將提示的主詞和動詞，以 be going to 的句型完成問句，並依提示以 be going to 的句型回答問題。

→ Unit 47 重點複習

1. What __*are*__ you __*going to do*__ (do) tomorrow night?

   *I'm going to do some shopping tomorrow night.* _____ (do some shopping)

2. When _____ you _____ (leave) ?

   _____ (at 9 a.m.)

3. _____ he _____ (call) her later?

   _____ (yes)

4. What _____ you _____ (say) when you see him?

   _____ (tell him the truth)

5. _____ they _____ (study) British Literature in college?

   _____ (Chinese Literature)

6. _____ your family _____ (have) a vacation in Hawaii?

   _____ (Guam)

**4** 自 Solutions 中選出適當的片語，用「I think I'll」的句型，寫出下列各項問題的解決方案。
→ **Unit 47 重點複習**

Problems

1. I'm tired. *I think I'll take a nap.*

2. It's too dark to see. _____

3. I just missed a phone call. _____

4. The grapes are ripe. _____

5. I received my phone bill. _____

6. It's my dad's birthday. _____

7. Emma is sick. _____

8. It's starting to rain. _____

Solutions

▲ buy him a gift

▲ take a nap

▲ bring my umbrella

▲ turn on a light

▲ check my voicemail

▲ visit her in the hospital

▲ pay it at 7-Eleven

▲ eat them right away

**5** 判斷下列句子的用法是否正確，正確的請打✓，錯誤的請改寫出正確的句子。
→ Unit 45–48 重點複習

1. Karl is working this weekend.

2. I think it's raining soon.

3. Harry is going to the grocery store later tonight.

4. I'm sure you aren't getting called next week.

5. Tina is going to write a screenplay.

6. Is Laura going to working?

7. I'll buy him a new bicycle.

8. In the year 2100, people live on the moon.

9. What are you do next week?

**6** 選出正確的答案。
→ Unit 45–48 重點複習

1. Kelly : What are you going to do today?
   Sam : I think _____ my car.
   Ⓐ I'll clean    Ⓑ I'm going to clean    Ⓒ I'm cleaning

2. Don't touch that pot. _____.
   Ⓐ You'll get burned    Ⓑ You're going to get burned    Ⓒ You're getting burned

3. Tom : It's time to pick up Ellen.
   Larry : _____ right now.
   Ⓐ I'll leave    Ⓑ I'm going to leave    Ⓒ I will be leaving

4. I have an idea for Janie's graduation present. I think _____ a briefcase for her.
   Ⓐ I'll buy    Ⓑ I'm going to buy    Ⓒ I'm buying

127

**7** 將下列句子改寫為「否定句」和「疑問句」。
→ Unit 45–48 重點複習

1. I'll be watching the game on Saturday afternoon.
   → *I won't be watching the game on Saturday afternoon.*
   → *Will I be watching the game on Saturday afternoon?*

2. You're going to visit Grandma Moses tomorrow.
   →
   →

3. She's planning to be on vacation next week.
   →
   →

4. We're going to take a trip to New Zealand next month.
   →
   →

5. He'll send the tax forms soon.
   →
   →

6. It'll be cold all next week.
   →
   →

**8** 判斷下列句子的「未來形式」屬於何種用法，選出正確答案。

→ Unit 45−48 重點複習

........... 1.　I'm thirsty. I'll get a drink.

　　Ⓐ Sudden decision　　Ⓑ Predictable future　　Ⓒ Intention

........... 2.　It will be winter soon.

　　Ⓐ Simple future　　Ⓑ Possibility　　Ⓒ Plan in advance

........... 3.　Be careful, or you will trip over a rock.

　　Ⓐ Sudden decision　　Ⓑ Possibility　　Ⓒ Simple future

........... 4.　There're only ten seconds left. We're going to lose the game.

　　Ⓐ Simple future　　Ⓑ Plan in advance　　Ⓒ Predictable future

........... 5.　I'm going to teach him a lesson.

　　Ⓐ Intention　　Ⓑ Simple future　　Ⓒ Sudden decision

........... 6.　All my friends will come to my birthday party.

　　Ⓐ Predictable future　　Ⓑ Simple future　　Ⓒ Intention

........... 7.　I'm going to buy a new car.

　　Ⓐ Simple future　　Ⓑ Intention　　Ⓒ Sudden decision

........... 8.　I'm visiting Mrs. Jones this afternoon.

　　Ⓐ Fixed arrangement　　Ⓑ Predictable future　　Ⓒ Simple future

........... 9.　Someone is knocking on the door. I'll see who it is.

　　Ⓐ Intention　　Ⓑ Possibility　　Ⓒ Sudden decision

........... 10.　The sky is dark. It's going to rain.

　　Ⓐ Predictable future　　Ⓑ Intention　　Ⓒ Plan in advance

........... 11.　I'm taking my dog to the vet on Saturday, so I can't go cycling with you.

　　Ⓐ Sudden decision　　Ⓑ Simple future　　Ⓒ Fixed arrangement

........... 12.　We will probably go to Greece for our honeymoon.

　　Ⓐ Sudden decision　　Ⓑ Possibility　　Ⓒ Plan in advance

## Part 6 Infinitives and -ing Forms
## 不定詞和動詞的 -ing 形式

### Unit 50

### Infinitives (1)
### 不定詞（1）

**1** 動詞有三種型態：不加 to 的不定詞、加 to 的不定詞、動名詞。

I can play the guitar. 我會彈吉他。

I want to play the guitar. 我想要彈吉他。

I enjoy playing the guitar.
我喜歡彈吉他。

| 不加 to 的不定詞<br>（動詞原形） | 加 to 的不定詞 | V-ing |
|---|---|---|
| be | to be | being |
| play | to play | playing |
| work | to work | working |

**2** 「不加 to 的不定詞」在形式上就是**動詞原形**，像是助動詞 do/does/did 和情態助動詞 can/may/will 等，後面都會接「不加 to 的不定詞（動詞原形）」。

My son can ride a bicycle.
我兒子會騎腳踏車。

We could eat crawfish for dinner.
我們晚餐可以吃小龍蝦。

She may start a new dance class.
她可能會開一個新的舞蹈班。

Did you go to the concert yesterday?
你昨天有去聽音樂會嗎？

Shall we call Grandmother after dinner?
晚飯後我們要不要打電話給奶奶？

**3** 「加 to 的不定詞」在形式上就是「to + 動詞原形」，許多動詞像是 decide、hope、learn、want、would like 等等，後面都會接「加 to 的不定詞」。

I can't afford to waste any time.
我沒有時間可以浪費。

I decided to start a new company.
我決定開一間新公司。

I expect to hit the big time any day now.
我隨時期待能飛黃騰達。

I have to learn many things about being in business.
關於生意方面的事，我有很多要學的。

I learned to chew gum and drink a soda at the same time.
我在還只能喝汽水的年紀就會嚼口香糖了。

I promise to remember you when I'm rich and famous.
我答應你，在我功成名就之後，還是會記得你。

I hope to retire at the age of 50.
我希望能在 50 歲的時候退休。

- David [1] _____ a new tablet.
  大衛想買一個新的平板電腦。
- Joanne [2] _____ 300 English words every week.
  瓊安希望每週能學 300 個英文單字。

## Practice

**1**

將括弧內的動詞以正確的形式填空。

1. I may _____ (watch) a football game this weekend.
2. I learned _____ (play) baseball last summer.
3. I can't _____ (fly) a kite.
4. He promised _____ (give) me a call when he arrives in London.
5. Mike hates _____ (go) to meetings.
6. Kate would like _____ (win) the race in the sports event on Sunday.
7. Did you _____ (hear) what she said?
8. I can _____ (play) baseball.
9. I will _____ (go) on an outing tomorrow.
10. I promise _____ (be) a good guy.
11. I want _____ (meet) your parents.

**2**

依據圖示，自右表選出適當的動詞片語，以正確的形式填空。

| | |
|---|---|
| pay the bill | quit drinking and smoking |
| look very happy | wear clothes |
| buy some red peppers | make good coffee |
| work 10 hours a day | |

**1**

She'd like _____ _____.

**2**

Help Joe _____ _____.

**3**

Ms. Jones can _____ _____.

**4**

Little Kuku does not _____. 

Maybe he doesn't want _____.

**5**

Jennifer has _____ _____.

**6**

He would like _____ _____.

# Part 6 Infinitives and -ing Forms
不定詞和動詞的 -ing 形式

## Unit 51

### Infinitives (2)
不定詞（2）

**1** 有些片語後面一定接「不加 to 的不定詞（動詞原形）」，例如：let's 和 Why don't we。

Let's go **to the beach.** 我們去海邊吧。

Why don't we walk **on the barrier island?**
我們何不到沙洲島上走走？

**2** 有些動詞通常先接受詞，再接「加 to 的不定詞」。

① ask 要求　　　⑤ tell 吩咐
② expect 要求　　⑥ want 要
③ invite 邀請　　⑦ allow 允許
④ teach 教　　　⑧ would like 想要

I asked Joan to call **my wife.**
我請瓊打電話給我太太。

The dean expects you to publish **two papers.** 院長希望你能夠發表兩篇論文。

Howard invited us to join **the tour group.**
霍華邀請我們參加旅行團。

Please teach me to dribble **the ball.**
請教教我如何運球。

The doctor told the patient to drink **lots of water.** 醫生要這名病人多喝水。

Mom doesn't allow me to go **out because I'm sick.**
我生病了，媽媽不讓我出去玩。

**3** 有些動詞，後面可接「不加 to 的不定詞」，也可以接「加 to 的不定詞」，意思都一樣，例如：help。

We'll help eat **the leftovers.**
= We'll help to eat **the leftovers.**
我們會幫忙把剩菜吃完。

help 後面如果**有受詞**，則會先接受詞，再接兩種不定詞。

Can you help me cook **dinner?**
= Can you help me to cook **dinner?**
你可以幫忙我煮晚餐嗎？

**4** 有些形容詞後需接「加 to 的不定詞」。

① easy 容易的　　　⑤ expensive 昂貴的
② difficult 困難的　⑥ stupid 愚蠢的
③ important 重要的　⑦ too 太……
④ possible 可能的　⑧ enough 足夠的

It's difficult to play **chess.**
玩西洋棋很難。

It is important to eat **fruit every day.**
每天吃水果很重要。

It isn't possible to drive **to Hawaii from California.** 從加州開車到夏威夷是不可能的。

I had too much to eat. 我已經吃不下了。

I had enough to drink. 我已經喝夠了。

**5** 不定代名詞 something、anything 或 nowhere 等，後面也可以接「加 to 的不定詞」。

I have something to tell **him.**
我有些事要跟他說。

She doesn't have anything to say.
她沒有任何話要說。

**1**

請填入正確的動詞形態，有些動詞有兩種正確的型態。

1. I want you _____ (finish) cleaning the house in thirty minutes.
2. Let's _____ (go) out to dinner.
3. Why don't we _____ (sit) on the sofa?
4. Please teach me _____ (fly) your airplane.
5. Let's invite your sister _____ (join) the party.
6. I want you _____ (call) her right now.
7. Would you like me _____ (call) her for you?
8. Can I help you _____ (make) some more phone calls?
9. It's easy _____ (have) a party.
10. This house is too small _____ (throw) a party.
11. There's nowhere _____ (sit) .

**2**

依據圖示，自右表選出適當的詞彙，以正確的動詞型態填空。

| | |
|---|---|
| bake cookies | read a story to you |
| finish the paper today | study for the exam |
| get the sausage on the plate | take a look at your answers |
| climb a tree | eat on a train |

1 Is it possible

_____

_____ ?

2 Let me

_____

_____ .

3 It's stupid

_____

_____ .

4 Am I allowed

_____

_____ ?

5 It's fun

_____

_____ .

6 I'm too tired

_____

_____ .

7 Do you want me

_____

_____ ?

8 Professor Butler expects us _____

_____ .

# Part 6 Infinitives and -ing Forms
不定詞和動詞的 -ing 形式

## Unit 52

### -ing Forms
### 動詞的 -ing 形式

**1** V-ing 形式經常被稱為**動名詞**，同時具有**動詞**和**名詞**的性質。有些動詞和片語動詞後面再接的動詞，必須是 V-ing。

| | |
|---|---|
| ① enjoy 享受 | ④ imagine 想像 |
| ② finish 完成 | ⑤ give up 放棄 |
| ③ mind 介意 | ⑥ feel like 想要 |

I enjoy listening to classical music.
我喜歡聽古典音樂。

He finished writing his first novel.
他完成了他的第一本小說。

I don't mind sitting in the dark.
我不介意坐在黑暗中。

Can you imagine living on the moon?
你能想像住在月球上的生活嗎？

Maggie wants to give up playing the piano. 瑪姬想要放棄彈鋼琴。

Do you feel like going to a movie?
你想不想去看電影？

**2** 談論**活動**時，常用「go + V-ing」的形式。（詳見 Unit 55 說明）

He went hiking in Switzerland.
他去瑞士健行。

We're going swimming at Silver Lake.
我們要到銀湖去游泳。

I go surfing in Indonesia every year.
我每年都到印尼去衝浪。

**3** 有些**介系詞**後面的動詞要用 V-ing 的型態。

| ① at  ② in  ③ for  ④ about  ⑤ before |
|---|

What about calling me when you finish?
等你結束後，打個電話給我如何？

I'm not very good at finding my way around a new city.
我不太擅長在新城市裡找到路。

Are you interested in helping me find out what happened?
你有興趣幫我查明發生什麼事了嗎？

This map is good for finding streets near the train station.
這個地圖可以幫你尋找火車站周邊的街道。

I will call before leaving in case you are free.
我會在出發前先打通電話，確認你有空。

**4** 有些**動詞**後面可以接「加 to 的不定詞」，也可以接 V-ing，意思都一樣。

| | |
|---|---|
| ① like 喜歡 | ④ start 開始 |
| ② love 愛 | ⑤ begin 開始 |
| ③ hate 恨 | |

Tommy loves listening to the blues.
= Tommy loves to listen to the blues.
湯米喜歡聽藍調音樂。

Kevin started learning how to fly a drone.
= Kevin started to learn how to fly a drone.
凱文開始學習如何使用空拍機。

John hates eating vegetables.
= John hates to eat vegetables.
約翰不喜歡吃蔬菜。

## Practice

**1**

依據圖示，自右表選出適當的動詞，以「V-ing 的形式」填空。

| | |
|---|---|
| play soccer | wait for his master |
| draw on canvas | sing a song |
| blow bubbles | bike |
| make clothes | walk in the rain |

1  He is good at

_____

_____ .

2  She is interested in

_____

_____ .

3  She loves

_____

_____ .

4  He feels like

_____

_____ .

5  He enjoys

_____

_____ .

6  She went _____

_____ with

her friend yesterday.

7  Gordon never gives up

_____

_____ .

8  She doesn't mind

_____

_____ .

**2**

請填入正確的動詞形態，有些動詞有兩種正確的形態。

1. Can I help you _____ (call) your family?

2. It's possible _____ (avoid) spending a lot of money.

3. I feel like _____ (drink) a Coke now.

4. I hate _____ (get up) early in the morning.

5. I'm not good at _____ (swim) .

6. Do you mind _____ (share) the table with this lady?

7. How about _____ (go) to Hong Kong with me?

8. He can't imagine _____ (live) a life without her.

9. I went _____ (run) twice last week.

10. I love _____ (go) to the movies.

11. Get all the papers ready before _____ (meet) with Mr. Lee.

12. Have you finished _____ (eat) your breakfast?

## Unit 53

### Purpose: "To . . ." and "For . . ."
### To 和 For 表示目的的用法

**1** 加 to 的不定詞可用來說明「某人做某事的原因」。

I am going to the market **to buy** some food. 我要去市場買些食物。

On winter mornings I eat oatmeal **to stay** warm.

冬天的早晨，我會吃燕麥粥來保持溫暖。

- Mindy went to the convenience store
¹ _____ some drinks.

敏蒂去便利商店買了一些飲料。
- Josh ran to her office ² _____ her the news.

喬許跑去她的辦公室，告訴她這個消息。

**2** 「for + 名詞」也可用來解釋「某人做某事的原因」。

He wants to buy a new suit **for his interview**.

他想要買套新西裝去參加面試。

She needs to get a second battery **for her cell phone**.

她需要買一顆手機的備用電池。

- Wendy is studying hard
³ _____ .

溫蒂為了考試正在用功讀書。
- My brothers are fighting with each other
⁴ _____ .

我的兄弟們正為了新玩具
打得不可開交。

**3** 「for + V-ing」則用來表示「東西的用途」。

A fax machine is **for sending** copies of documents over phone lines.
傳真機是透過電話線，傳送文件的複本。

FTP software is **for transferring** computer files over networks.
FTP 軟體可以透過電腦網路系統，傳輸電腦裡的檔案。

**錯誤**

for 不能接不定詞。

✗ I am running for ~~to~~ exercise.
我跑步是為了要運動。

表達**目的**時，用「加 to 的不定詞」或「for + 名詞」的**意義相同**。

- I run every day **to get** some exercise.
= I run every day **for exercise**.
我每天跑步是為了要運動。
- He went to the health club **to swim**.
= He went to the health club **for a swim**.
他到健身房去游泳。

**比較**

- Running is a good method **for exercising**.
跑步是運動的一種好方式。

## Practice

**1**

自右欄選出適當的詞彙來搭配左欄的地點，並正確選用「加 to 的不定詞」或「for + 名詞」的句型填空。

a library

a history museum

the aquarium

an art gallery

the amusement park

a zoo

1. You go to *a library to borrow books* .

2. You go to _____ .

3. You go to _____ .

4. You go to _____ .

5. You go to _____ .

6. You go to _____ .

fun

look at paintings

see the animals

see artifacts

borrow books

see the fish

**2**

自框內選出適當的動詞，用「for + V-ing」的形式說明右列交通工具的用途。

tow cars and trucks

put out fires

push soil and rocks

take the sick or wounded to the hospital

carry liquid cement（水泥）

1. A cement truck is a vehicle _____ .

2. A fire truck is a vehicle _____ .

3. A tow truck is a vehicle _____ .

4. An ambulance is a vehicle _____ .

5. A bulldozer is a vehicle _____ .

# Unit 54

## Review Test of Units 50–53
## 單元 50–53 總複習

**1** 將提示動詞以正確動詞型態填空。

→ Unit 50–52 重點複習

**surf**

1. I can _____ near my home in California.
2. I learned _____ during high school.
3. I love _____ and I go _____ every weekend.

**ski**

4. I might _____ this weekend.
5. I want _____ on Saturday afternoon.
6. We often go _____ on Mount Killington.

**drive**

7. Let's _____ for a while.
8. I'll help _____ if you get tired.
9. How about _____ into the city tomorrow?
10. It's easy _____ on the highway.

**2** 將下列句子以「加 to 的不定詞」或「for + 名詞」互相改寫。

→ Unit 53 重點複習

1. My parents went out to walk.

   → *My parents went out for a walk.*

2. Mr. Lyle went to the front desk to pick up his package.

   → _____

3. I have to get everything ready to attend the meeting.

   → _____

4. I jog every day for my health.

   → _____

5. I walked into the McDonald's on Tenth Street for two cheeseburgers.

   → _____

**3** 選出正確的答案。
→ Unit 50–53 重點複習

........ 1.  Do you enjoy ................ in cold water?

Ⓐ swim          Ⓑ to swim          Ⓒ swimming

........ 2.  I don't ................ coffee at night.

Ⓐ drink          Ⓑ to drink          Ⓒ drinking

........ 3.  Clive hopes ................ promoted in six months.

Ⓐ get          Ⓑ to get          Ⓒ getting

........ 4.  Why don't we ................ the baseball game on channel 74?

Ⓐ watch          Ⓑ to watch          Ⓒ watching

........ 5.  How about ................ a trip to France?

Ⓐ take          Ⓑ to take          Ⓒ taking

........ 6.  Can you help me ................ the dishes?

Ⓐ did          Ⓑ to do          Ⓒ doing

........ 7.  Do you mind ................ for fifteen minutes?

Ⓐ wait          Ⓑ to wait          Ⓒ waiting

........ 8.  My father taught me ................ tennis when I was eight.

Ⓐ play          Ⓑ to play          Ⓒ playing

........ 9.  He is depressed and wants to give up ................ to college.

Ⓐ go          Ⓑ to go          Ⓒ going

........ 10.  Jessie told me ................ the secret.

Ⓐ keep          Ⓑ to keep          Ⓒ keeping

........ 11.  It's difficult ................ Russian.

Ⓐ learn          Ⓑ to learn          Ⓒ learning

........ 12.  I have nothing ................ at the moment.

Ⓐ say          Ⓑ to say          Ⓒ saying

........ 13.  I would like you ................ the car on Monday.

Ⓐ return          Ⓑ to return          Ⓒ returning

........ 14.  Do you want me ................ the window?

Ⓐ open          Ⓑ to open          Ⓒ opening

........ 15.  Are you interested in ................ horror movies?

Ⓐ watch          Ⓑ to watch          Ⓒ watching

**4** 將圖片中的詞彙與地點搭配，並正確選用「加 to 的不定詞」或「for + 名詞」的句型填空。

→ **Unit 19–21 重點複習**

the beach / play beach volleyball

1. They went to *the beach to play beach volleyball* .

the water / get the ball

2. The dog jumped into _____ .

the supermarket / some milk

3. They walked into _____ .

the opera house / a concert

4. They went to _____ .

the store / buy a gift

5. They went to _____ .

my friend's house / see her new doll house

6. I went to _____ .

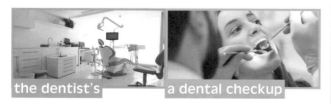
the dentist's / a dental checkup

7. She went to _____ .

the Starbucks / a cup of latté

8. She went to _____ .

the stadium / watch a baseball game

9. Andy went to _____ .

the market / buy some pumpkins

10. They went to _____ .

**5** 將錯誤的句子打✗，並寫出正確的句子。若句子無誤，則在方框內打✓。
→ Unit 50–53 重點複習

1. I might play basketball tonight.

   ☐ _____

2. I should to visit my sister.

   ☐ _____

3. Let's to go to see a movie.

   ☐ _____

4. I'll help make dinner.

   ☐ _____

5. I'll help to make dinner.

   ☐ _____

6. I want you call me next week.

   ☐ _____

7. Would you like that me to call you next week?

   ☐ _____

8. It's expensive to buy French wine.

   ☐ _____

9. When you finish to playing cards, call me.

   ☐ _____

10. I go to swimming every morning at 6:00.

    ☐ _____

11. Thank you for paying your rent on time.

    ☐ _____

12. Most people love to going on a vacation.

    ☐ _____

13. Ernie hates to eat liver and onions.

    ☐ _____

14. Kelly went to see the doctor for to have a checkup.

    ☐ _____

15. Kim went to the shop for some fresh sausages.

    ☐ _____

## Unit 55

### Go
**動詞 Go 的用法**

- go jogging 去慢跑
- go camping 去露營
- go mountain climbing 去爬山
- go hiking 去健行
- go dancing 去跳舞
- go swimming 去游泳
- go bowling 去打保齡球

**1** 「go + V-ing」常用來表達「從事某種活動」。

My father used to go fishing with me on the weekends.
我父親過去經常週末和我去釣魚。

I'm going shopping with Lucy this Saturday.
這個星期六,我要跟露西去逛街。

**2** go for 或 go on 加上某些名詞,也可以表達「從事某種活動」。

Would you like to go for a walk?
你想不想去散步?

Liz and John go for a swim every Sunday.
麗茲和約翰每週日都去游泳。

Who wants to go on a picnic?
　　　　　　　　↳ 強調 activity

= Who wants to go for a picnic?
誰想去野餐?　　　↳ 強調 go 的「目的」

Sam went on a trip to New Zealand by himself for two weeks.
山姆獨自前往紐西蘭旅行了兩個禮拜。

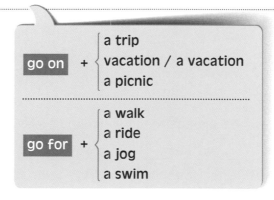

go on + { a trip / vacation / a vacation / a picnic }

go for + { a walk / a ride / a jog / a swim }

**3** 「go + 形容詞」可以表達「變成某種狀態」。

Everything went wrong! I don't know what to do.
什麼事都不對了!我不知道該怎麼辦。

The milk has gone sour. Don't drink it.
牛奶酸掉了,不要喝了。

### go 的常用片語

**go crazy** 發瘋
I'm going crazy with this project.
這個案子真是令我抓狂。

**go bad** 腐壞
Tofu goes bad easily if you don't put it in the refrigerator.
如果你不把豆腐冷藏起來,它很快就會壞掉。

**go by** 時間過去
His memories of the old days faded as time went by.
隨著時光流逝,他的往日回憶也逐漸模糊。

**go on** 發生
What's going on? 發生什麼事了?

**go Dutch** 各自付帳
Let's go Dutch. 我們各付各的吧。

## Practice

**1**

依據圖示，自下表選出正確的動詞，寫出「go + V-ing」的句型。

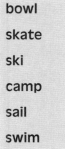

bowl

skate

ski

camp

sail

swim

go bowling

_____

_____

_____

_____

_____

**2**

自下表選出適當的詞彙，以正確的形式填空。

go

go on

go for

go by

1. The leftover soup _____ bad. Don't eat it.
2. The weather is good. Let's _____ a ride.
3. Seven years _____ since his wife died, and he still strongly misses her.
4. There's too much homework. I'm _____ crazy.
5. How about _____ a jog tomorrow morning?
6. Philip and Linda _____ a vacation in Belgium last month.
7. Tony _____ boating with his brother yesterday.

# Part 7 Common Verbs 常用動詞

## Unit 56

### Get and Take
### 動詞 Get 和 Take 的用法

**1** 「get + 受詞（人）+ 帶 to 的不定詞」可用來表達「叫某人去做某件事」。

Please get somebody to fix the toilet.
請找個人來修理馬桶。

I'll get him to give you a hand.
我會叫他去幫你。

**2** 「get + 受詞（物）+ 過去分詞」可用來表達「使某物接受某個動作」。

I'll get everything done as soon as possible.
我會盡快把所有的事情辦好。

Andrew, did you get the toilet fixed?
安德魯，你把馬桶修好了沒？

**3** take 的基本意義是「拿取」，但它也有「接受」的意思。

Why don't you take Amanda's advice?
你何不接受雅曼達的建議呢？

I really want to take the job.
我是真的想接下這份工作。

**4** take 經常用來表示「採取某種行動」。

Sally is taking a shower. 莎莉正在洗澡。

Would you like to take a look? 你要看一下嗎？

Take a seat, please. 請坐。

**5** 「take + 時間」用來表示「花費多少時間」。

It took me six years to get a medical degree. 我花了六年時間才拿到醫學學位。

It will take half an hour to get to the Central Station by bus.
搭公車去中央車站要半個小時。

## get 的常用片語

**get along** 相處
I think I can get along with Zoe.
我想我應該可以跟柔伊相處得很好。

**get over** 克服
You will get over your homesickness.
你會克服你的鄉愁的。

**get in** 進入（汽車）
Get in the car now. 快上車。

**get on** 上車（火車、公車）
You can get on a No. 16 bus at the bus stop two blocks away. 你可以在兩個路口之後的公車站搭 16 路公車。

**get off** 下車（火車、公車）
Get off the train at the Central Station.
在中央車站就要下車。

**get together** 相聚
Ben and Tommy get together twice a month. 班和湯米每個月要聚會兩次。

## take 的常用片語

**take a picture** 拍照
I took a picture of the scenery.
我把這景色拍下來了。

**take care of** 照顧
Sherry takes care of her grandparents.
雪莉一直照顧著她的祖父母。

**take off** 脫下衣物；起飛
Please take off your shoes before entering the house. 進屋子前請先脫鞋。

Our flight will take off in thirty minutes.
我們的班機將在 30 分鐘後起飛。

**take part in** 參與
Will you take part in the basketball game?
你會參加這場籃球賽嗎？

**take place** 發生
The accident took place in the middle of the night. 這場意外於夜半發生。

## Practice

**1**

將括弧內的動詞以
正確的形式填空。

1. Marty, will you get Sam _____ (finish) his dinner?
2. I can't get my students _____ (listen) to me. I'm so upset.
3. I'll get a plumber _____ (fix) the faucet tomorrow.
4. I'll get the paper _____ (do) first thing in the morning.
5. I'll get my hair _____ (cut) tonight.
6. Are you going to get your car _____ (wash) tomorrow?

**2**

哪些名詞經常搭配
take 組成慣用片語？
請在方框內打✓。

take _____

☐ a shower ☐ a walk ☐ a nap ☐ a jog

☐ a sleep ☐ a look ☐ a note ☐ a smell

☐ a picture ☐ a shortcut ☐ a chance ☐ a seat

**3**

選出正確的答案。

1. **Get on / get in** the bus here, and **get out / get off** at the fifth stop.
2. It **got / took** me five hours to finish this report.
3. Let's work together and **get over / get away** this problem.
4. **Get off / Take off** your dirty clothes and throw them in the laundry basket.
5. We're eager to **get part in / take part in** this reconstruction project.
6. We haven't **gotten together / taken together** for three months because we're both busy.
7. She took care **about / of** her grandfather last winter.

# Part 7 Common Verbs 常用動詞

## Unit 57

### Do and Make
### 動詞 Do 和 Make 的用法

**1** do 的基本意義是「做」，它的動詞三態是 do、did、done。

**What are you** doing? 你在做什麼？

**I think Mandy** did **it on purpose.**
我認為曼蒂是故意這樣做的。

**Have you** done **your project for school?**
你做完學校的案子了嗎？

### do 的常用片語

**do somebody a favor** 幫某人的忙
**Could you** do me a favor, **please?**
你可以幫我一個忙嗎？

**do one's best** 盡力而為
**Jessie** did his best **to find a home for the puppy.**
傑西已經盡力幫那隻小狗找到家了。

**do somebody good** 對某人有益
**Try to eat some fruit. It'll** do you good.
吃點水果吧，那對身體好。

**do exercise** 做運動
**My grandfather** does exercise **every morning.** 我爺爺每天早上做運動。

**do the dishes** 洗碗
**Andy, will you** do the dishes **tonight?**
安迪，今晚你洗碗好嗎？

**2** 「make + somebody/something + 動詞原形」可以用來表示「使某人或某物做某個動作」。

**I'll try to** make him agree **with this idea.**
我會試著讓他同意這個主意。

**Johnny's words** made everyone **in the room** laugh.
強尼說的話讓屋子裡的每個人都笑了。

**Is it possible to** make it happen?
有可能讓這件事發生嗎？

**3** 「make + somebody + 形容詞／名詞」可以表示「使某人成為什麼樣的人物或狀態」。

**Working hard will** make you a successful person. 努力工作，你就會成功。

**Brad tried so hard to** make his wife happy.
布萊德已經很努力討好他太太。

### make 的常用片語

**make somebody something**
幫某人做某樣東西
**I'm** making my sister a wedding dress.
我在幫我姊姊做一件結婚禮服。

**make a mistake** 犯錯
**Don't blame yourself too much. Everyone** makes mistakes. 別太自責了，人人都會犯錯。

**make a decision** 做決定
**You have to** make the decision **right now.**
你現在就必須做出決定。

| be made from something 用什麼做的（看不出材質的原形） | be made of something 用什麼做的（看得出材質的原形） |
| --- | --- |
|  |  |
| Paper is made from wood. 紙是用木材做的。 | This table is made of wood. 這張桌子是木製的。 |

146

# Practice

**1**

自下表選出適當的詞彙，搭配 make 或 do 填空。

- a wish
- the decision
- a favor
- a mistake
- good
- a speech
- his best

1. Johnny, will you do me ＿＿＿＿＿＿＿ by helping me move this box away, please?
2. He made ＿＿＿＿＿＿＿ by sending the package to the wrong person.
3. Regular exercise will do you ＿＿＿＿＿＿＿.
4. Don't blame him. He has already done ＿＿＿＿＿＿＿.
5. After everyone sang Happy Birthday, she made ＿＿＿＿＿＿＿ and blew out the candles.
6. Jennifer is going to make ＿＿＿＿＿＿＿ at Toastmasters. She is practicing right now.
7. He has made ＿＿＿＿＿＿＿ to marry his girlfriend. It's impossible to change his mind.

**2**

選出正確的答案。

1. Amy, can you **do / make** the dishes right now?

2. I'm going to **do / make** you a sweater this winter.

3. Years of practice has **done / made** him a good snowboard player.

4. Does Kim **do / make** exercise every morning?

5. The rings are **made of / made from** silver.

6. Cheese is **made of / made from** milk.

7. Reading every day will do you **good / well**.

8. Those columns are **made of / made from** stone.

9. Can Professor Dune make the pig **fly / to fly**?

10. Hearing the bad news made her **sadness / sad**.

147

## Unit 58

### Have
動詞 Have 的用法

**1** 「have + somebody + 動詞原形」
表示「**叫某人去做某件事**」。

**I'll** have him call **you back when he gets home.** 等他回來，我就叫他回你電話。

**The teacher** had the students make up **sentences using the verb "have".**
老師讓學生們用 have 這個動詞造句。

**2** 「have + something + 過去分詞」
表示「**讓某物接受某個動作**」。

**I'm going to** have my hair cut.
我要去剪頭髮。

**Joe** had his sprained ankle taped up.
喬把他扭傷的腳踝包紮起來了。

**We finally** had the shower fixed.
我們終於把蓮蓬頭修好了。

---

🗨 **比較**

Jason, please have your son do **his homework.** ↳ 最委婉

= Jason, please make your son do **his homework.** ↳ 最強烈

= Jason, please get your son to do **his homework.**

傑森，叫你兒子去 做功課好嗎？
↳ 三個句子的意義差不多，
但用 have 的語氣最委婉，
用 make 最強烈。

**have 常用片語**

**have a look** 看一眼
Janet, come here and have a look **at this.**
珍奈特，過來看看這個。

**have a walk** 散步
**My parents used to** have a walk **after dinner.**
我父母以前晚餐後都會去散步。

**have fun** 玩得開心
**Did you** have fun **in Bali?**
你去峇里島玩得開心嗎？

**have a good time** 玩得開心
**We** had a good time **last weekend.**
我們上週末過得很開心。

**have something to do with** 與……有關
**Does it** have something to do **with the professor?**
這件事和教授有關嗎？

**have nothing to do with** 與……無關
**It** has nothing to do **with me.**
這件事與我無關。

**have a baby** 生小孩
**Betty is going to** have a baby **next month.**
貝蒂下個月就要生小孩了。

## Practice

**1** 將下列句子以「have + somebody + 動詞原形」或「have + something + 過去分詞」的形式改寫。

1. He shortened the pants.
   → _____

2. Yvonne got her son to mop the floor.
   → _____

3. She washed the car.
   → _____

4. She asked her husband to replace the light bulb.
   → _____

5. He folded the paper.
   → _____

6. She packed the box with the books and sent it to the professor.
   → _____

7. He made his students read thirty pages of the book a day.
   → _____

8. I'm going to wrap this gift.
   → _____

**2** 自右表選出正確的片語，填空完成句子。

| | |
|---|---|
| have a look | have a haircut |
| have a good time | have something to do with |
| have your baby | have nothing to do with |

1. When are you going to _____ ?

2. Does it _____ Jeff? I saw him leaving the building yesterday.

3. No, it _____ Jeff. The police suspect someone else.

4. Can I _____ at your new cell phone?

5. Did you _____ on your last trip to New Zealand?

6. I'm thinking about _____ tomorrow.

**1** 選出正確的答案。

→ **Unit 55–58 重點複習**

..........1. George and Lulu ........................... shopping yesterday.

 Ⓐ went    Ⓒ did    Ⓒ made

..........2. It will ........................... 45 minutes to get to the airport.

 Ⓐ have    Ⓑ get    Ⓒ take

..........3. You should ........................... your fear of water.

 Ⓐ get over    Ⓑ get alone    Ⓒ get off

..........4. Would you like to ........................... a swim this afternoon?

 Ⓐ go    Ⓑ go for    Ⓒ go on

..........5. The festival will ........................... in Shanghai next month.

 Ⓐ take place    Ⓑ get together    Ⓒ have fun

..........6. I'll ........................... your advice and give it another try.

 Ⓐ get    Ⓑ take    Ⓒ have

..........7. The plane is going to ........................... in fifteen minutes. Please fasten your seatbelts.

 Ⓐ take place    Ⓑ take off    Ⓒ take over

..........8. Father ........................... a business trip to Hong Kong.

 Ⓐ has made    Ⓑ has gone for    Ⓒ has gone on

..........9. Why don't you ........................... his job offer?

 Ⓐ do    Ⓑ make    Ⓒ take

..........10. What's ........................... here?

 Ⓐ going on    Ⓑ getting on    Ⓒ taking off

..........11. The teacher wants us to ............................

 Ⓐ do a favor    Ⓑ do our good    Ⓒ do our best

..........12. He is a weird guy. I can't ........................... with him at all.

 Ⓐ get over    Ⓑ get together    Ⓒ get along

..........13. The shirt is ........................... 100% cotton.

 Ⓐ made of    Ⓑ made from    Ⓒ made on

..........14. This matter ........................... Jenny.

 Ⓐ doesn't have something to do with

 Ⓑ has anything to do with

 Ⓒ has nothing to do with

**2** 看圖自表中選出正確的片語，以正確的形式填空。

→ Unit 50–53 重點複習

| is made of |
| is made from |
| go for |
| go on |
| get along |
| get over |
| take part in |
| take place |

1. Cheese _____ milk.

2. My parents and I _____ a walk this afternoon.

3. Lucky and Puffy cannot _____ with each other.

4. Jessica _____ the play last week.

5. My family decided to _____ a vacation in Europe.

6. The music festival _____ in August, 2008.

7. _____ your fear and try parachuting.

8. This vase _____ glass.

**3** 將括弧內的動詞以正確形式填空。
→ Unit 56–58 重點複習

1. My brother made me _____ (finish) all the leftovers on the table.
2. Could you please get somebody _____ (change) the sheets and pillowcases?
3. Will you have everything _____ (finish) in twenty minutes?
4. Father had me _____ (clean) the bathroom on Sunday.
5. I'll have David _____ (apologize) to you.
6. The boss had everyone _____ (work) overtime last weekend.
7. I just want to get things _____ (do) as soon as possible.
8. Jason had his house _____ (paint) .
9. Please get someone _____ (remove) the stain on the wall.
10. I'll have him _____ (explain) to you in person.
11. I'll get my bicycle _____ (repair) tomorrow.

**4** 在問句的空格內填上正確的動詞，並依據事實，用完整的句子回答問題。
→ Unit 50–53 重點複習

1. Did you _____ your hair cut last week?
   → _____
2. Do you have to _____ a lot of homework tonight?
   → _____
3. Does your family _____ on a picnic every weekend?
   → _____
4. Do you like to _____ pictures of dogs and cats?
   → _____
5. Do you _____ care of your little sister when your parents are out?
   → _____
6. Do you like to _____ camping on your summer vacation?
   → _____
7. Do you _____ the dishes every day?
   → _____

152

8. Do you _____ a shower in the morning?

→ _____

9. Do you _____ crazy with your homework every day?

→ _____

10. Do you _____ a lot of mistakes?

→ _____

11. Have you ever _____ the dentist fill a cavity?

→ _____

**5** 將下列圖中所代表的名詞，依據其前面該用的動詞，填到正確的框內。
→ Unit 51-52 重點複習

| 1 ▶ do | 2 ▶ take | 3 ▶ make |
|---|---|---|
| _exercise_ | | |

a nap

exercise

friends

the laundry

a bath

a wish

a break

money

the shopping

## Part 8 Modal Verbs 情態助動詞

### Unit 60

## Can
## Can 的用法

**1** 情態助動詞是與另一個動詞連用，**表達特定意義**的動詞。
主詞不分人稱、單複數，情態助動詞的形式都只有一種。

**常見的情態助動詞有：**

- can
- may
- must
- should
- could
- might
- would
- shall

**2** can 是情態助動詞，後面只能接**動詞原形**，通常用來表示「**能力**」，此時用於現在式。

Buddy can run really fast.
巴弟可以跑得很快。

My dog can shake hands.
我的狗會握手。

Willy can dance, but he can't sing.
威利會跳舞，但不會唱歌。

He can play basketball. 他會打籃球。

**3** can 也可以用來表「**可能性**」。

I can meet you after 4:00 this afternoon.
我今天下午 4 點以後可以跟你碰面。

The director can see you next Tuesday.
主任下星期二可見你。

### 否定句的全形和縮寫

| | |
|---|---|
| I cannot play | I can't play |
| you cannot play | you can't play |
| he cannot play | he can't play |
| she cannot play | she can't play |
| it cannot play | it can't play |
| we cannot play | we can't play |
| they cannot play | they can't play |

### 疑問句的句型

| | |
|---|---|
| Can I play? | Can it play? |
| Can you play? | Can we play? |
| Can he play? | Can they play? |
| Can she play? | |

### 肯定和否定的簡答

| | |
|---|---|
| Yes, I can. | No, I can't. |
| Yes, you can. | No, you can't. |
| Yes, he can. | No, he can't. |
| Yes, she can. | No, she can't. |
| Yes, it can. | No, it can't. |
| Yes, we can. | No, we can't. |
| Yes, they can. | No, they can't. |

**4** 在情態助動詞的後面加上 **not**，可以構成**否定句**。
can 較為特別，它的否定形式是 **cannot**（連在一起寫），常縮寫為 **can't**，用來表示「**不能**」或「**不允許**」。

I can't speak French. 我不會說法文。

You cannot enter that room.
你不可以進那個房間。

**5** 情態助動詞的**疑問句**，是把情態助動詞移到句首。所以**把 can 移到句首**，就構成了**疑問句**。

Can you play the piano? 你會彈鋼琴嗎？

Can we park our car here?
我們可以把車停在這裡嗎？

# Practice

**1** 在各個圖示中，Ⓨ 表示 Chris 會演奏這種樂器，Ⓝ 表示他不會。
用 can 或 can't 造句，描述 Chris 會的樂器和不會的樂器。
左方列表有提示的樂器名稱。

flute
violin
guitar
piano
drums
saxophone

1. *Chris can play the guitar.*
2. 
3. 
4. 
5. 
6. 

**2** 依據事實，用 can 或 can't 回答問題。

1. Can you speak English?
   → *Yes, I can. I can speak English.*

2. Can you read German?
   → 

3. Can you hang out with your friends on the weekend?
   → 

4. Can you run very fast?
   → 

5. Can your mother cook Mexican food?
   → 

6. Can a dog fly?
   → 

7. Can a pig climb a tree?
   → 

8. Can we speak loudly in the museum?
   →

Unit **61**

## Could
### Could 的用法

| 否定句的全形和縮寫 ||
|---|---|
| I could not speak | I couldn't speak |
| you could not speak | you couldn't speak |
| he could not speak | he couldn't speak |
| she could not speak | she couldn't speak |
| it could not speak | it couldn't speak |
| we could not speak | we couldn't speak |
| they could not speak | they couldn't speak |

| 疑問句的句型 ||
|---|---|
| Could I speak? | Could it speak? |
| Could you speak? | Could we speak? |
| Could he speak? | Could they speak? |
| Could she speak? | |

| 肯定和否定的簡答 ||
|---|---|
| Yes, I could. | No, I couldn't. |
| Yes, you could. | No, you couldn't. |
| Yes, he could. | No, he couldn't. |
| Yes, she could. | No, she couldn't. |
| Yes, it could. | No, it couldn't. |
| Yes, we could. | No, we couldn't. |
| Yes, they could. | No, they couldn't. |

**1** could 也是情態助動詞，後面要**接動詞原形**，用來表示「**過去的能力**」。在表示這種意義的時候，常被視為是 can 的過去式。

He could read Japanese when he was five.
他五歲就看得懂日語。

He could speak five languages by the time he graduated from high school.
他高中畢業的時候，就會說五種語言了。

**2** could 的疑問句型，是將 could 移至句首。

Could he speak Farsi before he went to Iran? 他在去伊朗之前，就會說波斯話了嗎？
Could you please be quiet?
麻煩你安靜一點好嗎？

**3** could 也可以用於現在式，表示「**請求幫助**」，語氣比 can 更有禮貌。

Could you please help me?
↳ 用 could 較為正式、禮貌
請問你能幫我個忙嗎？

Can you give me a hand?
↳ 用 can 較不正式
你可以幫我個忙嗎？

**4** could 的否定形態是 could not，縮寫為 couldn't。

Peter couldn't skate before he met Jane.
彼德在認識珍之前並不會溜冰。

I couldn't speak when I saw him arrive.
I just cried with joy.
當我看到他來時，我喜極而泣，高興得說不出話。

# Practice

| | |
|---|---|
| make pots | paint landscapes |
| sculpt figures | shoot photographs |
| write calligraphy | paint pictures |

請依圖示，自右表選出正確的片語，用 could 的句型填空。

1 Lucy _____ _____ when she was 10 years old.

2 Johnny _____ _____ when he was 5 years old.

3 Sandra _____ _____ when she was 15 years old.

4 Kelly _____ _____ when she was 10 years old.

5 Laura _____ _____ when she was 65 years old.

6 Jane _____ _____ when she was 18 years old.

當你 12 歲的時候，你已經會做哪些事？還不會做哪些事？

請依據事實，用 could 的肯定或否定句型，寫出完整句子回答問題。

1. Could you play the piano when you were twelve?
   → _____

2. Could you swim when you were twelve?
   → _____

3. Could you use a computer when you were twelve?
   → _____

4. Could you read novels in English when you were twelve?
   → _____

5. Could you ride a bicycle when you were twelve?
   → _____

## Unit 62

### Must
### Must 的用法

**1** must 是**情態助動詞**，用來表示「**必要性**」或「**義務**」，後面要接**動詞原形**。

> **Drill Sergeant** Every day you <u>must</u> get up at 5:30 a.m. Every day you <u>must</u> run 10 kilometers and then <u>must</u> do 100 sit-ups and 150 push-ups.
>
> 軍隊士官長 你們每天早上要五點半起床，先跑 10 公里，再做 100 下的仰臥起坐和 150 下伏地挺身。

My passport is about to expire. I <u>must renew</u> my passport.

我的護照快要過期了，我必須更換新護照。

I have a problem with my tooth. I <u>must</u> go to the dentist tomorrow.

我的牙齒有毛病，我明天得去看牙醫。

**2** must 也可表示「**極有可能**」，具有「**一定是**」、「**一定要**」的意思。但要注意這種用法的 must 只能用於**肯定句**。

You <u>must</u> be Mrs. Smith. Your daughter has told me many good things about you.

妳一定是史密斯太太，妳女兒跟我提起很多關於妳的好事。

### 否定用法時

如果要表達否定意義「**極不可能**」，或疑問意義「**有可能嗎**」則必須用 can。

- He <u>can't</u> be at his office. I saw him in the grocery store just ten minutes ago.
  他不可能在辦公室呀，因為我十分鐘前才在雜貨店看到他。
- <u>Can</u> it be Jessica at the door?
  門外會是潔西卡嗎？

| 否定句的全形和縮寫 | |
|---|---|
| I must not use | I mustn't use |
| you must not use | you mustn't use |
| he must not use | he mustn't use |
| she must not use | she mustn't use |
| it must not use | it mustn't use |
| we must not use | we mustn't use |
| they must not use | they mustn't use |

| 疑問句的句型 | |
|---|---|
| Must I use . . . ? | Must it use . . . ? |
| Must you use . . . ? | Must we use . . . ? |
| Must he use . . . ? | Must they use . . . ? |
| Must she use . . . ? | |

| 肯定和否定的簡答 | |
|---|---|
| Yes, I must. | No, I mustn't. |
| Yes, you must. | No, you mustn't. |
| Yes, he must. | No, he mustn't. |
| Yes, she must. | No, she mustn't. |
| Yes, it must. | No, it mustn't. |
| Yes, we must. | No, we mustn't. |
| Yes, they must. | No, they mustn't. |

**3** must 的否定句型是 must not，縮寫為 mustn't，用來表示「**禁止**」。

You <u>must not</u> miss the Autumn Festival.

你不可以錯過秋季嘉年華。

You <u>mustn't</u> forget your mother's birthday.

你不可以忘記你媽媽的生日。

You <u>mustn't</u> touch the wall before the paint dries.

在油漆乾掉以前，絕不能碰牆壁。

**4** must 本身不使用於過去式，如果要表達過去必須做的事，請用 had to 來代替。

As a child growing up on a farm, I <u>had to</u> milk the cows every morning.

身為農場長大的小孩，我以前每天早上都得擠牛奶。

## Practice

**1**

哪些是該做或不該做的事？請將括弧內的動詞以 must、mustn't 或 had to 的句型來填空。

1. You _____ (finish) your homework before watching TV.

2. You _____ (smoke) cigarettes.

3. We _____ (clean) the house before the party started.

4. You _____ (fight) with your sisters or brothers.

5. Tell Billy that he _____ (come) home before dinner.

6. You _____ (finish) your dinner before eating dessert.

7. Tony forgot to bring his keys, so he _____ (break) the window to get into the house.

8. You _____ (eat) too much fast food.

9. Marie _____ (behave) herself at school.

10. I overslept yesterday so I _____ (run) to catch the bus.

**2**

自下表選出適當詞彙，用 must 或 mustn't 的句型回應各個句子。

- lose it
- hurry
- go to bed
- be careful
- eat something
- fight with them
- drink something

1. I'm late.
   → *You must hurry.* _____

2. I'm very tired.
   → _____

3. I'm starving.
   → _____

4. I'm extremely dehydrated.
   → _____

5. I'm cutting glass all day.
   → _____

6. I'm having a fight with my parents.
   → _____

7. I'm carrying a large amount of money in my wallet.
   → _____

## Unit 63

### Have To
### Have To 的用法

**1** have to 不是情態助動詞，但它的意義和 must 相同，常用來表示「**必要性**」和「**義務**」。

**You** have to **take out the garbage.**
你必須把垃圾拿出去丟。

**Young adult males** have to **serve in the military for one year.**
年輕的成年男子必須當一年兵。

**You** have to **pay the phone bill.**
你必須付電話帳單。

**2** have to 的否定句型是 don't have to 或 doesn't have to，表示「**不需要做某些事**」。

**We** don't have to **do any homework tonight.**
我們今晚完全不用做功課。

**Jim** doesn't have to **go to his office today.**
吉姆今天不用去上班。

**You** don't have to **return his call.**
你不需要回他電話。

**3** have to 的**疑問句型**，是在句首加上 **Do** 或 **Does**。

**Do we** have to **come home so early?**
我們一定要這麼早回家嗎？

**Does Helen** have to **cook dinner every day?**
海倫每天都必須做晚餐嗎？

| 肯定句的句型 | |
| --- | --- |
| I have to cook | it has to cook |
| you have to cook | we have to cook |
| he has to cook | they have to cook |
| she has to cook | |

| 否定句的全形和縮寫 | |
| --- | --- |
| I do not have to cook | I don't have to cook |
| you do not have to cook | you don't have to cook |
| he does not have to cook | he doesn't have to cook |
| she does not have to cook | she doesn't have to cook |
| it does not have to cook | it doesn't have to cook |
| we do not have to cook | we don't have to cook |
| they do not have to cook | they don't have to cook |

| 疑問句的句型 | |
| --- | --- |
| Do I have to cook . . . ? | Does it have to cook . . . ? |
| Do you have to cook . . . ? | Do we have to cook . . . ? |
| Does he have to cook . . . ? | Do they have to cook . . . ? |
| Does she have to cook . . . ? | |

| 肯定和否定的簡答 | |
| --- | --- |
| Yes, I do. | No, I don't. |
| Yes, you do. | No, you don't. |
| Yes, he does. | No, he doesn't. |
| Yes, she does. | No, she doesn't. |
| Yes, it does. | No, it doesn't. |
| Yes, we do. | No, we don't. |
| Yes, they do. | No, they don't. |

## Practice

**1**

自下表選出與圖片相符的片語，用 have to 或 has to 的句型描述圖中這些辦公室職員每天必須做的事。

| | |
|---|---|
| pack products | make copies |
| answer the phone | work on the computer |

1
> She has to pack products.

2

3

4

**2**

通常主管不需要自己做哪些事呢？

請依提示，用 don't have to 或 doesn't have to 描述這些事。

1
**deliver the mail**

2
**make coffee**

3
**show up every day**

4
**fax documents**

1. Judy

2. Mr. Taylor and Mr. Watson

3. James

4. Ms. Keaton

**Unit 64**

## Comparison Between "Must" and "Have To"

### Must 和 Have To 的比較

**1** have to 的過去式是 **had to**，
表示過去必須做某件事。
**had to** 也被用作 must 的過去式。

I had to **walk thirty minutes to school when I was a child.**
我小的時候，都要走 30 分鐘的路去上學。

**2** have to 過去式的否定句型是：
**did not have to** 或 **didn't have to**。

I did not have to **do the dishes last night because it was Jerry's turn.**
昨晚我不用洗碗，因為輪到傑瑞洗了。

I didn't have to **go to school last Friday because of a typhoon.**
上個星期五因為有颱風，我不用去上學。

**3** have to 過去式的疑問句型是：
**Did . . . have to . . . ?**

Did you have to **pass the Red Cross life saving test to become a lifeguard?**
你要先通過紅十字會的救生測驗，才能成為救生員嗎？

I had to **pass the life saving test to become a lifeguard.**
為了當救生員，我們要通過救生測驗。

He didn't have to **pass the life saving test because he decided not to become a lifeguard.**
他不必通過救生測驗，因為他決定不當救生員。

**4** 在肯定句型裡，have to 的語氣比
must 強烈。
must 只是表達**個人的要求或意見**，
have to 則有**必須強制執行**的意味。

**You must eat all your vegetables.**
↳ 我覺得你應該要把青菜吃完。
你必須把所有的青菜吃完。

**You have to pay the tax.** 你一定要繳稅。
↳ 法律規定

**You have to hand in your homework tomorrow.** 你們明天一定要把作業交出來。
↳ 學校規定

**5** 在否定句型裡，mustn't 的語氣比
don't have to 或 doesn't have to 強
烈，意思也不同。mustn't 指「**不可
以做某件事**」，don't have to 指「**不
需要做某件事**」。

**You mustn't walk yet.**
你還不可以走路。

**You don't have to put sugar in that coffee.**
↳ 可能是已經很甜了，不需要再加糖。
你不用在那杯咖啡裡加糖。

# Practice

**1**

說說看，你上個星期有哪些必須做的事？又有哪些不必做的事？

用 had to 或 didn't have to 來造句。

1. I had to go to school from Monday to Friday.
2. ....................................................................................
3. ....................................................................................
4. ....................................................................................
5. ....................................................................................
6. ....................................................................................

**2**

根據圖示中的標示，並利用括弧提供的動詞或片語，用下面的句型造句：

• You mustn't . . .
• You don't have to . . .

1. ....................................................................................
   (smoke) in the café.

2. ....................................................................................
   (pay cash) in this shop.

3. ....................................................................................
   (skateboard) in the park.

4. ....................................................................................
   (talk on a cell phone) in the movie theater.

5. ....................................................................................
   (pay full price) during a sale.

50% OFF

## Part 8 Modal Verbs 情態助動詞

## Unit 65

### May and Might
### May 和 Might 的用法

**1** may 和 might 是**情態助動詞**，後面要接**動詞原形**，用來表示「可能性」或「可能會發生的事」。

We <u>may upgrade</u> the operating system on the computer.
我們可能會將這台電腦的作業系統升級。

We <u>might buy</u> a new computer game.
我們可能會買個新的電腦遊戲。

**2** may 和 might 的差別不大，都是指「**未來可能會發生的事**」，但是 might 發生的可能性比 may 稍微少一點。

I <u>may order</u> a pepperoni pizza.
我可能會叫個義式香腸披薩。

I <u>may go</u> to my mother's house for dinner.
我可能會去我媽家吃晚餐。

I <u>might</u> even <u>cook</u> something myself, but I doubt it.
我甚至可能自己煮東西來吃，不過關於這點我很懷疑。

| 否定句的句型 | |
|---|---|
| I may not leave | I might not leave |
| you may not leave | you might not leave |
| he may not leave | he might not leave |
| she may not leave | she might not leave |
| it may not leave | it might not leave |
| we may not leave | we might not leave |
| they may not leave | they might not leave |

**3** might 可被視為是 may 的過去式，如果是**表示過去事件的可能性**，則要使用 might，常用於**間接引語**中。

Father said he <u>might go</u> to Hong Kong for business. 父親說他可能會去香港洽商。

Liz said she <u>might go</u> to a movie with Jason the next day.
麗茲說她隔天可能會和傑森去看電影。

**4** may 和 might 表示「**可能性**」的時候，通常**不會用於疑問句**。

✗ May you come shopping with us this afternoon?

✗ Might you go to visit your cousin this evening?

**5** may 和 might 也可以用來**請求許可**，這個時候使用 might 又更為**客氣**。

Pardon me. <u>May I borrow</u> your cart?
I need to move some computer equipment.
不好意思，我可以借你的推車嗎？我需要搬一些電腦設備。

<u>Might I ask</u> you a question?
↳ 更客氣
我可以請教您一個問題嗎？

## Practice

**1**

自下表選出適當的動詞片語，自由以 **may** 或 **might** 的句型填空。

| win the set（贏下這局） |
| win the race（贏得賽事） |
| clear the bar（跳過這一桿） |
| hit a home run（擊出全壘打） |
| block the shot（守住對方射門） |
| score a touchdown（達陣） |

This goalie __may__ __block the shot__.

This batter _____.

This tennis player _____.

This football player _____.

Horse No. 3 _____.

This pole vaulter _____.

**2**

利用括弧裡的 **may** 或 **might** 改寫句子。

1. Perhaps we will go to the seashore tomorrow. (may)
   → _____

2. Perhaps I will take you on a trip to visit my hometown. (might)
   → _____

3. Maybe we can pick up Grandpa on the way. (may)
   → _____

4. Perhaps we can visit my sister in Sydney next year. (might)
   → _____

5. Perhaps my sister will bring her husband and baby to visit us instead. (may)
   → _____

6. Maybe we can go to Hong Kong for the weekend. (might)
   → _____

7. Perhaps you will go to a boarding school in Switzerland. (may)
   → _____

8. Or maybe you will go to live with your grandparents. (might)
   → _____

# Unit 66

## Should
### Should 的用法

**1** should 是**情態助動詞**，後面要**接動詞原形**，可以用來**提供意見**。

You should use deodorant.
你應該要用體香劑。

Your hair looks funny. You should wash it or get a haircut.
你的頭髮看起來很好笑，你應該要洗一洗或剪個頭髮。

**2** should 也可以指「**我們認為正確的事**」或「**希望別人去做的事**」。

The government should ease immigration restrictions. 政府應當要減少移民的限制。

Laid-off workers should be given free classes to train them for new jobs.
應該要為那些被解僱的員工們，開辦輔導他們重新就業的免費課程。

**3** should 可表示「**現在**」或「**未來**」。

現在 I should go now or I will be late.
我得走了，否則我會遲到。

未來 I should depart after the next song.
下一首歌結束後，我就該走了。

現在 You should leave now or you will miss the bus.
你現在就應該出發，否則你會錯過公車。

| 否定句的全形和縮寫 | |
|---|---|
| I should not talk | I shouldn't talk |
| you should not talk | you shouldn't talk |
| he should not talk | he shouldn't talk |
| she should not talk | she shouldn't talk |
| it should not talk | it shouldn't talk |
| we should not talk | we shouldn't talk |
| they should not talk | they shouldn't talk |

**4** should 常用在以下句型：
· I think you should . . .
· I don't think you should . . .

I don't think you should have any more alcohol.
我想你不應該再喝酒了。

I don't think you should drive and drink.
我認為你不該酒後駕車。

**5** should 的疑問句，經常使用「do you think I should . . .」。

Why do you think you should be driving your car on the sidewalk?
你為什麼認為可以在人行道上開車？

Do you think Jessica should go to medical school? 你覺得潔西卡應該去念醫學院嗎？

| 肯定和否定的簡答 | |
|---|---|
| Yes, I should. | No, I shouldn't. |
| Yes, you should. | No, you shouldn't. |
| Yes, he should. | No, he shouldn't. |
| Yes, she should. | No, she shouldn't. |
| Yes, it should. | No, it shouldn't. |
| Yes, we should. | No, we shouldn't. |
| Yes, they should. | No, they shouldn't. |

## Practice

**1**

自下表選用適當的動詞，分別以 should 和 shouldn't 造句。

arrive
work
eat
yield
feed
take
cheat
respect

1. We _____ on a subway train.
2. We _____ seats to the elderly on a subway train.

3. Students _____ on an exam.
4. Students _____ their teachers and themselves.

5. You _____ late.
6. You _____ hard.

7. You _____ your dog French fries.
8. You _____ your dog out for a run.

**2**

利用題目提供的詞彙，分別用下面的句型造句：

• Should . . . ?
• Do you think . . . should . . . ?

1. I   call the director about the résumé I sent
   → *Should I call the director about the résumé I sent?*
   → *Do you think I should call the director about the résumé I sent?*

2. I   bring a gift with me
   → _____
   → _____

3. Mike   go on a vacation once in a while
   → _____
   → _____

4. we   visit our grandma more often
   → _____
   → _____

5. I   ask Nancy out for a date
   → _____
   → _____

6. Sally   apply for that job in the restaurant
   → _____
   → _____

# Unit 67

## Requests：May, Could, Can
### 表示請求的用語：May、Could、Can

**1** may、can、could 都可以用來表示**請求**。

May I please see the latest sales report?
請問我可以看最新的銷售報表嗎？

May I have a cookie and a glass of milk?
我可以要一片餅乾和一杯牛奶嗎？

Could you turn on the light so I can see it better?
可以請你把燈打開嗎？這樣我才可以看得更清楚。

Could I open this package and see what's inside?
我可以拆開包裝，看看裡面是什麼嗎？

Can I sit down at your desk while I read the newspaper?
我在看報紙的時候，可以坐在你的座位上嗎？

Can you run to the store and get some soy milk?
你可以跑去商店買一些豆漿嗎？

**2** 語氣上，may 比 could 和 can 更正式，而 could 又比 can 更禮貌。

| 最正式 | May I please have another waffle? |
| 禮貌，但不正式 | Could I please have another waffle? |
| 不正式 | Can I have another waffle? |
| 沒禮貌 | Give me another waffle. |

May I serve the wine now?
請問可以上酒了嗎？

**3** may、can、could 常拿來表示「**請求允許做某件事**」。

If nobody is going to eat it, may I have the last piece of cake?
如果沒有人要吃，我可以吃這最後一塊蛋糕嗎？

Could I finish the grapes?
我可以把葡萄吃光嗎？

Can I put my feet up while I digest all the food I just ate?
我剛吃的食物還在肚裡沒消化完，我可以休息一下嗎？

**4** could 和 can 可用來「**請求他人幫忙**」；may 則不能這麼用。

Could you help me with this test?
你可以幫我做這題測驗嗎？

Can you introduce me to her?
你能介紹我認識她嗎？

## Practice

**1**

服飾店裡有名男子正在挑選衣物，請按物品編號，依序寫出他會問的問題。從右表挑選適當的詞彙，並用下面的句型造句：

- May I . . . ?
- Could I . . . ?
- Can I . . . ?

pay with a credit card

get two more shirts just like this one

have three pairs of socks similar to these

have a tie that goes with my shirt

1. → *May I get two more shirts just like this one?*
   → *Could I get two more shirts just like this one?*
   → *Can I get two more shirts just like this one?*

2. → _____
   → _____
   → _____

3. → _____
   → _____
   → _____

4. → _____
   → _____
   → _____

**2**

自右表選出正確的用語，以提示的「情態助動詞」造句完成對話。

speak to Dennis  turn up the heat

borrow your father's drill  put my files here

move these boxes for me

1. _____ (may)

   Hang on, please. I'll get him on the phone.

2. _____ (may)

   I'm not sure. I'll ask him about it.

3. _____ (could)

   I'm sorry, but I think they're too heavy for me, too.

4. _____ (could)

   No problem. Is it warmer now?

5. _____ (can)

   Yes, of course. That shelf belongs to you.

# Unit 68

## Offers and Invitations: Would Like, Will, Shall
表示提供和邀請的用語：
Would Like、Will、Shall

**1** 「Would you like + 名詞？」
用來表「**提供對方某樣東西**」。

Would you like a vacation in Rome?
你想要去羅馬度個假嗎？

Would you like a free trip to Japan?
你想要免費的日本旅遊嗎？

1 _____ some more tea?
你要不要再來一點茶？

**2** 「Would you like + 帶 to 的不定詞？」
用來表「**邀請對方做某件事**」。

Would you like to take a look at this video about the moon?
你想不想看這部關於月亮的影片？

Would you like to go some place warm and sunny?
你想不想到一個溫暖且充滿陽光的地方去？

Would you like to visit a tropical paradise?
你想不想參觀一個熱帶天堂？

2 _____ to a movie with me?
你要不要和我去看電影？

**3** 「Would you like me + 帶 to 的不定詞」用來表示「**提供對方某種服務**」。

Would you like me to mail that letter for you?
要我幫你寄那封信嗎？

Would you like me to buy you a lottery ticket?
要我幫你買張樂透彩券嗎？

3 _____ that box for you?
你要我幫你打開那個盒子嗎？

**4** 「I will + 動詞原形」用來表「**願意幫忙做某件事**」，可縮寫成「I'll + 動詞原形」。

I'll do it. 我願意去做這件事。

I'll carry that box for you.
我會幫你提那個箱子。

I'll run out and buy you some ice cream.
我願意跑一趟，幫你買一些冰淇淋。

**5** 「Shall I + 動詞原形」這個句型的意思等於「Do you want me to . . . ?」，用來表「**提供對方某種幫助**」。

Shall I walk you out to your car?
要不要我陪你走去車子那裡？

Shall I call next week and see if you are free?
我下星期打給你，到時再看你有沒有空好嗎？

4 _____ the curtain for you?
我幫你把窗簾拉下來好嗎？

## Practice

| Would you like + 名詞...? | I'll... |
|---|---|
| Would you like me to...? | Shall I...? |

**1**

依照範例，利用題目提示的詞彙，分別用表中的四種句型，造出表示提供某樣東西的問句。

1. make some fruit salad
   → Would you like some fruit salad?
   → Would you like me to make some fruit salad?
   → I'll make some fruit salad for you.
   → Shall I make some fruit salad for you?

2. make some tea
   → _____
   → _____
   → _____
   → _____

3. squeeze some orange juice
   → _____
   → _____
   → _____
   → _____

4. make some pudding
   → _____
   → _____
   → _____
   → _____

**2**

依據圖示，自下表選出正確的片語，以「Would you like to...?」的句型完成句子。

go hiking
go fishing
go to the beach
play basketball
have some pizza

1

Would you like to go fishing _____ this Saturday?

2

_____ _____ tomorrow?

3

_____ on Sunday?

4

_____ next Tuesday?

5
_____ for lunch?

171

Unit **69**

Suggestions: Shall We, What Shall We, Why Don't We, Let's, How About
表示提議的用語：**Shall We**、**What Shall We**、**Why Don't We**、**Let's**、**How About**

**1** 「Shall we . . .」 用來表示「**提議**」，後面要接動詞原形。

Shall we **go** see Steven in the hospital?
我們要不要到醫院去看史蒂芬？

Shall we **help** your father paint the garage? 我們要不要幫你爸爸油漆車庫？

Shall we **join** a study abroad tour?
我們去參加遊學之旅好不好？

**2** 要「**詢問意見**」，則可以用**疑問詞**（what、where、when 等）搭配 shall we。

What shall we **do** today?
= What should we **do** today?
我們今天要做什麼？（美式較常用should）

Where shall we **meet** Ken and Gina?
我們要在哪裡跟肯和吉娜碰面？

When shall we **invite** them over?
我們什麼時候要邀請他們過來？

¹ _____ **during summer vacation?** 我們暑假期間要做些什麼？

**3** 「Let's (= Let us) + 動詞原形」也常用表示「**提議**」，通常用於**肯定句**。

Let's **visit** our high school math teacher, Mr. Chen.
我們一起去拜訪高中數學的陳老師吧。

Let's **go** to Canada. 我們去加拿大吧。

Let's **stay** up all night and see the sunrise.
我們來熬夜看日出吧。

**4** 「Why don't we . . .」也用來表達「**提議**」，後面要接**動詞原形**。

Why don't we **take a road trip?**
我們何不來趟公路之旅？

Why don't we **volunteer** at the library on Saturdays?
我們要不要每星期六都去圖書當義工？

Why don't we **visit** the Canadian Rockies after the tour?
我們何不在這次旅行之後，去參觀加拿大洛磯山脈？

**5** How about 也表示「**提議**」，後面要接**動名詞**（V-ing）或是**名詞**。

How about **visiting** the old neighborhood?
我們去拜訪一下老鄰居如何？

How about **calling** Jimmy to see if he is free?
我們何不打個電話給吉米看他有沒有空？

How about **a walk** in the park?
到公園去散個步如何？

How about **a trip** to the mall?
你覺得到購物中心如何？

² _____ Yellowknife and hunting moose?
你覺得到黃刀鎮去獵麋鹿怎麼樣？

## Practice

**1**

依照範例，利用各題目提示的動詞，
分別用右表的四種句型造句。

Shall we . . . ?
Why don't we . . . ?
How about . . . ?
Let's . . . .

1. play another volleyball game
   → _____
   → _____
   → _____
   → _____

2. go on a picnic
   → _____
   → _____
   → _____
   → _____

3. eat out tonight
   → _____
   → _____
   → _____
   → _____

4. take a walk
   → _____
   → _____
   → _____
   → _____

5. go to Bali this summer
   → _____
   → _____
   → _____
   → _____

6. have Chinese food for dinner
   → _____
   → _____
   → _____
   → _____

## Review Test of Units 60–69
### 單元 60–69 總複習

**1** 依據圖示，自下方表中選出正確的動詞，用 can 寫出問句，詢問是否會烹調圖中的食物。依據實際情況做出簡答後，再以完整句子描述事實。

→ Unit 60 重點複習

tea eggs

tomatoes

French fries

hamburgers

muffins

coffee

an egg

a bun

fry 油煎

make 泡

bake 烘烤

purée 製漿

boil 水煮

deep fry 油炸

grill 燒烤

steam 蒸

1. Q *Can you boil tea eggs?*
   A *No, I can't. I can't boil tea eggs.*

2. Q
   A

3. Q
   A

4. Q
   A

5. Q
   A

6. Q
   A

7. Q
   A

8. Q
   A

**2** 請用 「do . . . have to」 或 「does . . . have to」 填空完成下列問句。
→ Unit 63 重點複習

1. How old ＿＿＿＿＿ you ＿＿＿＿＿＿ be to get a motorcycle driver's license?

2. ＿＿＿＿＿ every person in a car ＿＿＿＿＿＿ wear a seatbelt?

3. ＿＿＿＿＿ you ＿＿＿＿＿＿ take a written test and a road test to get an automobile driver's license?

4. ＿＿＿＿＿ you ＿＿＿＿＿＿ pass an entrance exam to go to college?

5. ＿＿＿＿＿ every adult citizen ＿＿＿＿＿＿ pay income tax?

6. How old ＿＿＿＿＿ you ＿＿＿＿＿＿ be to vote for the President?

**3** 自下表選出適當的句型來完成下列餐廳與飯店內的對話，並且注意要用禮貌的語氣。
→ Unit 60–68 重點複習

| Can I |
|---|
| May I |
| I'll |
| Could you |
| Shall I |
| How about |
| Would you |

1. Waiter : ＿＿＿＿＿＿＿ take your order?

   Guest : Yes, I'll have a fish fillet and a bowl of onion soup.

2. Guest : ＿＿＿＿＿＿＿ have the table by the window?

   Waiter : I'm afraid it's reserved.

3. Guest : ＿＿＿＿＿＿＿ send someone to fix the towel rod in my bathroom?

   Receptionist : I'll send someone up right away.

4. Guest : It's a little stuffy in the room.

   Bellboy : ＿＿＿＿＿＿＿ turn on the air conditioner for you?

5. Waiter : ＿＿＿＿＿＿＿ like a tomato salad or a chicken salad?

   Guest : A chicken salad, please.

6. Guest : I didn't order fruit tea. I ordered a pot of milk tea.

   Waiter : I'm terribly sorry. ＿＿＿＿＿＿＿ bring your milk tea right away.

7. Guest : I want to have something light.

   Waiter : ＿＿＿＿＿＿＿ the chicken soup? It's popular among our guests.

8. Guest : I don't like chicken. Do you have anything else?

   Waiter : ＿＿＿＿＿＿＿ like to try Today's Special? It's steamed fish. It's a light dish, too.

**4** 從圖中選出適當的詞彙，用「Would you like . . . ?」的句型造問句，完成下列空服員（**F** Flight Attendant）與乘客（**P** Passenger）間的對話。
→ Unit 68 重點複習

1. **F** *Would you like something to drink?*

   **P** Yes, please. What do you have?

2. **F** ..............................................................................

   **P** No, thanks. I don't drink beer or wine.

3. **F** ..............................................................................

   **P** No, thanks. It's too sweet. Do you have anything hot?

4. **F** ..............................................................................

   **P** A cup of tea would be great.

5. **F** ..............................................................................

   **P** No, thank you. I'm not hungry.

   **F** Enjoy your tea.

a bag of nuts

some juice

a cup of coffee or tea

an alcoholic beverage

something to drink

**5** 將下列句子改寫為否定句。
→ Unit 60–66 重點複習

My dog can sing! → *My dog can't sing.*

1. I can walk to work.

   → ..............................................................................

2. Susie could dance all night.

   → ..............................................................................

3. I have to go to Joe's house tonight.

   → ..............................................................................

4. I have to go to see the doctor tomorrow.

   → ..............................................................................

5. I may go on a vacation in August.

   → ..............................................................................

6. I might go see the Picasso exhibit at the museum.

   → ..............................................................................

7. My friend can sit in the full lotus position.

→ ..............................................................................................................

8. I can finish all my homework this weekend.

→ ..............................................................................................................

9. I must stop eating beans.

→ ..............................................................................................................

10. John has to see Joseph.

→ ..............................................................................................................

11. The turtle may win the race against the rabbit.

→ ..............................................................................................................

12. My friend Jon should get a different job.

→ ..............................................................................................................

**6** 將下列句子改寫為疑問句。
→ Unit 60–66 重點複習

1. You can fry an egg.

→ *Can you fry an egg?* .............................................................

2. Paul could swim out to the island.

→ ..............................................................................................................

3. John must go to Japan.

→ ..............................................................................................................

4. Abby has to go to the studio.

→ ..............................................................................................................

5. George can play the guitar.

→ ..............................................................................................................

6. David must  finish his homework before he goes outside to play.

→ ..............................................................................................................

7. They have to cross the road.

→ ..............................................................................................................

8. I have to give away my concert tickets.

→ ..............................................................................................................

9. Joan has to stay at home tomorrow night.

→ ..............................................................................................................

**7** 選出正確的答案。
→ **Unit 69** 重點複習

___ 1. Bob : I'm bored. _____ go somewhere?

      Ⓐ Why don't we      Ⓑ Shall we      Ⓒ Both A and B

___ 2. Stan : _____ taking a ride on the subway?

      Ⓐ How about      Ⓑ Why don't we      Ⓒ Shall we

___ 3. Bob : Great. _____ go.

      Ⓐ Why don't we      Ⓑ Shall we      Ⓒ Let's

___ 4. Stan : _____ go to Forest Park?

      Ⓐ Shall we      Ⓑ How about      Ⓒ Let's

___ 5. Bob : _____ do at Forest Park?

      Ⓐ What shall we      Ⓑ Shall we      Ⓒ Both A and B

___ 6. Stan : _____ taking a walk in the park?

      Bob : No. That's boring.

      Ⓐ How about      Ⓑ Shall we      Ⓒ Let's

___ 7. Stan : In that case, _____ do?

      Bob : I want to go home and watch TV.

      Ⓐ what shall we      Ⓑ let's      Ⓒ why don't we

___ 8. Stan : _____ forget about it. You go home.

      I'm going for a walk in the park.

      Ⓐ How about      Ⓑ Shall we      Ⓒ Let's

___ 9. Stan : OK. _____ take a walk in Forest Park.

      Ⓐ How about      Ⓑ Let's      Ⓒ Why don't we

___ 10. Stan : _____ hop the next train?

      Ⓐ Let's      Ⓑ Shall we      Ⓒ What shall we

**8** 請將各個句子依據情態助動詞的作用，填入適當的分類編號。

→ Unit 59–69 重點複習

**A**
Asking for something
請求得到某物

**B**
Asking permission
請求允許

**C**
Asking someone to do something 請求他人幫忙

**D**
Offering something
供應物品

**E**
Inviting someone
邀請他人

**F**
Offering to do something
願意幫忙做某事

**G**
Asking for a suggestion
徵求意見

**H**
Making a suggestion
提議

1. Can I have a cookie, please?

2. Would you like one more croissant?

3. Why don't we visit Sam tomorrow?

4. Can you call the police for me?

5. I'll go get a bandage for you.

6. May I try on this shirt?

7. What should I do with my parents?

8. Would you like to play badminton?

179

**9** 依據對話的意思，用 must 或 mustn't 搭配括弧中的動詞完成對話。
→ Unit 62 重點複習

1. Jack：  Susan has been working for six hours.

    Olive：  She _____ (be) very tired. She should take a break.

2. Eddie：  Ken has gone to Japan for a vacation. It's his mother's birthday today.

    Yvonne：His mother says he _____ (visit) her in Tokyo.

3. Ada：  Bob hasn't eaten anything the whole day.

    Tim：  He _____ (be) starving. He _____ (eat)

    something.

4. Billy：  Cindy's phone bill is due today.

    Zoe：  She _____ (pay) the bill right now, or she can't call anyone

    with her phone.

5. Rick：  My little brother was taken to the hospital last night. He burned his fingers.

    Heather：He _____ (play) with matches any more.


**10** 依據對話的意思，用 may 或 should not / may not / must not 搭配括弧中的動詞完成對話。
→ Unit 65 重點複習

1. You _____ (have) one more piece of the pizza, but you

    _____ (eat) all of it.

2. You _____ (listen) to music on an authorized website, but you

    _____ (download) music from an illegal site.

3. You _____ (have) a cup of coffee a day, but you _____

    (put) too much sugar in it.

4. You _____ (drive) to the bank, but you _____ (find)

    a parking space anywhere near the bank.

5. You _____ (call) her in the middle of the night, but she _____

    (answer) the phone.

6. You _____ (watch) the lions in the zoo, but you _____ (try)

    to touch them.

180

**11** 依據對話的意思，用 should 或 shouldn't 搭配括弧中的動詞完成對話。
→ **Unit 66** 重點複習

1. Peggy： My dog Momo has been playing
   with his toy for twenty minutes.

   James：You ＿＿＿＿＿＿＿ (give)
   Momo some water to drink.

2. James：Snowbell is too fat.

   Anne： You ＿＿＿＿＿＿＿ (feed)
   her so much food.

3. Joanne： She looks so cute and friendly.

   David： I think we ＿＿＿＿＿＿＿
   (adopt) her.

4. Erica：Ted had a diarrhea this morning.

   Pete： You ＿＿＿＿＿＿＿ (give)
   him any more ice cream.

5. Peggy： Momo doesn't look happy today.

   James： He just wants to play.
   You ＿＿＿＿＿＿＿ (spend)
   more time with him.

6. Diana：Kiki is losing a lot of hair.

   Jacky：That's not good. You
   ＿＿＿＿＿＿＿ (take)
   her to a vet.

Unit **71**

## Affirmative and Negative Sentences
肯定句和否定句

**1** 肯定句是「**描述一個肯定事實**」的句子。

I have a large family. 我有一個大家庭。

Jim went to college last year.
吉姆去年上大學。

**2** 否定句是「表達否定意義」的句子，通常句子裡會出現**否定詞 not、never** 或 **rarely** 等。

I don't think it's a good idea.
我不認為這是個好主意。

I never lie to my parents.
我從不對爸媽說謊。

Nina rarely goes on a vacation. She's a workaholic.
妮娜很少去度假，她是個工作狂。

**3** 一般句子要構成否定句，如果是**現在式**，只要在**動詞前面加上** do not 或 does not；
如果是**過去式**，則在動詞前面加上 did not。

My grandparents don't like to live in the city. 我的祖父母不喜歡住在城市裡。

Brad doesn't believe in ghosts.
布萊德不相信世界上有鬼。

Carrie didn't take part in the competition last Wednesday.
凱莉上週三並沒有去參加比賽。

**4** 如果句子裡有 **be 動詞**或**情態助動詞**，則在 be 動詞或情態助動詞後面加上 not，構成否定句。

I am not mad at you. 我並不生你的氣。

Your father would not want you to stay in this industry.
你父親不會希望你待在這個行業裡。

Rene cannot scuba dive, but she loves snorkeling.
蕾妮不會水肺潛水，但是她愛浮潛。

## Practice

**1**

將右列肯定句改寫為否定句。

1. James is playing with his new iPhone.

   → *James isn't playing with his new iPhone.*

2. Vincent owns a shoe factory.

   → ................................................................................

3. They went to a concert last night.

   → ................................................................................

4. I enjoy reading.

   → ................................................................................

5. I can ride a unicycle.

   → ................................................................................

6. Summer vacation will begin soon.

   → ................................................................................

7. I had a nightmare last night.

   → ................................................................................

8. I am from Vietnam.

   → ................................................................................

**2**

將右列否定句改寫為肯定句。

1. Sue didn't watch the football game on TV last night.

   → ................................................................................

2. Rick can't speak Japanese.

   → ................................................................................

3. Phil and Jill weren't at the office yesterday.

   → ................................................................................

4. I couldn't enter the house this morning.

   → ................................................................................

5. Joseph doesn't like spaghetti.

   → ................................................................................

6. They aren't drinking apple juice.

   → ................................................................................

7. She isn't going shopping tomorrow.

   → ................................................................................

8. I won't tell Sandy.

   → ................................................................................

Unit 72

Question Forms: Types of Questions and the Question Words "What" and "Who"
疑問句：疑問句的種類和
疑問詞 What、Who 的用法

**1** 疑問句是用來提出疑問的句子，必須以「問號？」結尾。

Are you satisfied with the results?
你對這結果滿意嗎？

Did he apologize for being rude?
他為他的無禮表示歉意了嗎？

**2** 一般動詞的疑問句，如果是**現在式**，必須在句首加上 Do 或 Does，後面維持**動詞原形**；如果是**過去式**，則在句首加上 Did。

Do you spend your summer on a tropical island every year?
你每年夏天都去熱帶島嶼度假嗎？

Does he jog for fifty minutes every day?
他每天慢跑五十分鐘嗎？

Did I tell you that I had passed the exam?
我有沒有告訴你我已經通過考試了？

**3** be 動詞或情態助動詞的疑問句，則是將 be 動詞或情態助動詞**移至句首**。

Is there anything wrong?
有什麼不對勁嗎？

Shall we set off for the train station?
我們是不是該出發去火車站了？

Will you keep the secret? 你會保密嗎？

**4** 還有疑問句是在句首使用**疑問詞**。

常見的疑問詞：
1 what    5 who
2 where    6 how
3 when    7 which
4 why    8 whose

**5** what 用來詢問「**一般事物**」，通常指**動物**或**無生物**。

A What is your cell phone number?
B My cell phone number is 0928-332-432.
A 你的手機號碼是幾號？
B 我的手機號碼是 0928-332-432。

A What type of beverage is that?
B It's plum green tea.
A 那是什麼飲料？
B 梅子綠茶。

**6** who 用來詢問「**人**」。

A Who are you?
B I'm Jerry White.
A 你是誰？
B 我是傑瑞‧懷特。

A Who is your favorite author?
B Maybe John McPhee, but that's a hard question to answer.
A 你最喜歡的作家是誰？
B 大概是約翰‧麥克菲吧，不過這個問題很難回答。

## Practice

**1**

將右列句子改寫為
「疑問句」。

1. Jerry is good at photography.

   → *Is Jerry good at photography?*

2. Jane doesn't believe what he said.

   → ......................................................................................................................

3. He never showed up at the party.

   → ......................................................................................................................

4. Johnny gets up early every day.

   → ......................................................................................................................

5. I will remember you.

   → ......................................................................................................................

6. Julie asked me to give her a ride yesterday.

   → ......................................................................................................................

7. She was surprised when he called.

   → ......................................................................................................................

8. He's going to buy a gift tomorrow.

   → ......................................................................................................................

**2**

依據粗體字的提示，
將句子以 who 或
what 造出問句。

1. Q *What are you watching on the Internet?*

   A I'm watching **the news** on the Internet.

2. Q ......................................................................................................................

   A I'm interested in **painting scenery**.

3. Q ......................................................................................................................

   A **That man** is the vice president of the company.

4. Q ......................................................................................................................

   A My favorite musician is **Bach**.

5. Q ......................................................................................................................

   A He is looking at **a cat on the roof**.

6. Q ......................................................................................................................

   A **Jude** is writing an email.

Unit **73**

## Question Forms: "Who" and "What" Used as Subjects or Objects
### 疑問句：Who 和 What 作主詞或受詞的用法

**1** 疑問句中，who 用來指「**人**」，可以用來詢問句中**主詞**或**受詞**。

<u>Susan</u> **is calling** <u>Leo</u>. 蘇珊正在叫李歐。
主 詞　　　　　 受詞

 詢問主詞
Who **is calling Leo?** 誰在叫李歐？
主 詞

 詢問受詞
Who **is Susan calling?** 蘇珊在叫誰？
受 詞

**2** 疑問句中，what 用來指「**動物或無生物**」，可以用來詢問句中**主詞**或**受詞**。

詢問主詞
What **happened?** 發生什麼事？
主 詞

詢問受詞
What **did the dog eat?** 這隻狗吃了什麼？
受 詞

**3** who 和 what 用來詢問主詞時，**問句的動詞**和**直述句的動詞**是相同的。
詞語的順序不需要改變，也不需要另外加助動詞 do、does 或 did。

| 直述句 | 用 who 或 what 詢問主詞 |
|---|---|
| **Willy is eating a sandwich.** 威利正在吃三明治。 | Who is eating a sandwich? 誰正在吃三明治？ |
| **Debbie likes mountain climbing.** 黛比喜歡爬山。 | Who likes mountain climbing? 誰喜歡爬山？ |
| **Something has happened to Jim.** 吉姆發生了一些事。 | What has happened to Jim? 吉姆發生了什麼事？ |

**4** who 和 what 用來**詢問受詞**時，會改變語序，或者加上 **do**、**does** 或 **did** 來構成疑問句。

| 直述句 | 用 who 或 what 詢問受詞 |
|---|---|
| **Willy is eating a sandwich.** 威利正在吃三明治。 | What is Willy eating? 威利正在吃什麼？ |
| **Debbie likes mountain climbing.** 黛比喜歡爬山。 | What does Debbie like? 黛比喜歡什麼？ |
| **The vase is made of plastic.** 這個花瓶是塑膠做的。 | What is the vase made of? 這個花瓶是什麼做的？ |

## Practice

**1**

用 who 或 what 分別寫出詢問主詞和受詞的問句。

**1**

Johnny ate my slice of pizza.

→ *Who ate my slice of pizza?*

→ *What did Johnny eat?*

**2**

The boss consulted Lauren first.

→

→

**3**

Tom helped cook the fish.

→

→

**4**

My dog broke the vase.

→

→

**5**

Mom is making food for the baby.

→

→

**6**

Denise is standing next to Allen.

→

→

# Part 9 Types of Sentences 句子類型

## Unit 74

### Question Forms: the Question Words "When," "Which," "Where," and "Whose"

疑問句：疑問詞 When、Which、Where、Whose 的用法

### 1 when 用來詢問「時間」。

A When **do you start to work in the morning?**

B **My job starts at 9:30 a.m.**

A 你早上幾點開始工作？

B 我的工作是從早上 9 點半開始。

A When **did you move to Taiwan?**

B **I moved to Taiwan two years ago.**

A 你是什麼時候搬到台灣的？

B 我兩年前搬到台灣。

### 2 which 用來詢問「選擇」。

A Which **road do I take to get to Hsinchu?**

B **To get to Hsinchu, you should take Highway 1.**

A 我要走哪一條路才能到新竹？

B 要到新竹，你必須走國道一號。

A Which **do you want, the red apple or the green apple?**

B **I want the green one.**

A 你想要哪一種，紅蘋果還是青蘋果？

B 我要青的。

### 3 where 用來詢問「地點」。

A Where **did you study in Germany?**

B **I studied in Berlin.**

A 你在德國的哪裡念書？

B 我在柏林念書。

A Where **do you live?**

B **I live in the Netherlands.**

A 你住在哪裡？

B 我住在荷蘭。

### 4 whose 用來詢問「所有權」。

A Whose **chicken is this?**

B **That chicken belongs to Colonel Sanders.**

A 這個雞肉是誰的？

B 那個雞肉是桑德斯上校的。

A Whose **books are these?**

B **These books are mine. I just bought them.**

A 這些書是誰的？

B 這些書是我的，我剛剛才買的。

### 5 who's 和 whose 的意思與用法皆不相同。
who's 同 who is；
而 whose 則是who 的所有格。

Who's **going to clean up after the party?**
↳ = who is
派對後誰要負責清理？

Whose **cell phone is ringing?**
↳ whose 是 who 的所有格。
誰的手機在響？

188

## Practice

**1**

下列詞彙適合做哪一個疑問詞的回答？
將它們填入正確的空格內。

|  | Italy |  |
|---|---|---|
| this one | my brother's | in 2022 |
| the blue shirt | the large one | the cat's |
| the taller man | last December | the mall |
| Amber's | the office | the garage |
| tomorrow | Ms. Smith's | next month |

① which
this one

② where

③ when

④ whose

**2**

自下表選出正確的疑問詞填空。

where
when
whose
which

1. _____ was the Meiji Restoration in Japan?

2. _____ is Gary going to meet his client, in a café or in his office?

3. _____ city, Kyoto or Osaka, has the most beautiful temples?

4. _____ invention was the Walkman?

5. _____ is the British Museum located?

6. _____ was the steam train invented?

7. _____ bicycle is this?

8. _____ did you last see him?

9. _____ do you like better on pasta, olive oil or butter?

10. _____ does your school begin?

# Part 9 Types of Sentences 句子類型

## Unit 75

Question Forms:
the Question Words "How" and "Why"
疑問句：
疑問詞 How 和 Why 的用法

**1** how 用來詢問「方法」。

Ⓐ **How** do you get to the zoo?

Ⓑ Take the train to the last stop, and then walk past the mall to the zoo.

Ⓐ 你是怎麼去動物園的？

Ⓑ 搭火車到最後一站，然後再經過大賣場走到動物園。

**3** why 用來詢問「理由」。

Ⓐ **Why** did that chicken cross the road?

Ⓑ That chicken crossed the road to get to the other side.

Ⓐ 為什麼那隻雞要過馬路？

Ⓑ 過馬路是因為牠要到路的另一邊。

Ⓐ **Why** are you going to school?

Ⓑ I am going to school to study animal behavior.

Ⓐ 你為什麼要上學？

Ⓑ 我上學是為了研究動物行為。

**2** how 常和一些字搭配使用。

**How**

| | | |
|---|---|---|
| old 老的 | tall 高的 | long 長的 |
| much 多的 | many 多的 | often 常常 |

Ⓐ **How tall** was that dinosaur?
那隻恐龍有多高？

Ⓑ That dinosaur was 10 meters tall.
那隻恐龍有 10 公尺高。

Ⓐ **How long** was that dinosaur?
那隻恐龍有多長？

Ⓑ That dinosaur was 30 meters long.
那隻恐龍有 30 公尺長。

Ⓐ **How much** did that dinosaur weigh?
那隻恐龍有多重？

Ⓑ That dinosaur weighed over 2,500 kilograms.
那隻恐龍重達 2,500 公斤以上。

Ⓐ **How many** animal species have survived from the time of the dinosaurs?
有幾種動物從恐龍時代存活下來？

Ⓑ Only a few, such as sharks.
只有非常少數，像是鯊魚。

## Practice

**1**

自下表選出適當的
「疑問詞彙」來完成
句子。

How
How much
How old
How long
How many
How tall
How often

1. A _____ is your brother?
   B He is 25 years old.

2. A _____ is your sister?
   B She is 160 centimeters tall.

3. A _____ money do you have in your wallet?
   B I have about 500 dollars in my wallet.

4. A _____ times were you late for work this week?
   B I was late three times this week.

5. A _____ do I operate this machine?
   B You can follow the instruction manual.

6. A _____ do you see your boyfriend?
   B I see him every weekend.

7. A _____ is your winter break from school?
   B My winter break is about three weeks.

8. A _____ was your hamster when it ran away?
   B It was over two years old.

9. A This building is tightly guarded. _____ could he enter the manager's room?
   B He must be a smart thief.

10. A _____ is Taipei 101?
    B It is about 100 stories tall.

11. A _____ does a cup of pearl milk tea cost?
    B It usually costs 25 dollars.

12. A _____ do you go to Chicago to visit your relatives?
    B I usually go to Chicago to visit my relatives twice a year.

13. A _____ do you stay when you visit your family in Chicago?
    B I usually stay a week or so.

14. A _____ do I get to the airport?
    B Use a map.

## Unit 76

## Question Tags
## 附加問句

**1** 附加問句是附屬於句子結尾的小問句，用來提問或確認某件事情。

Tina is single, **isn't she?**
蒂娜還是單身，對嗎？

Jerry doesn't have a girlfriend, **does he?**
傑瑞沒有女朋友，對嗎？

I can introduce them to each other, **can't I?**
我可以介紹他們兩個認識，不是嗎？

**2** 肯定句會使用**否定的附加問句**，否定句會使用**肯定的附加問句**。

We are staying here, **aren't we?**
我們會待在這兒，對不對？

We aren't staying here, **are we?**
我們不會待在這裡，對嗎？

**3** 現在簡單式的附加問句，句子裡如果**沒有be動詞或助動詞**（can、may、should 等），附加問句就要用**do**、**don't**、**does** 和 **doesn't** 來構成。

You like to eat prunes, **don't you?**
你喜歡吃乾梅子，對不對？

Harry eats anything dead or alive, **doesn't he?**
不管活的還是死的東西，哈利都吃，不是嗎？

**4** 過去簡單式的附加問句，則用 **did** 和 **didn't** 來構成。

You didn't quit your job, **did you?**
你並沒有辭職，對嗎？

Larry stopped working at the airport, **didn't he?** 賴瑞不在機場工作了，不是嗎？

They got up early last weekend, **didn't they?** 他們上個週末很早起，不是嗎？

**5** 附加問句可以用來「**詢問問題**」，如果提問時**不知道答案**，語調要上揚。

This is my milk, **isn't it?**
這是我的牛奶，對不對？

唸唸看

He comes from Greece, **doesn't he?**
They aren't afraid of snakes, **are they?**
Ivy can't make rice pudding, **can she?**

**6** 附加問句也可用來「**確認事情**」或「**提出聲明**」。如果提問時已經知道答案，只是要做確認，語調要**下降**。

It's past your bedtime, **isn't it?**
現在已經超過你的上床時間了，對吧？

**7** 一般來說，**附加問句**的動詞和時態應該與前文一致，但也有例外。

She has a big house, **hasn't she?**
= She has a big house, **doesn't she?**
她有一棟大房子，對不對？

He wasn't leaving, **was he?**
他並沒有要離開，對吧？

例外

I am next, **aren't I?**
我是下一個，對不對？

# Practice

**1**

摔角選手 Hulk（HH）正在接受脫口秀主持人 DL 的訪問，請根據訪問內容，寫出正確的「附加問句」。

DL : Hello, Hulk. I can call you Hulk, ❶_____?

HH : I prefer Mr. Hooligan.

DL : You're joking, ❷_____?

HH : Of course. I don't look like a guy who stands on formality, ❸_____?

DL : You look like a guy who stands on other people's heads. I can say that, ❹_____?

HH : Sure. I'm proud of crushing my opponents under the heels of my boots.

DL : When you stand on your opponents, you don't hurt them, ❺_____?

HH : Hey! I haven't killed anybody yet, ❻_____?

DL : Let's go back to the beginning. You started wrestling as a child, ❼_____?

HH : My first real opponent was my older brother.

DL : You didn't fight with your sister, ❽_____?

HH : She was stronger than my brother, so I left her alone.

DL : You didn't wrestle with anybody else, ❾_____?

HH : We had a pet alligator.

DL : You have wrestled with alligators, ❿_____?

HH : Yeah, but my sister was tougher than any alligator.

DL : Who was uglier, your sister or the alligator?

HH : You don't want to make me mad, ⓫_____?

DL : No! You don't want to talk about that, ⓬_____?
Let's talk about your new TV show . . .

**2**

寫出右列句子的附加問句。

1. You're going to adopt a stray cat, _____?
2. He is not going abroad to study the law, _____?
3. You can't run fast, _____?
4. She will come to the class, _____?
5. I passed the exam, _____?
6. She doesn't believe me, _____?
7. The gift is for me, _____?
8. I'm chosen, _____?
9. It's midnight, _____?
10. Sam didn't cook dinner last night, _____?

# Unit 77

## Imperative Sentences
祈使句

**1** 祈使句是用來表達「**強烈要求或命令**」的句型,肯定句以「**動詞原形**」開頭。

Stop. 住手。

Watch **your head**. 小心你的頭。

Look **both ways before crossing the street**.
過馬路之前要記得左看右看注意來車。

Walk **this way**. 走這邊。

Wait **here**. 在這裡等。

Watch **your step**. 小心你的腳步。

**2** 祈使句的否定句會使用 do not 或其縮寫 don't,也可以使用 never。

Do not **touch the sculptures**.
不要碰這些雕像。

**Please** do not **take pictures**.
請不要拍照。

Do not **stand there**. 不要站在那裡。

Don't **touch the animals**. 不要摸動物。

Don't **step in the puddles**. 別踩進水坑。

### 祈使句的使用時機

**1** **Invitations** 邀請
**Please** join **our tour**.
一起去旅行吧。

**2** **Requests** 要求
Put **your tickets here**.
把票放在這裡。

**3** **Instructions** 命令
**Everybody** follow **me**.
所有人跟我來。

**4** **Warnings** 警告
Watch **out**. 小心。

**5** **Offers** 提供
Have **some green tea, please**.
喝點綠茶吧。

**6** **Advice and suggestions** 建議
Take **a break**. 休息一下。

**7** **Encouragement** 鼓勵
Don't give **up now**.
不要現在放棄。

**8** **Pleading** 懇求
Don't leave **now**.
現在不要離開。

**3** 祈使句前後可以加上 please 表示禮貌。

Please **hurry up**. 請快一點。

**Slow down**, please. 請慢下來。

Please **don't pick the flowers!**
請不要摘花!

# Practice

**1**

右列句子哪些屬於「祈使句」？請在祈使句前面打✓。

............ 1. Help yourself to that egg.

............ 2. You must talk to your teacher right away.

............ 3. Do not touch the stove.

............ 4. Can't you be honest?

............ 5. Please sit down.

............ 6. Tie your shoes this way.

............ 7. Nobody trusts Jason.

............ 8. Go back to bed now.

............ 9. I won't let you leave home.

............ 10. Don't feed your brother worms.

**2**

將右列句子改寫為「祈使句」。

1. Paul, I want you to close that door.

   → ...............................................................................................................

2. You should not go out at midnight.

   → ...............................................................................................................

3. You can't throw garbage into the toilet.

   → ...............................................................................................................

4. Can you go buy some eggs now?

   → ...............................................................................................................

5. I hope you're not mad at me.

   → ...............................................................................................................

6. You can take a No. 305 bus to the city hall.

   → ...............................................................................................................

7. You should be careful not to wake up the baby.

   → ...............................................................................................................

8. You don't have to worry about so many things.

   → ...............................................................................................................

9. You should relax.

   → ...............................................................................................................

10. Why don't you do your homework right now?

   → ...............................................................................................................

## Review Test of Units 71–77
### 單元 71–77 總複習

**1** 分辨下列句子是肯定句、否定句還是疑問句。在肯定句的前面寫上 A（affirmative），在否定句的前面寫上 N（negative），在疑問句的前面寫上 Q（question）。

→ Unit 71–75 重點複習

............ 1. You can't get into that room.

............ 2. That is the best movie I've ever watched.

............ 3. Betty is never late for work.

............ 4. Am I wrong about him?

............ 5. They're not from Peru.

............ 6. Did he make these cookies by himself?

............ 7. Timmy bought two boxes of chocolate in the store.

............ 8. Have you ever seen a whale?

............ 9. What happened last night?

............ 10. I'll come back in fifteen minutes.

**2** 用 Who、What、Where、When、Why、How、Which 或 Whose 等疑問詞，完成填空。

→ Unit 72–75 重點複習

1. ........................... can I pick up my dry cleaning? Tonight or tomorrow morning?

2. ........................... can I get new sports shoes?

3. ........................... is the most famous Japanese musician?

4. ........................... much does a lottery ticket cost?

5. ........................... left the refrigerator door open?

6. ........................... do you want to go on a vacation? Guam?

7. ........................... does the plane leave for Bali?

8. ........................... many brothers and sisters do you have?

9. ........................... did you hit your sister?

10. ........................... should people eat a balanced diet?

11. ........................... train did you take on Friday night, the 9:30 p.m. train or the one at 11:30 p.m.?

12. ........................... is the name of the tallest mountain in the world?

13. ........................... of these novels did you enjoy reading the most?

14. ........................... are the names of the movies you have seen this month?

15. ........................... scooter is blocking my car?

16. ........................... turn is it to use the bathroom?

**3** 依據粗體字的提示，將句子以 who 或 what 造出問句。
→ Unit 75 重點複習

1. **Eve** is visiting Charles.

   → *Who is visiting Charles?*

2. Eve is visiting **Charles**.

   →

3. **Edward** wants to meet Cathy.

   →

4. Cathy wants to meet **Edward**.

   →

5. **Mary's editing of the report** took her a long time.

   →

6. He took the **birthday cake** with him.

   →

7. Keith is dating **someone**.

   →

8. **Something** crashed.

   →

9. **Dad** answered the phone.

   →

10. **Someone** wants to marry Jenny.

    →

11. Dennis wants to buy **a new cell phone**.

    →

12. **Dennis** wants to buy a new cell phone.

    →

13. **Sylvia** wants to eat peanuts.

    →

14. Sylvia wants to eat **peanuts**.

    →

**4** 請在每一句的後面，加上正確的「附加問句」。
→ Unit 76 重點複習

1. Sightseeing is fun, _____isn't it?_____

2. Working 60 hours a week isn't good for you, _____

3. Chocolate chip cookies are tasty, _____

4. We aren't too old to have a good time, _____

5. You did a good job on the report, _____

6. You didn't get the letter in the mail, _____

7. The meeting was boring, _____

8. The project wasn't finished on time, _____

9. You liked the lentils, _____

**5** 請將下列錯誤的句子，更正重寫。
→ Unit 72–76 重點複習

1. Who Chris is calling?

   → _Who is Chris calling?_

2. What Irene wants to do?

   → _____

3. Who does want to stay for dinner?

   → _____

4. Who the last piece of cake finished?

   → _____

5. Who did invented the automobile?

   → _____

6. Who's dirty dishes are these on the table?

   → _____

7. What side of the road do you drive on?

   → _____

8. Rupert likes history, does he?

   → _____

9. They drive a minivan, don't it?

   → _____

**6** 找出下列對話中屬於「祈使句」的用法，畫上底線。
→ Unit 77 重點複習

Bob： How can I get to the station?

Eve： Go straight down this road. Walk for fifteen minutes and you will see a park.

Bob： So, the station is near the park.

Eve： Yes. Turn right at the park and walk for another five minutes. Cross the main road. The station will be at your left. You won't miss it.

Bob： That's very helpful of you.

Eve： Be sure not to take any small alleys on the way.

Bob： I won't. Thank you very much.

Eve： You're welcome.

**7** 將下列句子分別改寫為「否定句」和「疑問句」。
→ Unit 71–75 重點複習

1. Eddie is a naughty boy.

   → .................................................................................................................

   → .................................................................................................................

2. Jack walks to work every morning.

   → .................................................................................................................

   → .................................................................................................................

3. Sammi visited Uncle Lu last Saturday.

   → .................................................................................................................

   → .................................................................................................................

4. She will be able to finish the project next week.

   → .................................................................................................................

   → .................................................................................................................

5. My boss is going to Beijing tomorrow.

   → .................................................................................................................

   → .................................................................................................................

6. Joe has already seen the show.

   → .................................................................................................................

   → .................................................................................................................

## Unit 79

### Phrasal Verbs (1)
### 片語動詞（1）

> 片語動詞（phrasal verb）和**動詞片語**（verb phrase）不同。**片語動詞**是一組固定用語，**動詞片語**則是任何一組以動詞開頭的詞組。下列兩例就是動詞片語：
>
> - go **to work on time** 準時去上班
> - watch **the game on TV** 看電視轉播的賽事

**1** 有時，動詞後面會加上某些**介系詞**或**副詞**，如 up 和 down，形成一組**動詞片語**，我們稱這種固定的動詞片語為片語動詞。

- **get along** 相處
- **find out** 發現
- **watch out** 小心

**2** 這些介系詞或副詞，有時會**稍微改變動詞的意義**，但我們仍能從字面上探知意義。

Throw **the ball**. 把球丟出去。
↳ 動詞 throw：把球投擲出去。

Throw away **the ball**. 把球丟掉。
↳ 片語動詞 throw away：把球扔到垃圾桶裡。

Come in **from the porch**.
↳ 進來室內。
從走廊上進來吧。

Come out **to the porch**. 出來走廊上吧。
↳ 出來室外。

**3** 有些片語動詞的意義已經與原來的動詞不相同，**產生了新的意義**。

If you are going to throw up, go into the bathroom.　　↳ 吐
如果你要吐，就到廁所去。

The bank robber came out after the police cornered him.　↳ 出現
這名銀行搶匪在被警方包圍之後，只好現身。

**4** 片語動詞有四種類型。第一種是後面**不需要再加受詞**，可以單獨存在的片語動詞。

- **stand up** 起立
- **take off** 起飛

When you hear your name, please stand up. 叫到你的名字時請站起來。

Don't take off until I get back.
我還沒回去前先別出發。

**watch out** 小心
Watch out! There's a car coming.
小心！有車子來了。

**shut up** 閉嘴
Will you please shut up?
拜託你閉嘴好嗎？

**show up** 出現
Jason promised to come to the meeting, but he never showed up.
傑森答應要來開會，但一直沒出現。

**go off** 響起
The alarm clock went off while I was having a sweet dream.
我好夢正甜時，鬧鐘就響了。

**calm down** 冷靜
Calm down. I'll help you go through all this. 冷靜點，我會幫你度過這一切。

**hang out** 在某地逗留或與某人相處
We should hang out together at the mall sometime next week.
我們下星期找個時間在購物中心聚聚。

**give up** 放棄
Don't give up. 不要放棄。

# Practice

### 1

自右表選出正確的「片語動詞」填空，並做出適當的變化，完成句子。

| come along | take off | stay up | work out |
|---|---|---|---|
| move in | hang out | come in | |

1. My wife didn't _____ on the trip to Egypt.

2. Curtis needs to _____ at the gym more often.

3. Why don't we _____ together next week?

4. The plane has _____. You're too late.

5. You look tired. Did you _____ late last night?

6. Another family is _____ to the neighborhood.

7. _____, please.

### 2

選出正確的答案。

1. Her fondest dreams have at last come **true / out**.

2. Are we going to eat **up / out** tonight?

3. I think I'll try to encourage him. He shouldn't give **up / off**.

4. Did he show **up / down** at the party? I didn't see him.

5. I'm moving **in / out** tomorrow. We'll soon become roommates.

6. Don't stand there. Sit **up / down**.

7. I'm sorry for being late. The alarm clock didn't go **on / off** this morning.

8. Fay fell **out / down** and got hurt.

9. Can I have a plastic bag? I feel like throwing **out / up**.

10. Do you get **up / on** early every day?

11. Life has to go **out / on**.

12. Where did you grow **off / up**?

Unit **80**

## Phrasal Verbs (2)
## 片語動詞（2）

**1** 第二種片語動詞必須搭配**受詞**使用，受詞的位置又有兩種，可以互換。（下面的第一種句型較為常用）

**1** 動詞 + 介系詞／副詞 + 受詞

- take out 拿出去   - take off 脫掉

Can you help me take out the garbage?
可以請你幫我把垃圾拿出去丟嗎？
Take off your coat and hang it in the closet. 把外套脫下來掛到衣櫥裡。

- find out 發現

How did Jack find out everything about me? 傑克是怎麼知道我的每一件事情的？

**2** 動詞 + 受詞 + 介系詞／副詞

- bring in 拿進來   - bring up 養育

Bring the laundry in before it rains.
趁下雨之前把衣服收進來。
We are trying to bring our son up to be considerate and responsible.
我們盡力把我們的兒子培養得既體貼又有責任感。

假如受詞是代名詞，就只能放在**動詞和介系詞或副詞的中間**。

- bring up 告訴；提起   - carry out 進行

- I will bring it up with Craig.
  ↳ it= project
  我會對克雷格提起這項計畫。

---

**look up 查閱**
Pan looked up the word in the dictionary.
→ Pan looked the word up in the dictionary.
潘在字典裡查了這個字。

**fill out 填寫**
Please fill out the form.
→ Please fill it out.
請填妥這張表格。

**call off 取消**
They called off the game because of rain.
→ They called it off because of rain.
他們因雨取消了這場比賽。

**turn up/down 調大聲／調小聲**
Turn down the volume.
→ Turn it down.
把聲音調小一點。

**turn on/off 打開／關閉**
He turned on the light and started to read.
→ He turned the light on and started to read.
他開燈開始看書。

**hand in 繳交**
You have to hand in the paper on Monday.
→ You have to hand the paper in on Monday.
請在星期一繳交報告。

**put out 撲滅**
The firefighter put out the fire within an hour.
→ The firefighter put the fire out within an hour.
消防人員在一小時內撲滅了火勢。

**set off 點燃**
They set off the fireworks.
→ They set the fireworks off.
他們點燃爆竹。

**turn down 拒絕**
The manager turned down his proposal.
→ The manager turned his proposal down.
經理推翻了他的提議。

**1**

自下表選出正確的「片語動詞」來填空，並依照範例，用另外兩種句型來改寫句子。

set off
turn down
try on
call off
take off
fill out
throw away
bring up
turn off

1. Dick and Byron _____*set off*_____ the fire crackers.
   → *Dick and Byron set the fire crackers off.*
   → *Dick and Byron set them off.*

2. Don't _____ the price tag in case we have to return the sweater.
   → _____
   → _____

3. Don't _____ the offer right away.
   → _____
   → _____

4. We don't _____ bottles if they can be recycled.
   → _____
   → _____

5. You need to _____ the form and attach two photos.
   → _____
   → _____

6. Would you like to _____ these shoes?
   → _____
   → _____

7. Could you _____ the radio? I don't want to listen to it.
   → _____
   → _____

8. I'll have to _____ the meeting.
   → _____
   → _____

9. Lucy _____ her son by herself.
   → _____
   → _____

# Unit 81

## Phrasal Verbs (3)
## 片語動詞（3）

**1** 第三種也必須搭配**受詞**使用，而且受詞只能**放在整個片語動詞**的後面。

**3** 動詞 ＋ 介系詞／副詞 ＋ 受詞

- take after 相似
- pull for 支持

Your daughter takes after your wife.
你女兒很像你太太。

The crowd is pulling for the home team.
群眾全力支持地主隊。

### apply for 申請
I have already applied for the job.
我已經去應徵這份工作了。

### arrive in 抵達
Gina arrived in Athens on Saturday.
吉娜於星期六抵達了雅典。

### depend on 依靠
Success depends on hard work.
成功端賴努力。

### look after 照顧
Could you look after the baby on weekends?
週末都可以麻煩你照顧寶寶嗎？

### look for 尋找
Scientists are looking for some rare elements.
科學家們在尋找一些稀有元素。

### belong to 屬於
This suitcase belongs to Mr. Jefferson.
這個公事包是傑佛遜先生的。

### run into 遇見
I ran into an old friend on my way home.
我在回家的路上遇到一位老朋友。

**2** 第四種由「**動詞 ＋ 副詞 ＋ 介系詞**」組成較長的片語動詞，並且必須在最後面加上**受詞**。

**4** 動詞 ＋ 副詞 ＋ 介系詞 ＋ 受詞

- look forward to 期待
- move away from 搬離

Walter is looking forward to a break after finishing the IPO.
在完成公司初次公開上市的工作之後，華特很期待能小休一下。

Nicole is moving away from home for the first time.
這是妮可第一次離開家。

### keep away from 遠離
Keep away from the broken windows.
遠離碎裂的窗戶。

### keep up with 跟上
I can't keep up with you when we are jogging.
慢跑的時候我一直跟不上你。

### catch up with 趕上
You should study hard to catch up with your classmates.
你要用功才能趕上你同學。

### get along with 與……相處
I can't get along with Susan.
我跟蘇珊無法相處。

### put up with 忍受
I can't put up with him any more.
我再也受不了他了。

### fed up with 受夠
Shut up. I'm fed up with your lies.
不要再說了，我聽夠了你的謊言。

## 1

自下表選出正確的
「片語動詞」填空，
完成句子。

catch up with
come across
run down
watch out for
get over
put up with
fed up with
look after

1. It's hard to _____ other people's kids.

2. _____ the bucket on the floor.

3. You can leave now, and I will _____ you later.

4. I can _____ almost anything except screaming babies.

5. If you _____ any wooden napkin rings, please let me know.

6. Donna is _____ the street noise at her apartment and is planning to move.

7. The editor asked me to _____ the facts on this story.

8. She'll _____ her disappointment and face the reality.

## 2

自下表選出適當的
「介系詞」填空，
完成句子。

up
down
on
in
of
into
out of
to
from
off
for

1. I got _____ the train at Angel Street and got _____ at the main station.

2. It's starting to rain. Let's get _____ the car before it pours.

3. I ran _____ Jack this morning. He was in a hurry, so we didn't talk.

4. Thank you for coming. I look forward _____ seeing you next time.

5. After I got _____ the taxi, I went into the fish store.

6. We ran out _____ toilet paper. I'll buy some this afternoon.

7. Winnie applied _____ the scholarship last week.

8. I know I can rely _____ him.

9. Does this locker belong _____ Sean?

10. Norman arrived _____ New York yesterday.

11. What are you looking _____?

Unit 82  Review Test of Units 79–81
單元 79–81 總複習

**1** 自右表選出適當的片語動詞，填空完成句子。
→ Unit 79–81 重點複習

1. Please _____ me _____ at seven tomorrow morning.
   I don't want to sleep late.
2. Alison is going to _____ with her friends at the
   Internet café tonight.
3. The plane is going to _____ soon. We have to
   _____ the plane right away.
4. When are we going to _____ this report?
5. Sam _____ his old cell phone and bought a new
   one.
6. When are you going to _____ to your new
   apartment?
7. _____ the car now.
8. _____ the grass. Don't step on it.
9. Please _____ the registration form.
10. We are _____ each other very well.
11. She walks so fast. I can hardly _____ her.
12. Could you _____ Janet on your way to the office?
13. I _____ in the country, but I'm living in the city
    now.
14. Aunt Sally _____ her two kids all by herself.
15. Pete: Where is Tony?
    Ron: He is _____ at the gym.
16. The vice president is not available tomorrow. We'll have to
    _____ the meeting.
17. He finished the conversation with Zoe and _____
    the phone.
18. May I _____ this coat?

| |
|---|
| get in |
| throw away |
| take off |
| hang out |
| wake up |
| pick up |
| work out |
| call off |
| get on |
| hand in |
| grow up |
| fill out |
| get along with |
| bring up |
| move in |
| keep away from |
| hang up |
| keep up with |
| try on |

**2** 自下表選出適當的「副詞」或「介系詞」，搭配題目上方標示的動詞構成片語動詞，填空完成句子。
→ **Unit 79-81 重點複習**

| up | down | in | out | on | off | after | away | for |

### look

1. I'm _____ my wallet. Did you see it?

2. _____ the meaning of this phrasal verb in your electronic dictionary.

3. I have to _____ my little brother on Saturday.

4. _____! Don't trip over that wire.

### turn

5. Could you _____ the heat, please? It's too hot.

6. Why not _____ the TV and relax?

7. Don't _____ this offer, because it's the best you are going to get.

8. Make sure you _____ the lights before going to bed.

### take

9. Could you _____ the garbage now?

10. _____ your sunglasses so that I can see your eyes.

11. The plane will _____ in a few minutes.

12. I don't _____ my father. I look like my mother.

### put

13. It's cold outside. You should _____ a coat.

14. We _____ the campfire and left the park.

15. Don't _____ the plan until tomorrow.

16. He _____ his toys and went to bed.

### go

17. I'm back. Please _____ with the story.

18. The fire alarm _____ at midnight.

19. They _____ for a date.

**Unit 83**

## Adjectives
形容詞

不論描述的名詞是單數、複數，男性、女性，或者前面加什麼冠詞，形容詞的型態都**不需改變**。

- a new phone
- the new phone
- two new phones

- a tall boy
- the tall boy
- two tall boys

**1** 形容詞是「描述人物、地方、物品或狀況」的詞彙，用來修飾名詞。

an old computer
一台老舊的電腦

the smart dog
這隻聰明的狗

a fast car
一輛很快的車

**2** 形容詞經常放在**名詞的前面**。

① | 形容詞 | + | 名詞 |

**Watch out for the sharp edge.**
小心那鋒利的邊。

**He's an old professor.** 他是位老教授。

**That's a powerful squirt gun.**
那是把強力水槍。

**That's a warm coat.**
那是件溫暖的大衣。

**It's a deep river.**
這是條很深的河。

**3** 形容詞也可放在 **be 動詞或連綴動詞的後面**。

② | 主詞 | + | be動詞／連綴動詞 | + | 形容詞 |

**The news was sad.** 這則消息很感傷。

**The car looks cool.** 這輛車看起來很酷。

**My aunt feels lonely.** 我嬸嬸覺得很寂寞。

**The soup seems spicy.**
這碗湯好像很辣。

**The office is messy.**
這間辦公室很髒亂。

- **He's a** ¹ _____ **guy.** 他是個好人。
- **Those** ² _____ **people are laughing.**
  那群開心的人在開懷大笑。

- **Her husband** ³ _____.
  她的先生個子很高。
- **The fish** ⁴ _____.
  這魚聞起來很香。

# Practice

**1**

自下表選出適當的「形容詞」，搭配圖片的名詞完成填空。

big
small
old
new
soft
hard
curved
straight

1 pants

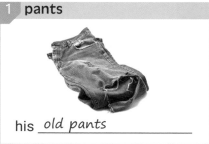

his _old pants_____

2 pants

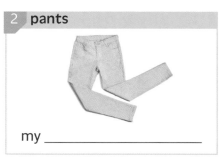

my _____

3 chair

a _____

4 chair

a _____

5 dog

her _____

6 dog

her _____

7 road

a _____

8 road

a _____

**2**

將右列各組詞彙重組，以正確語序完成句子。

1. he   in   lives   town   small   a
→ ....................................................................................

2. eyes   blue   she   has
→ ....................................................................................

3. smells   the lamb stew   good
→ ....................................................................................

4. two   I   have   kids   lovely
→ ....................................................................................

5. cute   is   my   teddy bear
→ ....................................................................................

Unit **84**

## Adverbs and Adverbial Phrases
## 副詞和副詞片語

**1** 副詞是用來修飾**動詞**、**形容詞**或是**另一個副詞**的詞彙。由好幾個詞彙所組成的副詞,則稱為**副詞片語**。

**I work in the Bangkok office** one week each month.

↳ one week each month 是副詞片語。

我每個月都有一星期到曼谷分公司上班。

**I** never **rest when I'm on the road. It's** always **hard work.**

↳ never 和 always 都是副詞。

我不曾在途中休息,這一直都是很辛苦的工作。

**2** 副詞經常由形容詞轉變而來。

❶ 形容詞直接加上 **ly**。
① **cold → cold**ly 冷地
② **beautiful → beautiful**ly 美麗地
③ **rapid → rapid**ly 迅速地

❷ 字尾是「子音 + **y**」的形容詞,去掉 **y** 再加 **ily**。
① **handy → hand**ily 便利地
② **ready → read**ily 敏捷地
③ **easy → eas**ily 輕易地

❸ 字尾是「子音 + **le**」的形容詞,去掉 **le** 再加 **ly**。
① **horrible → horrib**ly 恐怖地
② **possible → possib**ly 可能地
③ **simple → simp**ly 純粹地

形容詞 **It was an** easy **job.**
這是個輕鬆的工作。

副詞 **We finished the job** easily.
我們很輕鬆地完成工作。

**3** 有些副詞的構成較**不規則**。

❶ 副詞和形容詞完全不一樣。
**good** → well 好地

❷ 副詞和形容詞一樣。
**early** → early 早地
**fast** → fast 快速地

❸ 一個形容詞演變出兩種副詞形式,且意義相同。
**clean** → clean/cleanly 俐落地
**bright** → bright/brightly 明亮地

形容詞 **It was a** clean **getaway.**
這是一次徹底的逃脫。

副詞 **He got away** cleanly.
他逃得無影無蹤。

副詞 **He has** clean **forgotten it.**
他完全忘記這件事了。

**4** 副詞的位置通常在**動詞後面**,或者在**受詞的後面**。

**Henry clapped** wildly. 亨利熱烈地鼓掌。

**Paula welcomed me** warmly.
寶拉熱情地歡迎我。

**The agent signed the contract** sadly.
代理商傷心地簽下合約。

# Practice

**1**

寫出右列形容詞所對應的副詞。

1. sudden _____
2. real _____
3. early _____
4. quick _____
5. good _____
6. final _____
7. fast _____
8. lazy _____
9. entire _____
10. gentle _____

11. lucky _____
12. cheap _____
13. probable _____
14. special _____
15. cheerful _____
16. deep _____
17. merry _____
18. clean _____
19. simple _____
20. angry _____

**2**

運用粗體字的「副詞」形式，搭配括弧內提示的動詞，改寫各個句子。

1. He gave a **clear** answer. (answer)
   → *He answered clearly.* _____

2. He's a **bad** singer. (sing)
   → _____

3. He was **late** for school. (arrive)
   → _____

4. She's a **good** painter. (paint)
   → _____

5. She's a **fast** learner. (learn)
   → _____

6. He's a **noisy** worker. (work)
   → _____

7. She's a **professional** translator. (translate)
   → _____

8. It was a **terrible** earthquake. (tremble)
   → _____

9. She's a **fast** reader. (read)
   → _____

10. She's a **frequent** shopper. (shop)
    → _____

## Adverbs and Adverbial Phrases of Time and Place
## 時間副詞和地方副詞

**1** 時間副詞或副詞片語是用來指出「**事情發生的時間**」。
一般放在**動詞後面**，若句中有受詞，則要放在受詞**後面**。

* **later** 晚一點
* **early** 早
* **tomorrow** 明天
* **this morning** 今天早上
* **on Thanksgiving** 在感恩節
* **at midnight** 在半夜

**1**

| 主詞 | + | 動詞 | + | 時間副詞 | |
|---|---|---|---|---|---|
| The plane | | arrived | | late. | 這班飛機誤點了。 |
| Ladies | | go | | first. | 女士優先。 |

**2**

| 主詞 | + | 動詞 | + | 受詞 | + | 時間副詞 | |
|---|---|---|---|---|---|---|---|
| He | | brushes | | his teeth | | in the morning. | 他早上刷牙。 |
| She | | baked | | the cake | | before the party. | 她在派對開始前烤了一個蛋糕。 |

**2** 地方副詞或副詞片語是用來指出「**事情發生的地點**」。
和時間副詞一樣，地方副詞一般放在**動詞後面**，若句中
有受詞，則要放在受詞**後面**。

* **here** 這裡
* **there** 那裡
* **down** 下面
* **outdoors** 戶外
* **at the park** 在公園
* **to the club** 往俱樂部

**3**

| 主詞 | + | 動詞 | + | 地方副詞 | |
|---|---|---|---|---|---|
| He | | lives | | in the suburbs. | 他住在郊外。 |
| The newspaper | | was | | in the mailbox. | 報紙在信箱裡。 |

**4**

| 主詞 | + | 動詞 | + | 受詞 | + | 地方副詞 | |
|---|---|---|---|---|---|---|---|
| Wally | | parked | | the car | | in the driveway. | 華利把車子停在車道上。 |
| Erica | | took | | the box | | to the post office. | 艾麗卡把箱子拿去郵局。 |

**時間副詞**和**地方副詞**通常不會放在動詞和受詞的中間。

✕ We ate at the restaurant **dinner**.
✓ We ate **dinner** at the restaurant.
✕ We eat at 7 p.m. **dinner**.
✓ We eat **dinner** at 7 p.m.

**3** 如果句中有時間副詞也有地方副詞，通常時間副詞會放在地方副詞的**後面**。

**5**

| 主詞 | + | 動詞（片語） | + | 地方副詞 | + | 時間副詞 |
|---|---|---|---|---|---|---|
| Ronald | | ate his lunch | | behind the store | | after the delivery truck left. |

貨車離開後，雷諾在商店後吃午餐。

| Judy | walked | to Suzy's house | on Saturday afternoon. |
|---|---|---|---|

茉蒂在星期六下午走路到蘇西家。

| Trent | had a party | in his house | on Christmas day. |
|---|---|---|---|

聖誕節那天，崔特在他家舉辦派對。

## Practice

**1**

將右列各組詞彙重組，
以正確的語序完成句子。

1. over there   my parents   live
   → *My parents live over there.*

2. they bought   over 20 years ago   the house
   → _____

3. pays the mortgage   on the first day of each month
   my dad   to the bank
   → _____
   _____

4. went   he   to check the mailbox   downstairs
   → _____

5. to Wendy's house   were delivered   this morning   no packages
   → _____

6. Jack and Jimmy   at the café   are going to meet   this afternoon
   → _____

**2**

依提示回答問題。

1. When and where did you leave the bag?
   (in the cloakroom / at 4:30 yesterday)
   → _____

2. When and where did you last see him?
   (on January 22nd / at Teresa's birthday party)
   → _____

3. When and where did you buy that book?
   (last week / at the bookstore around the corner)
   → _____

4. When and where do you go swimming?
   (at the health club / on Sundays)
   → _____

5. When and where did you learn to dive?
   (three years ago / at the Pacific Diving Club)
   → _____

6. When and where did you eat lunch yesterday?
   (at Susie's Pizza House / at 12:30)
   → _____

Part 11 現在時態 85 時間副詞和地方副詞

213

## Unit **86**

### Adverbs and Adverbial Phrases of Frequency and Manner
### 頻率副詞和狀態副詞

**1** 頻率副詞是用來指出「**事情多常發生**」的副詞,通常放在**主要動詞的前面**。

- always 總是
- sometimes 有時
- usually 經常
- rarely 很少
- often 時常
- never 不曾

**1** | 主詞 | + | 頻率副詞 | + | 動詞 |

**Morty always eats lunch at his desk.**
莫提總是在他的辦公桌吃午餐。

**I rarely drink coffee at night.**
我晚上很少喝咖啡。

**We often develop plans as a team.**
我們通常團隊一起構思企畫。

**David never remembers his dreams.**
大衛從來不記得他做過的夢。

**2** 頻率副詞也可以放在 be 動詞的後面。

**2** | 主詞 | + | be 動詞 | + | 頻率副詞 |

**Frank is sometimes sent to pick up a customer at the airport.**
法蘭克有時會被派去機場接客戶。

**Cab lines are usually long at the airport.**
機場的計程車隊通常會排很長。

**I am always glad they send Frank to the airport, because I hate driving on the highway.**
他們派法蘭克去機場我都會很高興,因為我很討厭在高速公路上開車。

**3** 如果是頻率副詞片語,通常會放在**句尾**。

- every evening 每天晚上
- once a week 每週一次
- four times 四次
- every day 每天

**I buy a new teddy bear once a year.**
我每年都會買一個新的泰迪熊。

**I sleep with my teddy bear every night.**
我每天晚上都和我的泰迪熊一起睡。

**I watch the news on TV every evening.**
我每晚都收看電視新聞。

**4** 狀態副詞是用來描述「**事情發生時的狀態**」,一般放在**動詞或受詞的後面**。

**She is typing.**
她正在打字。

**She is typing fast.**
她正在迅速地打字。

**She reads carefully.**
她很仔細地閱讀。

**The car stopped suddenly.**
這輛車突然停下來。

## Practice

**1**

將右列各組詞彙重組，
以正確的語序完成句子。

1. he   misses   never   the mortgage payment
   → ......................................................................................

2. is   in the morning   always   the first customer   he
   → ......................................................................................

3. he   to work   walks   every day
   → ......................................................................................

4. the water   quickly   overflowed
   → ......................................................................................

5. exploded   suddenly   the volcano
   → ......................................................................................

6. many burglaries   lately   have been   there
   → ......................................................................................

7. entirely   their minds   that   changed
   → ......................................................................................

**2**

依據事實，使用「頻率
副詞」回答右列問題。

1. How often do you go to school?
   → ......................................................................................

2. How often do you exercise?
   → ......................................................................................

3. How often do you go on a trip to a foreign country?
   → ......................................................................................

4. How often do you go to a movie?
   → ......................................................................................

5. How often do you do the dishes?
   → ......................................................................................

6. How often do you visit your grandparents?
   → ......................................................................................

7. How often do you eat fast food?
   → ......................................................................................

8. How often do you work on Saturdays?
   → ......................................................................................

Unit **87**

## Comparison of Adjectives
### 形容詞的比較級與最高級

| | 原級 | | 比較級 | | 最高級 |
|---|---|---|---|---|---|
| young | 年輕的 | younger | 較年輕的 | youngest | 最年輕的 |
| big | 大的 | bigger | 較大的 | biggest | 最大的 |
| beautiful | 美的 | more beautiful | 較美的 | most beautiful | 最美的 |
| | | less beautiful | 較不美的 | least beautiful | 最不美的 |

**1** 形容詞有三種形態：**原級**、**比較級**和**最高級**，用來表示**修飾**的程度。

原級 **Look at that** old **ship.** 看那艘老舊的船。

比較級 **That ship is** as old as **my great grandfather.**
那艘船就跟我的曾祖父一樣老。

比較級 **If there is an** older **one, I don't see it.**
我還沒看過比這更舊的船。

最高級 **That is** the oldest **ship at the dock.**
那是碼頭裡最舊的一艘船。

**2** 比較級用來比較**兩個事物**；最高級用來比較**三個以上的事物**。

**Your kite is** higher than **my kite, but his kite is** the highest.
你的風箏飛得比我的高，但是他的風箏飛得最高。

**3** 形容詞比較級和最高級的構成方式：

**1** 單音節的形容詞，其比較級和最高級，是在字尾分別加 er 和 est。

| 原級 | 比較級 | 最高級 |
|---|---|---|
| tight 緊的 | tighter | tightest |
| small 小的 | smaller | smallest |

**2** 單音節的形容詞，若字尾是「短母音 + 子音」，其比較級和最高級必須先重覆字尾，再加 er 和 est。

| 原級 | 比較級 | 最高級 |
|---|---|---|
| big 大的 | bigger | biggest |
| hot 熱的 | hotter | hottest |

**3** 單音節的形容詞，若字尾是 e，其比較級和最高級，應直接加 r 和 st。

| 原級 | 比較級 | 最高級 |
|---|---|---|
| cute 可愛的 | cuter | cutest |
| late 遲的 | later | latest |

**4** 雙音節的形容詞，若字尾是「子音 + y」，其比較級和最高級必須先去掉 y，再加上 ier 和 iest。

| 原級 | 比較級 | 最高級 |
|---|---|---|
| sloppy 懶散的 | sloppier | sloppiest |
| foggy 有霧的 | foggier | foggiest |

**5** 雙音節形容詞，若字尾非 y，其比較級和最高級，是在形容詞前加上 more/less 和 most/least。more 和 most 具正面意義，而 less 和 least 則具反面意義。

| 原級 | 比較級 | 最高級 |
|---|---|---|
| special 特別的 | more special | most special |
| famous 有名的 | less famous | least famous |

**6** 三個音節以上的形容詞，其比較級和最高級，也同樣是在形容詞前加 more/less 和 most/least。

| 原級 | 比較級 | 最高級 |
|---|---|---|
| aggressive 進取的 | more aggressive | most aggressive |
| colorless 黯淡的 | less colorless | least colorless |

**7** 有些形容詞的比較級和最高級屬於不規則變化，請逐一牢記。

| 原級 | 比較級 | 最高級 |
|---|---|---|
| good 好的 | better | best |
| bad 壞的 | worse | worst |

## Practice

**1**

寫出右列形容詞的比較級和最高級。

1. big _____
2. tall _____
3. close _____
4. fast _____
5. sad _____
6. cute _____
7. spicy _____
8. thin _____
9. good _____
10. many _____

11. large _____
12. late _____
13. busy _____
14. simple _____
15. tiny _____
16. bad _____
17. useful _____
18. little _____
19. quiet _____
20. high _____

**2**

將括弧內的形容詞以「最高級」的形式填空，來詢問「誰是最……的人」。並依據事實回答問題。

1. Who is _____ (cute) in your class?
→ _____

2. Who is _____ (hardworking) in your class?
→ _____

3. Who is _____ (funny) in your class?
→ _____

4. Who is _____ (boring) in your class?
→ _____

5. Who is _____ (friendly) in your class?
→ _____

6. Who is _____ (tall) in your class?
→ _____

7. Who is _____ (smart) in your class?
→ _____

8. Who is _____ (creative) in your class?
→ _____

# Unit **88**

## Patterns Used for Comparison
## 表示「比較」的句型

**1** 我們可以用形容詞的**比較級**來比較兩件事物，後面需搭配 than 來使用。

**1** A + is/are + 形容詞比較級 + than + B

**The Nile River is longer than the Yellow River.** 尼羅河比黃河長。

**My running shoes are cooler than your running shoes.** 我的慢跑鞋比你的酷。

**Your hair is more colorful than my hair.**
你的頭髮顏色比我的鮮豔。

**2** 我們可以用形容詞的**最高級**來比較三樣或三樣以上的事物，前面需加 the。

**2** A + is/are + the + 形容詞最高級

**That is the tallest building in the city.** ↳ 這城市有三座以上的高樓。
那是這座城市最高的大樓。

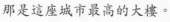

**She is the most amazing** ↳ 我見過三個以上令人驚嘆的女子。
**woman I have ever met.**
她是我見過最不可思議的女子。

**This is the worst restaurant I've ever eaten at.** ↳ 我吃過三家以上不好吃的餐廳。
這是我吃過最難吃的餐廳。

**3** 若要形容兩個人、事、物是一樣的，可用 as . . . as。

**3** A + is/are + as + 形容詞原級 + as + B

**Your cubicle is as ugly as mine.**
你的隔間跟我的一樣醜。

**Your hands are as cold as mine.**
你的手跟我的一樣冰。

**4** 若要形容兩個人、事、物是不一樣的，可用 not as . . . as。

**4** A + is/are + not + as + 形容詞原級 + as + B

**My boss isn't as bad as your boss.** 我老闆不像你老闆那麼壞。

**I'm not as slow as you.**
我才沒你那麼慢。

**5** 上述用法中，than 和 as 後面通常會接**受詞代名詞**。

**Even my grandmother is stronger than you.** 就連我祖母都比你還強壯。

**He sold as many computers as me.**
他賣的電腦和我一樣多。

**6** 如果在很正式的用法裡，than 和 as 後面會接「**主詞代名詞 + 動詞**」。

**My brother is smarter than I am.**
我弟比我聰明。

**I'm not as smart as he is.**
我沒有他那麼聰明。

**But I'm bigger than he is.**
但是我個子比他大。

## Practice

依據圖示，用下表的詞彙，以 A is . . . than B 的句型來描述 **Jim** 和 **Ken** 的不同。

**1**

| short | professional | fat |
|---|---|---|
| tall | casual | business-like |
| intense | lighthearted | |

1. *Ken is shorter than Jim.*

2. _____

3. _____

4. _____

5. _____

6. _____

7. _____

8. _____

Jim

Ken

**2**

將錯誤的句子打╳，
並寫出正確的句子。
若句子無誤，則在方
框內打 ✓。

1. Mt. Everest is highest mountain in the world.

   [╳] *Mt. Everest is the highest mountain in the world.*

2. The Japan Trench is deeper the Java Trench, but the Mariana Trench is deepest.

   [ ] _____
   _____

3. Africa is not as large than Asia.

   [ ] _____

4. Blue whales are the larger animal in the world.

   [ ] _____

5. A giant rabbit can grow as big as a labrador.   ★labrador：拉布拉多，一種獵犬。

   [ ] _____

6. China is not as more democratic as the United States.

   [ ] _____

7. The Burj Dubai is tallest than Taipei 101.

   [ ] _____

8. The Pacific Ocean is larger than the Indian Ocean.

   [ ] _____

Unit **89**

"Too" and "Enough" With Adjectives and Adverbs
**Too** 和 **Enough** 搭配形容詞或副詞的用法

**1** too 用來指出某人或某物「太……」，要放在**形容詞或副詞的前面**。

**1** too + 形容詞

I can't see. It's **too foggy**.
我看不見，霧太濃了。

**2** too + 副詞

Hurry up. You're walking **too slow**.
快一點，你走得太慢了。

**2** enough 的意思是「**足夠的**」，必須在**形容詞或副詞的後面**。

**3** 形容詞 + enough

You can't wear my clothes. You aren't **big enough**.
你不能穿我的衣服，你的體型不夠大。

**4** 副詞 + enough

I can't read your phone number. You're not writing **clearly enough**.
我看不到你的電話號碼，你寫得不夠清楚。

**3** too 和 enough 後面，可接「**for + 受詞**」。

**5** too + 形容詞／副詞 + for + 受詞

I found a studio apartment, but it was **too expensive** for you. 我找到一間公寓套房，但對你而言太貴了。

**6** 形容詞／副詞 + enough + for + 受詞

The apartment is **cheap enough** for me.
這間公寓對我而言夠便宜了。

**4** too 和 enough 後面，也常接「**加 to 的不定詞**」。

**7** too + 形容詞／副詞 + 受詞

This bar is **too noisy** to hold a conversation.
酒吧太吵了，無法談話。

**8** 形容詞／副詞 + enough + to V

This café is **quiet enough** to read.
這家咖啡廳夠安靜，可以讀書。

**5** too 和 enough 後面如果有受詞也有動作，就可以用「**for . . . to V**」的句型。

**9** too + 形容詞 + for + 受詞 + to V

It was **too noisy** for me to read.
太吵了，我無法看書。

**10** 形容詞／副詞 + enough + for + 受詞 + to V

It wasn't **quiet enough** for him to read.
不夠安靜，他無法看書。

**6** too 和 very 有時稱為**程度副詞**；too 表「**過量**」或「**超過需要**」；而 very 則是用來**修飾或強調形容詞**。

Terry is a fast swimmer. She swims **very fast**.
↳ very 用來強調她游得多快。

泰瑞是位游泳健將，她游得非常快。

Larry is not a good swimmer, and he has been underwater **too long**.
↳ too 表示他已超過他應該待在水底的時間。

賴瑞不太會游泳，他已經待在水底太久了。

## Practice

**1**

這些工作場合有什麼問題？請依據圖示，自下表選出適當的形容詞或副詞，用「too . . .」的句型造句，描述圖片中狀況。

noisy
dark
busy
talkative
many

1. Charlie couldn't talk on the phone because it was _____.

2. Amy couldn't take a coffee break because there were _____ phone calls.

3. Andrew couldn't see the keyboard very well because it was _____.

4. Jessica couldn't help her colleagues with their work because she was _____.

5. Jennifer couldn't concentrate on her work because her colleagues were _____.

**2**

使用右表的句型，改寫上一大題的句子。

**too . . . (for sb.) to . . .**

1. *It was too noisy for Charlie to talk on the phone.*
2. _____
3. _____
   _____
4. _____
   _____
5. _____
   _____

**1**　依據圖示，自下表選出適當的詞彙，用 is 或 look 來造句。
→ Unit 83 重點複習

| fat | healthy | tall | short |
| strong | weak | happy | thoughtful |

1. He is/looks strong.
2.
3.
4.
5.
6.
7.
8.

**2**　選出正確的答案。
→ Unit 83–84 重點複習

1. It was a **clear / clearly** day.
2. He loved her **dear / dearly**.
3. It was a **fair / fairly** shot.
4. The decision was **just / justly**.
5. It was a **wide / widely** river.
6. The bunny ran **quick / quickly**.
7. He was **wrong / wrongly** accused.
8. The balloon drifted **slow / slowly**.
9. She drove home **careful / carefully**.

**3** 將下列詞彙依正確的語序重組，並在結尾加上句號或問號，完成句子。

→ Unit 83-86 重點複習

1. guy  handsome  a  is  He

   → *He is a handsome guy.*

2. handsome  is  guy  That

   → _____

3. to his office  takes the subway  Ned

   → _____

4. to take a break  ready  Penny  is  always

   → _____

5. terrible  is  driver  a  Dennis

   → _____

6. Dennis  terribly  drives

   → _____

7. I'm  to  excited  too  wait

   → _____

8. these gifts  for  big  enough  isn't  This bag

   → _____

9. Do you  here  work  in this building

   → _____

10. Does Larry  with his brother  fight  every day

    → _____

11. Did we  at the Italian restaurant  meet  last Monday night

    → _____

12. Does Mr. Harrison  eat lunch  always  at the same time

    → _____

13. Is Greg  late  usually  for his tennis date

    → _____

14. Does Frederica  to the spa  go  every week

    → _____

15. Are you  too tired  to get up  sometimes  in the morning

    → _____

**4** 依據圖示，自字彙表選出適當的頻率副詞填空。
→ Unit 86 重點複習

1. Meg reads newspapers _____.

2. Tom drives to work _____.

3. Luke _____ drinks coffee.

4. Jason _____ eats French fries.

5. Steve _____ takes vitamins.

| never |
|---|
| often |
| twice a week |
| every day |
| sometimes |

**5** 依據圖示，自字彙表選出適當的頻率副詞填空，完成句子。
→ Unit 86 重點複習

| every week | every weekend |
|---|---|
| always | every Sunday |
| six times a month | |

1. Jason goes to church _____.

2. Lily goes to the gym _____.

3. Kate _____ goes swimming on Tuesday.

4. Timmy doesn't wash his laundry _____.

5. I go out with my friends _____.

**6** 將下列錯誤的句子打×，並寫出正確的句子。若句子無誤，則在方框內打✓。
→ Unit 88 重點複習

1. I see two talls guys.

   ☒ *I see two tall guys.*

2. That is a tall guy.

   ☐ ............................................................

3. Tony is tallest than David.

   ☐ ............................................................

4. Who is the most tall guy in the room?

   ☐ ............................................................

5. John is taller than Sam.

   ☐ ............................................................

6. James is gooder at math than Robert.

   ☐ ............................................................

7. Irving is a happily guy.

   ☐ ............................................................

8. Janice speaks English very good.

   ☐ ............................................................

**7** 依據圖示，自下表選出適當的「副詞」填空，完成句子。
→ Unit 88 重點複習

quietly
slowly
joyfully
eagerly

① ▶ Kitty is sleeping _____ on the grass.

② ▶ The sisters are pillow fighting ................................

③ ▶ Dori is chewing the bone _____.

④ ▶ My turtle swims _____.

**8** 用「not as . . . as」的句型，來比較圖中這些地方。
→ Unit 88 重點複習

Canada
Greenland
Area: 836,109 sq mi
Iceland
Germany
Sweden
Area: 41,285 km²
Switzerland
Russia
Area: 6,592,800 sq mi
Mt. Everest
Height: 8,848 m
Seoul
Per Capita Income: 30,644 US dollars
Area: 674,843 km²
France
Spain
Italy
Mt. Fuji
Height: 3,776 m
Mexico
Tokyo
Population: 37,393,000
Egypt
Manila
Population: 13,923,452
Brazil
Area: 3,287,597 sq mi
Madagascar
Area: 226,597 sq mi
Jakarta
Per Capita Income: 4,135 US dollars

1. Mt. Fuji and Mt. Everest (tall)

   → _____

2. Brazil and Russia (big)

   → _____

3. Madagascar and Greenland (big)

   → _____

4. Jakarta and Seoul (prosperous)

   → _____

5. Manila and Tokyo (densely populated)

   → _____

6. France and Switzerland (small)

   → _____

7. Iceland and Spain (far south)

   → _____

8. Italy and Germany (far north)

   → _____

9. Canada and Mexico (hot)

   → _____

10. Egypt and Sweden (cold)

   → _____

**9**  自字彙表選出適當的形容詞，用題目指定的句型寫出「表示比較」的句子。
→ Unit 88–89 重點複習

**. . . than**

1. An orange is _____ a lemon.
2. A coat is _____ a shirt.
3. Florida is _____ than Michigan.

big
high
terrible
tall
fast
hot
warm
sweet
cold

**the . . .**

4. The Antarctica is _____ place on earth.
5. The Jupiter is _____ planet in our solar system.
6. Taipei 101 is _____ building in Taiwan.

**as . . . as**

7. Earthquakes are _____ typhoons.
8. Can a horse run _____ a train?
9. Can a kite fly _____ an eagle?

**10**  依據題意，將括弧裡的單字搭配 too 或 enough 填空。有些題目可有兩種寫法。
→ Unit 89 重點複習

1. You have worked _____. (hard)
2. Don't work _____. (late)
3. This soup is _____. (salty)
4. This curry isn't _____. (spicy)
5. The way you speak is _____. (blunt)
6. Your music is _____. (loud)
7. This cell phone is _____. (expensive)
8. This computer is _____. (slow)

## Unit **91**

### Prepositions of Place: In, On, At (1)
### 表示地點的介系詞：In、On、At（1）

in the box
在箱子裡

on the box
在箱子上

at the bottom of the pole
在燈柱底部

**1** in 可用來指出「在某個三度空間裡」。

There's a fly in my soup.
我的湯裡面有隻蒼蠅。

I keep my emergency money in the refrigerator.
我把緊急備用的錢放在冰箱裡。

Barbara is in line to buy train tickets.
芭芭拉在排隊買車票。

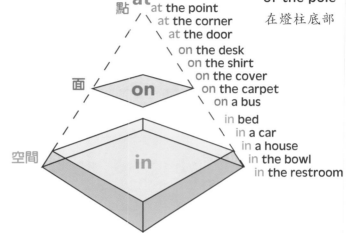

點 **at**
at the point
at the corner
at the door
on the desk
on the shirt
on the cover
on the carpet
on a bus
in bed
in a car
in a house
in the bowl
in the restroom

面 **on**

空間 **in**

**2** on 可用來表示「在表面上」。

Put the money on the counter.
把錢放在櫃台上。

Write your name and phone number on this paper.
把你的名字和電話號碼寫在這張紙上。

Put the stamp on this envelope.
把郵票貼在這個信封上。

**4** at 可用來表示「在某一點上」。

Meet me at the corner of 43rd Street and Lexington.
到列克星頓和第 43 街的轉角跟我碰面。

You can buy cheesecloth at the farmers' market.
你可以在農產品集貨市場買到薄紗布。

比較

- Your tablet is in my schoolbag.
  你的平板在我的書包裡。

- My schoolbag is on the table by the door.
  我的書包擺在門邊的桌上。

- I paused the bluetooth speaker at the beginning of the fourth song.
  我把藍芽音響暫停在第四首歌一開始的地方。

**3** on 也可用來表示「在一條線上」或「在某物的邊緣」。

There is a tag on the cable.
電纜線上有個標籤。

Hang the laundry on the clothesline.
把洗好的衣服掛在曬衣繩上。

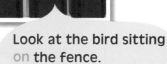
Look at the bird sitting on the fence.
你看棲息在籬笆上的那隻鳥。

## Practice

**1**

根據圖示，用 in、on 或 at 填空，完成句子。

1. This dog is _____ the sofa.

2. This dog is _____ the dog house.

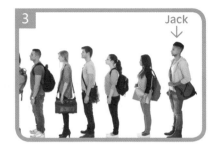

Jack ↓

3. Jack is _____ the end of the line.

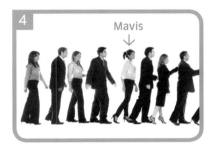

Mavis ↓

4. Mavis is _____ the middle of the line.

5. This cat is _____ the cup.

6. I'd like some whipped cream _____ my coffee.

7. There's a magazine _____ the table.

8. Ben is jumping _____ the bed.

9. The geese are standing _____ the edge of a river.

# Unit 92

## Prepositions of Place: In, On, At (2)
## 表示地點的介系詞：In、On、At（2）

in Australia
在澳洲

in Sydney
在雪梨

at home 在家

**1** in 常與**城鎮、洲名、縣市、國家、大陸**名稱連用。

**Sydney is in Australia.** 雪梨在澳洲。

**I live in Sydney.** 我住在雪梨。

**2** at 常與「**具體的小地點**」連用。
at home、at work 是慣用語。

**Otto is at the library, but he will be back for dinner.**
奧圖現在在圖書館，但是他會回來吃晚餐。

**I'll be at home if you need me.**
如果你需要我，我會在家裡。

**He is at home in the suburbs.**
他在位於郊區的家中。

**I'll be at work this afternoon from 1:00 to 5:00.** 今天下午 1 點到 5 點，我要上班。

**He is at work now if you want to call him there.**
他現在在上班，你可以打電話去那裡。

**3** at 也可表示「**在學習或研究的地方**」。

**She is a kindergarten teacher at Tiny Tots Language School.**
她是 Tiny Tots 語言學校的幼稚園老師。

**I saw Tom at school yesterday.**
我昨天在學校看見湯姆。

**4** at 和 in 可用來談論「**在某個建築物裡面**」。

**He met her at the multiplex movie theater.** ↳ inside or outside
他和她在電影城見面。

**The mayor's office is in the City Hall.**
市長的辦公室在市政廳裡。 ↳ inside

**5** 談論「**建築物本身**」時，要用 in 這個字。

**There is an elevator in the Eiffel Tower.**
艾菲爾鐵塔裡有電梯。

**There are spas in the rooms in the Hot Spring Hotel.**
溫泉旅館的房間裡有溫泉水療。

**6** 來看看 in、at 和 on 在「**地址**」裡的用法。

國家／洲名 → **in**
**I live in California.** 我住在加州。
**I live in the U.S.A.** 我住在美國。

城市／鄉鎮 → **in**
**I live in Mendocino.** 我住在孟得昔諾。

街道 → **on**
**I live on Flores Street.** 我住在福羅爾斯街。

門牌號碼 → **at**
**I live at 323 Flores Street.**
我住在福羅爾斯街 323 號。

樓層 → **on**
**I live on the fifth floor.** 我住在五樓。

**1**

用 in 或 at 填空，
完成句子。

1. There are many people _____ the airport.

2. The kids are _____ school.

3. There are some people _____ the train station.

4. Vicky is _____ the library.

**2**

依據圖示，用 in、on
或 at 填空，完成句
子。

To: Sherman Johnson
Apt. 3F, 223 Oak Street
Evansville, Indiana, 56082, U.S.A.

1. Sherman Johnson lives _____ the U.S.A.
2. He lives _____ the third floor.
3. He lives _____ Oak Street.
4. He lives _____ 223 Oak Street.
5. He lives _____ Evansville.
6. He lives _____ Indiana.

## Unit 93

### Other Prepositions of Place
### 其他表示地點的介系詞

❶ **in** 在……之內

in **the box** 在箱子裡

❷ **on** 在……之上

有接觸到

on **the box** 在箱子上

❸ **over** 在……之上

正上方 沒接觸到

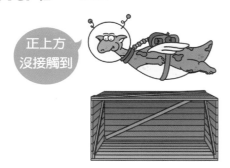

over **the box** 在箱子上方

❹ **under** 在……之下

正下方

under **the box** 在箱子下方

❺ **in front of** 在……前面

in front of **the box**
在箱子前面

❻ **behind** 在……後面

behind **the box**
在箱子後面

❼ **near** 在……附近／ **next to** 緊鄰著……

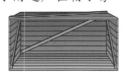

near / next to **the box**
在箱子附近／在箱子旁

❽ **between** 在……之間

between **the box** 在箱子之間

❾ **across**
穿越……

❿ **against**
倚靠著……

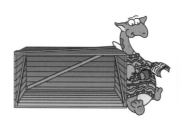

across **the line**
穿越繩索

against **the box**
倚靠箱子

# Practice

**1** 根據圖示，自下表選出適當的介系詞填空，完成句子。可重複選取。

| in | on | near | next to | in front of |
| behind | between | over | under | against |

1. The frog is _____ the leaf.

2. The woman is standing _____ the bicycle.

3. The boy is sleeping _____ the car.

4. The man is sitting _____ the bicycle.

5. The woman is resting _____ a tree and _____ a bike.

6. The girl is sleeping _____ the teddy bear.

7. The taxi stopped _____ the hotel.

8. The car is driving _____ the highway.

9. The man is hiding _____ the desk.

10. The seagull is flying _____ the ocean.

11. The dog is _____ the boys.

12. The white-headed cat is leaning _____ the black-headed cat.

## Prepositions of Movement
表示移動方向的介系詞

**① into**
到……之內

into the
telephone booth
到電話亭內

**② out of**
到……之外

out of the
telephone booth
到電話亭外

**③ onto** 到……之上

onto the box
到箱子之上

**④ off** 離開……

Off the box
離開箱子

**⑤ up**
往……上

**⑥ down**
往……下

up the hill
往山丘上

down the hill
往山丘下

**⑦ to** 往……

**⑧ from** 從……

from the city
從城市

to the city 往城市

**⑨ across** 橫越／跨越

across the road
橫越馬路

**⑩ along** 沿著／順著
along the road
沿著馬路

**⑪ past** 經過

past a traffic light
經過紅綠燈

**⑫ through**
穿越／通過

through
the tunnel
穿越隧道

**⑬ around**
圍繞

around the
traffic circle
圍繞圓環

## Practice

**1** 根據圖示，自下表選出適當的介系詞填空，完成句子。可重複選取。

| into | out of | on | off | up | around |
|---|---|---|---|---|---|
| through | across | along | past | down | |

The kids are partially ............................ the car.

The man is throwing garbage ............................ the trash can.

The man is walking ............................ the hill.

Someone is pouring water ............................ the instant noodles.

You need to drive ............................ the traffic circle.

The dolphin is jumping ............................ the water.

These taxis are driving ............................ the road.

The pedestrians are walking ............................ the street.

Are we going to drive ............................ the tunnel?

The kayaker in the yellow boat went ............... the other kayaker.

Gordon is looking ............... at Marty.

The woman fell ............... the bike.

## Prepositions of Time: In, On, At (1)
### 表示時間的介系詞：In、On、At（1）

**1** 「一天中特定的時間」，也就是「幾點幾分」，要用 at。

I have to turn in this report at 3:00.
我必須在 3 點交出這份報告。
At 5:00 I leave the office no matter what is happening.
不管發生什麼事，我都會在 5 點下班。

**2** 「一天中的某個時段」要用 in。

Breakfast restaurants are only open in the morning. 早餐店只有早上營業。
I like to drink coffee and read a book in the afternoon.
我喜歡在下午喝咖啡看書。

↗ at night

但「在晚上」卻用 at night。
• He always gets lost at night. 他晚上老是迷路。

**3** 「星期」要用 on。

We are going to meet at the night market on Friday. 我們星期五約在夜市見面。
On Saturdays I always sleep late.
星期六我通常睡到很晚。

**4** 「星期幾的某個時段」也要用 on。

I like to watch movies on Friday nights after the kids go to bed.
我喜歡在星期五晚上孩子們都上床後看電影。
Let's go to the farmers' market on Saturday morning.
我們星期六上午到農產品市集去吧。

**5** 「週末」常用 on。

Are you going to the Music Festival on the weekend?
↳ 英式用 at the weekend。
你週末要去參加音樂慶典嗎？
On weekends I catch up with all my housework.
我都在週末把所有的家事做完。

**6** 「假日期間」會用 at；
「假期當天」卻用 on。

We visit her every year at Thanksgiving.
我們每年感恩節都會去看她。
I always gain weight at Christmas.
我一到聖誕節就會變胖。
I love to eat turkey and stuffing on Thanksgiving Day.
我很喜歡在感恩節那天吃火雞肉和火雞裡的填料。
We stay up to see in the new year on New Year's Eve.
我們會在除夕夜徹夜不眠迎接新年。

# Practice

**1**

將列表這些表示「時間的詞彙」，依據其應該搭配的介系詞，填入正確的空格內。

**①** _____ in _____

**②** _____ on _____

the morning
Friday afternoons
National Day
the weekend
Sundays
Christmas
night
Monday
6 o'clock
the evening
Christmas Day

**③** _____ at _____

**2**

用 in、on 或 at 填空，完成句子。

1. Meet me _____ 5:00.
2. Let's go to a baseball game _____ Saturday.
3. The store isn't open _____ the morning.
4. I only play online games _____ night.
5. I do my laundry _____ Sunday afternoons.
6. The best time to go there is _____ Independence Day.
7. I need to get up _____ 6:20 tomorrow morning.
8. We usually go to the traditional market _____ weekends.
9. I'm going to give my mom a dress as a gift _____ Mother's Day.
10. What are you going to do _____ your birthday?

# Unit **96**

## Prepositions of Time: In, On, At (2)
## 表示時間的介系詞：In、On、At（2）

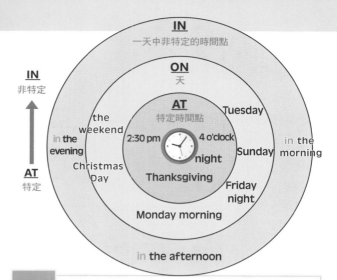

**IN**
一天中非特定的時間點

**ON**
天

**AT**
特定時間點

IN
非特定

AT
特定

the weekend
Christmas Day
2:30 pm
4 o'clock
night
Thanksgiving
Tuesday
Sunday
Friday night
in the evening
in the morning
Monday morning
in the afternoon

---

**1** 月分要用 in。

I suggest we take our vacation in August this year. 我建議我們今年八月去渡假。

My uncle wants to visit us in January.
我叔叔想要在一月時來拜訪我們。

---

**2** 日期要用 on。

Valentine's Day is on February 14.
情人節是在 2 月 14 日。

### February
| M | T | W | T | F | S | S |
|---|---|---|---|---|---|---|
|   |   |   |   | 1 | 2 | 3 |
| 4 | 5 | 6 | 7 | 8 | 9 | 10 |
| 11 | 12 | 13 | (14) | 15 | 16 | 17 |
| 18 | 19 | 20 | 21 | 22 | 23 | 24 |
| 25 | 26 | 27 | 28 | 29 |   |   |

Spring break starts on April 1.
春假從 4 月 1 日開始。

My wife's birthday is on July 10.
我太太的生日是 7 月 10 日。

**比較**

- Let's go in September.
  我們九月去吧。
- I am free on September 26th.
  我 9 月 26 日那天有空。
- Are you free on that day?
  你那天有空嗎？

---

**3** 年分要用 in。

He graduated from college in 1995.
他 1995 年從大學畢業。

The company was founded in 1888.
這間公司創立於 1888 年。

---

**4** 季節要用 in。

in the spring | in the summer
in the fall | in the winter

Flowers bloom in the spring.
花朵在春天綻放。

Mosquitoes bite most in the summer and fall. 蚊子在夏天和秋天的時候最為猖獗。

---

**5** 若已經用 this、next、every、tomorrow 或 yesterday 等表示「某特定時間」，便不可以再加 in、on 或 at。

Are you free this afternoon?
你今天下午有空嗎？

Do you want to go next week?
你下星期想要去嗎？

Let's go to the spa every Friday.
我們每星期五去做溫泉水療吧。

Can you spare an hour to help me tomorrow?
你明天可以抽出一小時來幫我嗎？

What happened to you yesterday?
你昨天發生了什麼事？

# Practice

**1**

將列表這些表示「時間
的詞彙」，依據其應該
搭配的介系詞，或者是
不需要介系詞，填入正
確的空格內。

| ① in |
| --- |

| ② on |
| --- |

this weekend

winter

tomorrow afternoon

May 5

next summer

yesterday morning

October

1998

last month

the fall

June 27

| ③ ✕ |
| --- |

**2**

用 in 或 on 填空，
完成句子。
若不需要介系詞，
請畫上「✕」。

1. He was born _____ 1971.

2. She was born _____ December 22, 1975.

3. The school basketball season is _____ the winter.

4. Edward is leaving this country _____ July 1st.

5. This book will be in print _____ April.

6. Jenny does her laundry _____ every Saturday.

7. We need to hand in this report _____ next Tuesday.

8. The museum is free _____ Sunday.

9. The room rates in this hotel are cheaper _____ December, January, and February.

10. Our hotel is always full _____ the summer.

Part

12

介系詞

96 表示時間的介系詞：In、On、At（2）

Unit **97**

Prepositions of Time o24r Duration:
For, Since (Compared With "Ago")
表示時間的介系詞：For、Since（與 Ago 比較）

**1** ago 是副詞，指「在……之前」，
只能用於**過去式**，不能用**現在完成式**。

**Steve left ten minutes ago.**
↳ 從現在算起的 10 分鐘前
史帝夫 10 分鐘前離開了。

**He graduated from Central University ten years ago.**
↳ 從現在算起的 10 年前
他 10 年前從中央大學畢業。

**I climbed the mountain three months ago.**
我三個月前去爬過山。

**I saw him five minutes ago.**
我五分鐘前見過他。

**2** 時間單位要放在 ago 的「前面」。

**two days** ago 兩天前
**two months** ago 兩個月前
**two years** ago 兩年前
**I played the song five minutes ago.**
我五分鐘前播放這首歌。

**3** for 用來表「**時間的長短**」，後面會接
「**一段時間**」。

**We have been working for hours.**
我們已經工作好幾個小時了。
**We stayed in Venice for five days.**
我們在威尼斯待了五天。
**I haven't seen him for three years.**
我已經三年沒見到他了。

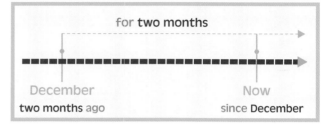

for two months

December — Now
two months ago — since December

**4** since 表示「**從當時到現在的時間**」，
用來討論過去到現在的這段時間裡所
發生的事。

**It has been two years since I last saw him.**
從我上次見到他到現在已經兩年了。
**We have been corresponding by email since then.**
從那次之後，我們一直都用電子郵件通信。
**I haven't talked to him since 2017.**
從 2017 年之後，我就沒和他說過話了。

**5** since 後面接「**事情開始的時間**」。

- since **11:00** 從 11 點起
- since **Monday** 從星期一起
- since **January** 從一月起
- since **2018** 從 2018 年
- since **my brother was born** 從我弟出生以來

**6** for 和 since 都可用於**完成式**，表達
「**從過去進行到現在的時間長短**」。

**He has been waiting since 10:00.**
他從 10 點等到現在。
**He has waited for one hour.**
他已經等了一個鐘頭了。

**1**

依據事實，用 ago
回答問題。

1. When did you move to your current apartment?
   → _____
2. When did you buy your cell phone?
   → _____
3. When did you have your last vacation?
   → _____
4. When did you meet your best friend?
   → _____
5. When did you have your last math exam?
   → _____

**2**

右列表示時間的詞
彙，應該搭配 for 還
是 since 使用？

請在空格內填入正確
的介系詞。

1. _____ Thursday
2. _____ last week
3. _____ one year
4. _____ 30 minutes
5. _____ 8 o'clock
6. _____ 2019

7. _____ last year
8. _____ two months
9. _____ a day or two
10. _____ we last met
11. _____ a while
12. _____ the beginning

**3**

依據事實，分別用
for 或 since 的兩種
句型回答問題。

1. How long have you been learning English?
   → _____
   → _____
2. How long have you lived in your current apartment?
   → _____
   → _____
3. How long have you had your own computer?
   → _____
   → _____
4. How long have you been styling your hair this way?
   → _____
   → _____

**1** 寫出下列詞彙的反義詞。
→ Unit 93-94 重點複習

1. in front of ⟷ .....................................
2. to ⟷ .....................................
3. over ⟷ .....................................
4. up ⟷ .....................................
5. onto ⟷ .....................................
6. into ⟷ .....................................

**2** 依據圖示，自下表選出適當的表示地點或位置的介系詞來填空，完成句子。
→ Unit 91–94 重點複習

| in | on | past | against | over | under | to |
|---|---|---|---|---|---|---|
| along | into | out of | down | behind | near | between |

The strawberries are ..................... the box.

The blueberry tarts are ..................... the plate.

I put some peanut butter ..................... the toast.

The apple is ..................... the books.

I poured some coffee ..................... the cup.

She is taking a jar of pickles ..................... the refrigerator.

He is putting some chicken ..................... his mouth.

The piece of ice is floating ..................... the sea.

The cheese is

................................................

the two halves of the bun.

Sheep B is standing

.................... Sheep A.

The bees are flying

.................... the flowers.

These camels are

walking .................... the

desert.

The crab is moving

.................... the beach.

This turtle is

swimming ....................

a group of fish.

The dog has a tennis

ball .................... his

mouth.

She is sitting ....................

her suitcase.

The lions are ....................

a car.

She is staying

.................... the surface

of the water.

The man is walking

.................... his room.

She is walking

.................... the stairs.

**3** 請用 at、in 或 on 填空，完成句子。
→ Unit 91–95 重點複習

1. The box is _____ the table by the door.

2. His office is _____ your bus route.

3. He is expecting you _____ 9 a.m.

4. He says he will be _____ work all day.

5. Are you going to be _____ school all day today?

6. Can you run another errand for me _____ the train station?

7. I need you to get some tickets _____ the lobby of the station.

8. Take the tickets to Tony's house _____ Glendale.

9. She is living _____ 109 Spring Street.

10. She is _____ the first floor.

11. She is _____ Apartment 110.

**4** 請用 in、on 或 at 填空，完成句子。
→ Unit 95-96 重點複習

1. My family always gets together _____ Thanksgiving Day.

2. My class starts _____ 8:10.

3. What are you going to do _____ Tuesday?

4. I'm going jogging with my wife _____ the morning.

5. He usually watches sports games on TV _____ night.

6. Aunt Betty goes to church _____ Sunday mornings.

7. Uncle Bob goes fishing _____ the weekend.

8. We get together with our grandparents _____ Christmas. We always have a feast _____ Christmas Day.

9. Mr. and Mrs. Smith are going on a vacation _____ July. They will leave for Australia _____ July 5.

10. The restaurant was founded _____ 1977.

11. Jeff always goes surfing _____ the summer.

**5** 依據圖示，自下表選出正確的介系詞填空，完成句子。

→ **Unit 93 重點複習**

| between | behind | near | opposite | next to |
|---------|--------|------|----------|---------|
| in front of | in | on | under | |

1

The ball is ........................ his foot. His foot is ........................ the ball.

2

The ball is ........................ the net.

3

Player A is ........................ Player B.

4

Player B is ........................ Player A.

5

Players A and B are ........................ Players C and D.

6

Player E is ........................ to Player F.

7

Player G is running ........................ Player H.

8

Player K is ........................ Players J and L.

**6** 以下內容是關於一名男子和他擁有車子的經歷，請用 ago、for 或 since 填空，完成句子。
→ Unit 97 重點複習

1. I drove my first car ＿＿＿＿＿＿＿ four years.

2. I crashed it while I was a college student, and I couldn't afford to buy another car ＿＿＿＿＿＿＿ a long time.

3. My father told me to save my money and buy a used car. I have owned several used cars ＿＿＿＿＿＿＿ then.

4. I bought my first used car 16 years ＿＿＿＿＿＿＿.

5. It was a piece of junk, and I only drove it ＿＿＿＿＿＿＿ two months before it broke down.

6. I drove my second used car ＿＿＿＿＿＿＿ three months, and then the transmission broke.

7. I bought my third "good" used car about 15 years ＿＿＿＿＿＿＿. I loved that car very much.

8. It lasted ＿＿＿＿＿＿＿ five years, and then the cost of repairs forced me to get rid of it. I decided to buy another "good" used car.

9. I have gone through five more used cars ＿＿＿＿＿＿＿ I got rid of my third used car. I'm still driving a used car, and I will probably continue to do so until I can't drive any more.

**7** 根據題目的內容，用 ago 重新造句。
→ Unit 97 重點複習

1. It's 4:00 now. Dana left the office at 3:00.

   → *Dana left an hour ago.*

2. It's 4:35 now. Nancy walked out of the office at 4:00.

   → _____

3. It's 9:00 now. Victor called at 6:00.

   → _____

4. Today is Friday. Julie came on Monday morning.

   → _____

5. This is July. It happened last month on the same date.

   → _____

6. It's 2022. We saw her last year.

   → _____


**8** 選出正確的答案。
→ Unit 97 重點複習

1. It's 6:00. The 5:00 bus left an hour **ago / since**.

2. My sister **left / has left** to go home two days ago.

3. We walked along the beach **for / since** three hours.

4. I have been visiting my grandparents **for / since** a week.

5. She has been visiting her grandparents **for / since** Saturday.

6. I have had this car **since / for** I was 21 years old.

Unit **99**

And, But, Or, Because, So
連接詞 And、But、Or、Because、So

**1** 連接詞用來**連接兩個詞彙、兩個片語**或**兩個句子的詞**。

- and
- so
- if
- but
- because
- before
- or
- when
- after

I'll take a hamburger and French fries.
我要一個漢堡和薯條。

I love fries, but I hate ketchup.
我喜歡薯條，可是我討厭番茄醬。

Sometimes I have a cola or a lemon drink.
有時我會喝可樂或檸檬飲料。

I eat fast food because it tastes good.
我吃速食是因為它好吃。

I know it's not healthy, so I don't eat it often. 我知道它不健康，所以我不常吃。

**2** and、but 和 or 可用來**連接句中個別的部分**。
and 是用來連接「**同類型**」的字。

My grandmother has two cats and two dogs. 我奶奶有兩隻貓和兩隻狗。

We have salty and sweet bread.
我們有鹹的和甜的麵包。

**3** but 用來表達「**相反的概念**」。

I went to his office, but he wasn't there.
我到他的辦公室去，可是他不在。

I tried to call him, but his voice mail kept picking up the call.
我打電話給他，但一直轉到語音信箱。

**4** or 用來表達「**多者擇一**」的可能性。

We could go on a vacation to Hong Kong or Macau. 我們可以到香港或澳門度假。

Are you married or single?
你已婚還是單身？

**5** because 用來描述「**原因**」，常連接子句。表示原因的子句會放在 because 後面。

I can't go because my wife won't let me.
我不能去，因為我太太不讓我去。

I can go because my wife is out of town.
我可以去，因為我太太出城去了。

**6** so 用來描述「**結果或目的**」，也是連接子句。表示**結果**或**目的**的子句會放在 so 的後面。

The meeting is cancelled, so you don't have to go now.
會議取消，所以你現在不用去了。

They want to meet you right now, so you have to come as soon as you can.
他們想馬上見你，所以你得儘快趕來。

## Practice

**1**

請用 and、but 或 or
連接右列句子。

1. I like soda. I like potato chips.

   → ....................................................................................................................

2. Do you want to leave at night? Do you want to leave in the morning?

   → ....................................................................................................................

3. I can't cook. I can barbecue.

   → ....................................................................................................................

4. I have been to Switzerland. I have been to New Zealand.

   → ....................................................................................................................

5. She isn't a ballet dancer. She is a great hip hop dancer.

   → ....................................................................................................................

6. Tom says he is rich. He always borrows money from me.

   → ....................................................................................................................

7. Will you come this week? Will you come next week?

   → ....................................................................................................................

8. Shall we sit in the front? Shall we sit in the back?

   → ....................................................................................................................

9. I read comic books. I read novels.

   → ....................................................................................................................

10. Do you like to eat German food? Do you like to eat French food?

   → ....................................................................................................................

## When, If, Before, After
連接詞 **When**、**If**、**Before**、**After**

**1** when 和 if 都連接子句。when 常用來表達「**將來確定會發生的事**」。

I'll drive you in the morning when you go to senior high school.
等你上高中的時候，我早上會載你去上學。

You can talk to him when he gets here.
當他到這裡時，你可以跟他談談。

I'll be your best man when you get married.
你結婚時，我會當你的伴郎。

**2** if 用來表達「**不確定是否會發生的事情**」。

We'll talk about buying you a scooter if your grades improve.
如果你成績進步，我們再談買機車給你的事。

We'll find the money if you get into UCLA.
假如你申請上加州大學洛杉磯分校，我們就出錢供你念。

I'll throw you a big party if you get that job.
如果你得到那份工作，我就幫你辦一場盛大的派對。

**3** when 和 if 的後面，都要用**簡單現在式**來表示**未來**，不可以用 will 的句型。

I will call you when I am free.
我有空的時候會打給你。

I will come if you invite me.
如果你邀請我，我就會來。

**4** when 和 if 放在句首時，句中需**加逗號**。

When you need a ride, give me a call.
當你需要人來載你時，打個電話給我。

If you come back to Taipei, give me a call.
如果你回來台北，打電話給我。

**5** before 和 after 也常連接子句。before 用來表示「**在某事或某時之前發生的事**」。

before          after

I have to finish this project before the manager comes back.
我要在經理回來之前完成這件案子。

Everybody left the party before Jacky arrived.
傑克還沒到，大家就已經走光了。

**6** after 用來表示「**在某事或某時之後發生的事**」。

I'll meet you at the basketball court after I finish cleaning my room.
等我整理完房間，我就去籃球場找你。

He set out for Paris right after he came back from Tokyo.
他從東京回來，旋即又前往巴黎。

## Practice

| | |
|---|---|
| lift weights | learn lots of things |
| read widely | become self-confident |
| practice writing | increase her stamina |
| practice public speaking | build up his muscles |
| skip dessert | stay slim |
| often go jogging | improve his communication skills |

**1**

依據圖示，分別自兩個右表選出適當的片語，用「if . . . , . . . will . . .」的句型造句。

1

If he lifts weights, he will build up his muscles.

2

3

4

5

6

**2**

利用題目給的片語，用「when she . . . , she'll . . .」的句型造句。

1. start jogging   finish stretching

    →

2. rest on a bench   get tired

    →

3 get home   eat breakfast

    →

## Unit 101 Review Test of Units 99–100
### 單元 99–100 總複習

**1** 以「I missed our date . . .」做句首，用 because 或 so 完成句子。
→ Unit 99 重點複習

1. my car broke down

   → I missed our date _____.

2. my boss needed me to work late in the office

   → I missed our date _____.

3. I could finish my report

   → I missed our date _____.

4. I had to bake cookies

   → I missed our date _____.

5. my dog was sick

   → I missed our date _____.

6. I could see my favorite TV show

   → I missed our date _____.

7. I had to take a sick friend to the hospital

   → I missed our date _____.

8. I had to help my mom clean the house

   → I missed our date _____.

**2** 請用 and、but 或 or 填空，完成句子。
→ Unit 99 重點複習

1. I love to eat pepperoni pizza _____ watch TV.
2. I like action movies, _____ my husband likes romantic comedies.
3. Are you going to see a doctor _____ not?
4. My mother _____ father want to come over this weekend.
5. You can quit school, _____ it's not a good idea.
6. Do you want to stay single _____ get married?
7. He has a double major in law _____ accounting.
8. I haven't graduated yet, _____ I will soon.
9. You can come with our group _____ go with the other group.
10. He will join the Army _____ go to graduate school.

**3** 請用 when 或 if 填空，完成句子。
→ Unit 100 重點複習

1. I want to be in the delivery room in the hospital ＿＿＿＿＿＿ the baby is born.
2. I will buy pink baby clothes ＿＿＿＿＿＿ it is a girl.
3. My brother will drive us home ＿＿＿＿＿＿ we leave the hospital.
4. I will take care of the baby ＿＿＿＿＿＿ it cries between feedings at night.
5. The baby will have a nice new crib ＿＿＿＿＿＿ it comes home from the hospital.
6. I can't wait to find out ＿＿＿＿＿＿ it is a boy or a girl.
7. ＿＿＿＿＿＿ the baby is two years old, I want to have a second child.
8. ＿＿＿＿＿＿ the first child is a boy, then I want a second boy.
9. Two boys can play together ＿＿＿＿＿＿ they are young.
10. ＿＿＿＿＿＿ we have a boy and a girl, I am worried they won't play together.

**4** 請依據提示，在第一格填入 when 或 if，並在第二格用簡單現在式或 will 的句型完成句子。
→ Unit 100 重點複習

1. ＿＿＿＿＿＿ I get dressed tomorrow morning, I ＿＿＿＿＿＿(wear) my holiest jeans.
2. Perhaps Linda will be at the party. ＿＿＿＿＿＿ I see her, I ＿＿＿＿＿＿(ask) her out on a date.
3. I'm definitely going to do it next time I see her. I'll give her my business card ＿＿＿＿＿＿ I ＿＿＿＿＿＿(ask) her out.
4. I hope she says yes. ＿＿＿＿＿＿ she agrees, I ＿＿＿＿＿＿(take) her to the aquarium to see the new killer whales.
5. Maybe that's too weird. She will probably think I am strange ＿＿＿＿＿＿ I ＿＿＿＿＿＿(tell) her we are going the aquarium.
6. I know what I will do. ＿＿＿＿＿＿ I ask her out, I ＿＿＿＿＿＿(give) her the choice of where to go.

**5** 請用 before 或 after 填空，完成句子。
→ Unit 100 重點複習

1. Spring comes ＿＿＿＿＿＿ winter and ＿＿＿＿＿＿ summer.
2. The lightning came ＿＿＿＿＿＿ the thunder.
3. It began to rain ＿＿＿＿＿＿ the thunder.
4. It rained heavily ＿＿＿＿＿＿ the sky turned bright.
5. Sometimes there will be a rainbow ＿＿＿＿＿＿ the rain.

Unit **102**

## Numbers: Cardinal Numbers
### 數字：基數

**1** 數字分三種形式：**基數**、**序數**和**分數**。基數是用來表達**明確的數量或範圍**。序數是表**先後順序**。分數是表非**整體或少於 1 的數目**。

- one 一
- two 二
- three 三

- first 第一
- second 第二
- third 第三

- one-third 三分之一
- two-thirds 三分之二
- one-fourth 四分之一

**2** 基數從 0 到 29 的寫法：

| zero | 0 | ten | 10 | twenty | 20 |
|------|---|-----|----|--------|----|
| one | 1 | eleven | 11 | twenty-one | 21 |
| two | 2 | twelve | 12 | twenty-two | 22 |
| three | 3 | thirteen | 13 | twenty-three | 23 |
| four | 4 | fourteen | 14 | twenty-four | 24 |
| five | 5 | fifteen | 15 | twenty-five | 25 |
| six | 6 | sixteen | 16 | twenty-six | 26 |
| seven | 7 | seventeen | 17 | twenty-seven | 27 |
| eight | 8 | eighteen | 18 | twenty-eight | 28 |
| nine | 9 | nineteen | 19 | twenty-nine | 29 |

**21 到 99 之間**的複合數字，中間都要加連字號。
- twenty-one
- ninety-nine

**3** 基數從 10 到 90，以十位數為單位的寫法：

| ten | 10 | sixty | 60 |
|-----|----|-------|----|
| twenty | 20 | seventy | 70 |
| thirty | 30 | eighty | 80 |
| forty | 40 | ninety | 90 |
| fifty | 50 | | |

**4** 數目 100 以上的數字，十位數和個位數之間，需加 **and** 來表示。

| one hundred | 100 |
|-------------|-----|
| one hundred and one | 101 |
| one hundred and ten | 110 |
| one hundred and twenty | 120 |
| one hundred and twenty-one | 121 |
| one hundred and ninety-nine | 199 |
| two hundred | 200 |

**5** 數字 1000 以上的寫法：

| one thousand | 1,000 | 一千 |
|--------------|-------|------|
| ten thousand | 10,000 | 一萬 |
| one hundred thousand | 100,000 | 十萬 |
| one million | 1,000,000 | 一百萬 |
| one billion | 1,000,000,000 | 十億 |
| one trillion | 1,000,000,000,000 | 一兆 |

**6** hundred（百）、thousand（千）、million（百萬）或 billion（十億）的後面，都**不可加 s** 表示複數。

- three hundred 三百
- three thousand 三千
- three million 三百萬
- three billion 三十億

**電話號碼**的唸法，通常是一個數字、一個數字地唸。

| 電話號碼 | 5236-8813<br>five two three six eight eight one three |
|----------|------|
| 台灣地區電話號碼（含國碼與區碼） | 886-2-7612-0096<br>eight eight six, dash, two, dash, seven six one two, dash, zero zero nine six |
| 含通行密碼、國碼、區碼和分機號碼 | 001-1-202-347-1000 Ext.2022<br>zero zero one, dash, one, dash, two zero two, dash, three four seven, dash, one zero zero zero, extension two zero two two |

**1**

請用英文寫出右列
數字的唸法。

1. 9 _____
2. 13 _____
3. 78 _____
4. 141 _____
5. 385 _____
6. 7,064 _____
   _____
7. 9,856 _____
   _____
8. 10,231 _____
9. 1,032,540 _____
10. 6,837,650 _____
    _____
11. 40,000,000 _____
12. 12,452,689 _____
    _____

**2**

請用英文寫出右列
電話號碼的唸法。

1. 911
   → _____
2. 8786-5239
   → _____
3. 318-926-5273
   → _____
4. 003-1-250-764-5320
   → _____
   _____
5. 02-3276-9370
   → _____
6. 0932-540-696
   → _____
7. 2364-5839 Ext.12
   → _____
   _____

## Unit 103

### Numbers: Ordinal Numbers
數字：序數

| 40 | 40th | fortieth |
| --- | --- | --- |
| 50 | 50th | fiftieth |
| 60 | 60th | sixtieth |
| 70 | 70th | seventieth |
| 80 | 80th | eightieth |
| 90 | 90th | ninetieth |
| 100 | 100th | one hundredth |
| 200 | 200th | two hundredth |
| 1,000 | 1,000th | one thousandth |
| 1,000,000 | 1,000,000th | one millionth |

**1** 序數用來表達**先後順序**。大多數的序數是在數字後面加上 **th**，但 1、2、3 的序數是例外。「零」則沒有序數。

| 1 | 1st | first |
| --- | --- | --- |
| 2 | 2nd | second |
| 3 | 3rd | third |
| 4 | 4th | fourth |
| 5 | 5th | fifth |
| 6 | 6th | sixth |
| 7 | 7th | seventh |
| 8 | 8th | eighth |
| 9 | 9th | ninth |
| 10 | 10th | tenth |

| 11 | 11th | eleventh |
| --- | --- | --- |
| 12 | 12th | twelfth |
| 13 | 13th | thirteenth |
| 14 | 14th | fourteenth |
| 15 | 15th | fifteenth |
| 16 | 16th | sixteenth |
| 17 | 17th | seventeenth |
| 18 | 18th | eighteenth |
| 19 | 19th | nineteenth |
| 20 | 20th | twentieth |

| 21 | 21st | twenty-first |
| --- | --- | --- |
| 22 | 22nd | twenty-second |
| 23 | 23rd | twenty-third |
| 24 | 24th | twenty-fourth |
| 25 | 25th | twenty-fifth |
| 26 | 26th | twenty-sixth |
| 27 | 27th | twenty-seventh |
| 28 | 28th | twenty-eighth |
| 29 | 29th | twenty-ninth |
| 30 | 30th | thirtieth |

**2** 序數前通常需要加 **the**。

**He was the first prize winner.**
他是第一特獎的贏家。

**The door to his office is the third one on the left.**
他的辦公室在左邊第三個門。

**4** 序數經常用來描述**日期**。

**Are you free on the fifteenth of November?**
你 11 月 15 日有沒有空？

**Our flight departs on the second of May.**
我們的班機 5 月 2 日起飛。

**3** 序數經常用來描述**樓層**。

**I bought the lipstick on the second floor of the department store.**
我在百貨公司的二樓買了這條口紅。

**I live on the fifth floor of this apartment building.**
我住在這棟公寓的五樓。

## Practice

**1**

根據右列的美國歷任總統表，依範例用序數來描述各任美國總統。

1. George Washington was _____

   President of the United States.

2. Thomas Jefferson was _____

   President of the United States.

3. James Madison was _____

   President of the United States.

4. Abraham Lincoln was _____

   President of the United States.

5. Warren Harding was _____

   President of the United States.

6. Franklin Roosevelt was _____

   President of the United States.

7. John Kennedy was _____

   President of the United States.

8. Richard Nixon was _____

   President of the United States.

9. Bill Clinton served as _____

   President of the United States.

10. Barack Obama is _____

    President of the United States.

| 1 | 1789–1797 | George Washington |
|---|-----------|-------------------|
| 2 | 1797–1801 | John Adams |
| 3 | 1801–1809 | Thomas Jefferson |
| 4 | 1809–1817 | James Madison |
| 5 | 1817–1825 | James Monroe |
| 6 | 1825–1829 | John Quincy Adams |
| 7 | 1829–1837 | Andrew Jackson |
| 8 | 1837–1841 | Martin Van Buren |
| 9 | 1841 | William Harrison |
| 10 | 1841–1845 | John Tyler |
| 11 | 1845–1849 | James Polk |
| 12 | 1849–1850 | Zachary Taylor |
| 13 | 1850–1853 | Millard Fillmore |
| 14 | 1853–1857 | Franklin Pierce |
| 15 | 1857–1861 | James Buchanan |
| 16 | 1861–1865 | Abraham Lincoln |
| 17 | 1865–1869 | Andrew Johnson |
| 18 | 1869–1877 | Ulysses Grant |
| 19 | 1877–1881 | Rutherford Hayes |
| 20 | 1881 | James Garfield |
| 21 | 1881–1885 | Chester Arthur |
| 22 | 1885–1889 | Grover Cleveland |
| 23 | 1889–1893 | Benjamin Harrison |
| 24 | 1893–1897 | Grover Cleveland |
| 25 | 1897–1901 | William McKinley |
| 26 | 1901–1909 | Theodore Roosevelt |
| 27 | 1909–1913 | William Taft |
| 28 | 1913–1921 | Woodrow Wilson |
| 29 | 1921–1923 | Warren Harding |
| 30 | 1923–1929 | Calvin Coolidge |
| 31 | 1929–1933 | Herbert Hoover |
| 32 | 1933–1945 | Franklin Roosevelt |
| 33 | 1945–1953 | Harry S. Truman |
| 34 | 1953–1961 | Dwight Eisenhower |
| 35 | 1961–1963 | John Kennedy |
| 36 | 1963–1969 | Lyndon Johnson |
| 37 | 1969–1974 | Richard Nixon |
| 38 | 1974–1977 | Gerald Ford |
| 39 | 1977–1981 | Jimmy Carter |
| 40 | 1981–1989 | Ronald Reagan |
| 41 | 1989–1992 | George Bush |
| 42 | 1993–2001 | Bill Clinton |
| 43 | 2001–2009 | George Walker Bush |
| 44 | 2009–2017 | Barack Obama |
| 45 | 2017–2021 | Donald Trump |

**1** 星期的**字首一定要大寫**，前面**不能加 the**，介系詞要搭配 **on** 來使用。

- Monday 星期一
- Tuesday 星期二
- Wednesday 星期三
- Thursday 星期四
- Friday 星期五
- Saturday 星期六
- Sunday 星期日

Call me on the Friday.
星期五打電話給我。

**2** 月分的**字首一定要大寫**，前面**不能加 the**，介系詞要搭配 **in** 來使用。

- January 一月
- February 二月
- March 三月
- April 四月
- May 五月
- June 六月
- July 七月
- August 八月
- September 九月
- October 十月
- November 十一月
- December 十二月

Let's go in the January.
我們一月去吧。

**3** 日期必須使用序數詞，完整的日期寫法，英式英語和美式英語不同。

| 英式英語 | 美式英語 |
| --- | --- |
| 15th January, 2025 | January 15th, 2025 |
| 15 January, 2025 | January 15, 2025 |
| 15.1.2025 | 1-15-2025 |
| 15.1.25 | 1-15-25 |

**4** 日期的介系詞要用 on。

We leave on January 10th.
我們 1 月 10 號出發。

Meet me on December 31st at 11 p.m. so we can ring in the New Year together.
12 月 31 號的晚上 11 點來找我，我們可以一起跨年。

**5** 年分的介系詞要用 in。

- in $^{1992}$ 在 $^{1992}$ 年
- in **2006** 在 2006 年

**年分的唸法**

❶ **年分的唸法**，1999 年以前的，會分成**前後**兩部分來唸。
  ① 1999  nineteen ninety-nine
  ② 1876  eighteen seventy-six
  ③ 1702  seventeen oh two (oh = zero)

❷ **年分的唸法**，2000 年以後的，則會唸成「**兩千 + 尾數**」，2010 年後的年分，亦可分成兩部分。
  ① 2001  two thousand one
  ② 2005  two thousand five
  ③ 2010  two thousand ten / twenty ten
  ④ 2012  two thousand twelve / twenty twelve

❸ **日期（幾月幾日）的唸法有兩種：**
  1 月 4 日
  ① the fourth of January
  ② January (the) fourth

## Practice

**1**

依據 **Mr. Simpson** 的
一週行事曆，造句描
述他每一天的行程。

1. Mr. Simpson is meeting Ms. Miller on Monday.

2. ................................................................

   ................................................................

3. ................................................................

   ................................................................

4. ................................................................

   ................................................................

5. ................................................................

   ................................................................

6. ................................................................

   ................................................................

7. ................................................................

   ................................................................

**Appointment Book**

**Mon.**
*meet Mr. Miller*

**Tue.**
*visit his grandma*

**Wed.**
*go shopping*

**Thur.**
*have dinner with Tom*

**Fri.**
*pick up Peter at the airport*

**Sat.**
*play basketball*

**Sun.**
*go to the movies*

**2**

用英文寫出右列日期
的唸法。

1. 20. 5. 19

   → ................................................................

2. 19. 6. 1996

   → ................................................................

3. 1. 3. 2018

   → ................................................................

4. 10-11-1502

   → ................................................................

5. 2-26-2010

   → ................................................................

6. 12-31-1876

   → ................................................................

Unit **105**

Time of Day
時間

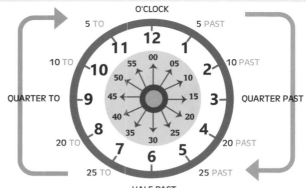

### 1 用 o'clock 來表示「整點」。

**nine** o'clock | **five** o'clock
9 a.m./9 p.m. | 5 a.m./5 p.m.
九點鐘 | 五點鐘

### 2 用 half past 來表示「幾點半」。（此為英式讀法）

half past **two** | half past **one**
兩點半 | 一點半

### 3 用 (a) quarter past 表「幾點過 15 分」；用 (a) quarter to 表示「差 15 分幾點」。（此為英式讀法）

a quarter past **twelve** | a quarter to **three**
十二點十五分 | 兩點四十五分

### 4 用 minutes past 表示「幾點過幾分」；用 minutes to 表示「差幾分幾點」。（此為英式讀法）

**twenty-six** minutes past **seven** | **twenty-two** minutes to **ten**
七點二十六分 | 九點三十八分

### 5 如果分鐘為 5 的倍數，就省略 minutes。（此為英式讀法）

five **past nine** | ten **past ten**
九點五分 | 十點十分

### 6 另一種說明時間的方法為「hour（時）+ the minutes（分）」。（此為美式讀法）

**two oh two** | **one fifty-two**
兩點零二分 | 一點五十二分

**seven thirty** | **twelve eighteen**
七點半 | 十二點十八分

## Practice

**1**

依據圖示，自下表選出
正確的時間填空。
（下面皆為英式讀法）

Ⓐ half past two

Ⓑ ten past ten

Ⓒ five to four

Ⓓ five o'clock

Ⓔ ten to twelve

Ⓕ two minutes to twelve

| | | |
|---|---|---|
| 1  D | 2  | 3  |
| 4  | 5  | 6  |

**2**

依據圖示，分別用兩
種方式，以完整句子
描述時間。

（第二題除外，第二
題只有一種寫法。）

 1  It's a quarter past nine.
It's nine fifteen.

 2

 3

 4

 5

 6

 7

Unit **106**

## Review Test of Units 102–105
### 單元 102–105 總複習

**1** 在空格內填入正確的星期或月分。
→ Unit 104 重點複習

1. The Chinese New Year is always in _____ or _____ .

2. Easter always falls on a _____ .

3. _____ is the third month.

4. _____ is the eighth month.

5. Mother's Day is on the second _____ of May.

6. _____ comes after Wednesday.

7. _____ the 13th occurs when the 13th day of a month falls on a Friday.

8. In Taiwan, typhoons occur mostly in _____ , _____ , and _____ .

9. Thanksgiving Day falls on the fourth _____ of _____ .

10. People born from late _____ to early _____ are Geminis.

**2** 用「the . . . of . . .」的形式，在空格內填入正確的日期。
→ Unit 104 重點複習

1. Christmas Day is on _____ .

2. New Year's Eve falls on _____ .

3. New Year's Day falls on _____ .

4. Valentine's Day is on _____ .

5. The Dragon Boat Festival is on _____ of the Chinese lunar calendar.

6. The Chinese Valentine's Day falls on _____ of the Chinese lunar calendar.

7. The Autumn Festival is on _____ of the Chinese lunar calendar.

8. Halloween is celebrated on _____ .

9. Is that true people born on _____ can only celebrate their birthday once every four years?

**3** 寫出下列各項資訊的唸法。
→ **Unit 104 重點複習**

電話號碼

1. 8930-7635

   → ..................................................................................................................................

2. 02-3478-9711

   → ..................................................................................................................................

3. 886-2-115-6730

   → ..................................................................................................................................

4. 4561-8932 Ext. 112

   → ..................................................................................................................................

5. 0965-321-578

   → ..................................................................................................................................

日期

6. 三月二十八日

   → ..................................................................................................................................

7. 七月四日

   → ..................................................................................................................................

8. 一月一日

   → ..................................................................................................................................

9. 九月十八日

   → ..................................................................................................................................

年分

10. 1459

   → ..................................................................................................................................

11. 1938

   → ..................................................................................................................................

12. 2009

   → ..................................................................................................................................

13. 2020

   → ..................................................................................................................................

# Progress Test

## Part 1 名詞和冠詞

**1** 下列名詞是可數還是不可數？請在可數名詞的括弧內填上 C，不可數填上 U。

1. (　) adult
2. (　) crown
3. (　) mouse
4. (　) bicycle
5. (　) salt
6. (　) box
7. (　) grass
8. (　) honesty
9. (　) bread
10. (　) market
11. (　) child
12. (　) time
13. (　) soup
14. (　) number
15. (　) company
16. (　) chocolate
17. (　) juice
18. (　) money
19. (　) knowledge
20. (　) paper

**2** 請寫出下列單字的「複數名詞」。

1. giraffe
2. dish
3. ox
4. life
5. duck
6. church
7. size
8. eraser
9. goose
10. television
11. pencil
12. oasis
13. cherry
14. species
15. library
16. datum
17. sheep
18. fairy
19. deer
20. witch

**3** 請用 a、an 或 the 填空，完成句子。

1. He is _____ singer.
2. Her face looks like _____ moon.
3. Have you got _____ credit card?
4. Does this library have _____ on-line catalog?
5. Have you ever eaten _____ snake?
6. _____ elephant stepped on my toe.
7. Mommy, I want to buy _____ dog.
8. _____ apple a day keeps _____ doctor away.
9. Do we have to wait _____ hour?
10. Please pick up _____ dry cleaning.
11. I thought it was _____ honest apology.
12. _____ pears were ripe and juicy.
13. He said it was just _____ quick trip.
14. Bob says _____ party starts at 10:00.
15. It's _____ integrated digital watch, cell phone, and GPS locator.
16. It's _____ big store, but they didn't have it.
17. I'll meet you at _____ bookstore.
18. The vice president will arrive at _____ city hall in _____ minute.

**4** 請依據圖示，用適當的「量詞」填空，完成句子。

1. some ＿＿＿＿＿ of mineral water
2. a ＿＿＿＿＿ of chocolate
3. a ＿＿＿＿＿ of toothpaste
4. two ＿＿＿＿＿ of tea
5. a ＿＿＿＿＿ of milk
6. a ＿＿＿＿＿ of facial cream
7. a ＿＿＿＿＿ of soda
8. a ＿＿＿＿＿ of soup
9. a ＿＿＿＿＿ of coconut milk
10. a ＿＿＿＿＿ of cabbage

**5** 請圈選正確的答案。

1. There is heavy traffic / traffics during rush hour.
2. We need a truck to move the furniture / furnitures.
3. Don't run while holding scissor / scissors.
4. How many glasses of milk / milks should I pour?
5. If it's OK with you, I'd rather have tea / teas.
6. Did you realize this store sells many kinds of coffee / coffees?

**6** 若空格處需要 the，請填上；若不需要，請畫上「ㄨ」。

1. Please put ＿＿＿ gas in the car.
2. When will we arrive at ＿＿＿ airport?
3. Buy me ＿＿＿ coolest cell phone you can afford.
4. Let's meet at ＿＿＿ 1:30 or 2 p.m.
5. When you get ＿＿＿ stock certificate, put it in a safe place.
6. ＿＿＿ report is due on Friday.
7. Are you going to the mall on ＿＿＿ foot?
8. I went to Nina's apartment by ＿＿＿ subway.
9. She's going to play ＿＿＿ violin at the concert.
10. Living in ＿＿＿ city is more convenient, but living in ＿＿＿ country is healthier.
11. Jeffery loves ＿＿＿ mathematics, but he doesn't like to study ＿＿＿ chemistry.
12. Does your father play ＿＿＿ golf on Sunday?
13. I need to get to ＿＿＿ station before noon.
14. ＿＿＿ dogs and ＿＿＿ cats are friendly animals.

**7** 將錯誤的句子打ｘ，並寫出正確的句子。
若句子無誤，請在方框內打✓。

1. The Calvin is a cool little kid.

   ☒ *Calvin is a cool little kid.*

2. Our vacation starts on the Friday, the January 20.

   ☐ ..................................................

   ..................................................

3. I am studying French, and I want to visit France.

   ☐ ..................................................

   ..................................................

4. The nearest airport is in the Canberra.

   ☐ ..................................................

5. Museum of Modern Art in the New York is 50 years old.

   ☐ ..................................................

   ..................................................

6. Great Wall of China is pretty amazing.

   ☐ ..................................................

   ..................................................

**8** 請將各名詞加上「's」、「'」或 of、of the。

1. Jane / hat ..................................................
2. my grandparents / house ...............................
3. side / road ..................................................
4. Beethoven / Fifth Symphony

   ..................................................
5. products / price tags ....................................
6. ruins / ancient civilizations

   ..................................................

**9** 下列句子是否需要加 the？將錯誤的句子打ｘ，並寫出正確的句子。若句子無誤，請在方框內打✓。

1. Don't go to bed too late.

   ☐ ..................................................

   ..................................................

2. We are going by bus to avoid parking problems.

   ☐ ..................................................

   ..................................................

3. Are you watching the TV or doing the homework?

   ☐ ..................................................

   ..................................................

4. Do you want to go to the theater or the cinema?

   ☐ ..................................................

   ..................................................

5. Helen has decided to learn piano.

   ☐ ..................................................

   ..................................................

6. The closest star to us is Sun.

   ☐ ..................................................

   ..................................................

**Part 2　代名詞**

**1** 請用正確主詞代名詞（I、**you**、**he**、**she**、**it**、**we**、**you** 或 **they**）填空，完成句子。

1. My name is Paul. _____'m on the baseball team.

2. Johnny! Why are _____ hitting your sister?

3. There's food for everybody. _____ should get plates and help yourselves.

4. Back on the bus. _____'re leaving in five minutes.

5. Tom said _____'d be back sometime today.

6. I called your mother and father. _____ said no problem.

7. Alison is the fastest runner in our class, and _____ just won another race.

8. That soup is too spicy. I can't finish _____.

**2** 請圈選正確的答案。

1. Do you want to sit with me / my?

2. Who did you bring with your / you?

3. Harriet said that she knew him / his from school.

4. I have known hers / her for many years.

5. Come to think of it / its, she has changed her name.

6. That dog belongs to our / us. We'll clean up after it.

7. You / Your can all sit down now.

8. I'm not sitting here with you guys. I'm going over there and sit with their / them.

9. That new guy is on your team. This guy is on ours / our.

10. I can't find my / mine basketball anywhere.

11. I'll drive my car. You drive yours / your.

12. Is this cottage your / yours?

13. Is this hat yours? I see your name on it. It must be yours / your.

14. My tennis racquet has my name on it. That's not my / mine.

15. I heard your excuse. What is hers / her?

**3** 請用正確所有格形容詞（**my**、**your**、**his**、**her**、**its**、**our** 或 **their**）填空，完成句子。

1. I'm a sales representative. Here is _____ business card.

2. This is where my parents, wife, children, and I live. It's _____ house.

3. The cat is licking the fur on _____ paw.

4. They bought a second car, but there's no room in _____ garage.

5. Beth looks different. Did she get _____ hair permed?

6. He loves mirrors. He's always looking at _____ muscles.

7. Do you want _____ meals on separate checks?

**4** 請用 some 或 any 填空，完成句子。

1. Jack has _____ laptops.

2. Larry doesn't have _____ laptops.

3. Do you have _____ laptops?

4. There were _____ phone calls for Ian.

5. There weren't _____ phone calls for you.

6. Were there _____ phone calls for me?

7. Would you like _____ chocolate milk?

8. Yes, _____ chocolate milk is great.

9. Have you tried _____ lobster sashimi?

10. No, I haven't eaten _____ lobster sashimi before.

11. You should try _____. It's tasty.

12. OK. I'll eat _____ at the seafood restaurant.

13. Have you been to _____ cold places recently?

14. No, I haven't been to _____ cold places.

15. Do Sam and Ann have _____ children?

16. Can I have _____ bacon for breakfast?

17. I don't watch _____ TV programs at night.

18. Did you see _____ worms in Puffy's food?

19. Yes, I saw _____, so I threw it away.

20. May I take _____ photos in the gallery?

21. No, you can't take _____ photos in the gallery.

22. Shall I buy you _____ food?

23. No, thanks. I don't want _____.

**5** 請用 some、any 或 no 填空，完成下列對話。

Boy: Don't touch my tops. You can't play with ❶_____ of them.

Girl: I can play with ❷_____. Mommy said so.

Boy: You can play with the flashlight.

Girl: There are ❸_____ batteries in the flashlight.

Boy: Do you have ❹_____ candy?

Girl: I have ❺_____ chocolate.

Boy: Give me ❻_____ and I'll let you play with a top.

Girl: ❼_____ chocolate unless you let me play with all your tops.

Boy: Can I have ❽_____ of the chocolate candies?

Girl: ❾_____ piece but this big one.

Boy: OK, but only ❿_____ of the tops. Deal?

Girl: Deal.

**6** 請選出正確答案。

_____ 1. How _____ do those strawberries cost?
ⓐ much      ⓑ many      ⓒ a few

_____ 2. Are there _____ art museums in the city?
ⓐ much      ⓑ a little      ⓒ many

_____ 3. I have _____ paintings by Japanese artists.
ⓐ much      ⓑ a lot of      ⓒ a little

_____ 4. Please give me _____ salad.
ⓐ many      ⓑ much      ⓒ a little

_____ 5. We need _____ good men.
ⓐ a few      ⓑ a little      ⓒ much

_____ 6. That's _____ for now.
ⓐ much      ⓑ enough      ⓒ a lot of

**7** 請用 little、a little、few 或 a few 填空，完成句子。

1. I have _____ money with me. I can't dine out with you tonight.

2. I noticed _____ spelling errors in your paper, but not many.

3. She got _____ help from her brother during the most difficult time in her life, but she has no complaint about it.

4. _____ spice in the soup will make it taste better.

5. She invited _____ friends to her house last night.

6. There are only _____ oranges in the refrigerator. I can't make enough orange juice for everyone.

7. I need to make _____ calls now.

8. There's _____ buzzing noise. What's wrong with your phone line?

**8** 請在空格處填上 one 或 ones，並寫出它在該句中所指的物品。

1. I don't need another glass of juice. I already have _____
   (= _____).

2. He needs to buy some new ties. The _____ ( = _____) he has are too old.

3. I bought two pairs of shoes. Which _____ (= _____) do you like?

4. Do you still have that old jacket, the _____ (= _____) with the broken zipper?

**9** 請自下表選出適當的不定代名詞填空，完成句子。

| | | |
|---|---|---|
| somebody | anybody | nobody |
| everybody | someone | anyone |
| no one | everyone | something |
| anything | nothing | everything |
| somewhere | anywhere | nowhere |
| everywhere | | |

1. I'm the only person here. _____ else has gone home.

2. You don't have a date, do you? I bet you haven't asked _____.

3. It looks as if you might be having a little trouble. Is there _____ wrong?

4. The phone call is for you. It's _____ from your office.

5. No, you can't drink any alcohol. We'll have _____ to drink when we get home.

6. That is a local flower. It grows here and _____ else.

7. I haven't said a thing. _____ has asked me about it.

8. Now you can make a cell phone call _____ in the world.

9. I'm hungry. I had _____ to eat all day.

**10** 請用 this、that、these 或 those 填空，完成句子。

1. Let's ask ＿＿＿＿＿ guy over there.
2. Let's ask ＿＿＿＿＿ child standing right next to you.
3. Let's ask ＿＿＿＿＿ policemen right here.
4. Let's ask ＿＿＿＿＿ man way over there by the shoe store.
5. Let's ask ＿＿＿＿＿ cab drivers on the opposite side of the street.

**11** 請自下表選出正確的「反身代名詞」填空，完成句子。

| | | | |
|---|---|---|---|
| myself | yourself | himself | herself |
| itself | ourselves | yourselves | |
| themselves | | | |

1. He is looking at ＿＿＿＿＿＿＿ in the mirror.
2. She never gives ＿＿＿＿＿＿＿ a break.
3. If we don't do it ＿＿＿＿＿＿＿, it will never be finished.
4. They moved their things ＿＿＿＿＿＿＿ without the help of a moving company.
5. She always says, "I can do it ＿＿＿＿＿＿＿," but then she never gets things done.
6. There isn't enough time for you to cook dinner ＿＿＿＿＿＿＿.

**▶▶▶ Part 3 現在時態**

**1** 請用 am、is 或 are 填空，完成下列段落。

I ❶＿＿＿＿ a traveling salesman. Today my sales meeting ❷＿＿＿＿ in Townville. Tomorrow my presentation ❸＿＿＿＿ in Smallville. I ❹＿＿＿＿ always busy. I ❺＿＿＿＿ an employee of Toothbrush Inc. We ❻＿＿＿＿ the biggest toothbrush company in the world. My job title ❼＿＿＿＿ Senior Sales Manager, but there ❽＿＿＿＿ no people for me to manage. It ❾＿＿＿＿ just me with my toothbrush samples. I have to visit two more stores, then I ❿＿＿＿ done for the day. That ⓫＿＿＿＿ my life.

**2** 請用 there is、there are、is there、are there、it is 或 they are 填空，完成句子。

Man: Let's go visit my Uncle Fred on his farm in Ruralville.

Woman: ❶＿＿＿＿＿ anything interesting to do in Ruralville?

Man: ❷＿＿＿＿＿ lots of interesting things to do.

Woman: Tell me about all those interesting things in Ruralville.

Man: Uhhh? You can enjoy nature. ❸＿＿＿＿＿ a quiet place.

Woman: ❹＿＿＿＿＿ many people?

Man: No, but ❺＿＿＿＿＿ a very nice place.

Woman: So, ❻＿＿＿＿＿ nothing interesting to do.

Man: Well . . . no.

Woman: You go visit the cows and the corn. I'm staying right here.

**3** 請用 have got 的正確形式填空完成句子。
（注意：have / has got，主要用於英式英文。）

1. I _____ a dog and a cat.

2. I _____ (not) any fish.

3. Tim: _____ you _____ any pets?
   Kim: Yes, I _____ .

4. They _____ two kids, but they
   _____ (not) any pets.

**4** 請將括弧內的動詞以「簡單現在式」填空，
完成句子。

1. I _____ (work) downtown in the city.

2. I _____ (take) the train to get to my
   office.

3. My wife _____ (commute) to work
   by bus.

4. How _____ you _____ (get) to
   your work?

5. I _____ (not drive) .
   I _____ (not know) how.

6. _____ you _____ (go) shopping at
   the new mall?

7. It _____ (take) me 20 minutes to
   commute to work.

**5** 請將括弧內的動詞以「現在進行式」填空，
完成句子。

1. What _____ you _____ (do) right
   now?

2. The phone in the kitchen _____
   (ring) .

3. I _____ not _____ (cook)
   dinner tonight.

4. My boss _____ (look) for
   someone to come in and provide some
   technical leadership.

5. _____ you _____ (work) now?

6. I _____ (plan) to take some
   days off.

**6** 選出正確的答案。

____ 1. Sometimes I _____ at this mini-mart.
   Ⓐ am shopping   Ⓑ shop   Ⓒ shops

____ 2. I usually _____ a cup of coffee at this
   café.
   Ⓐ am buying   Ⓑ buy   Ⓒ buys

____ 3. I _____ the newspaper right now.
   Ⓐ read   Ⓑ reads   Ⓒ am reading

____ 4. I always _____ the headlines before I
   read a newspaper.
   Ⓐ checks   Ⓑ am checking   Ⓒ check

____ 5. He _____ the newspaper every day at
   lunch.
   Ⓐ reads   Ⓑ read   Ⓒ is reading

____ 6. He _____ out an article from the
   newspaper.
   Ⓐ cut   Ⓑ cuts   Ⓒ is cutting

____ 7. Jim _____ tea and reads the newspaper
   every morning.
   Ⓐ drink   Ⓑ drinks   Ⓒ is drinking

____ 8. Ann: Are you reading a novel now?
   Bob: I _____ .
   Ⓐ do   Ⓑ am   Ⓒ is

____ 9. Kelly: Do you like to read novels on
   Sundays?
   Jimmy: I _____ .
   Ⓐ do   Ⓑ is   Ⓒ am

**7** 將錯誤的句子打✗，並寫出正確的句子。若句子無誤，請在方框內打✓。

1. I am wanting something to eat.
   ☐ ..................................

2. I am loving that dress you are wearing.
   ☐ ..................................

3. She has all sorts of new clothes.
   ☐ ..................................

4. I am thinking you are right about Jim.
   ☐ ..................................

5. Irene is having lunch now.
   ☐ ..................................

6. I was seeing some new shopping bags in your closet.
   ☐ ..................................
   ..................................

>>> **Part 4** 過去時態

**1** 請用 be 動詞的過去式填空，完成句子。

1. Pete: .......... Linda and Randy on vacation last month?
   Greg: Yes, they ...........

2. .......... that movie on TV last night?
   No, it ...........

3. Tony: .......... she attractive in her new dress yesterday?
   Randy: Yes, she ...........

4. Jason: .......... they at the party last night?
   Mia: No, they ...........

**2** 請用「過去簡單式」填空，完成對話。

Dad: ❶.......... you ❷.......... (go) to meet your girlfriend's parents?

Son: I ❸.......... (meet) them last Sunday.

Dad: What ❹.......... (happen)?

Son: We ❺.......... (eat) dinner and ❻.......... (talk).

Dad: What else ❼.......... you ❽.......... (do)?

Son: We just ❾.......... (stay) at their house.

Dad: It sounds like an adult dinner party.

Son: Yes, her parents ❿.......... (behave) themselves very well.

Dad: I ⓫.......... (mean) you.

Son: I ⓬.......... (be) well behaved, too.

**3** 請用「過去簡單式」與「過去進行式」填空，完成這篇故事。

I ❶.......... (stand) on Market Street waiting for my bus, and a guy in a black jacket ❷.......... (sit) on a bench across the street waiting for his bus. A pizza delivery woman ❸.......... (pull up) near the guy in the black jacket. The pizza woman ❹.......... (grab) one of the pizzas out of her car and ran into a nearby building. She had left her car with the motor running in the "No Parking" zone where the bus usually stops. I ❺.......... (notice) the guy across the street stand up. He ❻.......... (look) at the pizza woman's car. The guy ❼.......... (start) walking around the pizza car. I shouted at him as he ❽.......... (open) the car door, got in, and drove away. He had stolen the car and a stack of six pizzas. The pizza woman

**⑨** _____ (begin) to cry when she **⑩** _____ (discover) that her car and pizzas were gone.

**4** 請將括弧內的動詞以「現在完成式」填空，完成句子。

1. Mr. Keller _____ (be) a lawyer since 1984.

2. _____ you ever _____ (attend) a wedding on the top of a mountain?

3. Julie _____ (have) a perm and highlighting done to her hair.

4. Tim _____ (leave) and I hope he never returns.

5. Rocky _____ (be) out all night and has not returned yet.

**5** 請圈選正確的答案。

1. Who opened / has opened the boxes before I arrived?

2. I had / have had my present car for three years.

3. Have you been / Did you go to Australia?

4. Have you been / Did you go to Café Budapest last night?

**>>> Part 5　未來時態**

**1** 將括號內的動詞以「現在進行式」填空，完成下列表示未來意義的句子。

Dan: **❶** _____ you **❷** _____ (see) the doctor tomorrow?

Ann: No, I **❸** _____ (see) the doctor this afternoon.

Dan: I **❹** _____ (go) to the concert on Saturday. **❺** _____ you **❻** _____ (come) with me?

Ann: I wish I could, but I **❼** _____ (meet) an important client from Miami.

Dan: **❽** _____ you **❾** _____ (take) any trips in March?

Ann: I **❿** _____ (visit) some customers in Australia and New Zealand.

**2** 將括弧內的動詞以 **be going to** 的句型填空，完成下列表示未來意義的句子。

1. I am tired. I _____ (sleep) .

2. When _____ you _____ (visit) your friends in Hong Kong?

3. _____ you _____ (quit) your job after the company gives out bonuses?

4. Why _____ you _____ (move) to Japan?

5. _____ you _____ (live) with your parents?

**3** 將括弧內的動詞搭配 will 或 won't 填空，完成下列表示未來意義的句子。

1. He _____ (wonder) why I dumped him.

2. No way! I _____ (date) that jerk again.

3. He _____ (send) me some flowers and little gifts.

4. I _____ (screen) his calls and refuse to answer.

5. I _____ (respond) no matter what he does.

---

>>> **Part 6　不定詞和動詞的 -ing 形式**

**1** 將括弧內動詞以正確的形態填空，完成句子。

1. I can _____ (use) the computer.

2. I want _____ (use) the computer.

3. I like _____ (use) the computer.

4. We may _____ (finish) early.

5. Let's _____ (call) your cousin tonight.

6. I hope _____ (see) the museum soon.

7. Can you help _____ (stuff) the mailboxes?

8. It's too late _____ (start) now.

9. How about _____ (start) tomorrow?

10. Jane asked me _____ (send) her the contract as soon as possible.

11. Is it difficult _____ (learn) Japanese?

12. No, Japanese is easy _____ (learn) .

13. Are you good at _____ (play) video games?

14. Would you like me _____ (turn) on the lights?

15. Do you mind _____ (hold) the ladder for me while I change the light bulb?

**2** 請用 to 或 for 填空，完成句子。

1. He went to the store _____ some soy milk.

2. He wants soy milk _____ his breakfast cereal.

3. He went to the mini-mart _____ buy soy milk.

4. He drinks soy milk _____ stay healthy.

## Part 7　常用動詞

**1** 請將括弧內的動詞以正確的形式填空，完成下列句子。

1. I'm going _____ (shop) with Elaine tomorrow. Would you like to join us?
2. I can't get the car _____ (start). The battery must be dead.
3. Don't worry. I'll get someone _____ (fix) the car right away.
4. You can't make him _____ (do) anything he doesn't like.
5. I'll have him _____ (deliver) the package to your office.
6. Please have these boxes _____ (mail).
7. It took me thirty minutes _____ (walk) to the hospital.

**2** 請圈選正確的答案。

1. John and Lily went for swimming / a swim last Saturday.
2. My parents are going on to travel / a trip to Finland next month.
3. I'm thinking about taking / making the job he offered.
4. The statue of the lion is made of / from stone.
5. The meatballs are made of / from beef.
6. Did you have / get fun in Madrid?
7. David will make / do the dishes and I'll make / do the laundry.
8. The music festival will take place / part in November.

## Part 8　情態助動詞

**1** 請圈選正確的答案。

1. How many push-ups can / can't you do?
2. He can / cans drive his car with his eyes shut.
3. He can / can't always say something that makes everybody mad.
4. The director can / can't see you right now, because he is at a meeting.
5. Can you / Do you can please help me take out the garbage?

**2** 請將錯誤的句子打✗，並寫出正確的句子。若句子無誤，則在方框內打✓。

1. I could talk when I was one year old.
   ☐ _____

2. He can't swim but he loves taking baths.
   ☐ _____

3. If I can I would, but I can't so I won't.
   ☐ _____

4. He can climb up trees when he was young, but he couldn't get down.
   ☐ _____
   _____

5. If anybody who can do it, Bobby Brown is the guy for the job.
   ☐ _____
   _____

Progress Test

Part 5

Part 6

Part 7

Part 8

275

**3** 請將括弧內的動詞搭配 must 或 mustn't 填空，完成句子。

1. You _____ (tell) them who you are or they will throw you in jail.

2. You _____ (pay) your phone bill or they will cut off your service.

3. No, you _____ (eat) cookies before dinner or you will spoil your appetite.

4. He _____ (call) to apologize. He has to accept responsibility for what he did.

**4** 請自下表選出適當的動詞，搭配 should 或 shouldn't 填空，完成句子。

| ask | make | see | leave |
|-----|------|-----|-------|

1. Judy: I'm spending too much money on long distance calls.

   Sam: You _____ so many calls.

2. Judy: You have an appointment. Why are you still here?

   Sam: You're right. I _____ immediately.

3. Judy: I feel sick. Do I have a temperature?

   Sam: You have a fever. You _____ a doctor.

4. Judy: Why is my bonus so small? I sold more cars than anybody else.

   Sam: Do you think you _____ about how your bonus was awarded?

**5** 請用 must、have to、has to 或 had to 填空，完成下列句子。

1. You _____ drive at or less than the speed limit.

2. You _____ try the hot pot at this restaurant.

3. The dog _____ go to the bathroom.

4. My father _____ walk 5 km to work every day.

5. Did you _____ change all the estimates in the proposal?

6. You _____ finish by 5:00 or else you will end up working late.

**6** 請將下列單字重組為正確的句子。

1. in my account / the balance / check / can / you / ?
   → *Can you check the balance in my account?*

2. transfer / I / could / please / $20,000?
   → _____

3. an electronic fund transfer / the charges / you / could / go over / for / ?
   → _____

4. I / to fill out / this form / your pen / use / may / ?
   → _____

5. of / have / may / I / some extra copies / this EFT form / ?

    → ........................................................................

    ........................................................................

6. you / me / the baby / a bath / to give / like / would / ?

    → ........................................................................

    ........................................................................

7. the baby / while / to take / you / would / like / a break / I watch / ?

    → ........................................................................

    ........................................................................

8. for you / change / I'll / the baby's diaper / .

    → ........................................................................

    ........................................................................

9. I / some milk / your baby / for / warm up / should / ?

    → ........................................................................

    ........................................................................

10. for / I / a nap / put the baby / should / down / ?

    → ........................................................................

    ........................................................................

**7** 請用 shall、let's、why don't we 和 how about 填空，完成下列對話。

Max: The babysitter has finally arrived. ❶ ........................................ leave right now.

Faye: ❷ ........................................ go over a few details with her first?

Max: She's a babysitter. She knows how to take care of kids. What ❸ ........................................ we do tonight?

Faye: ❹ ........................................ telling the babysitter where we are going?

Max: Fine. Where ❺ ........................................ we go?

Faye: I don't know. Maybe we should go to see my mother.

Max: ❻ ........................................ I go to a movie with my friend, Wolfman?

Faye: OK. I'm coming. ❼ ........................................ leave now?

**1** 自下表選出適當的疑問詞填空，完成下列問答。

| what | why | which | whose | how |
|------|-----|-------|-------|-----|
| when | who | where | how old | how often |

1. Q ............ is your boss?
   A His name is Peter.

2. Q ............ is your job?
   A English Teacher.

3. Q ............ do you like more, books or movies?
   A Books.

4. Q ............ coat is this?
   A It's Albert's coat.

5. Q ............ is your car?
   A In the school parking lot.

6. Q ............ do you eat breakfast?
   A At 5:30 a.m.

7. Q ............ do you eat so early?
   A I have a long commute.

8. Q ............ do you get to work?
   A I drive on the highway.

9. Q ............ are your children?
   A They are 5 and 7 years old.

10. Q ............ do you see a dentist?
    A Never. I am afraid of dentists.

**2** 請依據題意，寫出問句完成下列問答。

1. Q *What are you doing?*
   A I'm watching a movie.

2. Q ............
   A The movie is about a man trying to save his daughter.

3. Q ............
   A The daughter was kidnapped.

4. Q ............
   A The man rescues his daughter at the end of the movie .

**3** 請填上正確的附加問句。

1. You're happy, ............?
2. It's late, ............?
3. Tom can't go, ............?
4. I'm not very tall, ............?
5. You have three aces, ............?
6. Frank won the game, ............?

**4** 自下表選出適當的動詞或片語填空，完成下列祈使句。

| pass | not forget | not take | sit |
|------|------------|----------|-----|
| come | move | call | |

1. ............ your mother right now.
2. ............ that ladder before getting the box.
3. Please ............ in and ............ down.
4. ............ the last piece.
5. ............ to write the financial report.
6. Please ............ me the peas and potatoes.

## Part 10 片語動詞

**1** 請選出正確的答案。

1. Everyone ran out of the building when the fire alarm _____.
   - Ⓐ went on
   - Ⓑ went off
   - Ⓒ took off

2. Can you _____ your father and mother in-law?
   - Ⓐ get over with
   - Ⓑ get away with
   - Ⓒ get along with

3. I feel like _____. Can I have an airsickness bag?
   - Ⓐ throwing up
   - Ⓑ throwing away
   - Ⓒ throwing off

4. _____ the volume or you'll wake up the kids.
   - Ⓐ Turn down
   - Ⓑ Turn around
   - Ⓒ Turn on

5. They _____ the trip to Korea because their grandma was sick.
   - Ⓐ called on
   - Ⓑ called off
   - Ⓒ called in

6. Winnie _____ a proposal at the conference last Thursday.
   - Ⓐ brought in
   - Ⓑ brought up
   - Ⓒ brought about

7. He's _____ his promise to stop playing video games on weekdays.
   - Ⓐ carried out
   - Ⓑ carried away
   - Ⓒ carried on

8. The police tried to _____ more information about the murder victim.
   - Ⓐ find out
   - Ⓑ find for
   - Ⓒ find about

**2** 請用正確的介系詞填空，完成句子。

1. The remote control airplane belongs _____ Johnny.

2. Keep away _____ the stove.

3. I'm looking forward _____ seeing you again.

4. Watch out _____ the falling rocks.

5. How can you put up _____ a man who never takes a shower?

6. Why are you searching the room? What are you looking _____?

## Part 11 形容詞和副詞

**1** 請圈選正確的答案。

1. This milk tea is too sweet / enough sweet.

2. The music isn't loud enough / enough loud.

3. Her attitude is too bitter / enough bitter for me.

4. Even decaf coffee is too / very tasty to drink.

**2** 將錯誤的句子打✗，並寫出正確的句子。若句子無誤，則打✓。

1. That's a cool computer.
   ☐ ................................................

2. It's a computer fast.
   ☐ ................................................

3. The screen is bright.
   ☐ ................................................

4. The machine light is.
   ☐ ................................................

**3** 將下列詞彙與片語重組，以正確語序完成句子，並在結尾加上正確的標點符號。

1. leave / I / at 10:00
   → *I leave at 10:00.*
   ................................................

2. at my house / pick me up / at 7:00
   → ................................................
   ................................................

3. always / to go dancing / dresses up / Greg
   → ................................................
   ................................................

4. to arrive / the first / never / Teddy / is
   → ................................................
   ................................................

5. were playing / the kids / yesterday / at the park
   → ................................................
   ................................................

6. she / five minutes ago / ran to the car / quickly
   → ................................................
   ................................................

**4** 寫出下列形容詞的「比較級」和「最高級」。

1. nice ................ ................
2. small ................ ................
3. sad ................ ................
4. busy ................ ................
5. pretty ................ ................
6. good ................ ................
7. bad ................ ................
8. much ................ ................
9. important
   ................................................
   ................................................
10. popular
    ................................................
11. successful
    ................................................
    ................................................
12. boring
    ................................................
    ................................................

**5** 請圈選正確的答案。

1. He is a little too smooth / smoothly.
2. Spread the frosting smooth / smoothly.
3. It was an awfully / awful performance.
4. He is so earnest / earnestly it makes me gag.
5. It was incredible / incredibly boring if you ask me.
6. I'd say they were artificial / artificially enhanced.

**6** 請圈選正確的答案。

*I'm a couch potato. I love watching TV and eating snacks. Guess how I rank walking, running, and exercising.*

1. A little bit of walking is bad / worse / worst.

2. Running and sweating is bad / worse / worst.

3. Heart pounding exercise like sit-ups and push-ups are the bad / worse / worst.

*Some people like tight clothes. Guess how tight these are.*

4. Those pants are as tight / tighter / tightest as a pair of socks, but they look good.

5. That shirt is tight / tighter / tightest than a swimsuit, and it shows everything.

6. Why are you wearing the tight / tighter / tightest possible clothing? It looks incredibly uncomfortable.

7. He doesn't look like an important / more important / most important guy with those old wrinkled clothes.

8. He is wearing a nice suit, and he looks important / more important / most important than most of the other managers here.

9. Wow. That guy is being followed by secret service agents. He looks like the important / more important / most important guy to arrive here.

---

**Part 12  介系詞**

**1**  請用 in、on 或 at 填空，完成句子。

1. Your earrings are _____ the table _____ the blue dish.

2. We live _____ the No. 12 bus line near the last stop.

3. He may be _____ work or _____ home, but I haven't seen him.

4. She is _____ school _____ the biochemistry building.

5. His flight was delayed, so he waited _____ the gift shop _____ the airport.

6. He used to live _____ 323 Hamilton Street _____ Evansville.

**2**  請用 in、on 或 at 填空，完成句子，若不需要使用介系詞，則畫✕。

1. From Monday through Friday I get up _____ 5 a.m. and go to bed _____ 9 p.m.

2. On the weekends I often take naps _____ the afternoon and go out _____ night.

3. My daughter was born _____ June 1st, 1991.

4. I like to take long walks _____ the weekends _____ the summer.

5. I'm not too busy _____ this weekend, so maybe we can meet _____ tomorrow morning.

**3** 請圈選正確的答案。

1. I parked my car near / in my apartment in front of / on a fire hydrant.

2. The pet store is next to / onto a Thai restaurant and down / opposite the Mayflower Department Store.

3. I slipped up / into this bad mood, and I can't get out of / under it.

4. When the tide was low, I walked from / to an island. Now the tide is high and I can't get off / between the island.

5. When I want exercise, I take the elevator past / up to the top floor, and then I walk down / round to the ground floor.

6. I have a short cut to my office, through / under an alley and off / across a parking lot.

7. The road goes over / between the highway and on / under the train tracks.

8. Walk past / through the old lady selling flowers and onto / around the breakfast vendor, and it's between / in the bus stop and the corner.

9. I went to / up the night market with lots of money, and on my way home between / from the market I realized I had spent it all.

**4** 將錯誤的句子打✗，並用 for、since 或 ago 改寫出正確的句子。若句子無誤，則在方框內打✓。

1. They left for lunch an hour since.
   [ ] *They left for lunch an hour ago.*

2. I graduated ten years ago.
   [ ]

3. We have been working on the report since 1:00.
   [ ]

4. I have been shopping since an hour.
   [ ]

5. I have been reading the newspaper for one hour.
   [ ]

6. The package has been here since Tuesday.
   [ ]

>>> **Part 13** 連接詞

**1** 請用 when 或 if 填空，完成句子。

1. I'll have to get used to the crying _____ my mom brings my baby brother home.

2. I want a wedding in Spain _____ I get married to Pablo.

3. I will buy a new house _____ I win the lottery.

4. _____ I graduate from barber school, I want to get a job cutting hair in the mall.

5. _____ I get up tomorrow, I am going to make my husband cook breakfast.

6. _____ my wife finds out, then I'm in big trouble.

**②** 請圈選正確的答案。

1. Those three people are Yuki, Kuan, and / or Sayed.

2. Would you like fish so / and chips?

3. I don't like fried fish, but / and I'll take an order of chips.

4. Are you single or / because married?

5. I am single or / because I can't find a wife.

6. I am married because / so I don't go to singles bars.

**③** 請用 because 或 so 填空，完成句子。

1. Yesterday I bought a present for my mother ........................ it was her birthday.

2. I put the package in the back seat of my car, ........................ I could take it to her house.

3. My mom was happy ........................ I remembered her birthday.

4. I offered to take her out to dinner ........................ I don't know how to cook.

5. I didn't tell her we were going to her sister's house, ........................ her party would be a surprise.

6. She suspected something ........................ she recognized several cars outside her sister's house.

7. I told her I had to pick up a gift, ........................ it would sound sort of reasonable.

8. The house looked empty when we walked in ........................ everybody was hiding.

9. Everybody waited a while before shouting surprise, ........................ she would be surprised.

10. My mom was really surprised ........................ waiting for two minutes really fooled her into thinking there was no party.

---

**▶▶ Part 14  數字、時間和日期**

**①** 寫出下列數字、日期或時間的唸法。

1. 34 ........................

2. 143 ........................

3. 1895 ........................

4. 8000 ........................

5. (03) 3459-8431 ........................

6. 9th and 10th ........................

7. April 20th ........................

8. 8:00 ........................

9. 8:30 ........................

10. 8:08 ........................

11. 8:45 ........................

**②** 填空完成句子。

1. The first two days of the week are ........................ and ........................ .

2. The first and second months of the year are ........................ and ........................ .

3. Saturday and Sunday are called the ........................ .

4. The season that comes after summer is ........................ .

5. Most people start working ........................ the morning and go to bed ........................ night.

# 彩圖 初級英文文法

## Let's See! 四版

Grammar Growth Curve

| | |
|---|---|
| 作　　　者 | Alex Rath Ph.D. |
| 審　　　訂 | Dennis Le Boeuf / Liming Jing |
| 譯　　　者 | 謝右／丁宥榆 |
| 校　　　對 | 歐寶妮 |
| 編　　　輯 | 賴祖兒／丁宥榆／陸葵珍 |
| 主　　　編 | 丁宥暄 |
| 內 文 設 計 | 洪伊珊／林書玉 |
| 封 面 設 計 | 林書玉 |
| 圖　　　片 | shutterstock |
| 圖 片 協 力 | 周演音 |
| 製 程 管 理 | 洪巧玲 |
| 出 版 者 | 寂天文化事業股份有限公司 |
| 發 行 人 | 黃朝萍 |
| 電　　　話 | +886-(0)2-2365-9739 |
| 傳　　　真 | +886-(0)2-2365-9835 |
| 網　　　址 | www.icosmos.com.tw |
| 讀 者 服 務 | onlineservice@icosmos.com.tw |
| 出 版 日 期 | 2024 年 6 月 四版三刷 |

國家圖書館出版品預行編目 (CIP) 資料

彩圖初級英文文法 Let's See!( 寂天雲隨身聽
APP 版 ) = Grammar growth curve. 1/Alex
Rath 著 . -- 四版 . -- [ 臺北市 ]：寂天文化事
業股份有限公司 , 2024.05
面；　公分

ISBN 978-626-300-258-6 ( 菊 8K 平裝 )
1.CST: 英語　2.CST: 語法
805.16　　　　　　　　　　113007162